BOOKS BY HELENA NEWBURY

Helena Newbury is the *New York Times* and *USA Today* bestselling author of sixteen romantic suspenses, all available where you bought this book. Find out more at helenanewbury.com.

Lying and Kissing

Punching and Kissing

Texas Kissing

Kissing My Killer

Bad For Me

Saving Liberty

Kissing the Enemy

Outlaw's Promise

Alaska Wild

Brothers

Captain Rourke

Royal Guard

Mount Mercy

The Double

Hold Me in the Dark

Deep Woods

CAPTAIN ROURKE

HELENA NEWBURY

FOSTER & BLACK

COPYRIGHT

© Copyright Helena Newbury 2017

The right of Helena Newbury to be identified as the author of this work has been asserted by her in accordance with the Copyright, Design and Patents Act 1988

This book is entirely a work of fiction. All characters, companies, organizations, products and events in this book, other than those clearly in the public domain, are fictitious or are used fictitiously and any resemblance to any real persons, living or dead, events, companies, organizations or products is purely coincidental.

This book contains adult scenes and is intended for readers 18+.

Cover by Mayhem Cover Creations

Main cover model image licensed from (and copyright remains with) Wander Aguiar Photography

ISBN: 978-1-914526-10-7

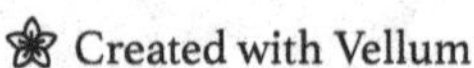 Created with Vellum

1

HANNAH

The first time I met Captain Rourke, I'd just arrived in paradise. And I wanted to escape as quickly as I could.

All around me, tourists were spilling out of the airport, pointing excitedly towards the palm trees, white beaches, and sparkling water. It was early morning, but it was already getting hot.

All I felt was cold. When I saw the waves crashing against the tiny island, eager to suck me out into the deep blue, the chill was as real as if I was already submerged.

All I wanted was to get the next flight home. The temptation to run straight back inside the terminal was almost overwhelming. By that evening, I could be back with Dad and Katherine.

But if I came back empty-handed, my sister would be dead in a week.

I hefted my bag of books onto my shoulder, picked up my suitcase and ran for the taxi rank. I gave the driver an address I prayed was still current and asked him to hurry.

The cab tore along the coast road, the acceleration pressing me back in my seat. I tried to ignore the ocean on my right and focused on the beautiful wooden houses whipping past on my left. Three hundred years ago, Nassau was home base for the pirates who stalked the Caribbean. This tiny island was where they drank and plotted and met their lovers, where governor's daughters in corsets pouted and flounced and were swept off their feet by roguish pirate captains. At least, that's how it was in my books.

Ten hours ago, I'd been driving through the wheat fields of Nebraska on my way to catch my first flight. *Culture shock* didn't even begin to describe it.

We pulled up outside a wooden house that looked abandoned. Its eggshell-blue paint was peeling from wood so dark with damp it was almost black. My stomach lurched: what if my great-grandfather had moved? I'd never find him in time. My trip would have been for nothing and my sister would be dead.

I knocked. No answer. *Oh God, please no....* I knocked again, harder. Tried the bell. Nothing.

I peered through the windows and saw furniture. It wasn't abandoned, just very run down. I'd just have to wait for him to come home. *Well, fine. I'll wait all day if I have to.* I wasn't giving up.

But as soon as I stopped moving, I swayed on my feet. The exhaustion and the jet lag and the worry all caught up with me at once. Between staying up all night with my sister at the hospital and then the traveling, I couldn't remember the last time I'd slept. I was in the house's shadow and, even in my cardigan and jeans, it was cool enough to make me shiver. And once I'd started, I couldn't stop.

I slowly turned around and looked behind me. The house faced directly onto the beach. I could wait there. But beyond the sand was the crashing, roaring—

The fear rose inside me and I quickly looked at my feet and took a slow, deep breath, fighting the panic back down. Then I took my shoes off and walked out onto the sand. As soon as the sun hit me, I felt better. My shivering stopped. But the beach was crowded: I couldn't sit down where I was.

Early-morning sun worshippers looked up at me from their towels and did a double-take at the fully-dressed woman laden with bags. I ignored the stares and giggles and plodded on, eyes down, trying to shut out the growing sound of the waves.

As soon as I found an empty spot, I dropped my suitcase and bag of books and sat down. Everyone else faced the sea, but I very deliberately turned around and faced my great-grandfather's house. I told myself it was so I didn't miss him coming home.

The real reason was, I didn't want to look at the sea.

I could feel it behind me, swelling and rising, never still, a bottomless pit that only the foolhardy venture out onto. I'd only ever seen it a couple of times in my life before.

And I'd only been in it once.

Just once.

The roar of the sea grew and grew in my mind and suddenly I was there, sliding down one side of a huge wave while Mom slid down the other, arm stretched out to try to grab me, her mouth open in a scream—

I took a deep breath and stared hard at the ground beneath my bare feet, then anchored my fingers deep into the sand for good measure. *You're safe. You're safe.*

What the hell am I doing here? How had I wound up on a tiny island, surrounded by the thing I was most scared of?

Because I had no choice. Not if I wanted to save her. And however hard I tried, that might not even be possible....

I closed my eyes tight, but it was too late. Hot tears sprang up behind my closed lids. I didn't want to cry so I reluctantly scooched around on the sand to face the sea and let the cool breeze bathe my face. I took long, slow breaths, trying to stay calm, but I was barely holding it together. What if my great-grandfather didn't come home? What if he couldn't help?

All around me, women in bikinis and men in shorts: tanned, perfect people, laughing and flirting, their only dilemma whether to go for a beer or a cocktail. And then there was me, a fully dressed woman with milky-white skin, arms wrapped round her knees, her bags piled around her. I've never in my life felt so alone.

And then I heard the slap of feet on wet sand, coming towards me from the ocean. As they came closer, I heard something odd in them: they weren't in rhythm, one step much quicker and lighter than the other. They came closer and closer and I waited for them to pass by.

But the footsteps stopped right in front of me. And then I felt a drop of water hit my outstretched foot. I couldn't help it, then: I opened my eyes and looked.

He was big: I had to crane my head back to see all of him. Even if I was standing, he would have been a good head taller than me, but sitting on my ass on the sand, he looked like a giant. But it wasn't his size that hit me most. It was that he was so... *hard.* So *solid.* He looked as if he'd been carved out of granite, everlasting and unshakeable, and the few hints of smoothness were the result of the battering of the sea. He looked as if a twenty-foot wave could slam into him and he wouldn't move an inch.

The ocean has always been all-powerful, to me, a force of nature we have no business messing with. But *he*...he looked as if he could actually take it on.

Water was streaming down, making his skin shine. He'd just emerged from the sea, but he wasn't panting and exhausted, like every other swimmer who wades ashore. He wasn't even breathing hard. He looked as if he'd just been out for a stroll, as if—

As if he belonged in the sea just as much as I belonged to the prairies.

In fact, now that he was on the beach, his feet were shifting and moving as if he didn't quite trust dry land. I followed his legs upward. His skin was a rich tan, almost caramel, gleaming and flecked with sand. The muscles of his calves and thighs were hard and sculpted but moved as smoothly as a big cat's. Working muscle, packed hard and tight from swimming, not the veiny, spherical look of a gym junkie.

The handle of a knife, bound with rough scarlet cord, rose out of a scabbard strapped to his right calf. *Who needs a knife, when they're swimming?* He was wearing trunks, so dark blue they were almost black, the fabric stretched tight over powerful thighs. And between them, a thick bulge—

I swallowed and quickly carried on up. The shorts gave way to—

God, he had the best abs I'd ever seen, every line deeply defined, water sliding over each hard ridge and gleaming along his centerline. But—

Something had marred the perfect symmetry. A line of scars, each one as big as my thumb, rising in an arch that led from one side of his body to the other. Something had—

No. That's insane.

But that's what it looked like. The idea throbbed and clanged in my head, an alarm, because if it was true then it meant that the ocean was even more terrifying than I'd thought. It looked like—

Something had bitten him. Something huge had closed its jaws on him as if trying to bite him in two.

I looked higher, craning my head back. The broad curves of his chest gleamed with water droplets and—God, there was just something about the width of that chest, the raw strength of his shoulders and pecs. He *loomed...* if he was atop you, pushing you down on the bed, he'd almost block out the light—

I flushed. My gaze flicked over his biceps, thickly strong from tearing through the water. In one hand, he held a blunt metal tube with a barbed arrowhead sticking out of the muzzle: a spear gun. A gleaming fish the length of his forearm was speared on it, its scales glittering in the sun.

He hadn't just been swimming. He'd been hunting his breakfast.

And now he'd stopped right in front of me. *I must be in his way,* I thought. And, me being me, I prepared to shuffle aside.

Then I saw the footprints he'd left. He'd waded straight up out of the ocean and then he'd veered. He'd veered towards... me. *That makes no sense!*

I finally lifted my gaze to his face, squinting against the sun. And found myself dropping headfirst into bottomless blue, the richest, *deepest* eyes I'd ever seen. Eyes you could drown in. God, he was gorgeous, and in a way I'd never seen back in Nebraska. His face was as gloriously hard as the rest of him, his cheekbones and jaw hewn from the cliffs and then smoothed by rain and wind. Yet his lower lip, pressed tight as he scowled down at me, looked so soft.

And that *scowl.* His gaze pinned me as firmly as if he'd had a hand on my throat. *Stay right there while I look at you, dammit.* It was angry, but it didn't feel threatening. It felt like....

It felt like he was angry with himself. As if I'd drawn him to me against his better judgment. *But I was just sitting here!*

And beneath that anger was something else, boiling out and expanding like storm clouds. Raw, hot need, a kind I'd never felt. A kind that didn't just lick over my body, focusing on my breasts and face and ass. A kind that reached right down into me, past all the fear and worry... and I felt something swell up inside me and answer, completely unexpected and so strong it took my breath away.

He was so close that the wind rushing in off the sea broke against his back and swept either side of us, enclosing us in a warm space where the air was still and the sun could soak into my bones. The heat brought home to me that he was standing there in just a pair of trunks; I was in a tank top, cardigan, and jeans, with all my bags around me. *I look ridiculous.* And yet, the way he was looking at me, I didn't *feel* ridiculous, for once. I felt—

I flushed. *Don't be stupid.* Katherine is the pretty one, slender and sleek with laser-straight hair. I'm all tangled blonde curls and hips and ass.

And yet he stared. And the heat inside me grew and crackled, every inch of my skin tingling as the feeling rippled through me. I had to look away from those eyes or I was going to be lost forever beneath the surface.

His black hair was still shining and dripping from the sea, the cut short and almost old-fashioned. At least a few days of stubble turned his tan cheeks dark. It was hard to gauge his age. His body looked like an athlete just out of college, but his eyes... his eyes looked like they'd seen every corner of every ocean in the world. And they were eating up every curve of my body, even through my clothes.

I flushed. *Thank God I'm not in a bathing suit.*

And then, just for a second, *I wish I was in a bathing suit.*

His eyes flicked up to mine again. The lust was even stronger now: the storm had spread to cover the whole of those gorgeous blue eyes.

And I started to catch something else, underneath, driving all that anger. *Pain.* Pain so raw and deep I wanted to press my whole body to him and wrap him into my arms. I'd never seen anyone hurt so much... or try so hard to hide it. I was suddenly aware that I was matching his breathing, my own chest rising and falling in time with his, locked onto him in a way that was so strong it was frightening.

And then I remembered why I was there. I checked over my shoulder and—

My heart leapt. Someone was walking up the path to my great-grandfather's house. Not an old man: a woman.

I stood up so fast I wobbled. Even standing, he towered over me. I felt like I had to say something before I ran off, but, when I spoke, my accent sounded ridiculous, a shy little Nebraska breeze against the might of the whole ocean. "I've got to go," I said.

The man frowned deeper and leaned forward. *No you don't.*

I drew in my breath, every inch of my skin prickling and alive under that glare.

And then he seemed to catch himself and straightened up. The anger in his eyes grew even stronger. As if he knew he was acting out of character and couldn't figure out why.

I shook my head, breathing fast. *This is crazy.* And whatever it was, I didn't have time for it. Heart thumping, I grabbed my shoes, grabbed my bags, and ran towards the house.

But I could feel his eyes on my back the whole way.

2

HANNAH

It started two weeks ago. I was singing in the shower, the one place on our farm where I'm sure no one can hear me. I was two verses into an old favorite when my dad banged on the door and told me we had to get to the hospital, *now*.

My sister Katherine had collapsed at a business meeting. She'd laid there writhing in such unimaginable pain that she'd cracked a molar from grinding her teeth so hard. She described it like *every nerve in my body being lit on fire*. And it had lasted for close to ten minutes.

The doctors did CTs and MRIs. They checked for epilepsy, brain tumors, and tropical diseases. Nothing.

They ruled out cancer and I was relieved. Then they ruled out everything else and I started to get really scared. They wondered quietly if it might be all in her head, but the blood tests showed there was definitely something wrong: her nervous system was under attack. They just didn't know from what.

We believe doctors are all-powerful. It was terrifying to see them stumped. *How can she be this ill, this suddenly?* She'd never been anything but healthy and she was younger than me, twenty-three to my twenty-five.

My dad started off stoic but, as the days went by, he started to get more and more stressed. Not worried, *stressed,* as if he was trying to make a decision. *What the hell's going on?*

And then, on the third day, as I sat talking to Katherine, it happened again. I screamed for my dad and the doctors and they all rushed in: her boyfriend, Chris, too.

Katherine thrashed so hard she kicked over a table and drew blood from her lip. The ECG machine went crazy, her heart rate so high that the doctors were worried she was going to arrest. The doctors tried drug after drug: nothing worked. I screamed at them to help her but there was nothing they could do. My sister was in unbearable, unimaginable agony and there was nothing I could do except hold her hand.

After fifteen minutes, the spasms died away and her heart rate began to slow. The doctors looked at one another, their faces sickly pale.

"The body's not meant to bear that sort of load," the doctor in charge of her case told us. "Not for more than a few seconds. Not four *minutes.*" He told us his best guess: the attacks would keep getting stronger and more frequent until they were constant. At that point, her heart would simply give out.

"How long?" asked Katherine. "No bull."

The doctor gave us the sad stare of a man defeated.

"Months?" asked Katherine, her voice cracking. Then, "Weeks?"

The doctor closed his eyes for a second. "A week."

And that's when my dad finally told us.

His big farmer's hands were bunched as he spoke. He'd worked the land his whole life, seen us through countless hard winters and drought-ridden summers. He'd never liked anything he couldn't touch and feel: he was one of those guys who sows by the feel of the soil, not by the calendar. When he told us, I wanted to throw my arms around him because this was about as far from his comfort zone as it was possible to get.

"They called it a curse," he said. "But it's not. Let's get that straight.

There's no such thing. Just folk back then didn't know medicine like they do now."

"Back *when?*" I asked.

"1700s," he said. "Best as we can figure. One of your ancestors, a woman, fell ill and....she died. No one knew why. Then her daughter fell ill, when she reached the same age, and *she* died. Then two of *her* daughters. That's when people started to say it was a curse." He swallowed. "The men in the family were all fine. And the other daughters. It only hit certain women and always in their early twenties."

The cogs were turning in my head. "Great-grandma Ellie?" I knew she'd died when she was young. I'd never met her.

My dad nodded. "Ellie was the last one. Your grandma's generation was fine. Your mom's generation was fine." He reached out and stroked Katherine's cheek. "That's why we never told you. We thought it was just superstition and coincidence: lots of women died young, in those days. We never—" His face threatened to crumple and he had to stop speaking.

A disease that killed through sheer, unbearable pain. A time bomb buried in our genes. I wanted to be sick. It wasn't just Katherine: we had seven female cousins roughly her age. How many of them was this thing going to hit? How many of *their* kids?

Over the next few days we met with a whole string of doctors, all with *genetics* somewhere in their job title. "But we know what this is," I kept saying. "It's some genetic defect, passed down the female line. It's in our chromosomes. You understand that stuff these days. You can treat it."

The latest doctor looked at me sadly. "There are a lot of abnormalities we can't detect. We know this is in your family's DNA but that doesn't mean we know *where...*or how it's attacking the nervous system."

"There's got to be *something,*" I told my dad savagely that night. We'd already lost Mom. I wasn't going to lose Katherine, too.

My dad put his arms around me. "I looked, pumpkin." He kissed the top of my head. "When you were born, I drove myself crazy trying to figure out if this thing was true or not. Talked to everyone. Even your great-grandpa called me up when he heard we'd had a daughter, trying to sell me on his theory."

I frowned. "Doesn't he live in Hawaii or something?"

"The Bahamas. Went out there after Ellie died."

"What was his theory?"

Dad squeezed me harder. 'Losing Ellie drove him crazy. That's why he went out there: he thought there was a cure there. He couldn't bring back Ellie, but he wanted to beat this thing, make sure it didn't hurt anyone else. He's been out there ever since. He must be in his nineties by now."

I looked at our reflections in the glass, searching his face. "But why *there*? Was there some magical plant that only grew there or something?"

I felt Dad shake his head. "He'd researched our family tree. Claimed some woman had been cured, hundreds of years ago. Spent all his money looking for what cured her. Even asked me for money."

"We should talk to him!"

He squeezed me. "He's a crazy old coot. And whatever he thought was out there, he never found it: you can be sure he would have told us, if he had." He sighed. "I'm not even sure he's still alive. Haven't heard from him in twenty years. The phone was disconnected, last time I tried."

I pushed back so that I could look at him. "I could go out there—"

"*No!*" His voice was so firm, I blinked. And then I saw it in his eyes. Mom was gone. Katherine was critically ill. I was all he had left.

I clutched him to me and we stood like that for a long time. He buried his face in my hair and, a few seconds later, I felt a couple of tears hit my scalp.

I'd never seen him cry, not even when Mom died. I think that scared me more than anything the doctors had said. This was real. Katherine was going to die. And then this thing was going to start picking off our cousins.

Unless someone did something. And the only hope lay in the Bahamas.

Katherine couldn't go and she needed her boyfriend here with her. No way would my dad leave and Mom was gone. That left me.

If I go and she dies while I'm away....

If I don't go and she dies....

After three hours pacing the hospital hallways, I was no closer to a decision. Then, in the early hours, Katherine screamed. I ran to her bedside and she crushed my hand in hers while she arched off the bed in agony. I watched her through a haze of tears. "*Make it stop!*" she screamed. "*Make it stop!*"

And all the hot emotion rose up inside me and hardened into iron. As soon as the attack was over, I packed a bag and drove to the airport.

Maybe my great-grandfather was crazy. Maybe there was no cure. And even if there was something in the Bahamas that could save Katherine, I was about the least suitable person in the world to go looking: a small-town librarian who'd only been out of the *state* a handful of times.

But I was damn well going to try.

I reached the woman just as she reached the door to my great-grandfather's house. When I touched her shoulder, she yelped and spun around. The box she'd been carrying clattered to the floor and cleaning products went everywhere.

"Sorry," I panted. I bent and started picking up spray-bottles and dusters. "I'm Hannah Barnes. I'm looking for my great-grandfather, Bertrand?"

The woman's jaw dropped. Then she grabbed my hand and stared into my eyes. She was smaller than me, but sturdily built, her graying hair held in place by combing shaped like orange butterflies. "Oh, heavens, child!" she whispered. She tugged me forward and I suddenly found myself crushed against her bosom. "I'm so sorry."

My stomach twisted in fear. "Where is he?"

She stroked my back. "Bertie passed last week."

I froze against her. I'd come all this way for nothing... and now Katherine had no hope at all.

3

———

HANNAH

The woman brewed me tea and insisted I call her Cynthia. She'd been my great-grandfather's housekeeper for thirty years.

I'd missed him by three days.

The house was run down, but still beautiful, with big windows giving views onto the beach and strong wooden shutters for the storm season. There were polished wood floors and an old-fashioned globe. I could imagine some rich colonist living there, back when the New World was just being settled. There was a faint, enticing smell I recognized but couldn't identify.

Cynthia had tried to contact our family, but all the contact details Bertrand had for us were years out of date. He hadn't stayed in touch with anyone in Nebraska. Whatever he'd been doing out here, it had obsessed him to the exclusion of everything else.

Cynthia began to clean and, ignoring her protests, I grabbed a mop and helped her. "Do you know what he was working on?" I asked.

She shook her head and nodded to a door. "He was never out of that study. Worked dawn till midnight. But he never told me what it was."

I sighed and started figuring out how fast I could get back to

Katherine. The next flight to the mainland wasn't for a few hours. I wanted to howl in frustration. By the time I got home, I'd have missed a full day and night of what little time she had left. *You idiot! Dad told you not to come!*

I helped Cynthia clean the rest of the house, figuring I might as well be useful to someone. She left me with a set of keys and I slumped down on the cracked leather couch to call a cab. I still had a while before my flight, but I figured I might as well wait at the airport. At least there I'd be further from the sea.

That made me think of *him.* The man on the beach. The one who seemed to love the water as much as I hated it. My opposite.

I relived that slow journey up his body again. Those muscles. Those eyes. That bulge in his shorts—surely not from staring down at *me?* I swallowed, remembering his gaze and the heat it had sent through me.

Don't be stupid. Men don't even look at me, let alone men like him. He was gorgeous and that whole beach was packed with slender beauties in designer bikinis. He probably took his pick of every tourist flight.

And yet... it hadn't felt like that. He'd looked almost angry with me, as if this was as out of character for him as it was for me. And beneath the lust, there'd been something else in his eyes, driving all that anger. I recognized it only because I'd seen it in the mirror, right after we lost Mom. *Pain.* Pain that was tearing him apart.

I shook my head. Whoever he was, I was never going to see him again. I dialed the cab company and, as the number rang, I gazed up at the cracks in the ceiling. My great-grandfather had obviously spent the bare minimum on maintaining the place. Yet I was sure he and my great-grandmother had been well off, at one point.

He'd spent all his money on this quest. Every single cent. How? What had cost so much?

I slowly turned to the study door. Then I looked at the set of keys: one of them must open it.

I knew he'd died without finding the cure: if he'd found it, he would have rushed back to Nebraska, victorious. I knew I'd come all the way out there on a wild goose chase, but I had to know how close he'd gotten. I had to know if there'd *ever* been hope, or if it really had all been the delusions of an old man.

"Triple-A Cabs," said a friendly voice in my ear.

I fingered the keys. *Make a decision, Hannah....*

"Sorry," I said. "I'll call you back."

I hung up and walked slowly over to the study door. Found the right key and unlocked it. Then I gingerly pushed it open....

The smell hit me first. That wonderful scent I'd caught when I walked into the house. The smell of old books. I closed my eyes and inhaled.

Books are my medicine. They have been ever since Mom died. When I need a lift, I reach for something light and funny. When I need to turn off my brain, I bury myself in a biography.

When Mom was ripped from us and Katherine was in Omaha and Dad was busy trying to keep the farm going and I needed *someone*...I immersed myself in an epic, sweeping historical romance box set, book after book until I knew the characters so well that I didn't feel alone.

And when I finish a long day at the library, doing everything from indexing to reshelving to sweeping floors because it's just me and my one, part-time helper...and I know that when I get home I have to help Dad sow a new crop because his back's giving him trouble again...and after that there's nothing waiting for me but sleeping in the same room I grew up in, the fairy wallpaper still peeking through the layers of paint I've plastered over it...and it's *just me,* because there's no time to see friends let alone think about a boyfriend and who'd want the girl who's still stuck in the same town after twenty-four years, too poor to move out of her dad's house, and I'm too shy to talk to them even if they did speak to me and—

When all *that* is in my head, I grab a book and escape.

So working at the library suits me. It's only recently that I've wondered if it suits me *too* well. Peaceful, but isolating. I look up and the sun's setting and I try to remember what on earth I did that filled a whole day. If I wrote *my* life down in a book, would anyone want to read it?

I opened my eyes.

The study was filled with books. Thousands and thousands of books.

The room was huge. Double height, with shelves stretching almost twenty feet into the air. They stretched on to the end of the room, maybe fifty feet away, where I could see a desk.

I walked reverently between the aisles, gazing in wonder. The newest books were at least a hundred years old: thick, leather bound monsters with gold-printed titles. Many were much older, some just binders of loose, yellowed pages. And there were hundreds and hundreds of them.

I thought *I* had a lot of books, but mine only covered two walls of my small bedroom. And my books cost maybe ten dollars a pop. These...I pulled a book from a shelf at random and checked the date: 1732. *This one book must be worth thousands....*

And it wasn't just books. There were piles of letters, some still bearing their glossy wax seals. And maps. New maps, freshly white and blue. Old maps, faded brown. And hand-drawn maps with the names of islands spelled in unfamiliar ways. Many of them seemed to be in Spanish. There were oil paintings, too, not displayed as art but leaned up against the walls as if they were *for* something.

I knew now what my great-grandfather had spent all his money on. But *why?* What did any of this have to do with a cure?

I bit my lip and looked back at the door I'd come through. If I wanted to get the next flight, I needed to go. By late that night, I could be back with Katherine and my dad.

But in a week, Katherine would be dead. I looked around the room. Would Bertrand have gone to all this trouble, spent all this money, if there wasn't at least a tiny shred of hope?

I closed the door, sat down at Bertrand's desk and began to read.

It took me twelve hours. For the first seven, I didn't leave the desk. Then, back aching and eyes throbbing, I made a huge pot of coffee, refueled and went back in.

Fortunately, my great-grandfather had kept a journal. That gave me a hint of the story but I had to go back and read all the sources before I could figure it out.

I had two things on my side. Firstly, a few years ago, Katherine had persuaded me to enroll in a Spanish class because she said it was a great way to meet men. It wasn't, but I'd enjoyed it and kept going so my Spanish was pretty good.

Secondly, burying myself in books is *what I do*.

Not many people understand it. They see a huge, thick book, one you need two hands to pick up, and they find it intimidating. But to me, that crisp white title page is like a smooth Egyptian cotton sheet. I want a book so big I could lie on the first page. Glowing red hot with my need for story, for information, I'd just burn my way through the pages, sinking down to the end.

Finally, late that night, I found the crucial stack of letters that made it all make sense. I sat bolt upright in Bertrand's creaky leather chair.

Way back in 1701, one of my ancestors, a woman named Elizabeth, had come out to the Bahamas with her husband. She'd fallen ill when she hit her mid-twenties and died within weeks. By that time, she already had two daughters, Isabelle and Margaret.

By 1722, both of them were approaching the critical age where the "family curse" was said to hit. But Isabelle's beauty had caught the attention of Marcus, a local merchant, and he started to woo her. Despite everyone's warnings—including hers—he'd married her when she was twenty-four and set about trying to save her.

His search took them all over the globe: to doctors in London and Paris, to herbalists in Asia and, finally, to a man in Africa he called a witch-doctor. By now, they were desperate. Isabelle was having attacks, just like my sister, and only had days to live. The man examined her and eventually gave the couple a "curious stone, black as night," with instructions on how to prepare it. The stone had to be ground up, mixed with oil and drunk.

And it had worked. Isabelle's symptoms disappeared and she went on to live a long life.

I drew in a ragged breath. *There's a cure!*

Isabelle hadn't forgotten about her sister. Margaret was now approaching her twenty-fifth birthday and was still in Nassau. I found the letter Marcus wrote to her, describing how he was carefully packaging some of the "curious stone" in a box, packing that box in a trunk and shipping it to her aboard a merchant vessel called the *Gwendoline.*

I was literally on the edge of my seat now, the letter gripped in my shaking hand. In those days, a voyage from Lagos in Africa would take almost a month. "But you will receive it in good time," Marcus reassured her.

And she would have done. But—

I snatched up the next letter in the pile.

Oh Jesus no.

The ship had never arrived.

In those days, communication was slow and it was weeks before Margaret received word: the ship had had to divert to another port after suffering some "terrible incident": its entire cargo had been lost, including the trunk containing the cure. Margaret had written to Marcus and Isabelle but by then they'd travelled to London to start a new life there. Another expedition to Africa was planned but, before it could even set out, the disease hit Margaret. She died just a week later.

I let out a guttural moan and slumped back in Bertrand's big leather chair. *A cure!* They'd actually found a cure, one that could save Katherine and all the other women in our family! I wanted to weep: it was so close I could taste it but, thanks to a storm or a mutiny or whatever had happened to that merchant ship, it was gone forever.

I gazed around the room in defeat. That was what it all came down to? Bertrand had traced the history of our family back three hundred years, only to discover that we'd been doomed by a cruel twist of fate?

My eyes stopped on a large table. Spread out on it was a piece of cloth, brown and ragged with age. A hand-drawn map. I couldn't make sense of all the numbers but I recognized some of the names of the islands: Nassau, Cuba, Haiti. And I could read the message written in flowing script across the bottom. *To my darling Esme. The path that leads to the Hawk.*

What the heck was the Hawk? And why had Bertrand been interested in it? As far as I could tell, he hadn't had time for anything that wasn't related to the cure. And why hadn't he come home to Nebraska when he discovered the cure was lost? From the dates in his journal, he'd found the letters almost a decade ago.

Maybe he hadn't wanted to admit defeat. I knew that feeling. Not only had I now missed the last flight of the day, I was going to have to go home and tell Katherine that I'd struck out. She was going to die and so were any other women in our family who were hit by the disease.

I trudged back into the living room. I'd have to sleep on the couch and get the first flight in the morning. I was exhausted but I knew I wouldn't be able to sleep, not with the guilt at having failed pounding through my head. I tried reading to calm myself but I'd been poring over texts for so many hours that the words swum in front of my eyes. I slammed the book closed. *Dammit!*

Now I'd stopped working, I couldn't shut out the slow crash of the waves outside. My skin began to crawl: I could feel the water soaking through my clothes, the heaviness of it sucking at me—

I stood up. If I didn't get out of there, the memories would come back and I'd lose it completely. There was no escaping the sound of the ocean, not on an island. But maybe if I could find a bar full of people, I could drown it out. I didn't relish the idea of walking into a bar alone but anything was better than remembering.

It was a weekday night and most of the bars were shuttered. But I saw an orange glow coming from McKinley's Inn: a squat, timbered inn that looked as if it had been there even in Margaret's day. From the noise inside, it was packed.

I pushed open the door...and it was like stepping back in time. Everything inside was made of dark wood and the place was lit only by sputtering candles that dripped wax onto the tables. The ceiling was low and the path from door to bar was worn smooth with age.

Heads turned. Conversation ceased. By the time I realized I was the only woman in the place, it was too late to turn back.

The bartender, a mustachioed man with a once-white apron, gave me a look that was halfway between pity and respect. I opened my mouth to ask for a drink: maybe beer, maybe wine. But he just gave me a tiny shake of his head, put a shot glass down on the bar, and poured liquor into it. Some local brand of rum. Then he nudged it towards me with a little nod.

I realized there was nothing behind the bar *but* liquor, most of it rum. I nodded my thanks for saving me the embarrassment and pushed a bill towards him.

The bar was still silent. I lifted the glass and almost reeled when I got a hit of the fumes rising from it. I never normally touched hard liquor. But maybe it would stop me thinking about Katherine...and how I was going to have to say goodbye.

I knocked back the shot...and then drew in a shuddering breath as it burned its way down my throat. When I exhaled, I felt as if I was breathing fire. Tears prickled at the corners of my eyes. *Holy— People drink this?!* A few seconds later, there was a slow-motion explosion of warmth down in my belly, strong enough to make me blink and press my lips together tight.

"Another," said a voice right next to me.

I turned. A man had slunk right into my personal space. He had tan, heavily tattooed skin stretched over heavy muscle and long, shaggy hair the color of mud. When he grinned at me, three of his teeth were gold.

I couldn't speak. My throat was seared from the rum and even breathing was difficult. But I shook my head and moved away from him.

And jumped as my hip bumped into another hard male body.

"Another," said the man who'd hemmed me in on my other side. He was shorter and paler, barely taller than me. He had a blond crew cut and was wearing a t-shirt that advertised some boatyard in Panama. He grinned at me and pushed his hip against mine, as if it was a game. I jerked away, which pushed me up against the first man. I saw they both had knives hanging from their belts. My stomach lurched. What the hell kind of place was this?

"I'm fine," I croaked.

But the short man had already grabbed the bottle of rum and refilled my glass, splashing some of it on the bar. The bartender cursed and glared but the man ignored him, slamming the glass down on the bar in front of me. The atmosphere was changing rapidly, ugly male aggression pressing in on me from both sides. *Just go,* I thought. *Just get out of here.*

I took a step back, turning to leave...and slammed into a wall of flesh. A huge man, wide as well as tall, his stomach bulging over his belt. My heart started to hammer: I could feel the whole situation slipping rapidly out of control. I tried to look confident and push my way past him.

But he pressed forward instead and I was driven back until my ass hit the bar. I was hemmed in by the three men. *Trapped.*

How did this go so wrong, so fast?

"Enough," snapped the bartender. But suddenly the long-haired man had his knife out, the tip thrust an inch from the bartender's face. The bartender swallowed and went silent.

The short man grabbed the bottle of rum. He brandished it in front of me, making the liquid slosh inside. "Let's give you a proper drink," he said. And he brought it towards my mouth.

I tried to push my way out but suddenly my arms were grabbed from both sides and I was pinioned against the bar. I shook my head as the bottle loomed closer and closer to my mouth but the men just laughed. As the short man chased my lips, he leaned in close. "Just enjoy it," he told me. "It'll make it easier." His eyes flicked down to my body. And then to each of his friends in turn.

I twisted away desperately, almost hysterical, now. They grabbed my hair and wrenched my head back, my mouth opening as I cried out in pain. The rim of the bottle nudged my lips once, twice, then slid sickeningly between them. Liquid gushed into my mouth. I fought against their grip but I had to swallow or drown. My eyes bugged out as I stared at the volume of rum in the bottle. *Jesus, that much will kill me!* Or at the very least, I'd be unconscious.

Unconscious, while they dragged me off somewhere and—

"Let her go."

Just three words and not even loud. And yet somehow they drowned out the men's sneering laughter as if it was nothing. The whole bar went quiet. The bottle was pulled from my lips and I spat and coughed, rum dripping down my front. My hair was released and I looked towards the voice.

Someone was moving in the shadows. He was moving towards us with awkward, jerky steps: each time he put his left foot down, his body would tense as if in pain and he'd quickly swing his weight over to his right. The three men around me were the sort who'd find that funny.

But none of them were laughing.

"Let her go!"

A snapped command. The three men all flinched as if hit and the space around me opened up a little but the short man still held my arm. This time, I picked up on the newcomer's accent. It wasn't anything Caribbean but it wasn't American, either. The consonants were hard and violent but the *o* was long, an echoing war cry. I couldn't place it but I still had that same, primitive reaction to it as everyone else in the bar: the hairs on the back of my neck prickled and my heart sped up. For thousands of years, hearing that accent meant *the barbarians are coming.*

The man stepped into the light and I caught my breath. It was *him,* from the beach, the scars on his torso now covered by a loose white shirt, those powerful legs now clad in sleek black pants with a silver-buckled belt. There was something hanging from it, still lost in the shadows. God, he looked even better than my memories of him:

the clothes just accentuated the roughness underneath: black stubble against white cotton, the shirt stretched across those magnificent pecs. Those deep blue eyes were locked on me, never blinking, as if—

As if he didn't care about anything else in the room.

It didn't matter that I was terrified. It didn't matter that one of the men still had his hand on my arm. That look, that burning, urgent look...it overrode everything. It blazed right to my core and melted me, the molten heat flooding straight down to my groin.

"I'll not ask a third time." The man's voice was unshakeable. The anger in his eyes was ruthlessly controlled, blistering heat frozen and carved into a weapon. I'd never understood the expression *cold fury* until that moment.

The short man glanced at the other two, ignored their warning glares, and raised his knife.

There was a musical whisper of metal and the short man froze, his neck craned back. The room went absolutely still.

It had happened too fast to see. And the blade was almost end-on to me so it was only when I shifted slightly and saw the candlelight on the shining steel that I could make out its shape. Even then, I had trouble accepting it. *That's a—No, of course it isn't—*

It was a sword. The man from the beach was holding the short man at sword point. *Who carries a sword?!*

The short man took two shuddering breaths. He dropped his knife and released my arm. The point of the sword was rock-steady at his throat. He ran for the door, the other two men right on his heels.

And then it was just the man from the beach and me.

4

ROURKE

One Hour Earlier

I shouldn't even have been at the inn. I had to be up early the next morning to work on the boat. But every time I tried to sleep, Edwards was there, nudging me in the ribs, telling me to go for one drink. One drink that might lead to one last crazy adventure, one last haul of treasure.

I told him all that was behind me but he wouldn't listen. He just put on that ridiculous Hawaiian shirt he always wore to McKinley's and stood by the door like a dog holding its leash.

Fine. One drink. It'd help me sleep, at least.

My leg was having one of its *bastard* days so by the time I reached the inn I was cursing, pain snaking up the damaged muscle and all the way into my thigh. I fell into a chair and slumped there in the dark until Benny brought me my rum. The conversation that had stopped when we came in slowly started up again and I let myself disappear into the shadows.

I'd accepted this as my future. Sitting in the dark in McKinley's, sleeping in the dark of my boat and then, finally, the sea would take me. She'd drag me down into her depths and I'd be in the dark forever. Where I belonged.

I was on my third rum when *she* walked in. The woman from the beach. She lit up that grimy place like a damn spotlight. Her golden hair cascaded down her back in soft waves, gleaming and bright: nothing had any right shining like that, in McKinley's. And her skin...in a room where every man had been scorched by the sun and whipped by the wind, she looked untouched. Her skin was creamy and perfect and those eyes: big and the palest blue, that blue you only get when the clouds clear right after a storm.

She didn't seem to be wearing any make-up: her lips were—I felt my chest tighten as I stared at them—Jesus, she had the most perfect, kissable lips I'd ever seen. I couldn't stop staring at them. They were a faint blush pink, soft, and delicately shining. When she realized the sort of place she'd walked into, she bit her lower lip nervously and—

Something moved inside me, something that had grown so heavy and cold, I'd forgotten it *could* move. I just wanted to grab her and pull her the hell out of McKinley's and Nassau and all of this. She wasn't a part of this. She wasn't like us.

She turned slightly and I saw her shape. A classic figure, not like some of the waifs you see today. She had full breasts and a proper, round ass; hips that gave her a glorious hourglass.

Jesus, they'd eat her alive, in this place. When men like us can't make an honest living, we do what we have to rather than give up the sea. Smuggling, gun-running, sometimes worse. Even the best men in McKinley's had broken plenty of laws. As for the worst men....

Cagol and Mackal were tipping the rum down her throat. The fat German brute they hang around with had joined them, hemming her in from behind, almost hiding her from my view. And nobody did a damn thing. The evil of the place seemed to boil out of the floor and the walls and surround her, oily and black against that pale skin.

I didn't want it to touch her. And for a second, I didn't want to be immersed in it myself.

I stood up, my left leg trembling and threatening to fail.

The men grabbed her arms. Pulled her taut against the bar, her head tipped back, and the bottle between her lips. I knew what would follow, once she was unconscious and unable to stop them.

I took a step towards them and my voice rang out before I'd even thought about speaking. I told them to let her go. And when they didn't obey, I drew my sword and put the tip right against Mackal's throat.

Everyone knows about my sword. Sergeant Watts, the cop who patrols the harbor, gives me grief about it but he looks the other way as long as I don't wear it into town.

I heard Mackal's knife clatter to the floor. Then his dirty fingers unwound from her pristine, pale arm and he ran. My eyes stayed on her arm, staring at the soft skin. I was imagining how good it would feel under *my* fingers.

I wanted to grip both of those slender arms and push her back against the hull of my boat, crush those blush-pink lips under mine. I'd press close enough that I could feel her warm body through our clothes, her breasts against my chest. One big hand on her cheek while I explored that perfect mouth—

I tore my gaze away...and found myself looking straight into big, pale blue eyes that were full of gratitude. *Aw, damn it!* I suddenly came to my senses.

She was a gorgeous, innocent wee thing. And I was a washed-up fucker with a limp.

I did the only thing I could do: I turned away and stalked back to my table. Back to Edwards.

5

HANNAH

I stood there panting. My throat was still raw and there were tears welling in my eyes. I was shaking: I couldn't stop shaking. But I was okay, thanks to him.

And yet he was walking away, each step difficult and painful. I put my hand out to touch his shoulder: I needed to thank him. But my hand froze in midair when I realized it was more than that.

Even through the fear, I'd had that same reaction to him as on the beach. I'd never had anything like that with a guy in Nebraska. I'd had attraction, I'd had lust, but this was much more than that. This man had a physical effect on me.

I stared at his back, his muscled shoulders rocking as he limped slowly across the room. I couldn't tear my eyes away. I'd never met anyone with such dark, brooding presence, such weight of personality. The bar was full of dangerous men but every one of them glanced up at him as he passed, unable to stop themselves.

I've often felt like I move through the world without leaving a trace: if I wasn't there, no one would notice. But this guy? He was like a massive battleship leaving a foaming, churning wake. I could feel myself caught in it, the raw pull of him like an ache that started in my chest and echoed down between my thighs. My heart was thumping, my breath quick. I felt my feet twitch, trying to go after him, and I flushed. *What are you doing? You don't even know him!*

But I wanted to. I was *fascinated.* Like the bar, he belonged to another century. Not old but...old-fashioned. And there was something else about him, something in his bearing and his gaze. Authority, but not the vicious, greedy arrogance of a CEO in a suit. Something older and deeper. I could see men shuffling out of his way to let him past. Big, tattooed men, guys who looked like they'd stab you if you glanced at them wrong. But they were meek and respectful to him. Why? Who was he?

He disappeared into the shadows. I turned back to the bartender, torn. I had questions but, after what had happened, dare I stay in this place?

The bartender was already holding something out towards me. Not more rum: a glass of cool water. He was giving me an apologetic look and I nodded that it was okay. He'd tried to help; he'd had a knife to his throat.

"You'll be okay, now," he said softly. "No one will touch you."

I blinked at him. Then I saw him glance into the darkness, where my rescuer had disappeared.

No one would touch me because I was *his,* in some primitive, caveman way this crowd understood. I should have been scared or outraged. Instead, I felt a twist of raw heat, deep inside me.

I accepted the glass of water and drank deep, washing away the taste of the rum, cooling my burning throat. "Who *was* that?" I asked when I put the glass down.

"Rourke." The bartender said it with a note of respect.

Rourke. I tasted the name on my tongue. Cold and hard as iron and there was something old fashioned about it: I could imagine it written on parchment with a quill dipped in glistening black ink. I turned, searching the darkness, but I couldn't see him. I wondered if he could see me. "Is he in here a lot?"

"Every night." The bartender wiped the counter. "He owns the place."

I blinked at him. I couldn't imagine the man I'd met doing something as pedestrian as owning a bar.

The bartender shook his head. "It's not *what he does*. He just owns it." He leaned close and lowered his voice. "Few years back, things were tough. Looked like I was going to close. Rourke walks in here and buys the place, so I could stay open. And so he'd always have a place to drink."

I frowned. "He's rich?" He didn't *look* rich.

The bartender considered it. "Used to be. Don't know how much is left. He lives cheap now, on his boat." He gave me a serious look. "Captain Rourke was the best."

Captain Rourke? Now it sounded even more old-fashioned. It felt like it should be written in elegant, looping script in some ancient ship's log, read by the light of a lantern.

"He has a boat," said the bartender. "Used to have a crew. But he gave it all up, a few years back." He nodded at the bar. "Most of the men here sailed with him, at one time or another."

That was it. That was what I'd seen amongst the men. A kind of respect I'd never known before. A captain: it fitted him perfectly. That authority, that confidence.... And then the name found the heat that was still blazing inside me. Twisted around it and tightened. *Captain Rourke.* Something about his glare, his commanding voice....

I flushed, realizing I'd crushed my thighs together.

You idiot. Sure, he'd saved me...but just as quickly, he'd gone back to his seat. If he was interested, he would have stayed. And I couldn't just go over there, even to thank him. Just thinking about it made my stomach lurch. I'd never approached a man in my life.

I turned towards the door. Then I glanced back to the shadows, biting my lip. I knew I should just leave, crash out on my great-grandfather's couch and wait for morning and then fly home to Katherine. That was the Hannah Barnes thing to do. I needed to get out of this bar, out of Nassau, back to the safe little burrow of my library.

But....

I can't explain it, but it felt as if leaving now and never seeing him again would be like slamming a book closed when it had barely begun.

I asked the bartender for a rum and then, willing my legs not to shake, I walked into the darkness in search of him.

The tables near the back were small and crammed close together. But as I neared, men shifted their chairs out of the way to let me pass. *They know I'm his.*

I saw his white shirt first and then he was looming up out of the darkness, bigger than the other men and sprawled in his chair, his left leg extended out in front of him. He was already looking at me. Had he been watching me, this entire time?

I could feel my heart racing. There was something about him, something solid and real and raw, something I reacted to like a drug. *What's wrong with me?*

But what really shocked me was that I could see it in his eyes, too. His gaze ate me up, like he was imagining throwing me down on a table and—

I felt myself flush.

And yet the closer I got, the more he glared. I walked slower and slower, drawn in by the heat of his gaze but held back by the fierceness of his anger. He wanted me. But he didn't *want* to want me.

I swallowed. "Can I sit down?"

He stared at me for one more breath. "No." Savage and hard, like a slap.

I turned to go. But just as I began to move, his hand whipped out and caught my wrist. His grip was warm and strong and rough with calluses. I could feel the power of him as he held me there. It should have been frightening but—

I hadn't realized how adrift I'd felt until he suddenly anchored me there.

I met his eyes. He was glaring, *furious* at me. For what? *I'm not doing anything!*

He nodded me towards a chair and I sat.

"I'm Hannah," I said after a few seconds. I put the glass of rum in front of him. "Thank you, for what you did."

He looked away as if embarrassed. Then, "Where the hell are you from, anyway? Kansas?" That accent again. *Yu,* as if it only had two letters. *Frrrom,* a rolling *r* that rippled the entire length of my spine. It was brutal and it was beautiful. It wasn't English.

"Nebraska," I said.

"That's a long way from the sea." He was still glaring at me, so hard I almost crumbled and fled. *I don't want you near me,* his eyes said.

No. Wait. I looked again.

I don't want anyone near me.

It suddenly hit me: he was in a room full of people who obviously knew him. Why was he sitting alone?

Everything turned around in my head. I wasn't the one person he was pushing away; I was the one person he'd grabbed hold of and allowed to stay.

"What is this place?" I asked.

Rourke looked around. "It used to be a pirate den." He took a sip of the rum I'd brought him. "It's gone downhill since then."

And that's when I identified the accent. *Scottish.* But what was a Scot doing all the way out here?

I leaned closer. The table's candle lit the hard line of his jaw, the rough stubble on his cheeks. All around us was dark wood, not a scrap of the twenty-first century to be seen anywhere. Rourke's loose white shirt was simple and classic enough that it was timeless: he could have sat in the same seat three hundred years ago, surrounded by pirates, and he would have fitted right in. "The bartender said you were the best," I said. "The best at *what?*"

He frowned at me. "You don't know?" He glanced around the room. "You don't know what we all do?"

I shook my head.

"We're treasure hunters."

My mind swam with images of sunken ships and chests full of gold. I blinked at him: was he joking?

But his face was stony. He nodded at the room. "Everyone's seeking their fortune. They're after that one big haul that'll make them rich. Some of them do it on their own. Some of them sign on with a captain and take a cut."

"A captain like you?"

Then the weirdest thing happened: Rourke glanced at the person sitting next to him. Right at them, making eye contact. Except....

Except the chair was empty.

He turned back to me. "I quit."

I swallowed. "So you...find treasure maps? *X marks the spot?*"

For the first time, he smiled: a lopsided, long-suffering grin that softened his whole face. "Mostly it's research. History. And a little rumor and instinct."

"Is there a lot of treasure?" The word *treasure* still sounded ridiculous to me. *There can't really be treasure, just sitting under the sea. Not these days.*

"Lots. This whole area was crisscrossed with trading routes. Merchant ships, treasure ships from Spain, pirate ships loaded with loot. There are plenty that we know went down but haven't been found yet, like the *Hawk.*"

A memory scratched in my mind. "The what?"

"The *Hawk*. She's the big prize, the one everyone here wants to find." The anger in his eyes eased a little and his voice slowed as he relaxed. The rolling *r's* became as smooth as malt whiskey. "There was a pirate by the name of Charles Mace. Attacked ships for years before the navy finally caught up with him. They chased down his ship, the *Hawk*, but lost him in thick fog. When the fog cleared, they found his entire crew in boats...but no Captain Mace and no *Hawk*. The crew said Mace had scuttled the ship and gone down with it, rather than let the navy hang him."

Rourke leaned closer. I found myself leaning in as well, lost in those blue eyes. They'd taken on a whole new look: there was a gleam there, a fire that had chased away all the anger and pain.

"But there's a rumor," said Rourke. "That Mace knew the navy would be coming for him. That he did scuttle the ship, but in a precise location. And that he left a map to it for his lover, so that she could recover the treasure after he was gone." He paused. "The *Hawk* hadn't put into port in weeks. Its hold was loaded with spoils, including the contents of a Spanish treasure ship. That gold would be worth tens of millions, today."

The memory was gleaming bright in my mind, now. "The pirate's lover," I said. "What was her name?"

"Esme."

I blinked, my mind whirling. Why would my great-grandfather have the map to a sunken pirate ship? It made no sense.

And then that question collided with another one that had been rattling in my mind all night.

Why did the ship carrying the cure never arrive in Nassau?

My eyes widened. "I have to go," I croaked. And ran for the door.

6

HANNAH

Please.

I left the front door to the house wide open. Went through the door to the study so fast it banged against the wall.

Please.

I raced around the desk and started rooting through the books and papers on the desk. Now I knew what I was looking for, it jumped out at me immediately: a Royal Navy communication ordering the capture of the pirate Charles Mace. There was a long list of Mace's crimes and I jumped to the most recent ones, ships he'd raided in his final weeks. The *Urca de Callao*—that must be the Spanish treasure ship—*entire cargo taken*. The *Apollo*: *entire cargo taken*.

The *Gwendoline*: *entire cargo taken*.

I drew in a huge, shuddering breath.

The *Gwendoline* was the ship that had been carrying the cure to Nassau. Charles Mace had seized everything on board when he raided it...including the trunk containing the cure.

And the *Hawk* hadn't put into port again until Mace scuttled it.

The cure was in the *Hawk's* hold. That's why my great-grandfather had been searching for the pirate ship. And sometime before his death, he'd found the map that led to it.

My heart was pounding against my ribs. A ship with tens of millions in gold was sitting on the bottom of the ocean and I was the one person who knew where it was. And in a trunk alongside all those riches was the cure that could save Katherine.

I jumped up but my legs had gone shaky. I leaned against the desk and ran a hand through my hair. *Think!* I had to be smart about this. I didn't know a thing about diving or boats. I needed an expert. I needed one of the men in that bar. But...my stomach twisted. I'd seen first-hand what some of them were like. Millions of dollars were up for grabs. If I chose the wrong one, they'd steal the map and I'd never get the cure.

I needed someone I could trust.

And there was only one who'd shown me compassion, however gruff and hostile he'd been.

The bartender had said he lived on his boat. I rolled up the map to the *Hawk,* put it in my purse, and set off for the harbor.

But when I got there, there must have been fifty boats. I had no idea which one was his. And there was no one to ask: it was after one in the morning and everything was dark and silent.

Except for one vessel. Light and music was coming from a huge white boat, its upper decks towering high above me. At the back, the hull extended like two arms surrounding a large square of water, as if the boat had its own mini harbor, complete with a crane and several small boats. The deck was cluttered with diving gear and tangled rope. Thumping bass and laughter spilled from an open doorway and I could hear the chink of bottles. The name on the side said *Pitbull.*

I was just wondering how to get their attention when a man wandered out, stumbling drunkenly, and picked up a crate of beer from the deck. He grinned when he saw me: an ugly, hungry smile.

"I'm looking for Captain Rourke," I said with confidence I didn't feel. "Can you please tell me which boat is his?"

The man turned, hawked, and spat over the rail. "*Rourke?* Why do you want *him?*"

I frowned. There was none of the respect the men in the bar had shown Rourke. Why not? I shuffled my feet, not liking the way his gaze was tracking down my body. "I just need to speak to him."

The man nodded at the open doorway behind him. "Come join us instead. We got plenty of beer." Another of those grins that made me shrink inside.

I shook my head.

The man sneered and nodded further down the harbor. "The fucking *Fortune's Hope*," he snapped. I heard him call me a few choice names under his breath and he disappeared inside.

I hurried down the dock. Right near the end, I found a boat as different from the *Pitbull* as it's possible to be. It was a sailboat, small and sleek where the *Pitbull* was huge and boxy. Its polished wood looked warm, next to the *Pitbull*'s alien, cold white fiberglass. And its deck was scrupulously tidy and clean.

There were no signs of life. I climbed carefully aboard and then caught my breath as I felt the deck move under me. *He lives here? On a boat?* I'd lived in the same house in Nebraska my entire life. I couldn't wrap my head around the idea of living somewhere so...impermanent.

But I knew this: If Captain Rourke's life was a book, it would be a heavy, thick book, a page-turner full of action and danger with elaborate silver lettering and a picture of a ship on fire. And mine? Mine would have a simple, beige cover and it would be a dull story no one would want to read.

He was my opposite. And right now, that was exactly what I needed.

I knocked loudly on the door that led below deck. "Captain Rourke?"

I waited. Nothing.

I knocked again. "Captain Rourke!"

Not a sound from below. I began to panic. What if I couldn't find him?

"Cap—"

The door swung open. Rourke stood there, his face only a foot from mine, his chest bare. "*What?!*" he snarled.

I swallowed. I tried not to stare at his chest, at those broad pecs that led to hard, bulging shoulders: God, he was so *big*, filling the doorway.... I tore my eyes away and then had to restrain a gasp as I saw the inside of the boat. Polished wood was lit by a flickering light. It was as neat inside as out, but the walls were loaded, every inch of space filled with cupboards and hooks for equipment and... what was *that?*

Mounted on the wall at the far end was a set of huge white jawbones, three times the width of my head. *A shark?!* There were photographs and weapons, a hammock—

I looked back to Rourke, forcing myself to keep my eyes on his face, this time. He was almost panting with anger. I could see the battle in his eyes again: furious that I was there, furious with himself for wanting me there. The heat in his gaze rippled down my body, soaking straight through my blouse and jeans. I flushed and my eyes dropped...but that left me staring at the hard slabs of his chest again. God, the man was carved out of rock—

"I found it," I blurted.

"Found *what?*" That Scottish accent, cleaving the air like a shining steel blade.

I managed to meet his eyes again. "I found the *Hawk!*" My voice was loud in the quiet harbor. "I know where she is!"

I saw the anger in his eyes turn to full-on rage. Then he grabbed my wrist and yanked me inside, my body slamming up against his.

7

ROURKE

Don't you ever say that again, I was going to scream at her. My lungs filled, my mouth opened—

But then she slammed into me, making me stagger back a step. I'd been so desperate to get her safe, I'd pulled her harder than I meant to. I was only wearing a pair of thin cotton pants and her legs pressed against mine, the warmth of her throbbing against my thigh. Her breasts pillowed against my chest and that was even more intimate, because only her blouse and her bra separated skin from skin. They were as soft and as weightily perfect as I'd imagined them...and I wasn't comfortable with *how much* I'd been imagining them, since she ran out of the bar. I could feel myself getting instantly hard. My leg was screaming from when I'd staggered but even the pain seemed to fade into the background, next to how much I wanted her.

What was this? Ever since I saw her on the beach, I'd been...*obsessed.* I was used to sex being just a physical need, something I'd work off from time to time with some tourist I found in a bar. But this was different: it was like her, good and clean and honest, a lust I hadn't felt since I was a teenager back in Scotland. The sort where every glimpse of exposed skin, even if it's just a flash of calf or a bare shoulder, makes you hard. I couldn't control it and that made me furious.

I stared down at her, panting. Those shining, blush-pink lips were only inches from mine. I felt an overwhelming urge to just lean down and kiss her—

I summoned up all my anger so I could deliver my speech. "*Don't*—" I began.

But she just looked up at me with those big blue eyes and I faltered. Looked away and cursed under my breath. I closed my eyes but that just made it worse: I could smell her, some soft perfume that made me think of wildflowers and sweet berries and walking barefoot through long grass with the sun on your back.

I rubbed the bridge of my nose. Dredged up my anger and started a third time, forcing my voice into a low growl.

"First of all," I told her, "you didn't find the fucking Hawk. Every tourist who comes here thinks they've found it because they've read some book or been sold some piece of tourist tat. People have been searching for it for *three hundred years!* Second, don't scream that you've found it." My voice grew firmer with each word, my fear for her fueling my anger. I grabbed her by the upper arms. "There are men here who'll kill for a sniff of that treasure, whether it turns out to be true or not! *Do you ken?*"

"What?"

"*Do you ken?*" I yelled.

"I don't speak Scottish!"

"Do you *understand?!*" I snapped.

"Yes!"

She was panting, scared. Well, good. She *should* be scared of the men around here. And if I scared her enough, maybe she'd leave me alone. That was what I wanted.

Beside me, I heard Edwards laugh.

That magnificent chest I loved so much was heaving up and down under her blouse. I had to look away for a second or I would have just grabbed her and kissed her right there. When I looked back, she was holding something out: a roll of cloth. I sighed.

"Please," she said.

That accent…I kept hearing different things in it. It was light and melodic, softly feminine. It sounded wrong, echoing around the hard wood of the *Fortune's Hope* where it's normally just Edwards and me arguing and joking and cursing. And yet it sounded so right.

I took the cloth. My face was already starting to twist into a grimace: I was going to have to tell her that she'd been sold a fake. I wasn't looking forward to stepping on her dreams.

But when I unrolled the cloth, the grimace didn't come. Instead, I felt something I hadn't felt in years: that little prickle on the back of your neck only another treasure hunter would understand.

You sentimental old bastard, I heard Edwards say. *You're as bad as her. It's a fake.*

But when I rubbed the cloth between thumb and forefinger, it didn't feel like a fake. It wasn't woven on a modern machine. And the ink had just the right color, the right spread at the edges….

I brought the map under the nearest light, a big oil lamp. I know it's old-fashioned but the smell's comforting.

"Well?" asked Hannah. "Is it real?"

I grunted noncommittally. But my heart was beating faster, my eyes taking in the lines of the islands, the flow of the handwriting. If this *was* a fake, it was the best I'd ever seen. That prickle on the back of my neck expanded, crackling down my spine. I leaned closer, checking the details, wanting to believe but not wanting to be fooled.

I knew how to check for sure. There's a rock just off the coast of Cuba. A real nasty one, because it's right where you'd swing by the western tip. It's sunk plenty of ships so it's well marked, but it only started to appear on maps after 1750. The Hawk sank in 1703 but most of the fake maps show the rock because the fakers don't know any better.

I checked. I double checked. The rock wasn't there.

I drew in a slow breath. Edwards put a hand on my shoulder and leaned close. *C'mon, that's crazy. Her? Three hundred years of people looking and she just stumbles across it?*

He was right. It was crazy. But….

But the thing is, treasure doesn't care. It doesn't care if you're an archeologist who's spent his entire life looking for a lost pyramid: it'll let you wander straight past and then show its secrets to some army patrol who come across it in a sandstorm. The wreck of the *El Cazador* was found by a fishermen who snagged it with their nets. A German U-boat was found by a ship laying undersea cables.

My heart was thundering, now. *And maybe, just maybe, the Hawk could be found by me.* One last haul, before the sea finally took me.

And then I remembered that that wasn't my life anymore. I remembered what happened the last time I'd gone seeking my fortune.

I rolled the cloth and handed it back to her.

"Is it real?" she asked urgently. "Can you help me get what's on board?"

I met her eyes but I didn't see what I expected. She looked desperate: this was beyond anything as simple as greed.

I realized I was still holding the map, our hands connected by it, the edge of my palm just brushing her softer one. "It's real," I muttered. Looking into those eyes, it was hard to get the words out. "But I can't help you."

"What? But you're the best!"

"*Was* the best."

"But it's the *Hawk!*" she said, eyes wide. "You told me it was the big prize. You said everyone wanted to find it!"

God, it sounded tempting. "Not me," I lied. "I quit."

She fell silent, just staring up at me as if cheated. As if she was realizing she'd been wrong about me. *I never said I was a damn hero!*

She swallowed and shoved the map back in her purse. "Okay, fine." Her voice was tight. "Well, thank you for looking at it. I'll find someone else." She turned to leave.

I couldn't help but stare at her divine, denim-clad ass for a second. She had her hand on the doorknob before I spoke up. "Wait!"

She stopped.

"You can't just go around the island telling people you've found the *Hawk.* The men around here...." I sighed. "They don't *just* hunt treasure. They do whatever makes them a quick buck. Some run drugs or guns. Most of them have killed. They'll kill you and take the map." My chest tightened at the thought.

She turned to look at me over her shoulder. God, the way her hair shone. It looked so soft.... "What *do* I do, then?"

I sighed. "Go home. That map'll bring you nothing but trouble. It's too much money, the kind that drives men crazy."

She shook her head. "I can't do that."

"Why not?" She didn't answer. *Does she owe money to someone? Is that what it is?* "Go to the government, then. Make it an official expedition, scientists instead of treasure hunters. You'll still get a cut."

"How long will that take?"

I shrugged. "Three, four months."

"No! I need to get there *now!*"

I frowned. "Why? Why the hurry?" She shook her head, turning to go, but I could see how scared she was and it made me mad. Whatever was threatening her, I wanted to run my sword right through it. I grabbed her. "Tell me!"

She looked down at where my hand gripped her arm. "Are you going to help me?" she asked in a choked voice.

I closed my eyes. I couldn't do it. I couldn't go back to all that. Not after Edwards. "No," I said at last.

She wrenched her arm out of my grip. "Then I guess it doesn't matter, does it?"

And before I could stop her, she was off my boat and running down the dock.

8

———

HANNAH

I spent a fitful night on my great-grandfather's couch. When the dawn flooded through the windows I was already awake, shaky from nightmares of Katherine in pain. I'd left my dad all alone, looking after her. *I should be there!*

But if I flew home now, she had no hope. I had to get to the *Hawk!*

I stumbled through to the study to think. I couldn't go to the government: that would take months and Katherine had less than a week. I had to go to one of the other treasure hunters...or criminals, as Rourke had described them. Like the three who'd grabbed me in McKinley's. The idea of putting my faith in men like that was terrifying. But what choice did I have? *I just want to be back in Nebraska. I'm the wrong person for this!*

I let out a sob of frustration and fell into a chair. The vibration dislodged one of the oil paintings that was propped up against the wall and it slid to the floor. I sighed, bent down and picked it up—

And found myself looking at Katherine's face.

No... not Katherine. But the resemblance was uncanny. The woman had the same blonde hair and blue eyes, the same cheekbones. There was another painting alongside the first and, out of curiosity, I picked it up, too. A different woman but the same hair and eyes.

I dug through Bertrand's notes until I found a catalog of sorts, matching the paintings to names. They were my ancestors...my *female* ancestors. Why had Bertrand been collecting paintings of them? Why had he needed to find out what they looked like?

A sudden chill went through me.

I gathered the paintings and separated them into two piles: women who'd died from the mystery disease and women it had skipped over. And I saw what Bertrand had seen: the disease was far from random.

Every woman with blonde hair and blue eyes had died. *Every. One.*

Every woman with some other combination had lived.

It *was* genetic...and now I knew exactly which women would be affected. I let out a moan of horror as I ran through my mental images of my cousins. Five of the seven women had blonde hair and blue eyes. Three were roughly Katherine's age and the other two would reach it within a few years. And at least two of the women already had kids of their own: I remembered the Facebook photos of little girls, most of them blonde. My heart felt as if someone was crushing it in my chest. I didn't know who I felt sorrier for: the blonde cousins who'd die or the brown-haired ones who'd live to see the disease steal their blonde daughters from them.

This wasn't just about Katherine, anymore. I'd known the other women in our family were at risk but now I could actually think of names and faces. Harriet would die. Gwen. Paula and Lindsey. *Chrissie! Oh God, Chrissie!* I wanted to throw up. Chrissie was three years old, a giggling, mischievous firework of a child with big blue eyes and golden curls. She'd be dead by twenty-five.

I stood up. *Screw* being scared. My family needed me. I had to go find another treasure hunter.

I dug my washbag out of my suitcase and had a quick shower. Pulled on a fresh blouse and jeans. I checked the mirror in the bathroom, ran a hand through my hair—

Oh Jesus. I froze and stared.

There was one blonde-haired, blue-eyed woman I'd forgotten about and I was looking right at her. I'd been so worried about Katherine and my cousins, I hadn't even considered myself. I was older than Katherine so I'd just assumed the disease had missed me the way it had missed my mom and my grandmother. But now I knew: it *would* hit me.

My stomach knotted. Bertrand's notes were clear: the older you were when the disease hit, the faster it progressed. Katherine had roughly a week. When it hit me, I might only have days.

The room spun and tilted around me. I took a long, shaky breath. *I am going to die.* The knowledge soaked into me like ice water. *I am going to die.*

I opened my mouth to call for Katherine. For my dad. For a friend. For *anyone.* And then I remembered I was thousands of miles from the nearest person I knew. The only sound in the house was my own panicked breathing.

The pain would be horrific, maybe even worse than Katherine's since the disease would hit me faster. And Katherine had gone through it with her family and boyfriend around her, in a hospital filled with doctors. If I collapsed right now, here in Nassau, there wasn't anyone to help me. No one would even find me. Hot tears burned at the backs of my eyes. *I can't do this! I have to fly home!*

But if I left now....

I squeezed my eyes shut. I thought of Katherine and her boyfriend, about the wedding they'd never have and the children they'd never raise. I thought about all of my cousins, about Chrissie, watching her mom die and knowing that was to be her fate.

I opened my eyes, took a deep breath, and set off for McKinley's.

~

I wasn't sure if McKinley's would be open: it was still only mid-morning. But it seemed to be the sort of place that was open whenever its patrons needed it...and they needed breakfast. There were benches outside and men were working their way through huge platefuls of bacon and eggs. The bartender frowned as I walked up. "You okay?"

I shook my head. "I just need to ask you some stuff—"

But he put a hand on my shoulder and gave me a worried look. "When did you last *eat?*"

"I'm okay," I said, shaking his hand off. I didn't have time for breakfast and I was too stressed to eat. But even as I thought it, my stomach rumbled noisily and I swayed, light-headed. Come to think of it, when *had* I eaten? Not since before my flight: about forty hours ago, now. I'd been too worried about Katherine.

The bartender took one look at my confused expression and pushed me down onto a bench. "*Wait there!*" he scolded. He strode away muttering. Moments later, he returned with a mug of tea and a plate piled high with slices of thick, rough-cut bacon, salty and perfect, slices of crunchy fried bread, and two eggs with golden yolks dripping down over everything.

"I can't eat all that," I said. And then ate it. My body knew what I needed, even if I didn't. As I ate, I could see the bartender watching over me from the doorway. *Because of Rourke.*

Something in my chest tightened, just at the thought of him. *Why didn't he help me?* When he'd saved me in McKinley's, I thought I'd seen something in him, some desire to do the right thing. I'd even had some romantic notion of a captain being...*honorable.* Well, he'd shown me how stupid that was. There was no honor in this place.

When I pushed my empty plate away, I felt better. The bartender came over and sat down opposite me. He waved away my thanks and the money I offered. "What do you need to know?" he asked.

"Who are the best treasure hunters?"

He crossed his arms. "The best one's Captain Rourke." That loyalty, again. That respect Rourke commanded.

"Other than Rourke."

The bartender studied me for a long time, then sighed. "The most *successful* is Grant Ratcher. Runs a big boat and a big crew. But you don't want to be messing with him."

The way he said it sent a warning chill down my spine. And I noticed he didn't call him *Captain* Ratcher, despite him still having a crew and Rourke being on his own.

"If you've got any other option," the bartender told me, "I'd take it."

But I didn't. I got Ratcher's address, thanked him again, and set off.

~

Ratcher's villa was high in the hills, a sprawling place with terraces and balconies, reached via a long, winding driveway.

I pressed the buzzer beside the gates. A camera panned to focus on me and a man's voice muttered, "Yeah?"

"Hannah Barnes, to see Mr. Ratcher."

There was a pause. The camera's glass eye stayed on me for a moment. Then there was a buzz and the gates unlocked.

A tanned guy with no shirt on, his chest a mass of twisting snake tattoos, led me through the huge house and out to a veranda at the back. A rabble of men, ten or more, chattered and cursed. It was barely past noon but there was already a pile of crumpled beer cans around them. A suckling pig was being turned on a spit over a fire.

The man turning it was big. Not as tall as Rourke but much wider, heavy muscles smothered with fat. Where Rourke was tanned, he was pasty, his white tank top disappearing into his pale shoulders where the straps cut deep into the soft flesh. His neck and back were bright pink and scarred from repeated sunburn.

The man leading me coughed to announce his presence but the big man turned the spit another three times before he bothered to turn around. His head was bald on top and shaved smooth on the sides and back, revealing a bumpy, uneven scalp. His head seemed to flow into his shoulders with no visible neck and it made him seem shorter and squatter, even though he was taller than me.

"Hannah," he said, grinning. That unsettled me, for some reason. With Rourke, it would have been *Miss Barnes*, the first time we met.

And something about the way Ratcher said it made my skin crawl. He almost smacked his lips and I writhed: I didn't want my name in his mouth.

Don't be stupid. You need him. I forced myself to smile.

"What can we do for you?" He was still grinning, being nothing but friendly, but it felt as if he was patronizing me. To my surprise, his accent wasn't American. He was British, some London accent I'd only heard in movies. Movies about bad neighborhoods and gangsters, that slow, sing-song dialect that can turn vicious and cruel in an instant.

I swallowed. "I want to hire you. Or do a deal with you—I don't know how this works. I've found the map to *The Hawk*."

The chatter around me stopped.

"Have you?" asked Ratcher thoughtfully. "Have you, now?"

I was keeping my eyes on him but I could feel everyone turn to look at me. I suddenly felt like a deer that had wandered into a pack of wolves.

"Can I see it?" asked Ratcher. He stepped closer, his bulk blocking out the sun. His size was intimidating: he might be fat, but there was still a lot of muscle there.

"I took a picture," I told him. And passed him my phone.

He lifted it up to his face and peered at it, his already small eyes made smaller by his squinting, His lower lip flopped over his upper as he concentrated. "Where's the rest?" he asked.

I swallowed nervously. I wasn't stupid: if I just gave him the map, he'd disappear with it and I'd never get the cure. I had to make him take me with him, even though that meant going *out there,* on the vast, open sea. That's why I'd very carefully covered the key part of the map with a blank sheet of paper before I'd photographed it. "You'll see the rest when we're on the way." I lifted my chin and tried to look confident. "Not before."

Ratcher stared at me incredulously. The hush around us deepened. I tensed, wondering if I was about to be hit by one of his ham-sized hands.

But then he burst out laughing: a big, ugly laugh that smelled of beer. He shook his head and pointed at me: *you rascal!* "No, no, very good! Very smart." He winked at me but his eyes weren't jolly: they were dead and cold. "Where's Fredericks?" When he didn't get an instant response, he yelled loud enough to make everyone jump. *"Fredericks!"*

A thin man with soft blond curls pushed timidly through the crowd. Ratcher shoved the phone in his face. "Is this real?"

Fredericks pushed his glasses up his nose and peered at the screen, zooming and scrolling. *He must be Ratcher's tame historian.*

Eventually, Fredericks looked up and nodded. Immediately, a ripple of excitement passed through the men. They started whispering and cursing, already muttering about how they were going to spend the money.

Ratcher called over a squat Hispanic man, a diving expert, to start figuring out what equipment would be needed. He'd surrounded himself with people who filled in for his lack of knowledge. What did *he* bring to the table? They had a muttered conversation, then Ratcher turned to me. "We'll do it," he said. "I'll take care of the costs of the operation. You supply the map. We split what we find fifty-fifty. Deal?" He stuck out a pale, flabby hand.

I stared at it. *Fifty-fifty?* Was that good? I had no idea what was normal. But I didn't care about the treasure anyway. Hell, they could keep all of it, as long as I got the cure. But I wasn't going to tell him that, not until that "curious stone" was in my hands. If Ratcher knew this was life-or-death for me, he'd have a frightening amount of power over me.

I took his hand and shook it. "Deal."

Ratcher turned to his men. "Alright. We move today, in case some other wanker's got wind of this. I want everyone geared up and ready to go by sundown."

The dive expert cursed.

Ratcher whirled to face him. *"You got a problem with that?"*

The man jerked back. "No!"

And suddenly I saw what Ratcher brought to the table: fear. His crew stayed for the money but he ruled by terror, not respect.

Ratcher turned to me. "We'll stop off at your place, so you can get your pajamas." He smirked as he said it, his eyes running over my breasts. "Then we'll go. My ship's down there: the *Pitbull*."

I looked where he was pointing but I already knew what I'd see: I remembered the name of the big, white, high-tech boat. Now I knew why that crewman I met hadn't respected Rourke. He was loyal to a different captain. And I remembered how his eyes had crawled over me.

This is a bad idea.

But what choice did I have?

Ratcher thrust a can of beer into my hand and clinked it with one of his own. I gave him a nervous smile and took a tentative gulp.

9

___

ROURKE

I was working stripped to the waist, using a plane to shave down a piece of wood before I fixed it in place. The boat was old enough that there was always something that needed replacing and I did all of the work myself. It helped fill the days and stopped me heading to McKinley's too early in the evening. I'd lose myself in it, listening to the ocean, and Edwards' watchful presence beside me. Normally, I got into a kind of meditative state and forgot everything else.

Today, though, I couldn't forget *her*.

I brooded on her all day, getting angrier and angrier as the sun got closer to the horizon. By the time the sun was kissing the water, I was livid. What the hell did she think she was doing, prancing around with something as dangerous as that map, tempting me?

Deep down, I knew that wasn't the problem. She wasn't *prancing around*. She'd been as smart as anyone new to this world could be. She'd come to me, not one of the others: it was me who'd turned her away. And as for tempting me...*yes*, she damn well did, but not deliberately. I had a feeling she didn't have a clue how gorgeous she was. It was all me. I couldn't take my eyes off the woman.

So why didn't you help her? asked Edwards, sprawled out on the deck next to me.

You know why, I thought bitterly.

The sound of engines made me look up. A convoy of SUVs roared up to the dock and started unloading men and gear. An expedition, and a big one. I watched as one car tore away from the pack and drove down the coast to a nearby cluster of houses. I grabbed my binoculars, a suspicion forming in my mind. The first person to haul himself out was...yes, Ratcher. And the second was—

I let out a groan as the sun caught her blonde curls. *Shit.* Not Ratcher. Anyone but Ratcher. Why had she teamed up with *him?*

Edwards gave me a pointed look. I told him to shut the hell up.

I watched as Hannah led Ratcher inside the house. I remembered Bertrand, the guy who'd lived there: he'd asked me questions about local history a few times, over the years. Was Hannah some relation to him? Is that how she'd got the map? *Why didn't I ask her, instead of chasing her away?*

Through the windows, I could see Hannah sitting on a bed, fiddling with what looked like a pair of jeans—I couldn't make out what she was doing to them. Meanwhile, Ratcher was quietly poking around in the other rooms, opening drawers and nosing in cupboards. The sight of it made my skin crawl.

Hannah grabbed a suitcase and a big travel bag so heavy she had to use both hands to heave it up onto her shoulder. Then she locked up the house and she and Ratcher got back into the car. I followed it back to the harbor, lowering the binoculars as it pulled up outside Ratcher's boat. Hannah hesitated at the gangplank. *Don't,* I willed her, unconsciously leaning forward.

Ratcher held out his hand for her. She bit her lip, casting nervous glances at the horizon. *She's scared of the sea.* So what the hell was she doing hunting sunken treasure?

I saw her take a deep breath and then she took Ratcher's hand and climbed aboard, her face pale. Ratcher bawled orders to his crew and they cast off. The harbor echoed with the sound of his ship's big engines and it growled out of the bay in a cloud of nose-wrinkling diesel fumes.

I lowered my head, focusing on my work. *It's her choice,* I told myself savagely. I put my hands on the plane and pushed it forward over the wood. *It's not your problem.*

I pulled the plane back and pushed it forward again: a less certain movement, this time.

On the third stroke, the plane slowed and then faltered to a stop.

I jumped up and ran to untie my launch.

10

HANNAH

Waves. Waves on every side of me. I could feel the panic rising and, as Nassau disappeared from sight, it got worse. I couldn't ignore the water beneath my feet. My breathing got faster and faster but, no matter how fast it got, I didn't seem to be getting enough air. We were in the middle of nowhere, suspended above a drop that might as well be bottomless, protected by a hull that suddenly felt very flimsy. I could already imagine the water soaking through my clothes and chilling my body. I was panic-breathing, now. If the boat sank, I'd be lost out here, the tops of the waves towering over me, the force of the ocean gradually sapping my strength until I sank beneath the surface....

I had to get away from the water. I went below deck...and entered chaos. The room was filthy and disorganized, the floors stained with oil and strewn with tangled rope. Muscled, tattooed men, high on excitement, cursed and yelled obscene jokes at each other. I stood in the middle of it all, clutching my bags, and my nerves only seemed to excite them more. They'd push past me, "accidentally" rubbing up against me, or throw a piece of diving gear across the room so it just narrowly missed my head. I felt like a high school geek, trapped by the football team in the locker room.

Ratcher rescued me at last. He showed me a corner where I could stash my bags and then led me to the mess hall, which reeked of sweat and fried food. God, how big was Ratcher's crew? There were at least ten sitting at long tables, working their way through plates piled high with ribs and French fries. There'd been another ten in the first room. And everyone seemed to have a beer in his hand.

Ratcher grinned as he saw the way I nervously eyed his crew. "Don't fret. They work hard, they play hard. But I can keep them in line."

I didn't miss the way he said it. *Can.* Not necessarily *will.*

He stepped closer, backing me into a corner. He came close enough that his stomach almost touched me, where it stretched out his tank top. Suddenly, I wanted to be back on deck, even with the waves.

"Why don't we take a look at that map?" he asked, that London accent sugary-sweet.

The room went quiet.

I swallowed. I might be new to all this but I wasn't stupid. Once he had the map, he wouldn't need me anymore. "Let's take it stage by stage," I said. "You know the rough area. Let's get there, then I'll show you the detail."

The cool softness of his belly touched me. As he pressed closer, it rolled outward to cover more and more of me. "I'd rather see it now," he said, a warning tone creeping into his voice.

One of his crew burst through the door. "It's not in her suitcase," he said. "And the other bag's just full of books."

What?! "You went through my *stuff?*"

Ratcher ignored me. "S'pose it must be on her, then." And he pressed hard against me, pinning me against the wall. I felt the soft squish of his stomach and then the muscles beneath, the reminder that he was as strong as he was big.

I gave a panicked gasp and tried to bolt to the side but he grabbed my throat with one big hand. He didn't choke me: not yet. But his hand was like iron. Then his other hand started working its way down my body. It was obvious that I wasn't hiding anything above my waist: I was only wearing a blouse and a bra. But his palm slid over my shoulders, under my arms and then.... I writhed in disgust, closing my eyes to shut out the sight of him as he cupped and lifted my breasts.

His hand slid lower, diving into the rear pockets of my jeans, taking the opportunity to squeeze my ass. Then the front pockets, his fingers probing.

He loosened his grip on my neck and I tore away from him, staggering on shaky legs.

"Think she hid it inside her?" asked the man who'd been through my bags.

Ratcher smiled. "If she does, we'll find it soon enough."

I wanted to scream but deep, chilling fear stole my voice. Men rose from their tables and ambled towards us. I took a step back.

"Think very carefully how you play this, girl," said Ratcher. He used *girl* as if it was an insult. "You hand me that map now, you can spend the whole trip with me, in my cabin with the door locked. But if you run, they'll come after you. And I won't be able to stop them once they catch you."

I was so scared, I wanted to throw up. How could I have been so stupid? This had been his plan all along: my only choice was whether I was entertainment for him...or the whole crew.

Ratcher grinned as he saw me weaken: he must have thought I was going to take his deal. And that superior smile made the anger jump and flare inside me, lending me strength. *You're going to have to catch me, first.*

I bolted across the room, heading for the nearest door. I didn't have any plan in mind, other than to get away. I heard Ratcher curse behind me: I'd taken him by surprise. But other men were already moving to grab me.

Two of them tried to corner me. They were grinning, enjoying the chase, which only made it worse. I dodged past them and sprinted through the door. I could hear laughter and footsteps behind me...but it didn't sound like they were running. *Why aren't they running?*

Then it hit me and my steps faltered and slowed. I had nowhere to run. We were miles from shore.

Footsteps behind me. I sped up again, determined. I didn't care if it was useless.

I raced around a corner and along the length of the ship. Seconds later, I burst back into the first room, the one where I'd left my stuff. Most of the men had left but a few were still there, rooting idly through my suitcase, holding up my bras and panties. They laughed when they saw me and stood up, taking a step towards me.

I ran up a set of stairs and burst out onto an upper deck, high above the water. My lungs were burning. The sun had pretty much set and all I could see around me was dark ocean. *A boat! I need a boat!* The idea of going out on the water terrified me but it was better than the alternative. I ran to a lifeboat that dangled over the water but I had no idea how to launch it.

The men started to emerge from below deck, appearing from stairways and doors. I swallowed and started to back away from them, but then my ass hit the rail. *Shit!* They were coming from both sides, surrounding me, muscles gleaming in the darkness, teeth white as they grinned. They'd enjoyed the chase, now they wanted their prize.

I looked behind me at the rail. The deck was at least twenty feet above the dark water and, if I jumped, it was too far to swim to shore. I had nowhere to go.

I looked back at the men. At their open, hungry mouths. *Oh Jesus, no....*

I turned to the rail and quickly climbed up onto it, closing my eyes to shut out the sight of the sea. I balanced there, sneakers squeaking on the rail, my heart hammering in my chest. *I'll jump. Even drowning's better than—*

"Don't," snapped Ratcher behind me. "Don't, you little—"

I bent my knees to jump. My eyes opened and I looked down—

And found myself looking into deep blue eyes set in a stern, tanned face. He let go of the rope he'd been climbing, grabbed the rail and vaulted over, pushing me down off the rail at the same time.

He had his sword drawn before his boots hit the deck. He straightened up and stepped between Ratcher and me, a protective wall of Scottish fury.

"No one's *fucking* touching her," said Rourke.

11

———

HANNAH

I stared at him, wide-eyed. How did he get here? And why was he saving me...how had he even known I was on board?

Ratcher stepped forward but I noticed that he stayed just out of reach of Rourke's sword. His crew pressed forward as well, a shrinking semi-circle around us. "What the *fuck* are you doing here, Rourke?" spat Ratcher.

Rourke didn't answer him. He just stood there, feet so surely rooted to the deck that he was almost part of the boat. He looked more sure-footed here on a swaying boat than he ever had on dry land. Without taking his eyes off Ratcher, he spoke to me. "Get ready," he said. "We're going to swim."

What?! I gulped and looked over the rail. The drop into the black water didn't look any more inviting now I had company. "Where's your boat?" I asked in a strangled voice.

"Behind us. Look a little to starboard."

Starboard? I had no idea which way that was. But then I saw something breaking the line of the waves, far behind us and shrinking rapidly. "All the way back *there?!*"

"Didn't have time to tie on," he snapped. "It's only a half mile."

I gulped. I'm a good swimmer but it's a long time since I swam half a mile...and that had been in a hotel pool. But, I realized, Ratcher's boat was still moving. With every second, Rourke's boat was slipping further out of reach.

I climbed up onto the rail again. Rourke waited until I was up, then backed up to the rail himself.

Ratcher and his crew pressed forward. "*Don't,*" warned Ratcher through gritted teeth. His whole face had turned red with fury. "The *Hawk's* mine and so's she. You do this, Rourke, and I'll hunt you down and fucking finish you!"

Rourke reached down and grabbed something off the deck: it looked like a big, net bag. "Ready?" he asked me, backing right up against the rail.

"No...."

Rourke suddenly turned, sheathed his sword, and scrambled up onto the rail beside me. Ratcher and his men surged forward. Rourke bent his knees, ready to jump—

I stared down at the dark water and swallowed. Twenty feet was much, much higher than I'd ever dived from. "Wait—"

A hand grabbed mine, warm and strong. Rourke jumped....

....and pulled me with him.

My legs kicked and I let out a long wail of terror. We plunged, my stomach left behind as the black ocean rushed up to meet us.

We smacked into the water and everything went dark. Salt water blasted up my nostrils, rushed up the legs of my jeans and then I was fully under, my hair streaming out around me—

Rourke's hand heaved on mine and I surfaced, spluttering and coughing. Somewhere high above us, I could hear cursing.

Rourke let go of my hand. "Wait right there," he told me. And to my surprise, he started swimming towards Ratcher's boat, one hand still gripping what I now realized was a fishing net. The boat was still moving and he reached it just in time to grab hold of the back before it left him behind. *What's he doing?* Already, the boat was starting to turn: Ratcher must have told the pilot to circle back to pick us up.

Rourke suddenly dived beneath the surface. A few seconds later, there was a screech of tortured gears and the steady roar of the boat's engine turned to coughs and splutters. There was worried yelling from up on deck. There was a screech of metal on metal, so loud I had to cover my ears...and then suddenly the engine stopped and everything was silent.

Rourke surfaced—from where the propeller was, I realized—and swam back to me. "Take 'em an hour to untangle that," he said as he arrived beside me. "Come on."

I just stared at him. It was slowly sinking in that I was *in the sea,* for the first time since—

I froze, barely able to tread water. The waves slapped and pulled at me, lifting me, and dropping me like I was nothing. I turned a slow circle, seeing nothing but vast, rolling blackness—

"Hannah?"

I didn't respond. My breathing went shaky. I was a kid again, reaching out for my Mom's hand, not quite able to grasp it—

"Hannah!"

I focused on Rourke. He was frowning, staring at me. *You alright?* his eyes asked.

No. My stomach twisted in panic and, simultaneously, I felt a hot rush of humiliation. *No, I'm not. I'm a fuck up who's scared of the sea just like a little kid and I shouldn't even be out here and—*

A big, warm hand found mine under the water and grasped it tight. A warm throb of security raced up my arm, pushing back everything else.

"Swim," he told me, the Scottish accent like whiskey over smooth ice. "Just swim."

And he tugged me forward, launching me in the right direction and then pulling ahead of me to lead the way. I somehow got my arms and legs going in a stroke. The ocean was still terrifyingly huge but I found I could shut it out—just—if I focused on him.

He swam with long, easy strokes, gliding through the water as if it was air, as if he was born to do this. Whatever caused the limp he'd had on land, it didn't seem to bother him at all, in the water. In fact, he had to keep waiting for me to catch up.

It wasn't just that I was out of practice, it was my clothes. Rourke's t-shirt and shorts didn't hold him back too much but my blouse was billowing out, filling with air and water like a parachute, and my jeans felt like they were made of lead.

"Take 'em off," snapped Rourke. That accent again. Rough-smooth, rasping right down my spine and making my toes dance. He hauled his t-shirt over his head as if to demonstrate and I tried not to stare at the smooth slabs of his pecs.

"I'm fine," I said.

Rourke wriggled out of his shorts, then looked over his shoulder and cursed. I followed his gaze. Ratcher's boat was still drifting but I could see men working at the stern, trying to launch one of the small boats.

"Take 'em *off!*" snapped Rourke again. This time, his eyes were blazing and.... I gulped. It was hard not to imagine him saying the same words as we stood beside his bed.

"I can swim like this," I lied.

Rourke just shook his head and dived. Before I could think about where he was going, I felt his hands on the fly of my jeans. My eyes widened and I looked down: all I could see was dark water but I could feel him there, his strong chest pressed against my legs. *"What—"*

I drew in my breath as I felt him pop the button of my jeans open, then tug down the zipper. The back of his thumb grazed the front of my panties and I flushed and stifled a gasp.

He tugged but the waistband of my jeans caught on the curve of my ass. His fingers hooked beneath the fabric to free it, fingertips skimming my ass cheeks, and this time I *did* gasp. Then he was pulling off my sneakers and hauling the jeans down my legs and off. He surfaced with them in his hand and just...*looked* at me. I'd never seen a stare like it: half lust, half anger, blazing right through to my core. I panted, treading water, my newly-naked legs kicking.

"The rest," he muttered. His eyes never left mine.

I swallowed and, knowing he'd do it if I didn't, I unbuttoned my blouse and stripped it off. He grabbed it from me as soon as it was free, wadding it up with my jeans, and gripping the bundle in one big hand. Then he just hung there in the water, staring at me.

Some of the waves were breaking high up on my chest, the water covering me. But some were breaking just below them, the night air cool through the soaked fabric of my bra. I could feel my nipples puckering and standing erect. I gulped, staring back into those deep blue eyes. I felt as if I was falling, plunging deep into molten heat....

Rourke turned and started swimming. I swam after him and now I could match his pace. I still wasn't used to swimming in the sea and kept getting hit in the face by waves, but I was determined to keep up. I tried not to think about the boat being launched behind us, or how quickly it would catch up.

It was completely dark by the time we reached Rourke's boat: a small launch only about fifteen feet long. I got my hands up on the edge and struggled to lever myself out. Suddenly, a warm hand was under my arm, thumb a half-inch from the soft flesh of my breast, and another hand was under my ass, hard fingers spread across my cheeks. He lifted me like I weighed nothing and I tumbled over the side and into the bottom of the boat. Rourke tossed in our clothes and then hauled himself in, water coursing down his body. He was wearing just a pair of jockey shorts, the fabric soaked, and clinging.

He loomed over me in the darkness, his height forcing me to look way up to meet his eyes. He was staring down at me just as he had on the beach, that same mix of raw need and fury. Except then, I'd been dressed.

Now, I was in my underwear...and it was soaked through and almost translucent. As his gaze tracked slowly over me, a fierce, crackling heat started at my groin and spread through my body, every inch of my exposed skin tingling and throbbing. I found I was taking big, shaky gulps of air. My eyes raced over the dripping slabs of his pecs, the deep lines of his abs, crisscrossed with scars, and—

His jockey shorts were black, soaked through and tight against his body, the bulge of his cock edged in moonlight. And as his eyes ate me up, I could see that bulge lengthen and swell—

He marched past me, grabbed the throttle, and rammed it to its limit. The boat leapt forward so fast I almost fell over. Behind us, I heard another engine start up. Ratcher's men had their boat in the water. They were coming.

It was a warm night but the air seemed freezing after the water and the faster we moved, the more the wind whipped across my wet skin. I hugged my knees and huddled in the bottom of the boat, eyes glued to the dinghy that was chasing us. It was smashing its way through the waves with brute force but our boat seemed to skip across their tops, in the air as much as it was in the water. I had to cling on tight to avoid being thrown out.

Rourke stood at the controls, legs bent to soak up the bumps, the muscles of his back standing out as he fought the wheel to keep us on course. Spray was blasting against his face and chest but he barely seemed to notice it.

I suddenly remembered something and grabbed for my jeans. I rolled up the left leg, praying....

No! It was gone!

I stared in horror at the jeans for a full ten seconds before I realized that, in the dark, I was holding them back to front. I turned them round and groped inside the *other* leg—

My fingers closed on the wad of cloth. I'd had to sew the map there in a hurry, while Ratcher waited in the next room of my great-grandfather's house. But it had worked: he hadn't found it. And my clumsy stitches had held in the water. If they'd come loose....

"We're nearly there," said Rourke. "Be ready. Need to move fast."

I'd been focused on the men chasing us. Now I looked to the front and saw that we were nearly back to Nassau's harbor. "What's the plan?" I asked breathlessly.

"I'm taking you aboard the *Fortune's Hope*," he grunted. "We'll lose them in the islands."

Almost as soon as he said it, we were there. Rourke swung the launch in a perfect arc, coming in behind the sleek lines of his yacht. He cut the engine at just the right time and jumped effortlessly aboard. I scrambled out behind him, not quite as gracefully. He bent to secure the launch. I pushed a lock of sopping hair out of my eyes. "What can I do to help?"

Rourke blinked at me as if he hadn't been expecting that. But he rallied quickly and nodded towards the front of the yacht. "Cast off. Two painters, fore and aft."

I looked at him blankly.

"Ropes," he said patiently. "One at the front, one at the back. Untie them."

I nodded and ran along the deck. It was only when my bare feet started slapping against the wood that it sunk in that I was in my underwear. And... *Oh God, all my clothes are on Ratcher's boat!*

There was no time to worry about that now. I could hear the dinghy that had been chasing us, its engine echoing around the harbor. I found the first rope and untied it, then raced to the front of the yacht and repeated the process there.

The engine roared as Rourke opened up the throttles and then spun the wheel to point us out to sea. Behind us, the dinghy with Ratcher's men in it was closing in. "Can we outrun them?" I asked.

"Not with just the engine." He grabbed my wrist and tugged me to the wheel. "Hold her steady."

My eyes bulged. *What? I don't know how to steer a boat!* But I grabbed hold of the wheel and held it, resisting the pull of the water that was trying to spin it back the other way.

Rourke raced out onto the deck. The limp was visible again, now, but it still wasn't as bad as when he was on dry land. There was something about being on the rolling deck of a ship that seemed to soak up the unsteadiness—where the movement threw me off balance, it seemed to suit him. As if....

I worked it out a moment later. Rourke was grabbing ropes and tugging them, unfurling the sails, and he didn't even have to look before he snatched each rope out of the air. He knew exactly where everything would be. *As if this is his home.*

The yacht surged forward as the wind caught the sails. A completely different feeling to the steady push of an engine: it felt as if we were being carried by a giant hand.

The dinghy chasing us started to drop back. As we moved out of the shelter of the harbor, Rourke really began to work the sails, turning and adjusting them to capture every bit of wind. He and the weather seemed to be in perfect sync: the wind would change and he'd already be swinging a sail across to compensate. We started to rush through the water, the yacht's sleek hull cutting through the waves where Ratcher's boat had battered them into submission. The dinghy following us dropped back and back...and eventually disappeared in the darkness. I realized there were no lights on Rourke's boat: we were running dark, like a smuggler. Yet Rourke seemed to know exactly where we were going, cutting around rocks and islands with ease. I realized he could probably sail these waters blindfold.

At last, he eased his grip on the ropes and stood listening at the stern. I stood there silently, barely daring to breathe, until he said, "They're gone. We lost them."

I let out a long sigh of relief.

And then it was just me and him, standing there all alone in the darkness.

12

ROURKE

My grandfather used to tell me tales about mermaids. Pale-skinned, golden haired creatures who'd tempt sailors with their beauty.

I never thought I'd see one.

But she was standing right there, alabaster skin lit silver by the moonlight, long golden hair falling in damp curls over her shoulders and breasts. Her breasts...oh, God, her *breasts*. Her body had been tempting in a blouse and jeans but *now*.... She was one of those women who tried to cover up her curves. Now, with her blouse gone and her bra turned gauzy by the water, she was unbelievable. I wanted to take each full, weighty breast in a hand, squeeze and lift and run my tongue between them while I stroked each pink, perfect nipple. And the rest of her...that hourglass formed by her waist and her flaring hips. Those legs that went on and on....

What really had me entranced, though, was her face. Something in those eyes, an innocence, an honesty that was like a sweet south wind. It stirred something inside me beyond the simple lust. Something I'd forgotten existed. And the more I felt it stir, the more frustrated I got, because I knew what that feeling was and I didn't want it.

Smitten. That's what my grandma back in Scotland would have called it. *You're smitten with that girl, Billy.*

She really was a mermaid: a creature from another world. Nebraska was far more distant and strange, to me, than any undersea kingdom. And she'd cast a bloody spell on me. Tempted? I'd sail my boat right onto the bloody rocks for her.

And then it got worse. Because she said, "Thank you."

I opened my mouth to tell her to stop it. I didn't want her getting any ideas about me being a hero.

But before I could, she said, "If you hadn't come, they were going to...."

The way she went pale said it better than words. My hands clenched into fists and I shook in fury. I wanted to kill every one of those bastards.

She saw my reaction and nodded her thanks. Then she gave me a tiny, timid little smile.

Aw, hell.... Something in my chest *lifted,* the way it hadn't since I was a bloody teenager. *No!* She'd better not—

She was still looking up at me—

No! Don't fucking like me, woman! Are you mad? No one likes me.

But she did. I could see it in her eyes. I had to cut this off at the fucking roots before it got any worse. Because whatever she thought I had to offer, it died a long time ago.

I forced it all down inside me, pushed past her, and started working the sails, not even glancing at her.

She came to stand behind me. "Where are we going?" she asked quietly.

"I'm going to circle around and take you to South Ocean Beach," I snapped. "Far side of Nassau. You can get a cab to the airport from there. Then you're going to ask someone at the airport for a light and you're going to *burn that damn map!*"

I heard her shake her head. Imagined those blonde curls tossing. "I can't," she said.

"You can."

"I thought the *Hawk* was the big haul everyone wanted. Don't *you* want it? You can help me find it!"

I shook my head, still not looking at her. "I told you: I don't do this anymore." I stared off to the side and cursed under my breath because now I was looking right into Edwards' pleading gaze. "It's too big for one person, anyway."

"I could help you—"

I spun to face her. "No!" I snarled.

She leapt back, scared. *Good,* I thought savagely. *She should be scared.* I wasn't going to have her in danger, much less put her there myself. I hauled harder on the ropes. The sooner she was off my boat, the better.

She went silent for a long time. As the lights of South Ocean Beach came into view, she said, "Rourke?"

I stared fixedly ahead and didn't answer.

"What's your first name?" she asked.

"*Rourke*'ll do fine," I snapped.

She didn't answer for a second but the silence was blackened and tainted, as if I'd slapped her. I silently cursed.

"I really need your help," she said, that sweet country voice barely a whisper.

My hand tightened on the rope it held. "This is no place for you. *Go home.*"

I caught movement in the windshield, up ahead of me, and—*oh, bloody hell.* I could see her reflection. And once I'd glimpsed it, I couldn't look away. Her head was lowered, or I would have been looking right into her eyes.

"That's not an option," she said, and I heard the crack in her voice. She was seconds away from crying.

"Why?" I snapped, my frustration making my voice vicious. "Why do you need the money so bad? You in debt?" I had visions of some thug back in Nebraska, backing her up against her living room wall, demanding money, and the anger made me squeeze the rope so hard that its rough weave dug into my palm.

"It's not the money," she said wretchedly. "It's not about the treasure."

"Then *what?* What else do you think you'll find down there?"

She finally lifted her head and our eyes met in the windshield's reflection. "A cure."

I wasn't even aware of my arms moving, but the ropes slackened and the boat slowed as we lost the wind. I turned around to face her, all those feelings I'd been struggling with swelling up and then contracting down into a cold, hard knot of worry. Silent tears were running down her cheeks and each one that fell to the deck felt like it was striking my heart.

It scared me, how much I felt for her.

I motioned with my head: *tell me everything.* She laid it all out for me: the illness, the history, and the letters she found.

The cure.

"How can you be sure it's down there?" I asked.

"It was definitely taken by the *Hawk* when she raided the *Gwendoline.* And you told me the *Hawk* didn't put into port again until Captain Mace scuttled her."

"Aye," I said grudgingly. I knew the story of the *Hawk* better than anyone and it made sense. "But even if it's there, some medicine's not going to have survived three hundred years."

She shook her head. "It's not a liquid, it's not something that would go moldy or decay. The letter said it was a stone."

I wrinkled my nose. "A *stone?* How could that cure...you think it's *magic?*"

She shook her head again. "No. Nothing like that. Look, I don't know how it works. I just know it cured one of my ancestors. Now it's my only chance of saving my sister. And the others."

My stomach tensed as she told me about her cousins...and their kids. *Ah, hell. Wee bairns, as well?*

"That stone is our only hope," said Hannah. "And you're my only hope of getting the stone."

I shook my head and looked away. But when I looked at her again,

Edwards was standing behind her, staring back at me. "I *quit*," I snapped at both of them.

Hannah swallowed. "Unquit," she said. "Please."

I closed my eyes. *No. Not this.* Diving and treasure...I knew where that road led. I wasn't going to let the same thing happen to her.

But if I didn't do it, half her family were going to die. I knew what that was like, to lose someone close.

I opened my eyes and looked right at her. And saw that flash there, that heat, the same heat that was raging inside me. *No. Jesus, no.* She *did* like me. But she had no idea what a mess I was.

I glanced at Edwards. She had no idea who else lived on this boat.

And I was too smitten with her. Being around her, in the close quarters of a ship, would be unbearable. This was my home, for God's sake, my sanctuary. *I don't want her here!* However much I *did*.

I looked back at Hannah, about to tell her *no*.

But...she was staring at me with those big, clear blue eyes. Thousands of miles from home. A damn mermaid who'd swum right into my world and for some reason had put her faith in me.

"Okay," I said. "Let's go find the *Hawk*."

13

HANNAH

I passed my soaking jeans to Rourke and he used his sword to slice through the stitches that held the map in place, then carefully wrung out the soaked cloth. Its time in the sea didn't seem to have damaged it. Most likely, it had been through far worse in the last three hundred years.

The wind was getting up. The boat lurched and I quickly sat down. This was nothing like Ratcher's boat. That had felt almost like a building. But here, the floor moved up and down in a way no floor should. It didn't so much rock from side to side as circle: a churning, lurching motion that left my stomach behind.

"You've gone pale," muttered Rourke as he examined the map.

I nodded and closed my eyes.

"Correction," said Rourke. "You've gone green."

I just sat there and took deep, calming breaths as the seat below me lifted me *up, up, up*...and then plunged me down.

I heard him sigh and stomp off. I thought he was leaving me to my fate but a few minutes later, he returned. "Here. Chew on this." He pressed something into my hand.

I grudgingly opened my eyes and saw an orange nugget dusted with sugar.

"Crystallized ginger," he said. "It'll help."

I blinked up at him, then nodded my thanks. I'd been expecting him to be scowling at me, despairing of the stupid landlubber. But he didn't have that expression at all.

He stared at me as I began to chew, the ginger fiery and sweet. "You really *are* from Nebraska, aren't you?" he grunted at last.

I nodded shamefully.

"It's not just getting seasick, though, is it?" he asked.

He hadn't missed the way I froze, when we jumped into the water. I looked away, flushing. I knew it must be impossible for him to even imagine being scared of the sea.

And yet his voice, when he spoke, wasn't cruel or disbelieving. It was gruff but kind...and almost embarrassed, as if he wouldn't want anyone to catch him being kind. 'You sure you want to be out here?"

I looked at the endless dark ocean around us and felt my chest contract with fear. Then I shook my head. "I don't want to be," I said quietly. "I have to be."

I looked up and caught his eye. For a second, he looked almost impressed. Then he remembered to scowl again. "We better find you something to wear," he muttered, and stomped below deck again.

He had a point: I wasn't as cold as I had been when we'd been racing across the water in the launch but the temperature was still dropping and I was still in just my soaking underwear. Rourke returned with a couple of towels and a bundle of clothes. I toweled off: it was strange, I'd been standing around in my soaked bra and panties for so long, I'd almost gotten used to it. Now, with a towel wrapped around me, I was suddenly aware that I was nearly naked, alone with a man I barely knew. A man who'd saved me twice. *Why is he doing all this?*

He pulled on a pair of pants and I tried not to stare at the hard muscles of his quads as he hauled the cloth over them. Then another of those loose white shirts, that magnificent chest slowly disappearing as he fastened it up. I realized I hadn't even started dressing yet and scrambled into the khaki t-shirt he passed me. Made for his much bigger frame, it hung midway down my thighs. A pair of his black shorts drowned me, too, but I managed to cinch them in just enough with a belt that they'd stay on. *There.* I was decent. Except....

"What?" he frowned, noticing how I was squirming uncomfortably.

I flushed and adjusted things again, but...*nope.* My soaking underwear was just too damp and cold against my skin. It would drive me crazy. "One sec," I told him. Keeping the t-shirt on, I fumbled about underneath it, unhooked my bra, and managed to extract it and drop it on the deck. My panties weren't so straightforward. I had to wrap the towel around my legs, drop the shorts, step out of the panties and pull the shorts on again, all while trying not to drop the towel. Finally, I was done. "There," I said with great relief.

And realized I'd just treated him to some sort of bizarre semi-clothed striptease. And now he was giving me *that* look, that scorching one that turned me molten inside, the one that said *you teased me. Now I'm going to pounce.*

I swallowed. *I didn't mean to—* But it was too late. I could feel the pull between us, just as I had at McKinley's. The air between us seemed to sing and crackle. I couldn't look away from those deep blue eyes, gleaming in the moonlight....

And part of me wanted him to. Part of me wanted him to just grab me, even though I hardly knew him.

Rourke tore his gaze away and stared off towards the horizon. I could see how his whole body had gone tense and hard, his biceps straining against the cotton of his shirt. When he spoke, it was through gritted teeth, as if barely controlling himself. "If the map's right, the *Hawk's* in shallow water, off the coast of an island. No point heading there now: it's too dangerous to dive at night. We should drop anchor here and sail on in the morning. We should be there before noon and I can dive down and take a look."

I nodded.

He looked me right in the eye. "Until then, we should get some sleep."

Where? In his cabin? How many beds are there on this thing? Does he mean...?

So many questions. But when he led me below deck, I forgot them all.

It was completely different to Ratcher's boat. I couldn't figure out why, at first. They were both made for the same thing: hunting for treasure. They both had to store equipment and have room for eating and sleeping and stuff. And yet....

Ratcher's boat had been all white fiberglass, giving it an almost alien feel. This was all polished wood and brass, warm where the other boat was cold. Where Ratcher's boat was dirty, this was scrupulously clean and tidy. And where Ratcher's was new but badly cared for, this was old but well-loved.

It felt like a home. That was the difference. Ratcher's ship was just somewhere he and the crew were based when they were out at sea: Ratcher lived in his villa. But Rourke slept here every night.

"Are these the cabins?" I asked. I opened a door...and stopped. It had been a cabin, once. But the bed's mattress had gone and it was piled with oxygen tanks. The closet doors were missing and I could see wetsuits inside. I had a feeling the other cabins would be the same: he'd given over the space to equipment.

He had no need of the space because he slept here all alone.

I spun and stared at him and he must have seen the realization in my eyes because he looked away, embarrassed. Why the hell was a guy as gorgeous as him all alone?

"I sleep here," he muttered, nodding his head at the main room. "But you can have it tonight."

I started to protest but he cut me off as soon as I opened my mouth. "I'll sleep fine out on deck," he told me.

I nodded shyly, grateful for the sacrifice. I was pretty sure *I* couldn't sleep out there, so close to the ocean. But then I looked around, confused. I didn't see a bed, or anything that could be turned into a bed. "When you say *here....*"

He pulled a tight roll of cloth from a nook and shook it out. It was only when he hooked one end to the wall that I remembered something I'd seen before, when I first came to his boat. *I'm going to sleep in a hammock?!*

He passed me the other end and pointed me towards the opposite wall but I couldn't find the ring where the hook went, at first. He had to squeeze past me to show me and, with the room being small and him so big—

Suddenly, we were chest-to-chest. The softness of my breasts rolled up against his pecs and I caught my breath. I'm big enough that it's very rare I don't wear a bra. I wasn't ready for how intimate it felt, the heat of him throbbing through the thin t-shirt. And—Oh God, my nipples were still standing out hard from being cold, scraping against him—

He swallowed, his eyes locked on mine. He took my hand in his big, warm one to guide it to the ring...but then he just paused there, gently squeezing it, as if he'd forgotten what he meant to do. Our breathing was in sync and every time that big, muscled chest lifted and expanded, my breasts were crushed harder against it. I was lost in those eyes again, speechless. I fumbled along the wall for the ring, hooked the hook into it—

Something heavy and warm and *alive* jumped onto my hand and scampered up my arm, heading straight for my face. I let out a scream and tried to move back, but the newly-hung hammock was behind me and all I did was stretch it until it was tight across my shoulders. Meanwhile, the *thing* had reached my elbow. I had a glimpse of fur and eyes and *claws* and then it was on my upper arm, my collarbone—

Tiny hands sunk into my hair. Tiny feet scrabbled on the upper slopes on my breasts. Two big, brown eyes stared into mine from just a few inches away and a mouth filled with white teeth shrieked *EEEEEEP!*

I kicked backwards with my feet to get away. The hammock twisted and I went with it, screaming again as my feet shot towards the ceiling and my head careened towards the floor in a graceless backward somersault. Only the fact that my hands were tangled in the hammock stopped me dropping to the floor. The thing on my face was still screeching, its screech and my scream blending together—

Strong hands grabbed my shoulders and pushed me back up to vertical. A leg hooked around my ankles and guided my feet until they found the floor.

And then he pulled the monkey from my face.

The monkey and I fell silent and just stared at each other, panting. It was about the size of my head, covered in brown fur except for a little pink face and tiny pink paws.

"Yo-Yo," explained Rourke.

'You—" I blinked. "You have a *monkey*."

Yo-Yo scurried up onto Rourke's shoulder and took cover behind his head, then peeked shyly out.

"Picked him up in Cairo." Rourke reached up to pet him. Yo-Yo grabbed hold of his finger and nestled his little face against Rourke's palm.

My heart melted: now that it wasn't leaping in my face, the thing was adorable.

"The guy who owned him wasn't treating him well," Rourke said with a grimace.

"So you rescued him?" My heart melted in a whole different way.

"No!" said Rourke defensively. "He didn't give me a choice. Rode out of there on my head and wouldn't let go. Edwards said we should keep him. And..." He looked away. "I like having the wee man around. He doesn't talk back to me."

I tentatively reached out and petted Yo-Yo. He tilted his head to one side as if deciding, then rocketed up my arm. This time, though, I was ready for it and let him scamper over my shoulder and onto my back. He buried his paws in my hair to hang on and cuddled up to the back of my neck, and I giggled. It was the first time I'd relaxed since Katherine fell ill. And, just for a second, I thought I saw Rourke give a little smile, too.

It was a happy moment. Then I ruined it. "Who's Edwards?" I asked innocently.

Instantly, Rourke closed off. It was as if a shutter had come down between us. "Head's in there," he said, pointing to a door. "I'll be on deck. Get some sleep."

Before I could ask what the head was, he was gone, the door closing behind him. *Shit!* What had I said? Who was Edwards, that he caused that kind of reaction?

I was too wired to sleep so I explored. I discovered that the head was the toilet and found a cupboard that held blankets. The other cabins were stuffed with equipment, just as I'd thought. There was a tiny kitchen, well-stocked with food. And that was it. A cozy little home...but God, it seemed like such a lonely life.

Something caught my eye, high in one corner of the room. It was almost hidden and I had to climb up on a cupboard to see it properly. A photo of Rourke, a few years younger. And next to him, grinning, a blond-haired man in a Hawaiian shirt. *Edwards?*

I was exhausted but my brain was still racing: I knew I wouldn't sleep yet. So I did what I always did: I reached for a book.

Shit!

My whole bag of books was still on Ratcher's boat! I closed my eyes and groaned. That actually bothered me more than losing my clothes. Being bookless, especially away from home, was like a physical pain. Disappearing into a book is how I normally switch my brain off and wind down.

Rourke must have a book. He lived here full time, after all. I began to search the shelves. It might even teach me a little about him...and I was so eager to learn more about him, it was embarrassing.

But a search of every shelf and every cupboard turned up nothing: not a techno-thriller, not a history book, *nothing.* The only thing I found was an old, gray reference book called *The Shipboard Doctor: A Guide to Emergency Medicine at Sea.*

That's it? He doesn't read for pleasure? I had trouble even processing that concept.

I fingered the book and then pulled it from the shelf. It was either that or have nothing to read and this was *me.*

It took me four attempts to get into the hammock—or at least to stay in. Yo-Yo retreated to a safe distance while I rolled and swung and was dumped unceremoniously on the floor. Only when I was finally in and cautiously relaxing did he spring across the room and land on my leg, which made me jump so much I almost tipped us both out again. Then he settled down on my bare feet, acting like a furry comforter, and I sighed in relief and opened the book.

The Shipboard Doctor managed to be both dull and terrifying, full of grave instructions on how to amputate a man's arm when it's been crushed between rocks, or what drugs to give following horrific jellyfish stings. I flipped to the front and wasn't surprised to find it had been written by another Scot: I could almost hear Rourke's growling accent as I read it. *In the case of air in the chest cavity compressing the heart, do not delay. Thrust a hollow needle into—*

I skipped a lot of the pictures.

But it did work to quiet my mind. And the ginger seemed to have done the trick with quelling my nausea. The soft rocking of the hammock was almost relaxing and the creaks and groans of the ship, which worried me at first, started to become familiar and comforting. It was almost as if it was alive. And it smelled good, like old wood and lamp oil.

The book flopped down onto my stomach. I hadn't been sure if I'd be able to sleep, given everything that was going on. But I was exhausted, it was warm under the blanket and having Yo-Yo cuddled up to my feet helped, too. I began to doze. And my mind started to wander.

Rourke. With his sword and the growly authority of a captain and that sense of honor he gave off...he felt like a man out of time. For all he kept saying this was no place for me, it almost seemed like it was no place for him: he might be bad-tempered and prickly but he wasn't cruel like Ratcher. He felt like a man who'd try to do the right thing, however hard he denied it. So how had he wound up in Nassau, surrounded by criminals?

And... I shifted slightly in the hammock. That chest, broad but narrowing down to that tight, powerful core. The way the water had coursed down it when he hauled himself up onto the launch, tan skin shining. The way he'd loomed over me, his size making me feel small.

I'm not a slender, delicate thing like my sister: I don't often get to feel small. But Rourke did it to me every time I was around him.

I shifted in the hammock again, straightening my legs and crushing my thighs together a little. I was on the edge of sleep, now, my thoughts slow and dreamy. I saw Rourke standing in just his jockey shorts, the bulge growing as he stared down at me. *That's crazy. Why would I do that to him? He can have any woman he wants.*

And yet he lived here all alone, snapping at everyone to keep them away.

And yet he'd agreed to help me.

A warm ache began in my groin. That moment when our chests had brushed together: I could still feel every tiny contact of my hardened nipples against his pecs. Just for a second, as he'd held my hand, I thought he was about to—

If Yo-Yo hadn't jumped out at me....

But then I'd gone and blown it by asking about Edwards. Now he was mad at me. And he was the only shot I had at saving Katherine and saving myself.

My hand had wandered down to the waistband of the borrowed shorts, my fingertips nudging underneath. I snatched it back. *No.* This had to stop now, before I messed things up and he changed his mind about helping me. Katherine had less than a week. And as for me.... I deliberately hadn't told Rourke that the disease would hit me, too. I was worried that, if I'd told him, he would have taken me straight to a hospital. But I knew a hospital couldn't help me. My only hope lay in that stone.

I couldn't afford to mess this up. From now on, I had to keep my distance.

With my clothes still on and Yo-Yo warming my feet, it was too warm for the blanket. I sleepily pushed it off onto the floor: *perfect.* I finally dozed off.

At first, everything was peaceful. But as the wind rose outside and the boat rose and fell, the feel of the waves dislodged memories.

I'd kept them pushed down inside me, buried under the safe, solid ground of the prairies. But now I was here, there was nothing to stop them bursting up to the surface, huge and dark, looming over me.

No! I twisted in my sleep and tried to fight my way awake, knowing what was coming.

But it was too late. I was already there.

14

HANNAH

We made the trip from Nebraska to California in two days of non-stop driving. Our folks good-naturedly bickered in the front, Katherine—age eight—acted out an elaborate princess-themed drama with her dolls next to me and me—age ten—steadily worked my way through a big bag of books. I'd look up every few hours, check that the highway looked the same, and immerse myself again. Only when I saw my first palm tree did I stop and gawp, open-mouthed. And then I saw the ocean, glittering and alive, indescribably beautiful.

For five days we took in the Golden Gate Bridge and Alcatraz and then Rodeo Drive and Hollywood Boulevard and Disneyland. But we kept putting off the beach. Finally, on the sixth day, Dad was visiting an old friend and Mom was driving us back to our motel. We were on a coast road and, suddenly, the sea was *right there*, beside the car.

Even fifteen years on, in a nightmare, my question still makes me wince. *It was all my fault.*

"Mom?" I asked. "Can we go in the sea?"

Mom shook her head. "We'll do a proper beach day soon."

"But tomorrow we're going to the Getty and then Dad wants to go to that battleship museum thing. We'll run out of time." We passed a perfect, deserted cove. "Look! We could go right there. Just for a minute? Please?"

Katherine loyally joined in. "*Pleeease?*"

Mom glanced across at the cove once, twice. I thought she was going to drive right past it. But at the last possible second, she gave one of her trademark long-suffering grins, slewed the car across the road, and pulled over. We whooped.

Minutes later, we were down on the beach. The sun was low in the sky and the sand was just the right temperature under our feet. The water was incredibly clear and at least as warm as the air. We paddled in a line, holding hands. I was entranced, watching the waves roll in towards us. I'd never seen the sea up close before. Katherine was giggling and even Mom looked glad we'd come.

"Can we swim?" I asked. We were all good swimmers: Mom had insisted we learn at the local pool. And I wanted to feel what it was like to be lifted by a wave.

Mom shook her head. "Not without your father here. I want to be able to keep an eye on both of you, in case a wave hits you."

"There are no waves *there,*" said Katherine, pointing.

We looked. She was right: just a little way down the beach, there was a stretch of water that was like a millpond, its surface barely rippling.

"Huh," said Mom, frowning. She walked us over to investigate. The water was as calm as it had looked from a distance. "Well...okay, I guess. Just for a minute."

We waded out and it was like a huge, warm bathtub. We giggled and sploshed and swam, as content as a family of otters. Minutes stretched into an hour: the sun had almost set.

Then Katherine turned around and frowned. "Mommy? We're a long way out."

Mom and I both turned and—

What I saw didn't match what I remembered. I was looking at distant cliffs and beaches, the highway just a thread of black. The cove we'd swum from was a tiny detail in the center. *How did we get so far out?*

"Okay, girls," said Mom, her voice carefully calm. "Start swimming back to shore, now."

I didn't argue. I could see how pale she'd gone.

We struck out for shore at a steady pace. *It's not so bad,* I reassured myself. *It'll be a funny story to tell Dad: we swam too far out and it took us forever to swim back in.*

But after ten solid minutes of swimming, we weren't any closer. If anything, the cove was retreating away from us. And that meant....

That meant we were heading out to sea.

I looked around me and that was the first time the sea changed in my mind, shifting from a fun stretch of water next to a beach, something you paddle and swim in, to being *the ocean,* that vast, cold, desolate thing that only big ships should go on. *We shouldn't be out here.*

We swam faster, Mom helping Katherine along, but it didn't do any good. My arms grew tired and then my legs and we *still* weren't any closer. I stopped and put my feet down for a second to rest—

And felt my toes search in vain. And remembered that we were way, way out of our depth. We *couldn't* rest.

Katherine was exhausted now, her little arms limp. Mom hustled her onto her back and we swam like that. I gritted my teeth and kept up but soon both of us were panting and exhausted and we were *still* getting further away. *Oh no. Oh no....*

Mom stopped, took Katherine in her arms, and treaded water. "Okay, don't panic," she muttered. "Someone'll see us." She raised one arm above her head and waved. "Help! Hey! *Help!*"

But the cove had been deserted and now the sun was sinking below the horizon. Immediately, the temperature started to drop. And as we were pulled further out, the waves were getting bigger. I looked at Mom. *No one knows we're out here,* I thought. And then, *this is my fault. I made her take us swimming.*

I couldn't even see the cove now over the tops of the waves. We were sliding down into the troughs and then rising up with the next wave and it wasn't fun like I'd imagined, not out here, not in the almost-dark. It was terrifying.

And then, quite suddenly, the sun went down completely and it was *black*. I couldn't see the waves properly and they took me by surprise, crashing over my head. "*Hannah!*" I heard my mom scream.

Somehow, she made it over to me and we all joined hands, treading water in a circle. "Stay together!" she told us, panting. She was exhausted: we all were. But she kept hold of our hands and hauled us up each time our legs failed, grunting with the effort. She tried to keep our heads above the waves, powering us up the sides of them so they didn't break over us. The lights were coming on the shore, now, and they were just tiny pinpricks in the distance.

The waves got higher and higher, pulling at us, trying to separate us. We were helpless now, the waves too big to swim over. We'd drop sickeningly into a trough and then the next one would crash down over us. Mom was almost sobbing with tiredness now, her arms on fire from hauling Katherine and me up. And then a huge wave broke over us and I felt her hand tear loose from mine. I coughed and choked and, when the water cleared from my eyes, she was sliding down one side of a wave and me down the other.

"*Mom!*" I went to let go of Katherine's hand to go after her.

"*No!*" she screamed. "*Keep hold of her! Keep hold of your sister! Don't let go of her!*"

I gripped Katherine's hand harder than ever and struck out towards Mom, towing my sister behind me. But Mom had already disappeared. It was too dark. "*Mom?!*"

Another wave broke over me and I pulled Katherine in close, wrapped my arms around her, and used my legs to keep us afloat. And even though I shouted again and again, tears streaming down my face, Mom didn't answer.

It was utterly black, now, and I couldn't tell where the water ended and the sky began. I only knew what was happening from the feeling in the pit of my stomach as I was lifted into the air and then dropped sickeningly down. The only warning I had of a wave breaking over me was the sound, a crescendo roar that filled my ears and burrowed deep into my brain. I'd hear that noise and then I'd be choking and drowning, coughing up water, desperately holding Katherine up. Time stretched out: I had no idea how long I'd been out there. I only knew I had to hold onto my little sister, no matter what.

15

ROURKE

After Edwards, I found I couldn't sleep in my cabin anymore. I'd wake in the middle of the night fighting the sheets, the metallic taste of aqualung air still in my lungs. I'd race across the boat to Edwards' cabin, convinced I could still save him, only to find his bed empty.

After barely sleeping for weeks, I started stringing a hammock up in the main room instead and the nightmares retreated, though they never went away. The rum helped, too. Later, I packed both our cabins with equipment, telling myself it was because I didn't like wasting the space.

But outside, on the deck, I always sleep like a bairn. I'd sleep there every night, if I had the excuse. Something about feeling the wind on my face and looking up at the night sky...I'm off in seconds. And tonight was perfect.

There was almost no light pollution, this far from shore. I'd turned on a few running lights just to make sure some cruise liner didn't smack into us in the dark, but other than that it was just darkness and about a billion stars above. The deck was rocking slowly, just the way I liked it.

And yet I couldn't sleep.

Part of it was being on the trail of treasure again. I had that buzz, that throb of excitement that never quite leaves you. I hadn't felt it since Edwards and my usual remedy would be to stay up half the night talking to him: planning, dreaming of the haul....

My stomach tightened. Edwards was gone. I had no one to share the excitement with.

I grunted and pushed the thought out of my head. But there was something else keeping me awake and it was harder to get away from. It was lying in my hammock, not ten feet away.

I kept thinking about her eyes. The delicate curve of her jaw. The way she stuck her lower lip out when she was being stubborn. I still couldn't believe she was doing this. She was so far out of her comfort zone: she was obviously scared of the sea and yet she was out here, trying to save her sister.

I cursed and turned on my side but sleep still didn't come. *Why can't I stop thinking about her?*

And then I heard something. Only a tiny noise: I wouldn't have heard it if I hadn't been lying there, silently fuming. A whimper, coming from below deck.

I got up, stumbled over to the door, and cracked it open. I could hear Yo-Yo's snores and the sound of Hannah breathing. As moonlight spilled into the room and struck her face, I saw her eyes were closed and I relaxed. God, she was beautiful. Blonde hair spilling over the side of the hammock like a sleeping princess. Sexy as hell even in my outsize clothes, her soft curves making me catch my breath.

But then she frowned and whimpered again and I saw that primal fear you only glimpse when someone's facing death. I crossed the room in two quick steps and stared down at her. A nightmare, a real bastard one. I knew the sort: I'd had plenty. *What happened to her? Is this why she's scared of the sea?*

She was shaking her head in her sleep, her eyes moving frantically behind their lids. My chest closed up tight. I had that same urge I'd had when I'd seen her in McKinley's and when I'd seen her with Ratcher: a need to protect her, stronger than anything I've ever felt. I wanted to scoop my hands under her and lift her out of the hammock and into my arms, whisper in her ear that it was alright....

Then I caught myself. I wasn't her husband or her boyfriend. If she woke in my arms, she'd scream her heart out. *Damn it, what's she doing out here? Why isn't she safe home, with someone who can look after her?*

It all rose up inside me, the need to protect her and the frustration that there was nothing I could do. I squatted down beside the hammock to get closer to her, even though holding that position made my leg howl in pain. I watched her face twist and her eyes grow wet and I cursed myself over and over that I wasn't *that* sort of man, the sort she needed—

And then, before I knew what I was doing, I reached out and took her hand, closing my big fingers around her slender ones. She squeezed back in her sleep. I stared at my hand, aghast. *What are you doing, man?* For a heart-stopping moment, she seemed about to wake. But then she slipped back into sleep...and the tension in her face started to ease.

After a minute or two, my leg felt like a garden hose with a knot tied in it, the pain building and building with nowhere to go. I wanted to throw back my head and scream with it, would have given a hold full of gold just for a second's relief.

But I wasn't going to let go of that hand. I stayed there for twenty minutes while her breathing slowed and her frown faded. Until she slept peacefully again.

I finally eased my hand from hers and stood up, the pain from my leg making me gasp. Her blanket was on the floor: she must have thrown it off during the nightmare. I carefully replaced it and then limped outside.

As I closed the door, my gran's voice came back to me again. *You're smitten, Billy.*

Yeah. Yeah, I was.

16

HANNAH

As the nightmare reached its peak, I felt something...or thought I did. I was still clinging onto Katherine but there was a hand holding mine, big and warm, helping me through it....

Suddenly, a blinding light lit up a circle of ocean around me. A man all dressed in orange plunged into the water next to me and then he was trying to get Katherine and me into a metal basket. I was so terrified that I didn't understand we were being rescued, at first. Then they winched us aboard the helicopter and I collapsed on the floor, my legs too weak to hold me.

Dad had been worried when we didn't show up for dinner and Mom didn't answer her phone. He'd got his friend to drive the route we'd taken and, after many hours, they'd spotted the car down in the cove, realized what must have happened and called the coast guard. Dad was there to meet the helicopter when it landed and his face, when he realized that Mom wasn't with us, was the most heartbreaking thing I'd ever seen.

They found Mom's body the next day, a mile down the shore. We'd been caught in a rip current. We'd missed all of the indicators because we hadn't known what to look for. And we hadn't known how to get out of it because this wasn't our world: we didn't belong there, should never have been anywhere near the ocean. Every time I closed my eyes, I could hear the waves, feel them lifting and dropping me. I never wanted to see the ocean again. I just wanted to be back in Nebraska, far away from the sea. Dad agreed and the three of us flew home that evening.

That night, there was a moment when I realized that things would be different, now. My dad was in his armchair, eyes squeezed closed, phone pushed tight to his ear, telling my mom's relatives what had happened. So I got Katherine unpacked and got her changed for bed. But she wanted milk to help her sleep and we were out because Mom had emptied the refrigerator before we went on vacation. I bit my lip. Dad was still on the phone.

So I went through Mom's things, found her purse and got a five dollar bill, pulled some jeans over my pajamas and snuck out of the back door. It was late and, except for the lights of passing cars, it was almost completely dark. I was terrified. But Mom was gone and Dad had enough to do. So I walked the half mile to the store, bought a carton of milk, brought it home, and gave it to Katherine. When she'd drank it, I saw her eyes go to the book on the bedside table. Mom read a chapter to us every night.

My heart twisted and crumpled. Mom *used to* read a chapter to us every night.

"Can you read some?" asked Katherine in a fractured voice.

I picked up the book, my hands prickling and numb. "I don't know if I can do it like she does it," I said, my voice strained. My eyes were getting hot and I was determined not to let them spill over in front of her.

"Can you try?"

I swallowed hard. *Yes,* I decided. *I can try.* And I opened the book.

My life changed direction that night. Like a train that's jolted onto an adjacent line, things ran in parallel for a while but as I got older they diverged more and more. Dad needed help on the farm and I made a decision: Katherine was the smart one, already acing math and science; all I was good at was English. So I started helping him in the fields after work, leaving Katherine free to focus on her homework. At night, to help me sleep, I'd bury myself in a book: when I was deep in a story, I wasn't missing Mom or imagining dark, towering waves crashing over me.

As I got older, it became obvious that there was no way my Dad could afford to send both Katherine and me to college. So as soon as I graduated, I took a job at the local library: I could walk there, so I didn't have to spend money running a car, and I could be home in time to help Dad before the sun went down. I took over the admin work Mom used to do. My ability to tease information out of thick, impenetrable texts came in useful for taxes and all the government red tape, or when I was scouring tractor manuals trying to help him solve a problem. I saved every penny I earned from the library and, between that and the farm, we scraped together just enough to pay Katherine's college fees.

By that point, Katherine had really come into her own, with crazy-good math skills. She majored in computer science and got a job with a software company in Omaha. The day she moved out to start her new life, I breathed a deep sigh of relief. *I did it, Mom. She's okay.*

I settled into quiet, small town life, helping my dad and fighting to keep the library open. I didn't date, had no idea *how* to date. I'd sort of missed all that stuff, growing up. Katherine kept attempting to set me up with men when she visited and I loved her for trying, but who'd want the pale, curvy girl who still lived with her dad?

The fear remained: I never once went near the ocean again. I couldn't even watch one of those disaster movies where a tidal wave sweeps over New York without wanting to throw up.

I didn't care. I didn't care that I was single or that I was still stuck in the same small town or that I was screwed up. I'd kept Katherine safe and I was a long way from the sea and that was all that mattered.

But now another dark monster was threatening to snatch my sister away from me. And I wasn't going to let it, even if it meant facing the ocean again.

~

I came groggily awake. Daylight was streaming in through the...*portholes?*

It took me a few seconds to remember where I was: on board the *Fortune's Hope*. And we were on....

The boat bobbed and creaked. The hammock swung. *Oh God!* All I could see outside was endless blue. The fear closed in from all sides: the boat seemed to drop away under me.

I dug my nails into my palms. *No!* If I let it win, I was finished. *Katherine* was finished.

I closed my eyes for a second, remembering the nightmare. The same one I'd had many times except...something had been different, this time. When I was lost in the sea with Katherine, I swore I'd felt someone there with me, helping me through it. A big, warm male hand holding mine.

I looked down at my hand and then at the door that led above deck. *Rourke?!*

As if to prove how crazy that was, the door opened and he limped in, gruff as ever. "We're underway."

I stared at him. "Great." The sun was high in the sky: he must have been letting me sleep in.

He ducked under the hammock, the top of his head passing a half-inch from the underside of my thighs. "You okay to eat some breakfast?"

I thought about it and found that I was. The fear of being at sea was still there but the seasickness had passed. I nodded.

He started messing with pans in the little kitchen: what was it called, the *galley?* I sat there in the hammock, staring at his back. *No. No way. I must have dreamt it.* I pushed back the blanket, preparing to get up....

Wait. Hadn't I thrown the blanket off before I went to sleep?

I turned and stared at Rourke again, my jaw dropping. He *had* been in here. He'd held my hand.

He must have felt my eyes on him because he turned. "What?" he grunted.

I shook my head and looked away. "Nothing."

17

———

ROURKE

I'd brought breakfast out on deck: now I was waiting for Hannah. She was below deck, changing into another one of my t-shirts. I'd dropped anchor for now but I was impatient to get going again.

I'd been up early and I'd been studiously building my anger back up while she slept, telling myself all the reasons I needed to get her off my boat. All that hand-holding at three in the morning had put some stupid ideas in my head and I didn't want them taking over. *Just get her to the damn wreck and get the cure. Then I can be rid of her—*

Hannah emerged from below deck. A fierce sun was beating down, turning the surface of the water into a million twinkling diamonds so bright they hurt your eyes. And as the sunlight hit her, she—

Well, she yawned and stretched. But that didn't even begin to describe the magnificence of the move. The sun hit all that golden hair at the same moment as her back arched and her chest strained upwards and—well, Christ, she wasn't wearing a bra. And she'd closed her eyes so I didn't even have to avert my gaze unless I wanted to.

There are times I've been a gentleman. This wasn't one of them. I drank it in: every glorious curve of that fine body, every line of that gorgeous face. *She really has no idea how bloody beautiful she is, does she?*

I got my eyes fixed on the mainsail a fraction of a second before she opened her eyes.

"Thank you for letting me sleep in," she said. "I needed it."

I grunted.

Breakfast was eggs fried on a skillet and crusty brown bread, toasted with lots of butter, together with plenty of coffee. Yo-Yo devoured an orange next to us. Hannah ate hungrily: had no one been feeding the poor girl? But her eyes never left the waves around us.

"You don't like the water," I said at last.

She glanced round at me guiltily. For a moment, I thought she was going to deny it: that gorgeous lower lip pushed out defiantly...but then she dropped her gaze. "I don't like the *sea.*"

I wrinkled my forehead. What had happened to her? How could I put it right? Then I caught myself. *What the hell am I doing?* I've never been much good at understanding women, even before I became a recluse. I had no hope of figuring out one with...*issues.*

And yet I wanted to. I couldn't stop wanting to.

Before noon, we neared the spot marked on the map: the bay of a small island. As we neared land, I could actually see the tension drain from Hannah's face. The island couldn't have been more than a half mile long and it wasn't much more than rocks but she looked at it as if it was the Promised Land. Her words made more sense to me, now. It was being *out at sea* that scared her: that huge, empty horizon. Funny: the exact thing I loved.

Soon we could glimpse the bottom through the water and the shallower it got, the more she relaxed. Before we got to the middle of the bay, I had to stop: it was no deeper than twenty feet and as shallow as six in places. I'd have to take the launch in. Not a problem in itself but....

"What?"

I'd been brooding at the rail and Hannah had noticed. I shook my head and rechecked the map. The location was right but you get a feel for these things, after enough years. And it didn't *feel* right.

She came closer. "What's the matter?" God, that sweet country accent. Cornfields and butterflies and messing around in the creek.

"It's too shallow," I said. "The *Hawk* was big. A wreck that big, this close to an island, and no one's found it in three hundred years?"

"You think the map's wrong?" I could see the sudden fear in her eyes. "You think it might be a fake after all?"

"Only one way to find out. I'll go down and take a look."

She moved towards the door that led below deck. "You need me to pass you something? A wetsuit? One of those big air tanks?"

I loved the fact she was ready to jump in and help. I'd taken a few tourists out, back when I was getting started with Edwards and we needed the money, and they'd sat on their asses the whole time. "No. It's shallow. Can you just get me a mask and snorkel, and some flippers?" I almost said *please* but managed to bite it back. Didn't want her to think I was soft for her.

I stood there waiting as she hunted for the gear. It would have been quicker to just fetch it myself but...

But I didn't want to hurt her feelings. *When did I start worrying about people's feelings?*

She emerged, triumphant, and handed me the gear. I untied the launch and was just about to set off when she said, "Be careful."

I blinked at her. I couldn't remember the last time someone had worried about me. The guys at McKinley's were probably running a book, each time I took the ship out, on whether I'd come back. They all knew I was ready for the sea to take me.

I grunted.

I cast off and started pulling on the oars. To get to the middle of the bay, I had to row all the way along the side of the boat and I couldn't take my eyes off Hannah as she stood on the deck, her golden hair blowing in the wind. God, she was beautiful. She really was from another world: I could imagine her standing in a wheat field: all she needed was a summer dress to complete the picture. *She'd look fantastic in a dress.*

She was keeping her gaze firmly fixed on the island but, every few moments, she'd check over her shoulder towards the sea, as if fearing the waves were going to creep up and swamp her. And the further I rowed away, the more uneasy she got. *She doesn't want to be on her own, not with the sea so close.*

I shook my head, furious with myself. *We don't have time for this.* But....

"Hannah!" I barked. My accent was hard around that soft "H."

She ran to the front of the boat.

"You going to be alright?" I almost spat it out, trying my best to be gruff. But I couldn't stop the concern that crept into my voice.

"Fine," she said. "I'll just stay here and re—" She broke off as if remembering something. She glanced at the waves. "I'll be fine," she said firmly. But when a particularly big wave rocked the boat, her head snapped around to look like a deer who's heard the hunter.

The launch was just drifting past the prow of the boat. I made a decision, grabbed on, and held the launch there. "Grab another set of gear," I told her. "You're coming with me."

Her eyes went wide. "What? I can't go—"

"It's six feet deep," I told her. "It's about as dangerous as a puddle. You'll be fine."

I saw her wavering, trying to decide, her gaze flicking back and forth between the waves behind her and the calm waters of the bay ahead of her. She didn't want to be in the water at all....

...but it was the sea she was afraid of. She nodded and ran below. A moment later, she reappeared holding a mask, snorkel, and flippers. I prepared to row all the way back to the rear of the boat to pick her up but she shook her head and clambered over the rail at the prow. I quickly dropped the oars and grabbed her feet, guiding her into the launch as she slithered down. Not many women—or men— would have tried that. She might be scared of the sea but she wasn't lacking in guts.

I swallowed. As she'd slithered in, my hands had slid up her legs and now I was holding her just above the knees. I looked up at the exact moment she looked down. Our eyes met.

"Take a seat," I muttered, trying not to think about how silky smooth her skin felt, or how those legs would feel stroking against mine as we thrashed and twisted in a bed. She sat, I picked up the oars, and we set off.

18

HANNAH

My heart was still thumping at the thought of going into the water but anything was better than sitting on the boat on my own, with endless horizon on three sides of me and the waves tipping the deck. The bay was different. It was so sheltered, there were barely any waves. And the bottom was so close I'd be able to touch it with my toes in places. It was water...but it didn't feel like the sea.

My underwear had dried so I'd slipped it on when I went below deck. I took off the borrowed shorts but Rourke warned me to leave the t-shirt on so my back didn't burn in the fierce sun. He showed me how to put the flippers and mask on and how the snorkel sealed itself if I dived below the surface. Then we jumped in together, the sea turning into white clouds of bubbles for a second. Then the bubbles cleared and....

I blinked behind my mask. I was in a whole new world.

I'd thought the water was clear when I was above the surface but now, without all the reflections, it was amazing. I was gazing down on lilac and topaz and sunset-orange coral. I could see a huge red crab crossing sideways beneath me and a clam the size of my head. I looked to my left and there was a bright yellow fish only inches from my mask, not scared at all: curious, in fact. It came right up to my face as if looking at its reflection in the glass, its fins dancing in the current. I'd never seen anything so beautiful. I could feel my eyes bugging out. *This was all down here, the whole time?*

Two-thirds of the Earth's surface is water. And I'd been just flying over it in planes.

The best thing was, there was none of that sense of panic and fear that I'd always thought was part of swimming. I'm a good swimmer but, subconsciously, I'd still always felt I was fighting the water, fighting to breathe. Here...I could just let my body go limp and float on the surface. The sun was dreamily warm on my back, I could breathe just fine through the snorkel and I only had to bat my toes a little for the flippers to push me through the warm water. It was effortless.

I knew we had no time to waste. Katherine had less than a week and I was already on borrowed time. But I couldn't help thinking that I never did anything like this, back in Nebraska. I was actually living, not just following the same routine every day.

We started to circle, searching for the wreck. Rourke went in front so, for the first time, I had a chance to really study him without him seeing. Again, he seemed more at home in the water than he ever did on land, his muscled back and shoulders letting him power through the water, his legs kicking in long, expert strokes. Only when the light caught his left calf did I see the jagged, messy scar there. *That must be what gave him the limp.* And there were other scars, too, on his forearms and upper arms. Thin, raised lines that could have been knife cuts. And small, circular marks. *Are those bullet wounds?*

Rourke suddenly sped up and I hurried to keep pace. We were coming to a point where the coral rose up, blocking our view of what was ahead. It was the only direction we hadn't checked. The wreck must be there!

I kicked hard and pulled alongside Rourke. We swum over the top of the rise...and stopped.

I looked left and right and then stared at Rourke in dismay.

We could see for hundreds of yards in every direction. But there was no wreck.

19

HANNAH

I'd grabbed Rourke's shoulder before I was even aware of it, fingers digging into the hard muscle. He was already turning to meet my big, panicked eyes. *Where is it?!* I tried to communicate.

To my horror, he gave a rueful shake of his head. *I don't know.*

I surfaced, tearing off my mask and pulling the end of the snorkel from my lips. I was bombarding Rourke with questions almost before he had his head above water. "Are we in the wrong place?" I wanted to know. "Was the map fake?" My voice was rising and a chill was soaking through my whole body, pushing back the warmth of the water. "*Where is it?!*" My mind was spinning. *Katherine! Oh God, Katherine! If we don't find it....*

His hands grabbed my shoulders, warm through the wet fabric of the t-shirt. He didn't say anything for a moment but his eyes commanded calm. I went quiet, but my breathing was still fast and ragged.

His fingers squeezed me gently, his hands big enough to surround my whole shoulders with heat. "I don't know," he said. "But we're going to keep looking until we find it."

I stared up at him. I knew he must be worried too but there wasn't a trace of it in his eyes. He was unshakeable. *Everything is going to be alright.* I felt it again: that authority, that leadership. The ability to tell his men they were heading into the storm and they were going to survive it: and to have them believe him. Where had he got that? Not just from commanding a ship full of divers hunting treasure, surely?

My heart slowed a little and I nodded. He gave my shoulders a last squeeze and then released me.

This time, we dived down to the bottom. I was nervous at first but soon got used to holding my breath: all I had to do when I needed to breathe was swim up and poke the snorkel above the water and I could fill my lungs again. We were only about ten feet below the surface and with the bright sunshine above and the warm, clear water it was no more threatening than a swimming pool.

I copied Rourke, grabbing handfuls of the coral and using it to pull myself along, keeping my eyes open for anything that looked like part of a ship. But there was nothing, not a single rotting timber. *Could it have rotted away to nothing? Are we in the wrong place?*

I was on my fifth dive when I thought I saw something: a hump in the coral that didn't look like the rest. Curving, but roughly rectangular. There was a hole in the coral nearby and I grabbed the lip of it to pull myself closer. My fingers nudged something inside and it *moved.*

I looked down at the hole and saw two green glowing eyes in the blackness. *What the hell's that?*

It erupted from the hole. Its silver-green body was as thick as my thigh and it was *long:* it just kept coming out of the hole, at least six feet of it. Its jaws opened and I had a glimpse of needle-like teeth. Then they snapped shut and I howled in pain, my hand buried in its mouth up to the wrist.

20

ROURKE

Shit! A Green Moray Eel, and a big one.

I raced towards her. Hannah was desperately trying to pull her arm out but eels have vicious, backward-faced teeth designed to stop you doing exactly that. Already, I could see blood clouding the water: luckily, I hadn't seen any sharks so far. Hannah started twisting around but the eel was clamped on tight. All she was doing was using up her air.

I reached her just as she gave up and tried to swim to the surface to take a breath. But the eel weighed a good sixty pounds: maybe she could have dragged it up there if she could swim with both arms, but she could only use one. And it was strong: it kept pulling and jerking at her, spinning her around and dragging her back down. As I reached her, her kicking foot hit me in the face, then in the ribs: she was in a blind panic, her eyes bulging as her lungs screamed for air.

I froze for a split-second, staring at her. I knew that look, that mortal fear as someone fights to breathe.

Then I snapped out of it, pulled my dive knife from its sheath on my ankle, and brought the hilt down with all my force on the eel's head. It went limp. But it was still dead weight pulling her down. We were too far from the surface. She needed air *now*.

I grabbed Hannah's face in both hands, pressed my lips to hers, and exhaled into her mouth. I felt her lungs fill and her panic eased a little.

Then I grabbed hold of the eel and slashed with my knife, cutting it off below the head. The body fell away and, free of its weight, Hannah kicked for the surface. I put my arm around her waist and helped her and we surfaced together, gasping and panting.

As soon as I saw the tears in her eyes, it did something to me. My chest contracted and nothing else mattered. "Shh," I told her. "Shh, it's okay. Let me look."

She turned away, closing her eyes, and held up her hand. I took hold of the eel's head and pushed it up her wrist instead of trying to pull it down and off. She grunted in pain but then let out a shuddering breath as its teeth came free. I forced its jaws wide, pulled it off her and threw it away, then examined her wrist. It wasn't too bad: red pinpricks where the teeth had sunk in but nothing was broken or torn. "You'll be fine," I told her. "Let's get back to the ship and I'll dress it."

Hannah nodded. Then: "No. Wait. I saw something, just before it bit me."

I stared at her. Her wrist would be fine but I'd been bitten a few times by those things and I knew it must hurt like a bastard. "I'll find it," I told her.

She shook her head. "No. I know what I'm looking for. And everything looks the same down there: what if we can't find it again?"

I blinked, astonished. She had a point. But I couldn't believe she wanted to go back down there, after what just happened.

We stared at each other. Her eyes were big with fear but that lower lip I was getting to love so much jutted out, determined. She *didn't* want to go down there...but she was going to do it anyway.

I nodded, impressed. She put her snorkel in place, took a few breaths to get her breathing under control and then we dived. For a few seconds she was uncertain, trying to get her bearings. Then she swam towards what looked like just another patch of coral.

I wouldn't have spotted it myself. The thing was so covered in coral that it was almost perfectly camouflaged. But as I reached it, I saw the hump of the lid and a hint of ancient brown wood.

A chest.

21

HANNAH

The chest was light enough until we got it above the surface, then suddenly felt like it was made of lead. I climbed into the launch and then reached down to help Rourke lift it in. My wrist was still bleeding but I ignored it. My heart was hammering: *is this it?* A little voice in my head was telling me that it made no sense: where was the wreck? And the letter told of a trunk, not a small chest. But I *wanted* to believe.

I was trying to convince myself because, if the cure wasn't in the chest, Katherine and I and all the other women with the disease were finished.

Back aboard the *Fortune's Hope,* we laid the chest down on the deck and knelt in front of it. Rourke broke away the corroded metal clasp with his knife. Put his hand on the lid.

I braced myself, holding my breath. And realized *he* was holding his breath, too.

He wanted it to be the cure. He wanted it as much as me.

Rourke swung back the lid and my eyes scoured the contents. Once, it might have been packed with velvet or some other cloth to protect the contents, but that had rotted away long ago. All that was left was a small glass bottle. I snatched it up. Thick, scalloped glass blurred what was inside. But there *was* something inside. *The cure!*

The top was sealed with red wax. Rourke passed me his knife and I used the tip to dig it away. Then I tipped the contents into my hand. A roll of cloth and something hard and dark. My heart leapt.

But it wasn't the black, curious stone my ancestor had described. It was a ruby the size of my thumbnail. I was dimly aware that it must be worth a fortune...but right now, I would have gladly swapped it for the cure. "What?" I asked, my voice tight.

I unrolled the cloth in case the cure was hidden inside. But there was only a message. *Esme,* I recognized at the top. And at the bottom it was signed, *C.* I squinted: the handwriting was spidery and difficult to read and the language was a mixture of Spanish and old English. It ended with "*and look in our secret garden.*"

I turned to Rourke. "Where's the wreck? Where's the treasure? Where's the *cure?!*" I shook the message. "What does this mean?!"

He gently took the ruby from me and turned it over in his hand. "I don't know," he said at last. "But I know a guy who will."

"Where? Back in Nassau?"

He shook his head and stood up. "We're going to Cuba."

22

HANNAH

I always get nervous, going through customs and immigration. Even just flying into Nassau with nothing more threatening than my bagful of books, I'd broken into a cold sweat as I walked past the security guards. Now I had to get into Cuba with no passport, no visa, and wearing oversized men's clothes. My legs were trembling as we walked up to the port guard.

But Rourke just stalked straight down the middle of the pier, scowling and limping and carrying a large box. The guard scurried to meet him, as if Rourke was the one in authority.

There was a rapid-fire conversation. Most of it was too quick for me to follow, but Rourke seemed very concerned with whether the authorities were taking proper care of their guards, these days, and sounded shocked to hear how many mouths the poor man had to feed. Rourke wished he could help but all he had was this case of twelve bottles of finest bourbon which needed to be surrendered to the authorities since it wasn't legal to import it. Oh! The guard could see that it got to the right people? How kind of him!

And suddenly, we were through. No passport. No paperwork. "Did you just bribe him?" I asked, stunned.

Rourke blinked at me as if all this was completely normal. That's when I realized it was, for him.

In moments, we were in a taxi: a cherry-red Chevy straight out of the 1950s, with bench seats and lots of polished chrome. Rourke sat back, looking like some unshaven visiting dignitary in his black pants and white shirt. Havana's streets seemed as familiar to him as Nassau. Back on the ship, I'd seen him root through a wooden box of currency and fill his wallet with Cuban Pesos. There'd been at least twenty other currencies there. Was there anywhere he *hadn't* been?

To me, though, it was all new and magical. I stared out of the window, entranced: beautiful old stone buildings, some of them painted in brilliant pastel shades; vintage cars; throngs of locals and tourists heading out for the night. The sun was just going down and everything was being lit up in golds, coppers, and reds. It hit me that I'd already had more new experiences, in the last few days, than I had in the previous few years back home.

Rourke had a muttered conversation with the taxi driver, both of them throwing glances my way. The driver laughed and nodded, then took us to a back street where shops had been set up in stone archways. Most were already dark and empty but one still glowed with light. Rourke opened my door for me and I climbed out...then turned and stared at Rourke in surprise. The archway was full of dresses.

He gave a little shrug. "You can't walk around in my clothes forever. But hurry. This place is about to close."

I blinked at him for a second, blown away by the gesture. But before I could thank him, he gave another shrug and looked away down the street. *He doesn't want me thinking he's nice.*

An elderly woman stepped forward, pointing warningly at her watch. I hurried into the archway.

All around me were racks of dresses. But not simple summer dresses. These were silky, ruffled creations with lots of skirt and low necklines and they were as brightly colored as everything else in Havana. I held one up in amazement, then turned to show Rourke. "Where did you bring me?!"

He rubbed at his stubble, looking embarrassed. "I told the cab driver you needed something to wear. But I think he thought you were my wife."

The old lady made *hurry up* gestures.

I grabbed a scarlet dress at random. The old lady motioned to the changing room: a blanket that hung down to knee level.

I darted behind it and stripped off the borrowed t-shirt and shorts, being careful of the bandage on my wrist. Then, when I saw how low-cut the dress was, I cursed and added my bra to the pile. Now I was standing in my panties, shielded from the street only by a blanket.

I was standing there trying to figure out if I should step into the dress or pull it over my head when I felt Rourke's gaze. I looked down, the dress gathered in my arms. The only bit of me that was visible to him was the naked backs of my calves, not a part of me I'd ever even thought about. And yet right then, I could feel them being studied, his stare so intense I wanted to shift from foot to foot. The heat that rippled up to my groin was stronger than I'd ever felt from some guy back home staring at my breasts, or ass, or even my whole body.

I struggled into the dress. It was clingy and tight all the way down to the skirt, which was slashed diagonally: one side went down almost to my knee but the other side came almost up to my groin, and it was finished with a long fringe that swished every time I moved. There was a zipper up the back but it was too low to reach and I was painfully aware the old lady was going to toss us out on the street any moment. "Um...Rourke?"

I heard the creak of Rourke's shoes as he walked closer. Then: "Hannah?"

I've always thought of *Hannah* as a farmer's daughter's name, a name you yell across the fields to get me to come in for supper, bawling that final *ah*. In Rourke's accent it was transformed. It became mysterious and quick: a rasp of the *H* and a quick ripple over the *ns*. A name said breathlessly. I flushed.

"I think I'm going to need you to zip me up," I said, keeping my eyes straight ahead.

I heard the blanket move aside behind me. Then nothing. He just stood there looking at me for far, far longer than was necessary. The exposed skin of my back prickled all the way from my neck to the top of my panties and another ripple of heat went through me.

I felt him take hold of the zipper and slide it up...slowly. The metallic rasp seemed to go on forever as the dress tightened around me and his eyes burned into my back. He was standing so close, I could feel each hot breath on my neck.

I turned around, looking down at myself at the same time. *Wow.* The dress clung to every curve: I'd never worn anything so figure-hugging. And there was a lot of pale leg and cleavage on display. *Where the hell do women wear dresses like this?*

Then I looked up.

Rourke was standing only a foot away, gazing down at me. His gaze didn't so much strip the dress from my body as burn it right off. His eyes slid down my neck and along the curves of my breasts. They followed the scarlet fabric as it went in and then out over my waist and hips and then tracked all the way down my bare legs. The heat blazed across my skin and then sank inward, growing and tightening. When he reached my feet, he came back up again even slower.

"I feel ridiculous," I said.

He looked me right in the eye. "You don't look ridiculous."

The old lady was complaining that she needed to close. Rourke hushed her, handed over some bills, and then asked me my shoe size. Moments later, I was slipping on a pair of scarlet heels. The old lady started to pull the shutters down even as we stepped back out onto the street.

"Thank you," I said, and I meant it. However over-the-top the dress was, it felt good to be wearing something that fit me again.

He gazed at me and it was a long time before he finally tore his eyes away and looked off into the distance. "You're welcome," he muttered at last.

As we got back onto the main streets, I didn't feel so self-conscious. Lots of women were wearing dresses like mine and lots of the men were dressed like Rourke, in pants and shirts. But why? Where were they all going?

"So who's this guy we're going to see?" I asked as we walked.

"Hobbs. A history buff."

"A friend of yours?"

He gave me a sour look. "I don't have friends. He helps me, sometimes, and I pay him."

I was still thinking how sad that sounded when he suddenly stopped and grabbed my hand. I looked down in shock at our joined hands and then up at him, my face flushed and my heart racing. But he wasn't looking at me. I followed his gaze down the street.

Ratcher had stepped out of a bar fifty yards ahead of us, his bald head gleaming with sweat. One of his crew burst out of another bar and shook his head at Ratcher, who barked orders. Other men I recognized from the villa were emerging from other bars: two, three, and four...God, Ratcher had his whole crew searching for us!

"*Fuck!*" said Rourke, squeezing my hand. *Fuck* would never sound the same to me again, after that. It just sounded right, said in his rough Scottish accent, the verbal equivalent of a brick through a window. He turned, still holding my hand, and led me in a fast walk in the opposite direction. "Don't look round!"

I nodded, panic driving all the air from my lungs. I tried to concentrate on putting one foot in front of the other, walking quickly but inconspicuously. But I could feel the presence of Ratcher behind me, every hair on the back of my neck standing up. Any second, I expected a hand to grab my shoulder. "How did he know we were in Havana?" I asked, my voice cracking in fear.

"Someone probably spotted the *Fortune's Hope* coming into port and tipped him off," said Rourke. "Or saw us in the street. People here know me." He suddenly stopped in his tracks. "*Bollocks!*"

Two more of Ratcher's men were coming the other way. I moaned in fear when I saw the knife one of them had on his belt. Then my stomach lurched: I could see the butt of a handgun poking out of the other one's waistband. We were trapped. I looked around in panic.

For all its color, Havana suddenly seemed to have a lot of dark alleys it would be easy for them to hustle us into. And they'd see us in another few seconds.

"In here!" Rourke snapped and pulled me into what I thought was a bar. It was only when we got inside that I discovered where all those women in dresses like mine had been heading. It was a dance club: crowds eight deep were watching as couples spun around a dance floor. Rourke pulled me into the crowd but, through the windows, I could see Ratcher's men approaching. They were searching each club in turn, I realized...and they were heading for ours.

I looked at Rourke just as he turned to me. When I saw his eyes, I caught my breath. The deep blue was lit up with protective fury. I'd never seen that before, never had any man feel that about me.

He pulled the message and the ruby from his pocket and stuffed them into my hand. "Take these," he growled. "Stay here."

I nodded. But as he moved toward the door, I saw him put his hand on his sword. I grabbed his arm. "Wait: *that's* your plan? There are two of them, plus all the rest coming down the street! One of them's got a gun!"

His hand wrapped around the hilt of his sword. "Aye," he said. "Well, I'm not—"

He bit back what he was going to say but he kept staring into my eyes. *I'm not going to let them get you.* My stomach flip-flopped.

The door opened and Ratcher's men stalked in, eyes everywhere. They didn't see us, but they started searching the crowd. Rourke pulled against my grip, trying to reach them before they reached us. I imagined the fight that would ensue. Rourke dragged into a back alley, a knife between his ribs. I looked around wildly but I couldn't see another exit.

Rourke tried to shake my hand off, his sword already drawn halfway. *No!* There had to be another way. But Ratcher's men were methodically working through the throng of people. They'd find us wherever we went in the crowd—

Unless we're not in the crowd.

My stomach lurched just at the thought of it. I'm basically a mouse. Give me a quiet place and a book to curl up with and I'm happy. Being the center of attention is *not* my thing.

But if I didn't do this, Rourke was going to wind up in a fight that'd cost him his life. He'd saved me. Now I had to save him.

I hauled on Rourke's arm. "Come with me!" I didn't give him a choice, dragging him deeper into the crowd.

"What are you doing?" he snapped. "Wherever we go, they'll see us!"

"Not—"—I shouldered my way past a couple of tourists—"if we —*excuse me*—" We reached the edge of the dance floor and I turned and grabbed his other hand. "...dance." I finished breathlessly.

23

___

ROURKE

I was ready to die, fingers wrapped around the hilt of my sword, thumb lovingly caressing the carved detail. Not a bad way to go out. Not the way I'd planned: I'd always thought it would be the sea that took me. But if that's what it took to protect her then so be it.

The only problem was, I wasn't sure I could stop all of them. And once I was dead, Ratcher would grab Hannah for himself.

And for his crew. My stomach twisted and my lips drew back over my teeth in a snarl. *No. No fucking way.*

Then Hannah was pulling me through the crowd. She was only a wee thing: I could have easily stood my ground. But I didn't want to hurt her by pulling out of her grip. And then we were at the edge of the dance floor and she was grabbing my other hand and telling me we had to dance.

Dance?! I stared at her. We were trying to hide and she wanted to make us the center of attention?

She nodded over my shoulder. "They're checking the *crowd*," she said hotly. "They're not checking the *dancers*."

I looked and... damn, she was right. Ratcher's men expected to find me propping up the bar or buried in the crowd, watching. They weren't even glancing towards the dance floor. And if we got right out in the middle, we'd be hidden by all the other couples. It was actually a good plan.

Except...*dance?!* I'd rather take my chances with Ratcher's men.

She pulled me out into the middle of the dance floor but I just stood there. *I can't do this. I've got a gammy leg, for God's sake.*

But then, as if to tempt me, she started to dance.

She wasn't like the other women on the dance floor, a mix of locals and confident tourists. She didn't know the moves that went with the fast, Latin beat. But she had a beauty that eclipsed all of them and her body....

I swallowed. Aye, she had the body for it. The dress's diagonal slit exposed all of one leg, right up to the hip, and the heels made her already long legs seem endless. As she turned and flexed to the beat, her ass came into view, ripe and full and perfect. It swayed and dipped before me, hypnotic. I wanted to grab hold of it with both hands and *squeeze*.

And her breasts. Dear God, her breasts, the creamy weight of them pushing forward as she arched her back. She bent her knees, grinding to the beat, long legs flashing...and then she met my eyes and beckoned me forward.

Something snapped inside me. I stormed forward and grabbed hold of my woman.

24

HANNAH

At first, I was terrified. I felt like every woman around me was staring, wondering what the hell the pale, curvy American thought she was doing. I slinked and twisted and writhed and felt like a complete idiot.

But when I focused on Rourke, all of that disappeared. Watching him was like watching a huge, powerful attack dog snapping and growling, desperate to reach me, held back only by a chain. And the chain—his self-control—was weakening. His gaze sent a rush of heat through me, my skin throbbing. The people watching ceased to exist: it was just me dancing and him watching. And I didn't feel like a timid mouse, anymore. The dress helped: it was like being dressed in liquid sex, hugging my curves, and swishing around my legs. I rolled my hips, shook my ass and beckoned...

And suddenly, Rourke was storming towards me. One big hand clasped mine. The other took hold of my waist and—*God,* I wanted to melt into it, it felt so *right*. Strong and warm and confident, guiding me, *controlling* me. I had to look way up to meet his eyes, we were so close, and I gasped at what I saw there. The lust had filled his eyes completely: he'd let himself go, given himself up to raw need. For a second he just held me there, my breasts pillowed against those hard pecs.

And then, to my amazement, he danced.

It wasn't the fast, *look at me* moves of the men around us. That wouldn't have worked, with his imposing size. This was simple and classic, masterful and confident. From the moment he took my hand, there was no question of who was leading whom.

At first, I was confused as to why his leg wasn't bothering him. Then I saw the pain in his eyes: it was hurting like hell...but his lust, his need for me, was overriding it. The thought of that rippled down through me, lighting me up, turning to molten heat in my groin. He was hardness and power and brute strength, marching me like *this*, then twirling me around like *that*. I caught my breath: for the first time in my life, I felt graceful. And I'd never felt so alive.

He twirled me, one arm overhead, his eyes never leaving mine. He marched me, thigh-to-thigh, and I could feel how hard he was and that he knew that I knew. *Where the hell did he learn to dance?* Was it a British thing? I could imagine James Bond dancing like this. Did they teach all the Brits at school?

As the music reached its peak, he pulled me tight to him. Leaned me back over his arm, my hair sweeping towards the floor. His lips descended until they were a hair's-breadth from mine....

And the music ended. My eyes fluttered open and I saw him gazing down at me, eyes blazing. He lifted me upright but didn't let go of me. The other couples around us were kissing, giggly and excited as they walked away. But Rourke was the opposite: he was stone-cold serious, solid, and immovable in the middle of the dance floor as the others flowed around us. His hand cupped my cheek, tilting my head up towards him. His thumb stroked across my skin and a tremor went through me. For fully three seconds, he stared down at me, those deep blue eyes scalding hot, melting me, and destroying me. *This is* your *fault,* he told me sternly. *Your fault.*

And I swallowed and panted as he leaned down to kiss me.

25

———

ROURKE

Those blush pink lips. Those blue eyes gazing up at me. It was too powerful to fight.

I leaned down to kiss her.

My lips were a half-inch from hers when my leg erupted in white-hot pain. I fought it back, just like I had all the way through the dance. But it was enough to remind me. *You damn fool. She's a wee thing with her whole life ahead of her.*

And I was a cripple who lived on his boat because it was all I understood. Who talked to Edwards and a damn monkey instead of having friends. Who looked at the horizon every day and wondered if today was the day the sea would take me.

The proper place for her was Nebraska. Where some damn farmer could play guitar to her under a tree and make her a bloody picnic and all that stuff. *He'd* get to kiss her. They'd get married, have two children and a faithful dog.

My job, my only role in the life of this woman, was to make sure she lived to see that future.

I twisted away and looked around. Ratcher's men were gone.

I turned back to Hannah. She was blinking up at me, confused.

Then—my heart twisted—*disappointed*. Oh Jesus, if she'd known how close I'd come. Once my lips touched hers, I wouldn't have stopped kissing her until we were in a bunk.

"They're gone," I grunted. "Come on."

And I led the way out of the club.

26

HANNAH

Even with his limp, Rourke walked fast, slamming his good foot against the sidewalk as if it had personally wronged him. When he stepped onto his left leg—the injured one—he didn't make a sound, didn't let his face betray the pain. But I could see the sweat breaking out on his brow. The dancing must have left him in agony.

"How far is it?" I asked.

"Not far." He'd nearly kissed me. I was sure of it. Now he wouldn't even look at me. "A mile."

A mile. And he was going to walk it all because he didn't want to show weakness. I could almost see the pain radiating up his leg, tightening his ass and lower back and even his shoulders, each time he took a step. *God, he's—*

I bit my lip as realization hit. *He's as stubborn as I am.*

I stopped. "I can't walk any further in these heels."

He turned and glowered. "It's only a mile."

"I have blisters," I lied. I lifted one foot and nodded at my shoe. "*You* put me in these things. We're getting a cab."

For a second, his scowl disappeared. His eyes widened, full of concern that he'd in some way hurt me. Then he frowned again. I could tell he suspected it was a ruse. I stood firm, staring back at him.

"Fine," said Rourke grudgingly. He finally looked me in the eye. "We'll get a cab."

~

"The library?" I asked as we pulled up outside the massive stone building. "The library's open *now*?" It was well into the evening.

"It is for Hobbs," grunted Rourke. He passed some bills to the driver and we climbed out. "They like him, here. Let him do his research at all hours." He limped up the steps and held the door open for me. "He donates some of the old books he finds to the library." Rourke sighed as we made our way through the huge, echoing building. "And... he speaks their language."

"Spanish?"

Rourke grimaced and pushed open a door. "*Intellectual.*"

The reading room was small and lined with thick leather-bound volumes that deadened all sound from outside. An ancient grandfather clock ticked a slow heartbeat. A man sat hunched over an enormous book, its pages edged in gold. He was wearing a tweed suit and white cotton gloves, keeping his place with one finger while he scrawled notes in a notebook with the other. I couldn't see much more than tousled blond hair and the tops of his gold-rimmed spectacles.

"Hobbs," said Rourke bitterly.

At his voice, the man's head jerked up like a startled rabbit. He had one of those happy, cherubic faces that mustn't have changed much since he was sixteen: I pegged him at about thirty, now. He broke into a wide, excited grin. "*Rourke!*" he said, delighted. "Wonderful!" His British accent was amazing: it spoke of country estates and horses and a stiff brandy in the evening while reading *The Times.*

Hobbs ran around from behind his desk, grabbed Rourke's hand and pumped it up and down, barraging him with questions about where he'd been, how the *Fortune's Hope* was doing and *if the fine weather was agreeing with him.* He spoke as if he'd been ripped from the last century. I liked him immediately.

What I couldn't understand was why Rourke seemed so cold towards him. Watching Hobbs, you would have thought they were best friends but Rourke was nothing but terse and sour in return.

"And who is *this* fine lady?" asked Hobbs.

I blinked and then flushed.

Rourke rolled his eyes and introduced me. "Listen," he barked. "We've found the map to the *Hawk*."

Hobbs's eyes widened. He stared at Rourke for a beat to check that he was serious. Then his lungs slowly filled. *"Good heavens!"*

"The map led us to a point just off an island. But when we got there, there was no ship," I told him. "Just a chest, lying in shallow water, with this message and a ruby." We laid our finds, together with the map, on the desk. Hobbs leaned over them and stayed there for several minutes, transfixed. Every now and again, he'd mutter something like, "Quite extraordinary," or "Well, I *do* say...."

Rourke gave me a look, as if to say, *see?* But I just shook my head at him. I couldn't work out why he disliked the man so much. I thought he was adorable. If Hobbs was a book, he'd be a scholarly textbook from a small London publisher, with the price in shillings on the cover and a quote in Latin at the start.

At last, Hobbs straightened up. He went to the back of the room, slid out a thick, leather-bound volume, and plucked a hip flask and two glasses from behind it. "Rourke has told you the story of Charles Mace and his lover, Esme, I take it?"

I nodded.

"Though knowing Rourke, I suspect he glossed over the more romantic parts," said Hobbs.

Rourke let out a sigh and rolled his eyes. I leaned forward eagerly.

"Esme was a gypsy dancer, said to be the most beautiful woman on all these shores. Her family didn't want her running off with a pirate captain and she wouldn't leave her people and run away with him, so they had to meet in secret. Esme was a strong swimmer and a fine sailor: they'd meet by moonlight in secret harbors and caves all around the area."

I was entranced. *So romantic!* Next to me, Rourke gave a despairing grunt.

"So: picture the scene," said Hobbs. "Mace knows he's going to be caught. He doesn't want the British to get his treasure. He wants to leave it for Esme. But she's penniless and alone: if he sends the *Hawk* to the bottom and leaves her a map to where he sunk it, how will she recover the treasure? She has no boat, no crew...."

Now Rourke was grudgingly leaning forward as well. "So...?"

"Well, understand that I'm hypothesizing here, but...it would make sense for Mace to leave Esme a map to a smaller haul, first." He picked up the ruby. "This would be something she could easily trade for a boat and a crew. That would let her go after another, bigger cache of treasure that would let her pay for a *bigger* boat and crew, and so on. Finally, she'd get to the *Hawk* and, by that point, she'd have what she needed to recover the main treasure."

I picked up the note we'd found in the bottle. "But why all the writing?" I asked. "Why not just give her another map?"

"Because Mace knew everyone would be after the treasure," said Rourke. "He was worried someone other than Esme might read the note."

"Exactly," beamed Hobbs. "So it describes where to find the next haul in terms of places only the two of them know."

I re-read the note. Not all of it made sense, yet, but it did seem to be full of references to things that had happened. *That place where we... The time when we.... And look for our secret garden.* "How many clues?" I asked urgently.

Hobbs pointed to a line in old English I'd had trouble deciphering. "Three," he said. He poured whiskey into the two glasses. "This is the first one. It'll lead you to the second one, that will lead you to the third one and *that* one will lead you to the *Hawk.*"

Two more clues! A longer journey than we'd thought: we'd have to move fast to save Katherine. But there *was* hope. Hobbs handed me a glass and raised his in a silent toast. I started to drink, then remembered Rourke didn't have a glass and looked at him guiltily.

"He knows I only drink rum," Rourke explained.

I drank, the whiskey smoky and mellow. Then I realized something. "Wait: these clues are designed so that only Esme can understand them?" My heart sank. "We're screwed! We don't know what she knew! We don't know all their secret meeting places or their history or—"

And just then, I felt it: a crackling streamer of pain that seemed to erupt from the floor and snake up through my foot and leg—

Oh God! I knew what this was....

The pain exploded through my whole body. I dropped my glass and screamed so hard my throat ached. It felt like every nerve had been plunged into acid. My legs buckled and I stumbled: would have fallen, if Rourke hadn't grabbed me around the waist.

The room vanished in a blurry haze and I was only dimly aware of being gently placed in a chair. I heard Hobbs say, "Dear lady!" and then Rourke was leaning over me, his eyes wild with fear...and then I saw that fear deepen.

He'd realized what I hadn't told him.

It was the worst pain I'd ever felt, like a thousand butcher's knives had been shoved deep into me and someone was slowly twisting them. Pain is meant to be momentary. A burn, a cut, a broken bone...it hurts, but the pain always recedes. There was no relief from this: it was like I'd pressed my whole body against a hot stove and I *couldn't move away.* All I could do was pray for it to end.

And what if it didn't? I'd known that the disease would hit me hard when it came, because I was older...what if I'd skipped straight to the final stage? What if the pain just went on and on until my heart gave out?

I wanted to writhe and thrash but the slightest movement made the agony worse. I felt my fingers locking around the arms of the chair. My eyes were screwed shut, now, but I could feel that my cheeks were wet. I was sobbing.

And then I became aware of a presence, right next to me. Rourke's big body, hunkered over me like a bear, his grizzled jaw next to my cheek, and his lips at my ear. "*What can I do?*" he said in a hoarse whisper. I could hear the frustration in his voice, the anger at being helpless. Beneath all the pain, my heart swelled. He wanted to help me. It killed him that he couldn't.

But I couldn't even answer him. I could only sit there, rigid as a statue, tears flowing down my cheeks. After a while, he began to stroke my hair with his big, calloused hand, and that helped, a little. I was dimly aware of him muttering to Hobbs, explaining the disease and the cure.

At last, I thought I felt the pain start to recede: like looking up from the bottom of the sea and seeing the tide drawing back. I didn't want to hope too soon in case it started again. But bit by bit, it ebbed away and my taut muscles started to relax. I slumped there panting like I'd run a marathon. I was soaked in sweat and everything ached from being tensed so long. The one thing that felt good was Rourke's hand on my head. When I managed to open my eyes, both men were standing over me. Hobbs looked worried but Rourke looked terrified.

"How long?" My voice came out as a croak and my jaw ached from grinding my teeth together.

"Twenty minutes," said Hobbs. He passed me a glass of water.

Rourke ran his hand over my hair one last time and then awkwardly dropped it to his side. I immediately felt an ache of loss. He turned to Hobbs, his fists bunching. "How do we work out the clues?" he roared. "We need to find the wreck!"

It wasn't the first time I'd heard him shout but the other times had all been simple anger. This was different: there was a thread of panic woven into the rage. Hobbs heard it, too. I saw his gaze flick from Rourke to me, astonished, and I caught my breath. *He's never seen Rourke worry about anyone else, before.*

Hobbs nodded and pushed his spectacles up his nose. "I have something that might help." And he hurried from the room.

Rourke took a step towards me and I thought for a second that he was going to smooth my hair again: that would feel *so* good. But he hesitated and then clasped his hands behind his back as if to remove the temptation. "You should have told me!" he snapped.

"You wouldn't have taken me to the *Hawk*," I croaked.

He fumed silently for a while. "Aye," he said at last. "I might not have done." Then, forcing out the words, "How long do you have?"

I swallowed some more water, still trembling from the memory of the pain. "Days."

Rourke cursed under his breath and stared at the floor.

I had no idea what to say. So I said, "Why are you such an asshole to Hobbs?"

Rourke looked at me and scowled. "I'm not an—" He sighed and went quiet for a moment, brooding. "He's just not like me." He looked at the door Hobbs had vanished through. Just for a second, I saw a hint of pain there. Then he shook it off. "I used to cut him in on the haul, when he helped me find something. You know what he spent his share on?"

"Books," I said immediately.

That threw Rourke. "...yes," he said. "Waste of money."

"And buying a bar just so you can drink in it *isn't*?"

He glared at me. "You should be in a damn hospital."

"Hospitals can't help me," I said. "Only that stone can." My strength was slowly returning but I was still shaking. The knowledge that the pain could return at any time, without warning...that scared me so much I wanted to throw up.

Rourke laid a warm hand on my shoulder and I shook a little less.

At that moment, Hobbs returned, carrying a carved wooden box that he set on the desk. He lifted the lid and unfolded layers of silk the color of blood. Then he lifted out a thick book bound in shining brown leather. "Be careful," he told us. "It's three hundred years old."

I eased myself out of the chair and stumbled over, my legs still shaky. The book didn't have a title or an author on the cover and it didn't have the grand, showy bindings of an expensive book. But it was well-loved, worn from constant use. I opened it to a page at random.

There was a date and a carefully written entry. *I waited until night and slipped out of our camp. Charles was waiting for me with a horse and a bottle of wine. The moonlight lit up his eyes and it was like falling into water so deep you couldn't see the bottom—*

I looked at Hobbs. "This is her diary," I said in wonder. "*Esme's diary!*"

Hobbs nodded. "I acquired it about five years ago. Cost me a great deal of money." He looked at Rourke and me. "It's yours."

I threw my arms around him and hugged him. But when I straightened up, Rourke was glowering off into the distance. What *was* it with him? If you only watched Hobbs, you would have sworn they were best friends. If you only watched Rourke, you'd swear they were mortal enemies.

And then I glanced at Hobbs's disappointed face and I got it. They *were* friends. That's why he was helping. Rourke just didn't show it...ever.

Well, I wasn't going to let him get away with that. I elbowed Rourke in the ribs and he cursed and stared at me, puzzled.

I glanced meaningfully at Hobbs.

Rourke growled and looked away. Looked back and saw I was glaring at him. By now, Hobbs was carefully packing the diary back into the box.

"Hobbs," said Rourke reluctantly.

Hobbs looked up, a puppy hoping for a treat.

"...thank you," said Rourke.

A slow smile spread across Hobbs's face. He nodded and pushed the box into my hands. "Godspeed," he told us.

I hurried down the steps of the library, the box clutched to my chest. Rourke fell in beside me. "Where now?" I asked. "Back to the *Fortune's Hope?*"

Rourke shook his head. "Ratcher'll be waiting for us. He's probably got his boat moored right next to ours."

Ours. Our boat. I knew it was just a slip of the tongue but I liked the way that sounded. "So what do we do?"

Rourke rubbed his stubble. "Well, we can't leave. Even if we got past him and away, he'd just follow us. We need to tie him up here in

Havana for a while." He studied me as he thought...and then he got that look in his eye, his thoughts forgotten. His gaze soaked into me and immediately, the slumbering heat awoke. God, how did he do that to me?

Rourke finally tore his gaze away. "The Chief of the Harbor Police owes me a favor," he said. "And a bottle of rum." He took out his phone.

"Why does the Chief of—"

Rourke sighed as he dialed. When he'd comforted me, in Hobbs's office, I'd seen a different side of him but now I could sense all his defenses sliding back into place. "Sometimes, when I was back and forth around ports, I used to bring in stuff that wasn't...strictly allowed."

My eyes widened. "You're a smuggler, as well?"

"*Was* a smuggler," he muttered. His whole mood was darkening. "And it wasn't like that." He put the phone to his ear and turned slightly away from me.

I should have shut the hell up but I was too shocked. I was realizing how much I didn't know about him. He'd hinted that he and the people he used to work with were into some shady things, but I hadn't thought—"What did you smuggle? Drugs? *Guns?*"

"For God's sake, lass!" he snapped. "What does it matter?"

Then the call connected and he turned from me, speaking in rapid-fire Spanish into the phone. It was strange, hearing Spanish with a Scottish accent, like an exotic spirit stirred with a razor-sharp knife. Any other time, I would have just listened, entranced. But I couldn't enjoy it. My face was burning as if he'd slapped me. Maybe I was just shaky after the attack, but his snapping at me...*hurt*. The dress, the dancing, then the way he'd comforted me when I was in pain. I'd thought we were connecting. *I thought he liked me.*

I turned my face up to the heavens and let the cool night air bathe my eyes, blinking back the beginnings of hot tears.

Rourke finished the call and turned back to me. I quickly turned to face the street, arms wrapped round myself against night's chill. I felt him watching me, the back of my neck prickling. I could feel the anger rolling off him in waves. I still didn't understand what I'd done wrong. *Why is he so angry?*

But the longer he gazed at me, the more his anger seemed to subside. And it wasn't replaced by the hot lust I'd felt before. This was something else. Something tender.

He sighed. "I'm not used to this," he muttered. "Been a long time since I talked to a girl."

"You can tell," I said, still hurt.

"Even longer since I danced with a girl."

"That, you *can't* tell," I mumbled. I finally turned to face him. Just looking at him made me take a quick little breath. God, he was gorgeous. And those deep blue eyes were staring right into mine with such intensity. There was still anger there, but not at me. At himself.

"The Police Chief's going to help, but it'll take a wee bit," he said. "We can't go back to the *Fortune's Hope*." He glanced behind me. "But I know a place...."

I turned and looked over my shoulder. There was a dark doorway between two buildings, with stairs leading down. A pink neon cocktail glass was the only sign it was a bar: there was no name, no indication of what to expect inside. I turned back to Rourke.

He'd moved closer and he towered over me, his body dwarfing mine. Every muscle was tensed, as if he was ready to face off against an army. His voice was low enough to put the fear of God into any attacker. And yet his eyes were everywhere but on my face: he was awkward as a teenager. "Look, do you want a damn drink?" he blurted.

An apology. Or as close as Rourke got to one.

And I thought I knew why he'd suddenly blown up at me, when I'd asked about the smuggling. He didn't want me thinking he'd done bad things.

He met my eyes and that heat throbbed straight down inside me again, slamming into my groin and radiating out.

I nodded.

And he took my hand and led me into the bar.

27

HANNAH

The steps were steep and I had to go carefully, unused to the heels. I could hear singing, in Spanish. Then the cellar came into view: bare brick walls and a small stage at one end, the whole room packed with locals. It was dark and warm, the tiny tables lit only with candles that cast everything in a flickering orange glow. Up on stage, a man was just finishing a ballad, struggling to hit the high notes. But everyone cheered and clapped anyway, and he waved happily and hurried off stage. A woman replaced him. It was some sort of open mic night, I realized.

We found a table near the back, so small our knees were nearly touching. Rourke grabbed a spare stool and put his left foot up on it, then gave a long sigh of relief. It was the first time I'd seen him really acknowledge the pain in front of me. But I wasn't going to ask about it. Not yet. Not after the way he blew up at me outside.

"Where did you learn to dance?" I asked, trying to keep things light.

Rourke grimaced, but in embarrassment, not anger. "Officer's ball," he said. "It's a tradition. Dinner jackets or kilts. Canapés and dancing."

"You were in the army?"

"Navy."

I nodded silently. Now I knew where that authority came from, why he *commanded* where Ratcher just raged and yelled at his crew.

We were interrupted by the waitress, a beautiful, leggy woman with long dark hair. She looked how I imagined Esme had: glamorous and sultry, in a way I could never be. "Hello, Rourke," she said coolly, her tray tucked under one arm.

I saw the way she was looking at him. The way she was looking at *me.* My stomach hit the floor.

"Carla," said Rourke with a nod, his voice carefully level.

"And who's *this?*" asked Carla, eyeing me.

My face felt as if it was on fire. My stomach tightened. Nerves and self-consciousness and...something I hadn't been expecting: a fierce rush of jealousy. *Her and him....*

"Hannah," said Rourke carefully. "I'm helping her."

If Carla was a book, it would have been one of those bodice rippers with a big, sweeping title in gold embossed text. And a sultry maiden in a peasant blouse wrapped around the hero and sex scenes that would make you flush and check no one was reading over your shoulder.

She was sexy and adventurous and darkly alluring in a way I could never be. *They're perfect for each other,* I thought miserably.

We ordered drinks and Carla strutted out of sight. "We used to have a thing," Rourke said, by way of explanation.

Used to? My heart leapt. But then why had he brought me here? Did he *want* to make me uncomfortable? I mean, he couldn't have brought me here, to this one particular bar, knowing his ex worked here, without even considering....

Then I studied his face and groaned. *Yes. Yes, he could.* Rourke was *exactly* that man. I bet he'd been coming to this bar for years, every time he came to Havana. He'd been here before he met Carla and while he was with Carla and he'd kept coming here after they broke up. He hadn't considered that it might be a bad idea to bring a woman here because—

My stomach flip-flopped. *Because I'm the first woman he's ever brought here.*

Carla returned and set Rourke's rum in front of him, then my mojito in front of me. I thanked her and it was a little less awkward, this time. At least I knew where I stood.

I made the fatal mistake of relaxing. That's when Rourke's phone rang.

He put it to his ear. "What? I can't—" He sighed and stood up. "I barely have a signal, down here. I'll just be a minute."

I felt my eyes widen and I think I gave a kind of horrified moan as he limped off towards the stairs. *What? Wait! Don't leave me alone with—*

Carla slid her perfect ass onto Rourke's vacated stool. I turned to her in dismay, just as she leaned forward across the table. *"So!"* she said, picking up Rourke's rum.

I swallowed. She was like a cat, prowling and watchful, trying to decide exactly how she was going to tear my eyes out. She crossed her legs and I saw three different men around us swivel to gawp at her. "So?" I asked in a shaky voice.

She took a long sip of Rourke's rum. Her eyes were so dark brown they were almost black. "You and Rourke." Her accent was smoky and dark, almost a growl.

I took a sip of my cocktail and shook my head. "He's just helping me," I told Carla.

"Really," said Carla.

I nodded.

She leaned an elbow on the table. Her perfectly-toned, smoothly tan forearm would have made a personal trainer weep. She rested her cheek on her hand and drummed blood-red nails against her scalp. "See, the problem with that is...Rourke doesn't help people. Not since he quit."

I took another gulp of my cocktail for strength. "He doesn't even like me," I told her. "He's grouchy. Bad-tempered. He snaps at me." With each word, Carla's face soured. *"What?!"* I asked.

"That's what he does to someone he really likes," said Carla. "He cares enough about you to push you away."

I stared at her, stunned. And thought of Hobbs, and how Rourke treated him.

Carla leaned back from me and drank the rest of Rourke's rum in one gulp. The anger seemed to have gone out of her, now that she knew what was going on.

"Did he push you away?" I asked tentatively.

At first, I thought Carla wasn't going to answer. She stared at the woman who was singing another ballad on stage. *Does no one sing anything but love songs in this place?* But eventually, she spoke. "It was...before. He was different, in those days. He and Edwards used to come in here with fresh scars and a new haul of treasure. They were inseparable. They'd buy the crew drinks. Rourke and I would...." She trailed off, remembering.

"Edwards?" I asked. I remembered Rourke mentioning the name. "Rourke has a friend?" I couldn't imagine Rourke being inseparable from anyone.

Carla said nothing. But when she looked at me again, her eyes were shining with tears.

Oh God. He'd *had* a friend. And something had happened, something so awful that it had changed Rourke forever.

Carla turned back to the stage and went silent for long minutes. "Do you sing?" she asked, nodding towards the woman.

My face flushed at just the thought of someone actually hearing me. "No!" I said quickly. "I mean, not that you'd want to hear."

Carla took another minute to compose herself, then continued. "Afterwards...Rourke would still come here but he was hurting." Her tone was bitter. "And I couldn't pull him out of it, however hard I tried."

I looked away, embarrassed. For days, I'd been desperate to know more about Rourke. Now I felt like I was invading his privacy.

But then I felt a soft hand on my face. Carla was leaning across the table again, gripping my chin between thumb and forefinger. She gently turned my head to look at her. The anger had gone from her eyes. "*I* couldn't pull him out of it," she said softly. "But I was only ever a warm bed to him. You...."

I flushed, eyes wide. "I'm not—"

But Carla shook her head. "I saw the way he looked at you."

I stared at her in amazement and my heart wanted to lift and soar. I wrestled it back down. "I'm not part of...*all this*," I said, waving my hand at the bar, at Havana, at treasure and bribing officials and men with guns. "I'm a librarian. Rourke is some...treasure hunting, rum-drinking, smuggler."

"Smuggler?" asked Carla. She shook her head. "The only thing Rourke ever smuggled was medicine, for the doctors."

The whole incident in the street flipped around in my mind. He hadn't been angry because I discovered he did something bad. He'd been angry because I came close to discovering he did something good.

He doesn't want me to like him.

At that moment, Rourke walked up. "It's happening," he said as I turned to him. "We need to get to the harbor, now." Then, when I just stared at him, "What?"

"Nothing," I said in a choked voice. I turned to Carla to say goodbye, but she was already stalking off across the bar.

Rourke picked up his empty glass, eyed the lipstick on the rim, and glanced at Carla's departing back. He shook his head ruefully and I saw that pain again, the same pain I'd seen when I'd asked why he was an asshole to Hobbs. *He doesn't want to be like that. He wants friends. He's...*

I thought about the *Fortune's Hope* and its solitary hammock. Rourke was the most independent, self-contained man I'd ever met but...*he's lonely.*

"Come on," he grunted. "We need to go."

28

———

HANNAH

The habor was in uproar. A crowd had gathered to watch as at least twenty harbor police officers swarmed over Ratcher's boat, which was anchored next to the *Fortune's Hope*. Ratcher himself was on the dock, screaming at a placid, silver-haired cop whose generous belly stretched out his uniform pants. I was guessing he was the Police Chief Rourke had called.

"This is bollocks!" yelled Ratcher. "We're *clean!*"

"Then as soon as we've conducted a thorough search, you can be on your way," said the police chief smoothly. He took out a cigar and took his time lighting it. "Contraband is a very serious issue."

Ratcher saw us. "*You!*" He surged forward and two police officers grabbed his arms. Even so, he managed to keep inching along the dock towards us until a third grabbed him from behind.

Rourke and I hurried aboard and I helped him cast off. Moments later, we were gliding forward and... for the first time, I felt a little ripple of excitement. I was still terrified of the open ocean but there was something about being on *our* boat, being able to set a course for wherever we wanted. I was beginning to understand why Rourke loved this life so much.

There was a growl from the dock and I turned to look. Ratcher had used his bulk to throw the cops off him and charged back aboard the *Pitbull*. He raced along the deck, separated from us only by a thin strip of water. "*Rourke!*" he bawled. "You're finished! You're fucking finished! You *and* your boat." Then he looked right at me. "And your bitch!"

Rourke had been ignoring him but his head whipped around at that last word. He stared at Ratcher with such vengeful fury it was chilling...but at the same time, it made me go warm inside. And then we were past Ratcher's boat and heading out to sea, and I let out a long sigh of relief.

Rourke anchored us far off the coast of Cuba, where Ratcher wouldn't be able to find us. I went below deck, made a nest in the hammock, and cuddled in with the diary. Within minutes, Yoyo had made himself comfortable on my chest: I'd found he'd happily sit there for hours as long as I kept stroking him.

The diary was amazing. Everything was there, from the first time she met Captain Mace to when he set off on that fateful final voyage, and I devoured it in big, hungry chunks. I read late into the night and then carried on the next day. But not long after breakfast, I was surprised to hear a voice outside that wasn't Rourke's. I looked up in panic. Had Ratcher found us?

Rourke walked in carrying a big cardboard carton. "It's okay," he said. "We had to leave in a hurry, so I had one of the fishermen buy us some supplies and bring them out." He nodded to the carton. "Got some stuff for you."

I rooted through the carton. He must have sent the fisherman on a shopping trip around Havana because there were tank tops and shorts, a swimsuit, underwear and toiletries. "Thank you," I said with feeling.

He shrugged as if embarrassed. "I just wanted my t-shirt back," he grunted.

He went outside to work on the boat: maintaining it seemed to be a full-time job. By the time he returned, it was almost noon. "You're *still* reading?" he asked.

I was so deep into Esme and her feelings for Captain Mace that it took me a couple of seconds to re-surface. "Hmm?" I shook myself back to reality. "It's just so romantic! Did you know Mace didn't want women on his ship—?"

"Smart man," muttered Rourke.

"...but she couldn't bear to be apart from him, so she snuck aboard and hid in his cabin while the ship was in port, and by the time they were at sea it was too late, so he had to take her with him?"

"So she didn't do as she was told either," grunted Rourke.

"And when the British were hunting Mace, they came to the gypsy camp and took her prisoner, to try to lure him into a trap," I said. "But Mace took a boat of his men and just...*descended* on them and wiped them out. He burned a whole British fort, just because they'd taken her."

I looked up and caught Rourke's eye. Just for a second, there was a gleam there, as if he understood what it was like to feel that way. As if he'd do that for me.

"Bloody fool," he muttered at last. And limped out into the sunshine.

I kept at it, losing myself in the pages, and soaking up Esme's life. Rourke refueled me with mugs of steaming coffee and thick slices of the local bread. Rich and yellow, it was baked with coconut and sugar and tasted amazing toasted and spread with butter.

One by one, I figured out each of the four references in the clue. Each was about something that had happened to the couple and each one was a number. The first two were easy: the number of charms on her bracelet when they met (six) and the number of days she'd made him wait before they'd finally made love for the first time (fifty-one). The third answer was *the date when you woke the whole village, from the bell tower.* I hadn't yet found anything relating to bell-ringing. And I was horribly aware that time was ticking away. Katherine had only days left. Me, maybe even less.

Wait. *There.*

Mace had met Esme early one morning and they'd crept through the village and into the bell tower, where they wouldn't be disturbed. And Esme had screamed and, yes, she'd woken everyone in the village and they'd had to flee before they were discovered. I scrunched up my forehead. Why had she screamed? Some of the English was very old-fashioned and Esme had a tendency to slip into Spanish, too. I re-read the paragraph. Her clothes were tangled. Why would she scream because her clothes were tangled?

Wait: her clothes were tangled *on the floor.*

Oh. *Oh!*

I stood naked and bent for him, my hands on the window ledge. He pressed his body to mine from behind. One hand captured my breast while he slowly entered—

"So do we know where we're going?" asked Rourke.

I slammed the diary closed, my face going beet-red. He'd come in without me hearing him. We stared at each other and I tried *not* to see him as Captain Mace and to *absolutely not think* about him entering—

"Almost done," I squeaked.

He gave me a curious look, grunted and left.

I opened the diary again. The fourteenth. That was the date Esme had...screamed. 14, 6, 51...one more number to go. The last answer was the date a fire destroyed her home town. *Shit!* It was something Esme would know, but it happened way before the diary started.

Hobbs. Hobbs might be able to find out. I borrowed Rourke's satellite phone, a bright yellow waterproof thing, and called him. I imagined him in a wingback chair, picking up the handset of some antique phone.

"Warrington Hobbs?"

His first name was *Warrington?* "It's Hannah." I explained the progress I'd made and asked whether he knew of a fire that burned down Esme's home town. With his local knowledge, it only took him a few minutes to find the right book and get the date: the 16th. *14, 6, 51, 16.*

"It's a location," said Hobbs. And he translated it into longitude and latitude for me.

I wrote it down and thanked him. Then, while I had him on the phone, "Hobbs? Rourke was in the navy, right?"

"Indeed. Captained a ship."

"That's how his leg was injured?"

"He never shared the specifics with me, but yes. Some unpleasant incident off the coast of Africa." While I was still digesting that, Hobbs continued. "You know, you're the first person he's let on that ship in two years."

I crept to the door that led out onto the deck and peeked out. Rourke was hauling on a wrench, tightening up the bolts that secured an eyelet to the deck. He'd stripped off his shirt and the muscles of his back stood out, his wide shoulders hulking and powerful. He was glaring at the bolt, that ever-present anger radiating out of him. Anger from the pain. Anger at whatever had injured him. Anger at whatever had happened to Edwards. "I don't think he wants me here," I whispered into the phone.

"That's funny," said Hobbs. "Because I think he really does."

29

ROURKE

We were flying. The wind had filled the sails, the prow was slicing through the blue with a slender slash of foaming white, and the hull barely seemed to touch the water as we sped along. It was my idea of heaven. Sailing like this, I'd slip into a kind of meditative state where even the pain dropped away. I'd focus on the horizon and the boat and me would almost blend into one.

Except today, I couldn't keep my eyes on the horizon. They kept drifting to *her,* as she sat at the prow, her long hair streaming out in the wind as if she was the boat's figurehead.

She'd put on the new tank top and shorts. I don't know if it was the scoop-neck tank or the new bra but everything seemed to be pushed up and together and my mouth damn well watered every time I laid eyes on her. And the shorts...I should have specified something long because the fisherman had brought her tight khaki things that only came a few inches below her ass. Every time she shifted position on the deck, the ropes would go limp in my hands as I forgot what I was doing and just stared, transfixed by her legs. God, she was beautiful. And special: bright and vibrant in a way I'd forgotten existed. I was starting to feel things for her that went far beyond simple lust. I *liked* having her on board, however much I protested: the boat felt alive, with her here, in a way it hadn't since Edwards died. Even the damn monkey liked her. And when she was around, I could almost forget the pain in my leg.

She was smart, too. I'd taught her port and starboard, fore and aft and she'd picked them up fast. She'd deciphered the clue and figured out the location we were heading to now. And she saw things, things I didn't want to admit to myself. I *was* rough on Hobbs. I just didn't want him or Carla or anyone else thinking they were my friends. Not after Edwards. I wasn't going to go through that again. And I didn't want anyone making me remember. If I was nice to Hobbs, the next thing I knew he'd be coming aboard and drinking rum with me and then he'd want to *talk* and then—

I didn't need friends. And my strategy had worked just fine ever since Edwards died: stay angry, snap and growl until people had no choice but to stay away. Except...for some reason, it didn't work on Hannah. She wasn't scared of me the way the others were. And when I did manage to push her away, I ached like a lovesick kid.

Maybe she wasn't a mermaid. Maybe she was a siren, singing some sweet song that had got inside my head. Because I'd been starting to have thoughts where my story didn't end with the sea taking me, where I had some sort of a future...with her. Dangerous bloody nonsense like that. Seeing her in agony at the library had been the most gut-wrenching experience of my life.

I realized I'd let the ropes slacken again and growled, hauling them tight. I had to get this done, find the cure and then get her off my boat so she could go back to Nebraska and I could go back to the end of my life.

But when we arrived, it wasn't that simple.

The heading took us to a point just offshore of another small island: a lifeless, barren rock. More rocks littered the sea around it. They stuck up through the water like vicious teeth, some as big as houses, and I had to slow right down to thread us through them.

I knew we were in the right area but there was nothing marking the exact spot other than this "Secret Garden" the message mentioned and we didn't know what that was. Hannah said Esme hadn't described anything like that in her diary so I'd just have to search and hope I recognized it when we found it. I figured I probably had a square mile to cover and that may not sound like a lot on the surface, but it's a huge area underwater.

I put on scuba gear and dived but within minutes I was grinding my teeth in frustration. The rocks were even more of a pain beneath the water. They blocked my view so I couldn't just gaze around the way you would in a field. And it wasn't like we were looking for a huge shipwreck. We knew now it would be a chest. I'd have to laboriously swim up and down in a search pattern, examining every square foot.

After two trips back up to the surface for fresh air tanks and three solid hours of swimming, I was exhausted. I got the launch back to the *Fortune's Hope*, climbed aboard, and collapsed panting on the deck. After a few seconds, something blocked out the fierce sun: a woman's body. All I could see was a silhouette but—*God, is she naked?!*

My eyes adjusted and I started to make out details. She wasn't naked but she'd changed into the swimsuit I'd bought her and it hugged every glorious curve of her. Deep, lush green, it set off that golden hair and made her pale skin look even more milky and perfect. She leaned down over me and I wanted to weep at how her breasts bobbed and swayed.

She reached beneath me and helped me shrug off the straps of my air tank and pull the mask off my face. "You okay?" she asked, concerned. I was hypnotized by those blush-pink lips, close enough to kiss.

"Aye," I muttered. "Give me a minute and then I'll go back down." I told myself I was resting but, in truth, I just wanted to be close to her for a few minutes.

The deck shifted and she changed her stance for balance, putting a foot either side of me. I swallowed as I looked up at her: the smooth muscles of her legs, the soft skin of her inner thighs....the swimsuit was pulled tight at her groin and my eyes locked there for a second.

I'd been thinking about that part of her. I couldn't *stop* thinking about it. I'd imagined it a thousand times: how the blonde curls would feel against my thumb, how she'd gasp when I spread her and entered her....

"If I went down with you," Hannah said, "we could cover twice the area."

"No," I said immediately. She was right: we could swim side by side, just six feet between us, and together we'd cover a stripe of the search area twice as wide. But this wasn't about bloody logic. I didn't want her down there, where it was dangerous. "You're not diving," I growled. And I started to get up, raising my knees and getting my hands under me.

But she didn't move, just stood there straddling me. God, she was as stubborn as I was. She was forcing me to stay and argue because it was either that or invade her personal space. I felt the anger flare and pulse. Didn't she know I was just trying to protect her?

She glared down at me and crossed her arms, not giving an inch.

Well, *fine.* I pulled my feet up and stood right where I was. She drew in a gasp as I started to come up. Leaned back a half inch...and then caught herself and forced herself to stand her ground.

My head came first, rising straight up her body, my face an inch from where that tightly-stretched Lycra covered her groin. If I'd exhaled, she would have felt it.

I got my legs under me, wincing as my bad leg protested, and pushed up. My chest was close enough that it skimmed her stomach, her torso...*she* wasn't moving, so *I* didn't give an inch, either. We locked eyes, challenging each other, both anticipating the moment—

And then it happened: my chest hit the underside of her breasts and I felt that soft, warm weight and it took everything I had not to buckle and just grab her and kiss her right there. I rose and they lifted with me, compressing against my chest. *Oh Jesus!*

And then I was standing, gazing down into her eyes, her breasts pushed tight against me.

I glared at her.

She glared at me.

We were so close, I could feel her heartbeat, and it was racing just as much as mine. I could feel the heat of our bodies throbbing into one another.

I drew in my breath, fighting to control it. But I couldn't. The closeness of her, those eyes, those soft lips, the honeysuckle smell of her hair.... *Dammit, I'm going to kiss her....*

Her eyes suddenly went huge and scared, then screwed shut.

"Hannah?" I asked, frowning.

She fell. She fell like someone had cut her strings and it was only because I was so close that I managed to grab a hand. I let her slowly down to the deck, fear flooding through me. *"Hannah?!"*

Her body began to move but it wasn't under her control. I watched in horror as every muscle began to contract, becoming as tight as her joints allowed and then *tighter,* knotting and spasming as her nervous system short-circuited. Her face twisted into a howl of agony but no sound came out, just terrified, irregular panting. I dropped to my knees beside her and stared into her eyes and she stared up at me in terror.

A ripple of pain passed through her from head to feet, so strong that her body inched along the deck. Her legs kicked, her hands clawing at the deck. Sweat was breaking out on her forehead and tears filled her eyes. My own chest contracted tight. *She needs a doctor!* She'd said they couldn't help but it didn't matter: I was past reason. I looked around for help—

And saw only pure, unbroken blue. There was no one to help, no nearby hospital or medical center because, like a fool, I'd taken her all the way out here even after I knew she was ill. *You idiot, Rourke! You fucking idiot!* I moaned in dismay and stroked her hair, running through my options. The satellite phone? Even a coast guard chopper would take a good half hour to reach us, all the way out here, plus as long again to transport her somewhere....

Her back arched. Not just a reaction to pain: this was her body fighting against itself. My stomach knotted as I watched her bend higher and higher. The body is terrifyingly strong, when it's out of control. In the navy, I'd seen victims of nerve gas who'd bent and twisted so hard they'd snapped their own spines. I grabbed her shoulders and pressed her down to the deck, even though it made her sob in pain. I felt my own eyes grow hot. It was the helplessness: she was going through sheer hell and there wasn't a damn thing I could do.

Except hold her.

I hunkered over her, clumsy as an ox, and gripped her tight, pressing her against me and trying to soak up the worst of the spasms so that she didn't wrench something out of its socket or break her back. I held her there for what felt like hours. Her tears were wet against my cheek and I felt a big, hot up swelling of...*something. What if this is it, this time?* She'd said she reckoned she only had days left. What if she just—

She went limp in my arms. I drew in a horrified breath and felt for her pulse but I couldn't find it. Edwards had always been the one who was good at this stuff, sewing up someone's arm or checking them for concussion. *Where is it? Where is it?*

There. Weak and irregular, but there. I let out a shaky breath. Not knowing what else to do, I stroked her hair back from her forehead and kept stroking it as our breathing slowed. I'd been so caught up in her and her pain that I hadn't noticed that my bad leg was screaming from my awkward position, but now it hit me. I scooped her up into my arms, swung my legs around, and wound up sitting on the deck with her across me, her head cradled on my bicep and her ass in my lap.

She opened her eyes and looked up at me. The confirmation that she was alive, and okay, was the sweetest sight I'd ever seen. I went to say something angry, to call her an idiot for being out here when she was so ill, to push her away, but....

But I just couldn't. She was so beautiful. So strong, so stubborn and yet she lay broken in my arms. However deep I reached for the anger, I couldn't find it.

She swallowed. Then, her voice weak, "I have to go down with you."

I shook my head. "If this happens again, down there, you'll die."

"If I *don't* help you, and we don't get through these last two clues and find the cure, I'm dead anyway. And so's Katherine."

Jesus. She was still more worried about her sister than herself. I looked around us. There *had* to be another way. This ship used to be filled with people! Time was, I could have had ten men diving at once, searching for this thing. We'd have found it in an hour!

But I'd chased them all away. The only person I saw, as I looked around, was Edwards, leaning against the rail near the prow. He nodded at me.

It was her or nothing.

"Okay," I said. "Let's teach you to dive."

30

HANNAH

Sitting on the deck, Rourke gave me a crash course in scuba diving. He was serious and intense, his Scottish accent making it even more somber: he made absolutely sure that I knew how dangerous it could be. He wanted me scared and I *was* scared: the open ocean all around me would have made me twitchy at the best of times but we'd be going down into its depths, out of easy reach of the surface. I'd be relying on a machine to let me breathe.

Rourke showed me how the regulator and mouthpiece worked and explained how I'd have about forty-five minutes of air. He gave me a weighted dive belt that would cancel out my body's buoyancy and help me stay down. Then we got into the launch and headed out. When I was sitting on the edge of the launch, ready to go in, the fear started. This wasn't like snorkeling: I couldn't see the bottom. I felt the fear spread, bone-deep and chilling. I'd avoided the ocean for years. Now I was about to willingly sink right into its depths. *What if I can't get to the surface? What if I get trapped? Why the hell am I doing this?*

Because if I didn't, Katherine was dead.

Rourke put his hands on my bare upper arms. "Okay?" he asked, concerned.

I gulped. And nodded.

And before he could talk me out of it, I jumped off the boat.

At first there was total panic. I was in a cloud of bubbles, falling headfirst. Falling *fast* and my head was underwater. *I'm drowning!*

I had to force myself to breathe in, my body tensing as it anticipated water. But cool air filled my lungs instead. Another breath and I began to calm a little. I was breathing...underwater!

The bubbles cleared and I saw Rourke. He made the sign for *okay?*

And I cautiously returned it. I *was* okay. I looked around in wonder. I was floating a little beneath the surface, not sinking and not rising, just hanging there as if I'd gained the power of flight. A brightly-colored fish swam past my nose, flicking its tail. Then, a massive turtle, its shell at least two feet across, cruised slowly by.

I watched and, after a few moments, my breathing slowed and settled. It was amazing: if snorkeling had let me glimpse another world, scuba diving let me fly around in it. I didn't have to keep returning to the surface: already, I'd been under longer than I could have held my breath. I turned to Rourke, my eyes wide with wonder. And I thought I saw the corners of his mouth twitch.

He led the way down to the bottom and we began the search. I couldn't believe how colorful everything was. I'd always imagined the bottom of the sea as being flat, pale sand. But there was coral in orange, purple and pink, lush green seaweed and fish in electric blue and canary yellow. We swam over dark crevices, some of them geysering bubbles and heat. We passed the wreck of a fishing boat. The freedom was intoxicating. Why had I only discovered this *now*? I turned to look at Rourke, though I had no idea how I was going to explain, without words.

I found him looking right at me. His gaze was tracking inch by inch along my bare legs as they kicked through the water. I could feel it as clearly as if he'd been touching me: up my thighs, up over my groin, over my stomach. He spent a long time on my breasts, the heat of his gaze throbbing steadily into me, turning into a twisting, lashing energy deep in my core.

Then he reached my face and realized he'd been caught. He looked quickly away and we swam on, my whole body feeling scalding hot against the water.

After only a short while, Rourke tapped my arm and made the hand sign for *ascend*. I blinked at him: was something wrong? But I nodded and swam up with him. "What's up?" I asked when we'd hauled ourselves into the launch.

"Nothing. Time to come in." And this time, he couldn't hide his grin. "It's been forty minutes. Your air's almost up."

What? I'd lost all sense of time. But he was right: my gauge was almost on empty. His had a little left. "Why did I use more air? I'm smaller than you."

"Aye, but I breathe slower. You will, too, with practice."

We went down twice more that day. Swimming side by side, we covered ground fast. Luckily, the water was shallow enough that we didn't have to waste time decompressing each time we came up. But there was a huge area to search. When the sun set, we still hadn't found the next clue.

The instant we returned to the *Fortune's Hope*, a warm, furry lump whacked into my chest and swarmed up my body to my shoulder. Yoyo grabbed hold of my ear and chirruped loudly, disgruntled at being left alone all day. He only relaxed when I gave him some serious stroking. "I swear you're part cat," I muttered, not minding at all.

Yoyo blew a raspberry and plucked a hair grip from my hair, then tried unsuccessfully to clip it into his own hair. He was always imitating us and he was a borderline kleptomaniac when it came to small, shiny things: two of my hair grips had disappeared completely. I grabbed a banana and used that to distract him while I plucked the hair grip from his head.

That night, I searched again for something to read. I'd pored over Esme's diary for so long that I could recite it in my sleep and I wasn't sure I could face more of *The Shipboard Doctor's* terrifying medical conditions. But on a low shelf at the very back of the room, I found the one other book on board: the ship's log.

I read for hours, losing myself in it. If Esme's life was a searing romance, the log was a real-life adventure novel that stretched from the Caribbean to the coast of Africa and all the way south to Argentina. Rourke, Edwards and their crew had searched for lost Mayan gold, Spanish treasure ships, and the riches the Nazis had smuggled out of Europe in World War II. The *Fortune's Hope* had been through the Panama canal, been briefly seized by the Colombian authorities after they'd been mistaken for drug runners and had taken fire from pirates off the coast of Mozambique. Rourke had been bitten by a snake, thrown in jail by a corrupt dictator and was once lost at sea for two days with nothing but a bottle of rum. Edwards, who came across as the softer, gentler of the two, had tangled with an octopus, had a brief but tempestuous fling with the daughter of the aforementioned corrupt dictator and had been quarantined after the *Fortune's Hope* was used to transport doctors to an Ebola outbreak in Africa (thankfully, his symptoms turned out to be flu).

And through it all, they'd been there for each other. I looked towards the door, towards the deck where Rourke slept. They'd been close as brothers....

I found the last entry that mentioned Edwards. They'd been on a diving expedition to search for Spanish gold. There were four days of happy, routine entries...and then nothing. A whole page had been ripped from the log. That was two years ago. Since then, it had just been Rourke on his own, sailing gradually farther and farther from shore.

My stomach tightened. *Almost as if he wants something bad to happen to him.*

That was why he kept pulling away. He was helping me, trying to save my life. But as far as he was concerned, his was already over.

The next day, we dived again, starting at first light and continuing all day with only quick breaks for food. I gradually got more confident in the water and we ate through a lot of the search area. By late afternoon, we only had about a fifth of it to go. We'd either find it soon or...*what if I got the clue wrong? What if we're in the wrong place?*

Don't think like that. We were running out of time. If we had to start all over again, we were screwed.

We worked on, exhausted but feeling the tension. Neither of us wanted to quit or even take a break, not when we were so close to the end. I was almost out of air, swimming quickly over the coral, when everything suddenly went dark beneath me. Had a cloud covered the sun? I made out the edges of a shadow, cast by something above and behind me. A boat?

I twisted onto my back to look. No. Not a boat.

The thing was right above me, close enough to touch. It was at least twice as long as I was tall, its body blue-gray, the color of gun barrels and death. It parted its jaws, showing teeth that were serrated like knives.

And then the shark swam straight towards me.

31

HANNAH

The fear wasn't like the sick dread I got when I looked around and saw the empty, endless horizon. That happened in my head: it could be argued with, sometimes rationalized away. This was down in the pit of my stomach, deep and primal, a racial memory that stretched back millions of years. *Shark!*

I knew I had to move but I just hung there, hypnotized. The mouth coming towards me filled my vision. All I could see was darkness, edged with teeth. I remembered the scars on Rourke's stomach, a warning I'd completely ignored. I'd left the safety of land and come down here into its world. Now I was prey.

The shark gave a flick of its tail and accelerated, jaws wide. I closed my eyes.

Something barreled into my side, knocking me sideways and twisting me around. When I opened my eyes, Rourke was staring at me from six inches away, his hands on my shoulders. He kicked hard and hauled me up—

We broke the surface twenty feet from the launch. Suddenly, my muscles unfroze: I knew what happened now. I imagined my legs as seen from below, pale and tempting as they hung down....

I raced for the launch. The sun was low in the sky, turning the surface of the water gold. I couldn't see down through it, couldn't see if the shark was right below me, jaws opening—

I grabbed the side and frantically scrambled in. Then I turned and saw Rourke still treading water: he'd waited for me to get in first, ready to help me if I'd needed it. I saw movement in the water behind him and let out a moan of terror. I grabbed him under the arms and pulled, terrified that any second he'd scream as teeth snapped closed below his waist—

We toppled back into the boat together, him on top. We were pressed hard up against each other but I was so scared, there wasn't room for it to be sexual. My arms were clasped around him where I'd pulled him in and I hugged him like a giant teddy bear, clinging to his chest.

"It's okay," he said in my ear. "It's okay, lass. We're in."

My breathing gradually slowed. I loosened my grip and he rolled off me so that we were both on our backs, looking up at the sky. I tentatively raised my upper body and looked around.

A fin cut through the water no more than six feet from the boat. Smooth and effortless, horribly fast. Instead of swimming past, it turned. Circling us.

"Where did it come from?" I asked in a choked voice.

Rourke was watching it grimly. "Sharks migrate. It's probably moving through the area."

"So we can just wait for it to move on?"

"Aye." He stroked his chin. "But now that we've disturbed it, it might hang around for hours."

"Fine. We'll wait until tomorrow." I moved to the back of the launch: Rourke had showed me how to work the outboard motor. "Pull up the anchor, we'll head in."

But he didn't move. Instead, he looked at the water.

My stomach lurched as I saw where this was heading. "We can wait until tomorrow!" I insisted.

He looked at me. Then he picked up a fresh air tank.

"You can't go back down there!" I grabbed the air tank. "Wait! We'll come back tomorrow!"

He locked eyes with me. "There's still some daylight left. We're *close*. I can feel it. Can't you feel it?"

I went quiet. I *could* feel it. We'd nearly covered the search area. Whatever this "secret garden" was, we must be right on top of it. "But —" I started.

He put a thumb against my lips. "If we wait," he said, "it's another day."

My lips moved against his thumb as I tried to think of an argument. But he was right. If we found the next clue *now*, we could travel overnight to the next one. If we waited until the next morning, we'd lose all that time. Time Katherine and I didn't have.

My protest died in my throat and I nodded. He left his thumb on my lip for another second before he removed it.

He checked the new air tank and strapped it on. Then he pulled on his mask and I finally woke up and started moving. "I'm coming with you," I told him.

He rounded on me. "No!" he snapped. Then, in a softer voice, "I know how to swim with sharks. I can stay quiet. The more people there are moving around down there, the more it'll get riled up."

My chest tightened. "I'm not letting you—"

He fixed me with a look and then just nodded firmly. He *was* going to go down there for me, whether I wanted him to or not.

I bit my lip. "I'm not worth—"

His eyes narrowed in a way that made my heart lift and swell. *Yes. Yes you damn well are.*

I was still reeling from that when he moved to the edge of the launch. "Whatever happens, *stay on the launch*," he told me. "I'll be back before dark."

He flipped over the side and, with barely a splash, he was gone.

There was nothing I could do but wait. *He knows what he's doing,* I told myself. *He'll be okay.*

But I couldn't forget the shark's serrated teeth. Or the scars on Rourke's stomach from the last time he'd faced one. *If something happens to him....*

I sat there scanning the water for any sign of his return. The sun sank lower and lower in the sky, turning the water orange and then red. He'd said he'd be back before dark. Another twenty minutes, maybe. I stared at the water, willing him to appear....

A noise right next to me made me jump clean off the seat. The high-pitched tone had to cut through the air a second time before I realized what it was: the satellite phone was ringing. I let out a shuddering sigh of relief and answered it. "Hello?"

"Miss Barnes!"

Hobbs! It was good to hear a friendly voice. But he sounded worried. "What's up?"

"My office was broken into, sometime earlier today. I just got back and found it. I suspect it was someone working for Ratcher." His voice became urgent. "Miss Barnes, they took my notes. I'd written down the location we worked out. *He knows where you are!*"

I turned in a slow circle, the phone still clamped to my ear. And saw the ugly white bulk of Ratcher's boat cruising towards me.

32

HANNAH

S*hit. Shit, shit shit!*

I hunkered down in the launch. Luckily, both it and the *Fortune's Hope* were mostly hidden by the rocks that surrounded the island. I was pretty sure Ratcher hadn't seen either of them yet.

But he didn't have to find us. He had twenty men and lots of equipment. He could scour the whole search area in a few hours, even in the dark. If he found the clue first and took it, we were finished. I'd never find the *Hawk*.

I looked at the water. And if Ratcher's men found Rourke down there.... My stomach twisted. He'd be outnumbered and completely unprepared. I had to warn him.

The sun was sinking fast. *He'll be up in another fifteen minutes.* But Ratcher wasn't wasting any time. I could hear his voice echoing across the water, bawling orders. There were splashes as divers hit the water: he must have had them geared up and ready to go the instant they arrived.

With shaking hands, I pulled on a fresh tank of air. There was no Rourke to do a safety check on my gear or make sure I had everything adjusted right. I just had to hope I'd remembered what he'd taught me.

I looked at the water. Where the sun hit it, the waves were orange and crimson. But in the shadows it had already turned to deep, impenetrable black.

I took a deep breath...and jumped in.

It was even darker than I'd imagined. Anything beyond fifty feet was just blackness. And the shark could cover that distance in a heartbeat.

I struck out in the direction Rourke had gone in, heart hammering in my chest. Every flicker at the edge of my vision made me twist to check if it was the shark. Every change in current against my ankle made me spin around, expecting to see jaws closing on my leg. I was close to all-out panic. I could just make out the launch's anchor chain behind me. The urge to swim back to safety was almost overpowering.

No. Rourke was down here because of me. I couldn't leave him.

I forced myself to stare straight ahead and just *swim.* I went faster and faster, shoulders burning and legs aching, imagining jaws opening behind me—

Rourke loomed up out of the darkness and I was going so fast I whacked breathlessly into his chest. For a few seconds he just stared at me in disbelief. Then he grabbed my shoulders and glared at me, furious and worried. *What are you doing here?!*

I mimed frantically but there wasn't a hand gesture for what I needed to communicate. Eventually, I tore free of his hands, swam down to the bottom, and scrawled *Ratcher* in the sand.

Rourke went stock still. Then the anger in his eyes evaporated, to be replaced with gratitude. We started swimming back towards the launch and the relief of not being on my own anymore was incredible. The darkness was rapidly closing in. By the time we reached the launch's anchor chain, I couldn't see more than twenty feet in front of me.

Rourke pointed up and we started to ascend, me first. I was almost at the surface when a black shape slammed into him.

At first, I thought it was the shark. Then I made out the arms tangled around him and the flashing silver of a blade. One of

Ratcher's men, in a wetsuit. And beneath the surface, far from any laws, he was going to carry out Ratcher's threat and finish Rourke for good.

I made a clumsy turn and swam back down. I had no idea what I was going to do, just knew I needed to help him. The man had grappled Rourke from behind and had his knife to Rourke's throat. He was struggling to slash it across while Rourke strained to keep it away, the blade jerking and twitching, millimeters from his flesh.

I didn't know what to do so I just grabbed the man's arm and heaved it away from Rourke. The man span around, slashing wildly, and I felt a momentary flash of pain. Then Rourke thumped into him from behind, his own knife drawn. The two turned to face each other and hung there in the water, eyeing each other. At least now it was a fair fight.

My hand throbbed and stung. I looked down and saw threads of red rising from a slash across my palm, the blood curling and blooming in the water.

Oh shit.

Everything I'd heard about sharks flooded my mind.

Oh SHIT!

I clenched my hand into a fist but the blood kept escaping. I saw Rourke look towards me and his eyes went wide with fear as he saw the blood, too.

I whirled around, trying to see in all directions. And saw the shark shoot out of the darkness, heading straight for me.

33

ROURKE

Hannah bolted, swimming for her life. But I knew in my gut she had no hope of outrunning it.

I was ready to kill Ratcher's man for harming Hannah, but every second I spent fighting him, she and the shark got further away. So I used an old Navy diving trick: I swam up above the guy, lunged down and slashed through his air hose where it joined his tank. He shot away, kicking hard for the surface so he could breathe again.

Hannah and the shark were already out of sight. I shot off in the direction I'd last seen them, legs powering me forward, arms back to streamline me. All I could see was darkness. My heart was slamming against my ribs: I knew I was faster than her, but so was the shark. At any second, I expected to see a cloud of blood in front of me, the shark biting and tearing—

I still had my dive knife in my hand and my fingers crushed the hilt. I'd bury it in the thing. I'd gut it, if it had taken her from me.

The shark's tail loomed out of the darkness. As I watched, it lunged forward and butted up against something. I swam closer, staying behind it so it didn't see me.

It was the fishing boat we'd swum past the day before. Some of it had rotted away but the wheelhouse was still intact and Hannah was inside, terrified, her back pressed against the far wall as the shark rammed its jaws again and again against the glassless windows. They were too small for it to fit through but the wood was already starting to crack. Riled up as it was, the shark was more than capable of smashing the boat to pieces to get at the blood it could smell.

Hannah looked up at me with big, frantic eyes. *What do I do?*

I stared at her, then looked at the shark. There was only one way to get it away from her. I brought my dive knife up to my hand.

Hannah saw what I was maneuvering to do and shook her head. *Don't!*

I ignored her and pointed to the launch, telling her to go straight there as soon as I did this. Then I put the blade of the knife against my palm.

Hannah stared at me, eyes shining with tears behind her mask. *No!*

I slashed right across my palm and the blood billowed out in a red cloud towards the shark.

34

HANNAH

*N*o!

But it was too late. Rourke flapped his hand, spreading the blood around. The shark was just lining up to ram my hiding place again when it suddenly broke off and turned. Its black, dead eyes stared right at Rourke. Then it flicked its tail and shot forward, right towards him.

He powered away, moving much faster than I could...but the shark was already gaining as they disappeared into the darkness. *It's going to catch him!*

I swam out through the boat's window and made for the launch. My limbs were already exhausted from swimming from the shark but I forced myself forward. As I drew near, I glimpsed Rourke and the shark up ahead. The shark surged forward and Rourke twisted and dived beneath it, almost losing his mask as a fin clipped him. The shark circled around, jaws open and ready. It was only a matter of time.

I swam towards the launch...and then froze.

Beneath me, in the area we hadn't searched yet, rocks lay in a rough circle. And between them, invisible unless you were directly above it, was a carpet of green seaweed. Pink, blue, and yellow coral bloomed like flowers. *Their secret garden!* It had to be. I could imagine Esme and Mace swimming here, finding it, and naming it.

Ahead of me, Rourke glanced my way and saw that I'd stopped. He pointed frantically to the launch and then had to dodge out of the shark's way again.

I swam for the launch...then stopped again. I knew I had to get out of there: Rourke could only distract the shark for so long. But once we were back to the launch, we'd have to leave: we were massively outnumbered. Then Ratcher's men would find the clue...and Katherine would die.

I kicked with my flippers and swam down to the bottom. There was a clear patch in the center of the garden and some small stones had been piled there as a marker. I shoved them aside and started digging in the sand with my hands. The water turning cloudy but there was a pink tinge to the clouds. *Shit!* Digging was making my hand bleed more.

I glanced up. Rourke had just evaded the shark again and—*Oh God.* The shark was circling around to get back to him. It would pass right over me and, if it smelled easier prey this way....

I squeezed my hand into a tight fist and prayed. The shark's shadow fell over me and it seemed to hesitate...then it flicked its tail and swam back towards Rourke.

I dug frantically and—*yes!* The hard wood of a chest, much bigger than the first one. I cleared away the sand and heaved it out of the hole, panic lending me strength. There was no way I could get it to the surface, though, and we weren't going to be able to come back down for it with the shark around.

Thinking fast, I heaved it over to the launch's anchor chain. Rourke was gesturing wildly for me to surface, his expression flicking between fury and fear for my life. I lifted the small anchor from the sea bed and looped the chain around and around the chest as if I was tying a parcel, then hooked the anchor into the chain. I'd just have to hope it held.

Too late, I spotted the blood clouding the water: messing with the chain had opened the cut in my palm right up. The shark seemed to twitch...and then it suddenly twisted in the water and shot towards me.

I kicked with all my strength for the surface. I came up right next to the launch, got my hands up on the side, and heaved my upper body in.

There was an explosion of water behind me as the shark surfaced. I felt a pull on my leg and my blood turned to ice water.

Then I tumbled forward into the boat. Seconds later, Rourke surfaced and hauled himself up and over the side.

I lay on my back, panting in fear, and examined my foot. The whole front part of my flipper was gone, the ragged bite mark ending an inch from my toes.

Rourke hunkered over me. "You *fucking...stupid wee—*"

Water sprayed over our faces and there was a crack as loud as a gunshot, right behind my head. The whole boat tipped and I smelled blood and rotten meat.

Rourke grabbed my shoulders and heaved, throwing himself backwards and pulling me with him I landed on top of him, twisted around to look...and screamed.

The whole end of the boat was *gone*. The shark had rammed us, smashing the prow to splinters. It had its jaws in the hole: my head must have been inches from its teeth. It was weighing down that end of the launch, tipping us. As I watched, anything not tied down—a spare regulator, a flashlight, the satellite phone—skittered down the deck and tumbled into the shark's mouth. And then *we* started to slide towards it, too.

Rourke's spear gun slid past us. He grabbed it just as the shark swallowed and lunged forward to crush more of the boat. There was a high-pitched hiss that hurt my ears and then the shark was falling back, a metal spear protruding from its back.

The boat fell back into the water and we lay there panting.

By now, it was fully dark. Thick cloud covered the moon and blocked out most of the stars: it was hard to see where the sky ended and the water began. Rourke got to his knees and pulled me up as well. His hands were hard on my upper arms and he was shaking, his eyes a maelstrom of rage and fear. I braced myself to be yelled at. He tried to form words once, twice....

Then he just pulled me to his chest and folded his arms protectively around me. I clung to him, all the fear that had been kept at bay by the adrenaline suddenly hitting me. It looped around and around in my mind: the shark lunging at him; the moment it had turned towards me; the sickening pull on my leg.... Both of us had been inches from death.

I pressed my face into the valley of his chest, soaking up his warmth and the immovable *solidness* of him. I wanted to never let him go.

The water lapping at our legs made us finally break apart. The hole the shark had made was just barely above the waterline. We weren't quite sinking but we were taking on some water every time a wave hit us. I used a mask to bail while Rourke hauled on the anchor chain. It went taut and he grunted, his muscles straining with unexpected effort. He frowned....

Our eyes met as both remembered. *The chest!*

Rourke dug deep and heaved, drawing in the chain and its load inch by inch. I held my breath: if it slipped out of the chain now, there was no way we could get it back.

My heart leapt as the top of the chest broke the water. Both of us leaned over the side and *pulled*. It took everything we had to wrestle it over the side but we did it. I wanted to punch the air.

Then I let out a low moan of horror. The extra weight pushed the hole below the waterline. Water gushed in, faster than I could bail.

"We need to get out of here," Rourke said. He looked around and cursed.

I looked up and saw why. It was fully dark now and all I could see was black in every direction. I couldn't even figure out which direction the *Fortune's Hope* was in. And there were rocks all around us. The launch was already crippled: if we ran into something, it would break apart completely and we'd be in the water with the shark.

"Flashlight?" I asked.

"In the shark's belly," said Rourke. "And Ratcher would see it. On a night like this, you can see a light for miles."

I'd completely forgotten that Ratcher was out there somewhere, looking for us. A shudder went down my spine as I remembered the fury on his face when we'd escaped him in Havana

"We'll have to go slow," Rourke whispered. He picked up the oars. "And very, very quiet. Sound travels over water."

I nodded. Despite everything that was going on, his low whisper, in *that* accent, sent a delicious ripple right down my spine: it was like being stroked with a soft paintbrush loaded with warm, liquid silver.

The water was rising so I started bailing again, as quietly as I could. Rourke sat down and stared around him for a moment. *How can he see?* It was pitch black.

He hauled on the oars and we slid silently into the darkness.

35

ROURKE

Jesus, it was dark. One of those nights where the air seems solid, a blanket that hides the rocks until it's far too late.

But my family had been doing this for a long time. Back in 18th century, my ancestors used to smuggle liquor and tobacco into Scotland. The sea was in my blood. I couldn't see the rocks but I could hear the waves breaking against them, feel the change in the wind against my face as we came into the lee of them. I got the oars slicing the water with barely a splash and Hannah was managing to keep the bailing quiet, too. We slid over the water like a ghost, threading past rocks I could only see in my mind. All it would take would be to clip one and our momentum would crush the damaged hull like an eggshell. Then we'd be in the water with an injured, vengeful shark.

Steady, said Edwards beside me. And I took a deep breath and focused.

Seconds later, I heard voices and laughter. The clink of beer bottles. Then Ratcher's voice, snapping at his crew, telling them to keep it down.

I leaned forward and tapped Hannah on the shoulder, trying to ignore how good that smooth skin felt. She stopped bailing and sat there frozen.

I concentrated and gave one last hard pull on the oars to keep our momentum up. Then I lifted them clear of the water and held them there. We glided past a rock the size of a house and—

Ratcher's boat was right there, it's stern towards us. They'd killed their lights but Ratcher hadn't been able to stop his crew smoking. I could see the glowing tips of their cigarettes, cherry red in the darkness. And inside the wheelhouse I could see the glow of screens and control panels: Ratcher was too nervous a sailor to shut down his technology. We were going to drift by less than ten feet from him.

The voices became distinct. "It's too dangerous," said one man. From his accent, it was Trujillo, Ratcher's dive expert. Not a bad guy: he'd just signed on with the wrong boss. "Grainger said he saw a shark."

They were just silhouettes in the darkness but I recognized Ratcher from his bulk. Heard Trujillo's gasp as he was lifted clear of the deck. "Rourke and the bitch are down there somewhere," spat Ratcher. "The divers keep going until either we find the fucking clue or we find *them* and get it off them." He dumped Trujillo on the deck. "If they're too scared, tell them I'm raising the bounty on Rourke. Ten thousand. That'll get them moving. And fifteen if they bring him in alive. I want that Scottish bastard to watch while I fill our hold with gold. Then he can watch while I throw *her* face-down over one of the chests and fuck her 'till—"

I forced myself to tune it out but I couldn't stop my hands tensing in white-hot fury. An oar twisted. Water dribbled and dripped.

I heard Ratcher's feet move as he spun around. "What was that?" The words came straight towards me out of the darkness. He was staring right at us. I held my breath. We were still moving but more slowly, our momentum running out. And I didn't dare row again.

"Give me a flashlight!" Ratcher snapped.

I closed my eyes and prayed.

I heard Trujillo rooting around in the disorganized mess that was Ratcher's deck.

"Now!" yelled Ratcher. "*Fucking now!*"

Trujillo finally found a flashlight and handed it to Ratcher. Ratcher fumbled for the switch, turned it on and—

A circle of ocean three feet behind us turned blazing white. Ratcher cursed and we drifted silently on, my heart pounding so hard I was amazed they didn't hear it.

Moments later, we reached the *Fortune's Hope*. But as we approached, I saw a trail of bubbles from a diver moving away. *Shit!* They'd found our boat. Had one of Ratcher's men just happened across the anchor chain, moments ago? Or had they found it earlier and he'd just completed some sabotage mission? Had they just put a damn hole in our hull?

I tied up the launch and then put a hand on Hannah's shoulder. "*Wait here,*" I whispered. I was worried there might be more of Ratcher's men waiting for us aboard.

I stepped onto the deck, my dive knife drawn. Silently inched open the door that led below deck—

Something flew out of the darkness and hit me in the face. I staggered back, knife coming up—

A brown, furry face stared back at me from three inches away. Yoyo tilted his head, then kissed my cheek.

My whole body was shaking with adrenaline. I very gently plucked him from me and set him down, then crept below deck.

Nothing. I searched the whole ship. No one was on board and nothing looked to have been disturbed. I couldn't see water coming in anywhere, either. Maybe that diver *had* only just found us.

Maybe. I made a mental note to dive down and check our hull, once it was light.

I hurried back outside and got Hannah aboard. I raised the anchor and unfurled the sails, wincing as the fabric snapped taut in the breeze. We swept off into the night with barely a whisper. And, once we were far out of sight and sound of Ratcher, I slumped down on the deck and rested my head on my knees, utterly exhausted.

All of the fear hit me at once, then: how many times had I nearly lost her, in the last few hours? I was weak with it, shaky with it. Ever since Edwards, I'd been living without much fear of my own death. Now I was suddenly remembering what it was like to be scared for someone else.

This is exactly why I couldn't let her get any closer. I already cared too much. *Get her the cure. Get her off the boat.* She was smart and gorgeous and damn well perfect. And that meant...I forced my heart to harden. That meant she deserved better than a washed-up cripple.

She likes you, said Edwards, next to me.

A washed-up cripple who hears ghosts, I corrected.

I pushed myself up to standing, wincing as my leg twinged, and then headed below deck to check she was okay. I swung open the door—

She was naked.

I swallowed. She was standing in front of the half-height closet where she'd been storing the clothes I bought her. The door was open but it only blocked my view of her from mid-thigh up to just above her breasts. And the door was narrow: beyond its edge, I could see the curve of her hip. My eyes locked on the smooth, bare skin where the waistband of her panties should have been.

She flushed. "I'm running short of dry clothes," she said. "Have you got anything I could put on?"

She gave a tiny shiver. It was getting late and the night was cooling fast. I nodded, rooted in another cupboard, and found an old cable-knit sweater. I tossed it to her over the top of the door—

God, just a glimpse, a tiny glimpse of the side of her swaying, milky breast as she leaned sideways a little to catch it.

She lifted her arms over her head. I knew I should avert my eyes. I didn't.

She wriggled into the sweater, which was like a dress on her. Even though the door blocked everything I was hard as iron, watching her. Imagining the rough wool sliding down her bare skin. Then she found some dry panties, stepped into them, and pulled them up her legs, twisting a little as she did it. God, I was *aching.* It was more erotic than any striptease.

She closed the cupboard door. We stared at each other again. It kept happening, however much I willed it to stop: one look at those clear blue eyes and I was lost, drawn to her so hard I had to grit my teeth to keep from stepping forward. *Don't!*

But I was wavering. Nearly losing her had stripped my self-control down to a slender thread.

"Can we look?" she asked.

I actually cocked my head to the side in puzzlement.

"The chest!" she said.

It was like a bomb going off in my mind. A three hundred year-old chest, heavy with treasure…and I'd forgotten all about it. How the hell had I done that?

Beside me, Edwards was laughing his ass off.

"*Aye,*" I snapped, and strode out to the launch. *Treasure.* That was exactly what I needed. That'd cut through all this nonsense and remind me who I was. I grabbed the chest and heaved it into my arms, then staggered below and laid it on the floor. Kneeling down in front of it, I felt that rush I always got. *This,* I understood. I'd missed it, ever since Edwards. It's a feeling I couldn't describe to anyone. It's not about the money. Numbers in a bank account mean nothing to me. It's something deep and basic, something that's been in the human spirit for centuries. It's what drove men to cross oceans and conquer cities. It's like a drug and no one but us treasure hunters ever understand—

Then I glanced sideways at Hannah and froze.

She was staring at the chest with the exact same look in her eyes.

She was one of us, now. For the first time in two years, I had someone to share it with. Something swelled in my chest, unexpected and powerful. I looked around at Edwards and he was staring at her, too.

I swallowed. Then I nodded at the chest. "You should open it," I said, my voice thick with emotion.

Her eyes grew wide. "*Me?* Are you sure?"

"You found it."

With shaking hands, she freed the iron hasp. Then she slowly swung back the lid.

The light from the lantern hit what was inside...and the entire room lit up gold.

Hannah sucked in a long, shaky breath. Her hand grabbed for mine and squeezed it. The warmth in my chest expanded, growing tight.

The chest was brimming with coins, so full that just opening the lid caused a few to slide out and clink to the floor.

"Those," I said slowly, "are doubloons." I picked one up and showed it to her. It was heavy with gold, nothing like the nickel coins of today. I fished out a few large, silver coins. "And these," I told her, "are *Real de a Ochas*. Spanish dollars." I showed her the "eight" in Roman numerals. "Better known as—"

She grabbed my hand, eyes wide as a child's *"Pieces of eight?!"* She stared in silent wonder for a moment. Then, in a small voice, "How much...?"

I considered. "Coins will go for between five hundred and a few thousand dollars each. There's maybe a thousand here. So...a million dollars?"

She leaned closer to the chest, awestruck. As she shifted, her breasts moved under the sweater and—

It was handmade and old, the loops of wool loose and uneven. And I could see, through one of the holes, the delicate pink of her nipple.

That fragile thread of my self-control stretched, thin as spider silk. *Don't,* I told myself.

Hannah suddenly thrust her hand into the coins. "What about the message?" she muttered. "What if it isn't—?"

But then she drew her hand back, clutching another of the glass bottles sealed with wax. She slumped in relief, showing me the rolled cloth inside. But she'd dragged out something else, as well. Caught on a finger was a thin gold chain that disappeared beneath the coins. I took hold of it and pulled it free.

She clapped her hand to her mouth. I'd never seen a lass actually do that and it was bloody adorable. *"That's the necklace!"*

"What necklace?"

"The necklace Charles Mace gave Esme!"

I looked at it. The gold chain was made to look like twisted rope. The pendant was another ruby, a bigger one, this time, shaped into a teardrop. It almost looked like a drop of blood.

"Mace said his heart hurt every time he was away from her," said Hannah breathlessly. "So he gave her this on the carriage ride to the port, just before—what are you doing?"

I'd undone the clasp and was leaning forward towards her neck. I looked her in the eye and she gulped.

"You're crazy," she said. "It must be worth hundreds of thousands."

"A necklace like this deserves to be worn. Not put in a museum."

She swallowed. Then, with shaking hands, she gathered up all that shining golden hair and lifted it away from her neck. I slipped the chain on and fastened it, trying to breathe slow and steady, even when my thumbs brushed her skin.

"There." I leaned back. God, she looked beautiful. Eyes wide and excited, those blush-pink lips so soft, so inviting. The necklace was nothing compared to her.

My self-control stretched even more, so thin it was barely there. *Don't!*

She plunged her hands into the chest and lifted them out, letting the coins run through her fingers. She was grinning in wonder and excitement. I remembered that feeling. I remembered *my* first time.

She turned slightly.

The light caught her *just so.*

And my control snapped completely.

I grabbed her by the shoulders and kissed her as hard as I could.

36

HANNAH

I think I made a noise like *whelp!*

It all happened so fast. Rourke grabbed my shoulders with his big, warm hands and then his lips were pressing down hard on mine. The realization roared through me like a hot hurricane: *this is real. He's kissing me.* And the kiss wasn't like anything I'd ever known.

There were no mind games.

There was no hesitation.

He didn't ask for permission.

He just damn well kissed me, old-fashioned and full-on and wonderful. I felt myself flower open under him, the kiss rippling right down to my toes. I suddenly felt so soft, so weightless and insubstantial, against those hard lips. The kiss moved and changed, exploring me, his thumb stroking beneath my chin as he pressed and spread me and pressed again.

He lowered me to the floor and then lowered himself full-length atop me, taking his weight on his forearms so his muscled frame didn't crush me. But he still pinned me to the ground, the hard contours of his chest pressed tight against the softness of my breasts, those powerful thighs heavy against mine. I couldn't escape and I didn't want to.

He broke the kiss. I was red-faced and panting: staring up into his eyes, I felt like I was tumbling into that bottomless blue. His eyes clouded with lust, his gaze becoming darker and hotter, scorching me until I squirmed and crushed my thighs together. I opened my mouth to speak. I'm not sure what I was going to say. Maybe a nervous *umm*.

I didn't get the chance. As soon as I drew in breath, his thumb was against my lips. Every nerve ending in my mouth was trembling and alive, the stroke of his rough skin against my softness electrifying. "Hush, lass," he growled.

And then he grabbed the bottom of my borrowed sweater and tugged it all the way up to my neck, baring my breasts. I let out a strangled moan and started panting harder, my brain trying to catch up. I could feel every millimeter of my skin as cool air breezed over me, followed a heartbeat later by the heat of his gaze. His eyes ate me up, every curve, and I felt his cock swell and press even harder against me. I caught my breath: I'd never had a man so obviously *relish* me.

Then he filled his hands with my breasts, lifting and squeezing, thumbs rubbing across my nipples. Then his mouth enveloped me. I arched my back and cried out as those hard lips found my softness, as his tongue sought out the stiff peak of my nipple and lashed around it.

His mouth moved to my other breast and he took the first in his hand, thumb rubbing over my spit-shiny nipple. Glowing ribbons of pleasure shot down to my groin and began to twist, pulling taut.... I wanted to thrash and buck but he had me pinned so thoroughly I could barely move. I had to settle for grinding my ass against the floor, coins clinking and shifting under me.

He started kissing me again and tugged me up to half-sitting so that he could get the sweater the rest of the way off. We were panting and desperate, kissing open-mouthed and hungry. I wanted to sit all the way up so that I could get his shirt off, but he was kissing me so hard, I had to keep scooching my ass back along the deck, or I'd have toppled backwards. He finally managed to get the sweater off over my head and toss it away and then I felt something solid behind me I could use to lever myself up to sitting. I groped behind me, put my hands on the edge of the thing and *pushed*—

It tipped and I dropped with it. There was a tinkling metal roar I'd only ever heard in movies and I was engulfed in a tidal wave of gold.

I'd just tipped over the chest.

Coins flooded over my shoulders and down my body. They swept over my stomach and rolled down my legs, glittering and chinking. When it was over, my whole upper body was covered, only my head and breasts visible.

I caught my breath, eyes wide. The coins were cold but, against my heated, naked skin, they felt wonderful. I moved a little and gasped as I was caressed by a thousand smooth, cool fingers.

Rourke looked down at me and grinned: that big honest, Scottish smile that lit me up inside. I gave a shaky, nervous laugh and then he was kissing me again and I gave myself up to the sensations: his hot mouth, the cool coins, his hands sliding over my breasts. Both of us were out of control now, hands frantic as we explored each other's bodies.

His hands moved lower and I felt him pull off my panties. I lifted my ass to make it easier for him. I was lying on a shifting carpet of coins and, already, they were warming from our body heat.

He tossed my panties behind him and moved forward but I stopped him, my hands on the top button of his shirt. I couldn't wait any longer, had to see him, and had to feel him against me.

He growled, impatient, and I could feel the heat of him throbbing through the thin cotton as I pushed buttons through holes as fast as I could. A triangle of tan skin slowly appeared: that deep valley between the slabs of his pecs. His nipples were pink and perfect and I ran my thumb over one, making him growl. God, he was so hard, midsection tight and powerful from swimming, his abs deep ridges I had to stop and run my hands over, fingertips tracing each line. I traced the scars, too, the fierce teeth marks the shark had left. They didn't mar him: they told the story of who he was and showed his strength: he'd fought that monster and survived.

He let me finish the last button and then ripped the shirt from his shoulders and threw it away. He hunkered down over me, gripped my thighs just above the knee, and *pushed.* I drew in my breath as my legs folded and opened, coins shifting under me. His blistering, almost angry gaze locked on my eyes for a second and then slid down, over breasts that had started to rise and fall in urgent, gasping rhythm, over my stomach, still strewn with gold, and down to my groin. And then he just *looked.*

I should have been self-conscious but there was no room for that. He was gazing at me with such a mixture of hunger and reverence that it took all my fears away. I'd never felt anything so deeply hot.

"So beautiful," he whispered. His voice was tight with lust and his Scottish accent shaped the words into poetry.

He cupped me. A finger parted me and—God, I was soaking. He stared into my eyes and I bit my lip, rolling my hips as he pushed the finger into me all the way to his palm, groaning along with me.

Then he was unfastening his belt and kicking off his pants. His cock sprang out, iron-hard and ready, and I ground my ass into the coins as I saw it: long and *God* thick, a satiny head of purple-pink atop tan perfection. It had that same solid weight to it as the rest of him, not just big but somehow *heavy.* When he moved atop me and it nudged my thigh, the heat of it made me gasp.

I heard the rubber sound of a condom. Then he used one hand to guide himself to me, the head of him nudging up against my folds. The other hand he slid into my hair, palm cupping my cheek, thumb brushing my cheekbone.

He pressed forward, his muscled hips sinking between my thighs, and I rocked my head back and cried out at how good it felt. He filled me in one long, slow, perfect thrust, not stopping until the base of his cock kissed my folds. I looked up at him, eyes wide, nostrils flaring as I took quick, shuddering breaths. I could feel him throbbing within me: so hot, so *solid.*

He lowered his head so that he could kiss me again and it was slow but deep, lips trembling as we panted, both of us overwhelmed by sensation. He looked down the length of my body, all the way from my face to where he was buried in me and then on down my legs. "You're like a dream, lass." His voice was thick with lust.

I wriggled under him, embarrassed but glowing. No one had ever said anything like that to me before. Then he rose up on his forearms, his broad shoulders blocking out everything behind him, and he began to move.

He withdrew and I groaned: it was like a loss, an ache. Then those powerful thighs and hard ass *flexed* and I caught my breath as he drove into me again, his size making me gasp. His chest rasped over my nipples, sending streamers of pleasure lashing down to my groin, and my fingers clawed at his shoulders. His mouth was at my ear, cursing at how good it felt: how good *I* felt.

He was staring down at me with such intensity, relishing every silken drag of his cock inside me. His weight pinned me to the deck as he began a steady rhythm and for long minutes our fevered panting was the only sound in the room.

He took me higher and higher, until I was begging. Then he lifted himself on his elbows and cupped my breasts. I'd been tossing my head in pleasure and a lock of hair had wound up lying across my chest. He stroked hair against skin, the silk of it and the press of his heated thumb making me gasp. I heard him mutter something under his breath, almost in wonder, something that might have been *mermaid*. Then he squeezed, making me grind and thrash atop the coins, and began fucking me even harder.

The pleasure was expanding, filling me to bursting point. I had to release the pressure and it came out not just as pants but as words: *yes*es and *oh God*s and his name, over and over. At first, it was just under my breath but that wasn't enough: it rose until I was saying it, *shouting* it, I couldn't help it—

His thrusts became hard and then almost brutal, the feel of a man driven beyond control. My hands were frantic, running up and down his back. Every inch of him was like rock and I wanted to explore all of him. The feel of his muscles flexing under my palms as he drove into me was intoxicating and every tight thrust was making the pleasure swell and tighten—

My legs bent, heels coming up off the deck and digging into the hard cheeks of his ass to urge him faster, faster. My eyes widened as I felt myself do it: I'd never done that before. But I felt him harden and swell even more inside me: he liked that I was as out of control as he was. The coins shifted in musical tides under us as his rhythm sped up. Our hands found each other and interlaced, the pleasure blossomed and then drew tight—

I tipped my head right back, coins cool against my cheek, and cried out long and hard, my scream of ecstasy filling the *Fortune's Hope*. And that seemed to set Rourke off because he slammed into me twice more and then held there, hilted in me, and I felt the pulse of his release.

37

HANNAH

I'd thought about two people in one hammock but had decided it was impossible. Even if we fitted, how the hell would we climb in?

It turned out, I didn't need to worry. Rourke simply lifted me to my feet and moved to stand behind me. He took a second to enjoy my body, running those big hands up over my breasts and down my thighs. Then he crushed me to him, shuffled us backwards a few feet, and *sat*. I yelped: suddenly, I was sitting on his lap on the edge of the hammock, our feet swinging back and forth above the floor. Then he twisted us and lay down, spooning me from behind, and we were in.

The warm, weighty feel of him behind me was heavenly: as our bodies cooled and the temperature dropped, I didn't even need a blanket. I just snuggled my shoulders back against his chest, he draped an arm around me, and it was perfect. The hammock rocked gently as the boat moved. A few days ago, the reminder of the sea outside would have terrified me. Now, wrapped up in Rourke's warmth, it was restful.

Rourke. I couldn't keep calling him *Rourke.*

"Rourke?" I asked carefully.

He knew what I was asking without me saying it. "Will," he said, his Scottish accent a soft silver lash against my ear.

William. William Rourke. The name was just as old-fashioned as everything else about him. It suited him perfectly. And in his arms, I drifted into a deep, peaceful sleep.

When I woke, it was dawn. Rourke was still sleeping behind me and I lay there trying to process what had happened between us. What would happen now? Where did I stand? Why had he picked *me,* after pushing everyone else in his life away?

I'd always thought Rourke would suit someone like Carla, or Esme: some sultry, adventurous woman who could match him story for story. A brave woman. Whereas I was...well, a mouse. I was a librarian, for God's sake. I wasn't sultry like Carla, with her heels and her hypnotic, ass-wiggling walk. And I wasn't adventurous, or brave. I'd still be in Nebraska if it wasn't for Katherine getting ill. I wasn't suitable for him.

Which got me thinking about Captain Mace and Esme. Mace had loved Esme with all his heart. He'd even scuttled his ship so that she could have his fortune after he drowned.

Something occurred to me and I was so surprised, I said it out loud. "She never found it."

Behind me, Rourke grunted sleepily. "Who? What?"

I didn't have any room to turn around to look at him, plus I was enjoying the warmth of him against my back too much. So I stared ahead of me, at the chest and its spilled coins. "Esme. She never found any of the treasure. She didn't even follow the map to the first clue, or it wouldn't still have been there."

Rourke grunted again. "Lucky for us."

"But it's so *sad!* Mace went to all that trouble to make sure she got his fortune, to make sure she'd be rich after he was dead, and she didn't get *any* of it! Something must have happened before she got the map."

"Maybe it was best that he died, though," Rourke said. "For her."

Now I *did* turn around, even though it was difficult. "For the best? How? They should have been together forever!"

He shook his head. "Mace was like me. He belonged on the sea. If he had lived, what life would she have had?"

I wanted to say, *a romantic one!* Full of adventure and travel and sunsets. But I just stared at him.

"The sea's no place for women. It's no place for anyone but lone men who no one'll miss if they don't come back. You haven't seen how heartless it can be, how it can tear someone away—" He broke off, staring into my eyes. "I'm sorry, lass. Maybe you have."

I couldn't speak past the sudden lump in my throat.

"But men like Mace and me...it's best not to get too involved with us. Aye, Esme lost her man but it happened young enough that she could find some respectable fella instead and have a *real* life."

"But—But she loved him! He loved her!"

Rourke just stared at me for a long time. I could see the emotion in his eyes, the battle between what he wanted to say and what he thought I needed to hear. At last, he said, "Men like us only love two things. Treasure and the sea."

I nodded, biting my lip, and then turned my back and spooned with him again. I knew now where I stood. He didn't regret what had happened but he was laying down the rules: he wouldn't let this turn into something long term. He wanted to send me back to Nebraska when this was over and be out here on the sea alone because...because *why?* I knew it was connected to Edwards and whatever had happened to him.

And unless I could figure it out, we'd never get any closer: he'd push me away the same way he'd pushed away everyone else.

38

ROURKE

I plunged into the water and, immediately, I felt better. The sea is isolating, be it a few feet of water above your head or miles of ocean around you on the surface. People think it's lonely but it lets you *escape*.

And it always helps me think. My head was throbbing, my whole body hot with rage and emotion. I needed the water to cool me down.

Telling her I didn't love her...that had been the hardest thing I'd ever done. Why couldn't I be some normal guy, someone who could make a life with her? Because a life with Hannah...damn, that would be a prize worth more than anything on the *Hawk*. She was smart and kind and *good*. The sex had been unbelievable, even better than I'd imagined. And afterwards, I'd cuddled up to her perfect body and I'd *slept*. Slept in a way that made every night's sleep I'd had since Edwards feel like a brief, shallow doze. Hannah actually calmed me more than the sea, something I'd never thought was possible.

I forced my heart to harden. She had no future with someone like me. She needed to be safe on land. And I didn't deserve her, didn't deserve anything more than being sucked down into the sea's black depths. That's why I'd had to tell her what I did. That's why I had to keep pushing her away. However hard it was.

Cursing, I speared a Red Snapper for breakfast and swum for the surface. I hauled myself aboard the *Fortune's Hope,* grimacing as the leg took my weight again. Then I paused there, dripping wet and frowning. There'd been something I'd meant to do, the next time I was in the water.... I racked my brains but the memory was gone: all I could think of was Hannah's soft skin and the way her hair felt against my fingers. *It'll come back to me.*

Still dripping, I stalked over to the door that led below deck. I reached down inside me, hauling the anger up like a man drawing lava from a well. I needed to be savage and hard with her, like I was with Hobbs and Carla and everyone else. I had to show her that I wasn't someone she wanted to be with—

I hauled open the door and froze. In that single second, all the anger slipped between my fingers.

She was pacing.

As she passed each porthole, the sunrise lit up her golden hair with pinks and oranges. She was indescribably beautiful but it wasn't just that.

She was clutching the note we found in the chest of coins, muttering to herself furiously as she glared at it. She was the very picture of the frustrated academic: all she needed was a pair of glasses. But it wasn't just that, either.

It was the fact that Yoyo was mimicking her, pacing along the cupboards in time with her, grumbling like her, even scowling like her. I felt my own scowl dissolve.

I could harden myself to her looks, to her bravery and kindness. But...*dammit* the lass could be so cute, it just completely disarmed me.

I went to close the door but it was too late: she glanced up and saw me. For a second, we just stared at each other. I could see the need in her eyes. She needed me to tell her how I felt about her. Tell her it had been much more than just sex, tell her that I wanted to be with her.

She needed me to tell her the truth. And, dammit, I wanted to.

But if I let her in, then what? This was no place for her. I wasn't going to let the sea take her. It had taken Edwards and one day it would take me—I deserved that. But not her. She deserved safety, a long happy life in Nebraska with some farmer. Some guy with a working fucking body—

I looked away. "What's the matter?" I grunted.

She didn't answer, just stared at me, hurt. I felt like the filthiest, most diseased bilge rat: I wanted to slip right down beneath the decks. *All she wants is for me to put my arms around her and tell her I—*

I stood my ground. I swore I felt Edwards kick me in the shin but I ignored it. And at last, Hannah looked away.

"I can't figure out the next clue," she said. "It's not like the first one, it's not questions where the answers are numbers. It's...*vague*. Talks about how he trusts Esme and the treasure's only for her, no one else."

I waited for more. When there wasn't any, I rubbed my jaw. "That's it? That *is* vague."

Hannah sighed and sat down cross-legged on the floor. The sweater rode up and I tried not to stare at the tops of her thighs. "We're missing something. We need to get inside his head."

I grimaced. *Get inside his head?* Sounded like a load of touchy-feely bollocks. Way outside my comfort zone. And the last thing I wanted was to be talking when there was all this tension between us. I wanted to go outside and mess with the sails, or splice a rope.

Then I remembered the fear, as she'd lain thrashing and kicking in agony on the deck. If we didn't figure this out, she was dead. If this is what it took, this is what it took.

I sat down next to her, my big form filling most of the space. "Okay," I growled.

"What was he *like*?" she asked. "What were pirates like?"

I snorted. "Bunch of thieves. They wrapped it up in a lot of talk about honor and some of them stuck to some sort of a code. But they're not what you'd call trustworthy."

"More like Ratcher's men than...." She didn't finish the sentence but she nodded at me. *More like Ratcher's men than you.* As if I was some sort of angel.

I scowled and then nodded. "Like Ratcher's men," I allowed.

Hannah turned and stared at the chest. The sweater pulled tight over her breasts and I caught my breath.

Her brow furrowed in concentration. "What's the first thing Ratcher's men would have done, if they'd found the chest before us? Or the first thing some gang of pirates would have done, if they'd found it before Esme?"

I reluctantly drew my eyes from her breasts and looked at the chest. "Helped themselves, probably," I muttered. "Taken a handful of coins before they gave it to their captain. Slipped out a few more whenever they could."

"What if that's it?" asked Hannah. Her voice started slow as she worked the idea through in her head, but it gained in pace. "What if it's something to do with...if pirates found it, they'd divide the treasure, and steal some, and lie to each other about how much there was...but if Esme found it, she'd—Oh God, she'd have *every single coin! It's the number of coins!*"

I blinked and stared. That *did* make sense. No way would a pirate crew get a chest full of treasure aboard without a bit of pilfering going on. If the heading was the number of coins then even one or two missing would throw it way off. "But we need *two* numbers," I said. "Heading and distance."

We stared at each other for a moment and then got it at the same time. "*Silver and gold!*" That's why there were doubloons and pieces of eight.

"All we need to do is count the coins!" Hannah's voice was tight with excitement. Then she looked around the boat and her face fell.

We hadn't exactly been careful with the treasure, the night before. Most of the coins had spilled out of the chest and they'd rolled into every damn nook and cranny.

"Right," I said grimly. "We need *every single one.*"

For three hours, we worked on our hands and knees, collecting up the coins, sorting them into silver and gold and stacking them in piles of ten for easy counting. It didn't help that a rocking boat isn't the ideal place to deal with coins that slide and roll. I chased coins into dark corners and banged my head more times than I could count.

And yet every moment of frustration was countered by the sight of Hannah's perfect ass as she crawled to look under something, or the way she tossed her hair out of her face as she bent over the chest. I had to reach up and take hold of a hatch cover, at one point, just to keep from grabbing her and pulling her to me. By the end of it, I was bruised and sore-tempered and horny as a sailor on shore leave.

But we'd done it. There were no more coins anywhere and we had our two numbers. I grabbed a map, plotted the course..., and sighed.

"What?" asked Hannah, worried?

I showed her the line I'd drawn. It smacked into an island long before it reached its destination. "We're missing some," I said.

We both searched the floor for about the fifteenth time but couldn't see a coin anywhere.

"Maybe someone found the chest, years ago. They couldn't get it to the surface but they took a handful of coins," I said.

"Or one of Mace's men stole some, before Mace even hid it," said Hannah in a small voice.

We were so close! I stood up, growling in frustration. Yoyo jumped onto my shoulder and snuggled in, probably trying to make me feel better.

Hannah suddenly got to her feet. "Wait," she said. "Where does Yoyo hide the things he steals?"

I blinked at her. Then limped quickly along the length of the boat. "Up here," I said, my voice hoarse. "He makes a nest, in this coil of rope—"

I felt inside the dark little hiding place...and pulled out two of Hannah's hair clips, six bottle tops..., and a doubloon.

We raced back to the chart. I redrew the line, adding one degree...and this time, the course cut clear between two small islands and finished just offshore of a third. "Now *that* looks right," I muttered. I turned to Hannah—

Only to find her right next to me, her chin almost on my shoulder as she stared excitedly at the chart. As I turned, my hand brushed hers and my fingers closed on it automatically. She looked up at me expectantly and *God* those lips.... It wasn't just that I wanted to grab her and push her back against the wall, rip her panties off her and bury myself between those sweet thighs—

It was worse than that. I wanted to celebrate with her. I wanted to be a team with her, just like I'd been a team with Edwards.

Working out that clue had been damn near genius: *I* sure as hell wouldn't have got it. But if I told her how much I thought of her then I knew I'd slip: I wouldn't be able to stop myself telling her everything else I liked about her—

I silently cursed. *More* than liked about her.

So I just muttered, "That was smart, working that out." And stalked off to get us underway.

When we arrived, I persuaded Hannah to wait on board while I did a quick dive to check things out. She was shocked when I surfaced after less than five minutes. "It's a cave."

"A *cave?*"

I nodded. "Underwater. About twenty feet down."

"How do you know the final clue's in there?"

I climbed up the ladder and onto the deck. She immediately started helping me off with my air tank: I resisted at first and then let her. "Because the water here's too deep for Esme to get to the bottom. But she could get to the cave and follow it...*if* she knew where she was going."

Hannah frowned. "It isn't just a cave?"

"I shone my light in there and there are different passages leading off it. But there are symbols on the walls. I'm guessing they meant something to Mace and Esme."

Hannah thought for a second and then ran off and returned with the diary. "Are these them?"

There were several pages filled with hundreds of elaborate, circular glyphs, each one subtly different. "Yeah."

"Gypsy magic. Hexes and good luck charms, all that stuff. Mace taught Esme about sailing a ship: she wanted to teach him something in return, so...."

I sighed and glowered. *Romantic nonsense.* But exactly the sort of thing the love-struck couple would use. The good symbols would mark the way to the clue. The bad symbols would lead to dead ends. To Esme, it would be simple, but anyone else would get lost and run out of air. "Right." I thought for a second. "We'll need to copy that page onto something waterproof and I'll need more lights and—"

"I know them," she said.

"...what?"

She flushed. "I'm good at picking things up from books. And I've been over this page about a thousand times. I know which symbols are which. It's not that hard, once you understand the rules." She leafed through several dense pages of text. "Esme explains it all."

I groaned. I knew what was coming. "You're not going down there!" She started to speak but I cut her off. "Cave diving is the most dangerous sort there is. It's dark down there—"

"We have lights—"

"Doesn't matter, it's easy to get confused. Before you know it, you're in a dead end with no air."

"But it can't go on far. Esme had to be able to swim to the clue just holding her breath!"

I hesitated. She was right, but Esme had been a superb diver: she could probably hold her breath for at least a few minutes.

Hannah took hold of my upper arms. Her slender, cool fingers felt amazing on my sun-warm biceps. The temptation to just yank her towards me and kiss her was almost too much. "Look," she said softly, "you can go down there handfuls of paper and try to match the symbols and be there all day...or I can go with you and we can be done in a few minutes."

I sighed and glowered at her but she was right. Any other time, I would have happily accepted the slower, safer method where she stayed on the surface. But she was overdue for another attack of the disease. We didn't have a whole day to waste playing it safe. I put my hands on her shoulders, unable to stop myself squeezing gently. "You do *exactly as I tell you...*"

She nodded. And a half hour later, we dived.

39

HANNAH

I knew, in the pit of my stomach, that I'd made a mistake. I knew it as soon as we hit the water but it wasn't until we were at the mouth of the cave that I admitted it to myself.

It was dark. We each had a head-mounted flashlight but their beams just revealed how dirty the water was. There was no current to keep things moving and the water was thick with plankton and other debris: it was like swimming through thick soup, claustrophobic and unsettling. I could only see a few feet in any direction.

Rourke had given me some underwater flares for emergencies but I was trying hard not to think about them, or the sort of situation that would require them: trying not to think about rock falls or getting stuck or getting lost in the dark—

I squeezed my eyes shut for a second and tried to slow my breathing. *He was right. I shouldn't be down here.* But I had no choice, not if I wanted to save Katherine. We were running out of time.

A hand caught mine and squeezed. My eyes fluttered open and I found myself looking into Rourke's deep blue eyes, his brows knitted with concern. Just his physical presence was reassuring: his wetsuit was stretched tight over the hard slabs of his muscled chest and the thickness of his arms. He was so solid and warm in the cold darkness.

My breathing eased. As long as we stuck together, I'd be okay. *Ten minutes. Fifteen at most and we'll have the clue and be out of here.*

Just as Rourke had said, there were passages leading off the main cave: three of them, each with one of the circular symbols carved in the rock next to them. Captain Mace must have spent days preparing this, holding his breath and diving down to carve the symbols a few minutes at a time.

I swum closer and hung in the water as I examined the symbols. Rourke had found me a wetsuit to wear and I was glad of its insulation: without the sun to heat it, the water down here was uncomfortably chilly. But the wetsuit had been sized either for a man or for a woman less curvy than me: I was a little self-conscious about how tight it was across my breasts and ass. Rourke definitely approved, though. When I'd come back above deck having struggled into it, his gaze had felt like it was melting the fabric right off me. He still wanted me as much as he had the night before...but now he was holding back.

And I knew why. He'd made clear that he wasn't offering anything long term and, because he was an honest-to-goodness gentleman, he wasn't going to tumble me into the hammock for sex. That left me half-frustrated and half grudgingly impressed with him being so honorable. *I* didn't want it to be just sex, either. And the longer I was around him, the more certain I was that it could be so much more. If he'd only give me the chance and open up....

I shook my head. *Focus.* Two of the symbols were curses. The one in the center, though, was for good luck and I swam into that passage, Rourke right behind me. It was narrow enough that I had to be careful not to bash my elbows on the rocks and, when I looked behind me, Rourke's big body almost filled the passage. The sight made me tense. *There's no way out, if he gets stuck behind you. You'll be trapped here in the dark with your air running out.*

Stop it!

I rounded the next bend...and stopped, frowning.

We'd entered a huge tunnel that went left to right across us. On the far wall were at least twenty other passages. Some were only big enough for fish but I saw at least seven that might lead to the treasure. I sighed. We'd have to swim across and check each one until we found a symbol.

I swam forward. Rourke suddenly grabbed for me but I was just too fast, his hand closing an inch from my forearm. I twisted around, still drifting forward, to see what had worried him—

And saw him firmly shake his head, eyes wide. He was making a savage sweeping motion with his hand from left to right.

That's when I noticed something. All of the dirt in the water wasn't just hanging there, anymore. Ahead of me, it was beginning to move, slowly at first but faster and faster, so fast it blurred. The big cross-tunnel was some sort of underground river...and I was drifting right into the current.

I screamed as it hit me full force in the side and carried me along with it. It was like I'd been hit by an invisible train, pinned to its cab as it thundered through the tunnel. I twisted and saw Rourke straining to reach me...and then he was gone, his light just a speck in the darkness.

I started to tumble, panic-breathing and flailing for something, *anything* to grab onto. But the rock walls were whipped by too fast. And they were terrifyingly close to my face. If I hit my head...I stopped trying to grab on and focused on just trying to stay clear of the sides.

I flashed past several dark openings and that's when it hit me: these caves were much, much bigger than we'd thought. Captain Mace had laid his trail for Esme in one small corner of the maze, marking only the tunnels he needed. The rest of the tunnels weren't marked *at all.*

I'm not going to be able to find my way out!

Even as I thought it, I tried to desperately memorize what I was passing. But there was no hope: the tunnel had already split and rejoined several times and—

The tunnel twisted sharply. The first warning I had was when I saw the rock looming out of the darkness ahead of me, my momentum carrying me forward. I desperately back-pedaled. *No, no, no, no—*

I slammed into the rock. There was a cracking sound and my light went out.

And then there was only darkness.

40

___

ROURKE

For a second, I just hung there in the water, staring, as the woman I loved was ripped away into the darkness. *An underground river!* Cold, fresh water, rocketing through the caves under pressure. It would carry her god-knows how many miles underground....

Further than her air would last her.

I finally reacted, launching myself forward and letting the current grab me and carry me. *Christ,* it was fast. My stomach tightened as I saw that it branched: I had no way of knowing which way Hannah had been taken. All I could do was let myself go limp and pray the water carried me the same way. I checked my air and grimaced: I was already down to twenty minutes. Hannah would be using up her air faster: *much* faster, if she was panicking. And we'd need air to get back through the caves and up to the surface.

I had to find her. I had to find her *now.*

41

HANNAH

Without light, there was no up or down. I could feel the force of the water blasting me through the tunnels but I had no way of knowing whether I was in a tight passage or a large room, except when an elbow or knee whacked against rock. Each time I went around a bend, my back or arms would grate along the wall: if it hadn't been for the wetsuit, my skin would have been shredded. I wrapped my arms protectively around my head. My head was still ringing from the first hit: another one and I'd fully lose consciousness, drop my mouthpiece, and drown.

Suddenly, the current dropped away. I could still feel it tugging at me, but I could make progress against it and I could feel calm water off to one side. I clawed blindly at the water, trying to pull myself in that direction—

And then I came completely free of the current. The water around me went suddenly slack and calm. And for the first time in what felt like hours, I stopped moving.

It was absolutely black.

It was darker than the root cellar under the farmhouse in Nebraska, darker than the night I lost Mom. The terrifying realization hit me: I was deep below the rock and *that* was deep below the sea. I was separated from the nearest light by a million twists and turns of dark passageway and even they were filled with thick, dirty water.

There is no way out.

My whole body was shaking as I took deep, shuddering panic breaths. It was worse because I had nothing to touch. My weighted dive belt meant I just floated in the middle of the passage: I had no idea how close the walls were. Everything was silent: I hadn't been aware of the rush of water in my ears, while I'd been in the current, but now that it was gone I wanted it back more than anything. The silence was terrifying. Between it and the darkness, it was like I was already dead.

Oh God.

I couldn't feel the water through my wetsuit and that completed the sensory deprivation. I didn't feel like I was underwater, anymore: I was just floating in suffocating blackness.

Oh God I don't know what to do—

I lost all sense of time and place. All I could feel was my own panicked breathing, sucking air through the mouthpiece, exhaling it as bubbles.

And then something changed. The air I was inhaling felt different. Tight. Like I was sucking on a straw, chasing the last drops of soda in a bottle.

My air was running out.

42

ROURKE

I checked my air again: less than ten minutes. Hannah would be scared, breathing fast: she'd be close to using up all her air already.

Maybe she already had.

The thought pushed me faster, legs driving me through the water, arms outstretched to grab hold of a passage opening and stop myself if I glimpsed her. But there were too many openings, too many points where the river divided. I might already be a half mile away from her, heading in the wrong direction.

My chest ached with the need to call for her. On the surface, it would be so simple: one good shout and she'd hear me and answer and I could home in on her voice. But down here it was just silent blackness. *Jesus, she'll be terrified!*

I should never have brought her down here. I tried to force the thought from my mind, knowing where it would lead, but it was too late. *She's going to die down here. She's going to die just like—*

Shut up!

Just like—

I grabbed hold of an outcropping and clung on: it took all my strength to hold myself there against the current. God, I'd never known fear like this. The thought of losing her....

I stared at my air supply display to make myself focus. Six minutes, maybe seven. I squeezed my eyes shut for a second. If I let myself get caught up in Edwards and the past, we were both dead. Because no way was I running and leaving her here. I either found her, and got us both out, or I'd die trying.

I opened my eyes, blinking in the sudden brightness of my dive lamp. And I suddenly knew what I had to do. The only hope of finding her was to go dark myself and pray I could make out the faint glimmer of *her* light in the distance.

It meant fighting every primitive instinct I had. I had to force my fingers to press the button and shut off my lamp. Then, as blackness enveloped me and the panic and nausea rose in my chest, I had to fight the urge to switch it back on.

I took a deep breath, let go of the rock and felt the current snatch me into motion. As I sped along, I strained my eyes against the black, searching for any faint hint of brightness.

I'd just have to pray her lamp was still working because, if it wasn't...we were both dead.

43

HANNAH

At first, I tried to tell myself it was just my imagination. But each breath was a little more difficult, as if the tube I was sucking through was getting longer and longer. My lungs had to strain and yet, each time, they filled a little less and I had to breathe again sooner. The harder it got, the more I panicked and the more I panicked, the more air I used. I couldn't even check how close to running out I was because there was no light to see the gauge.

I was starting to get hot, sweat beading on my face behind the mask. I had to fight the urge to rip the mouthpiece from my mouth and gulp down the coolness that was all around me, telling myself it was water, not air.

Somewhere out there, I knew Rourke must be looking for me. But how would he find me, in the maze?

He wouldn't. I felt it like freezing water, leaking into my veins. He'd die down here searching for me.

I was getting warmer and warmer and started to feel soft and sleepy. My limbs began to relax and my hand brushed something that hung from my belt, a shape like a thick pencil. Why was I carrying pencils?

I felt my eyes close. It didn't make any difference and it seemed so

much effort to keep them open. There was a strange sensation in my
chest that I didn't recognize, at first. I was breathing in but nothing
was happening. It was as if someone had their hand over my mouth.
But none of it seemed very important, suddenly. I was so tired....

My limbs went heavy and I felt myself slump until I was hanging
in a fetal position in the water. The pencil-things clattered
soundlessly against my thigh. Why was I carrying so many pencils? I
screwed up my forehead, trying to remember. Rourke had given me
them: gorgeous, angry Rourke. They wrote in bright white ink—

The thought of Rourke made me fight against the sleepiness. *No,
not ink. Not pencils. Think!*

Flares! They burned bright, that's what I was thinking of. *Bright.*
Bright enough that he might find me. I reached down and fumbled
for one but it felt as if I was wearing twenty pairs of gloves. I pulled it
off my belt but immediately dropped it. I pulled a second one free but
then just drifted there, trying to remember how to light it. Twist?
Pull? I was almost asleep, my hands moving through sheer
stubbornness.

Twist *and* pull.

My world exploded. The light was so bright, I thought at first that
the flare had exploded in my hands. My pupils were huge from being
in total darkness and the light was so overwhelming that at first, I
couldn't see anything. Then, as my eyes adjusted, I saw rocky walls
around me, the passage lit up as if by noon day sun.

The shock of it cut through the fog and I got one, brief second of
clarity. I realized that I wasn't breathing, that I'd stopped some time
ago and was down to whatever oxygen I had in my lungs.

I was dying.

The flare dimmed a little as my eyes closed again. I felt it slip from
my fingers and sink slowly down to the floor, the light flickering like
an old movie.

And then my brain used up the last of the oxygen in my blood
and there was nothing at all.

44

ROURKE

Nothing. Nothing but blackness. The rush of water against my body told me I was still moving but I couldn't see a damn thing. I was bruised and battered from bouncing off walls, my hands scraped from pushing myself free when the current rammed me into a dead end. But I was no closer to finding her.

I'd always known it would end like this: deep under the sea, no light, no air. I'd accepted it as my fate years ago. Now, I was raging against it. *You can have me,* I wanted to scream aloud. *You can have me, dammit! Just let me save her first!*

The current swept me on. I twisted and—

There!

I star fished, sending out arms and legs in every direction to try to find something to cling onto, but it was long seconds before my hand found an outcropping and I clung on.

I'd seen something. A flickering off to my left. It was gone now that I was past it but I was sure it had been there.

The current was too strong to swim against. I had to haul myself along hand over hand, feeling for each handhold in the blackness. I didn't dare switch my lamp back on: I needed to keep my night vision so I could see the faint hint of light. My muscles were soon burning:

the passage must be narrow because I could feel the water straining against my shoulders and head, trying to dislodge me like a blockage in a high-pressure pipe. I realized I was breathing hard: *that* wasn't good. I couldn't have much air left. But one problem at a time.

I levered myself up to the opening of the passage and saw it again: a flickering ahead of me. I hauled myself in and, free of the current, I started to swim like crazy. I rounded two corners, the light getting brighter and brighter. I rounded a third—

My heart contracted into a tight, icy ball.

One of the flares was burning on the floor, its brilliant white light turning the water clear: it almost looked as if the passage was full of air. Floating in it, as if in space, was Hannah.

Slumped over.

Head down.

Unmoving.

I was too late.

I dived for her, not wanting it to be true. But her chest wasn't moving. And her air gauge was tight against the red line that meant *empty*.

I went to check for a pulse and then pulled my hand away: there was no time. Instead, I pulled out her mouthpiece, sealed my lips to hers, and exhaled. I saw her chest inflate but there was no response. Her hair had come loose from the band she'd used to tie it back and it had billowed out around her head in a golden cloud. She looked like a mermaid, even in death.

I took a deep breath of air from my tank and breathed it out into her lungs. Nothing. *Come on, lass, come on!* My vision was blurry and wet.

She didn't move. I reached for my mouthpiece again—

The flare went out and we were plunged into blackness.

Shit! I found my mouthpiece, sucked deeply on it, then groped for her. My fingers found the floating strands of her hair, then her cheeks. I pressed her back against the rock wall, using it to pin her. I searched for her lips with mine and found them. I breathed into her

45

HANNAH

Rourke grabbed my arm and pulled me forward along the passage, away from the current. I understood: there was no way we could fight our way back against it so we had to find another way. But I'd also done the math in my head and, when I got a glimpse of his air gauge, my chest constricted in panic. *We're not going to make it!*

He must have seen me tense because his head snapped around and he glared at me with the full force of that stubborn, Scottish determination. His hand crushed mine so hard it almost hurt. *Yes. Yes we are.*

We kicked hard, racing through the tunnels. Each time he passed me the mouthpiece, I tried to take only a tiny breath of air, even though my lungs were screaming at me to gulp. But as the minutes ticked past, I could see the needle on the gauge sinking and sinking.

I had no idea where we were going but Rourke didn't hesitate: either he had some diver's instinct that let him estimate the right direction or he was just guessing and hoping, knowing that uncertainty and hesitation meant certain death.

The problem was, the place was a maze. We could pass right by a passage that led to the surface and we wouldn't even know it—

Wait!

I stopped and grabbed Rourke's ankle as he raced ahead of me. He pulled up short and twisted around to look. *What?* His eyes were wild. He jerked his head. *We have to go!*

I pointed frantically to the wall. Next to an opening was a circular symbol: a gypsy charm for wealth. We'd somehow stumbled across part of the route Esme was meant to follow.

Rourke shook his head. *We don't have time!*

He turned to go but I grabbed hold of his shoulders and wrenched him around. Then I pantomimed diving and holding my breath and finally tapped an imaginary watch.

He blinked as he got it. We'd thought Esme's route must be only a few minutes long, because she had to swim it, grab the treasure, and get back, all in one breath. But if we were still finding new symbols this deep in the caves, the route must be longer than that. There was no way even a good swimmer like Esme could get in and out in one go.

The only possible explanation was: the chamber that held the treasure also held air, so she could fill her lungs for the trip back.

I plunged into the passage, Rourke right behind me. I was barely slowing to look at the symbols, now: desperation was sending the adrenaline pumping through my body and my eyes were wide and staring, each carving as clear as if it was ten feet tall. And their meanings flashed up in my mind as if I was Esme herself. *That way: long life. That way: many children. No, not that way, that one's poverty. There! Bountiful harvests.*

God bless my thirst for information.

We swam through an opening and—

What?

The cave was circular and only about eight feet wide. There were no other openings. We'd hit a dead end.

No! That can't be! And almost immediately, the crushing guilt. *I led us the wrong way!* I must have got one of the symbols wrong, but I had no idea which.

Rourke suddenly grabbed my arm, hauled me around, and

shoved the mouthpiece into my mouth. I didn't understand at first. Then I felt it: the tightness as I inhaled. *Oh God!* The air had run out.

I took a breath and went to pass it back to him. But he knocked my hand away. I tried again and this time he shook his head fiercely and used both hands to keep it jammed in my mouth.

He knew it was over. We weren't getting out. But he wanted me to live as long as possible.

I shook my head. He pinned me with those deep blue eyes and nodded solemnly. And then he wrapped me in his arms.

I could feel tears running down my cheeks to pool in the bottom of my mask. *No!* I didn't want him to sacrifice himself for me. *I'm dead anyway, you stubborn, Scottish bastard!* But he wouldn't let go of me, wouldn't unpin my arms from my sides.

And then the air ran out completely. Thanks to him, I had enough air in my lungs that I could last maybe a minute, holding my breath. Then I'd have to gulp in water and—

He felt me stop breathing and gently released me. I pulled the mouthpiece from my mouth and struggled out of the air tank's straps. Then I pressed myself up against him. I wanted to die feeling his warmth against me.

He put his arms around my waist. He looked angry for a moment, angrier than I'd ever seen him. Furious that I was going to die and that there was nothing he could do about it. *It's not your fault,* I tried to communicate with my eyes. *It's mine! I dragged you down here. You could have been back in Nassau, drinking rum!* I was sobbing and my chest was burning: I'd already used up the air in my lungs and I needed to breathe—

He put his hand on my cheek. Rubbed his thumb across my cheekbone. And all at once, his anger subsided and he looked almost peaceful. Happy, because he'd figured out that there was one thing he *could* do. He leaned forward—

No! No, don't do that!

Too late. He grabbed my cheeks, forced my lips apart and—

No! Rourke, no!

He exhaled every scrap of air he had in his lungs. I felt mine fill as he gave me his last bit of life.

And then he was pushing me gently away and falling backwards, down to the bottom of the chamber. He didn't want to drag me down with him, wanted me to have every chance, even if it was useless.

No! I reached for him but he was falling fast, the chamber dimming fast as he carried away the only source of light. Blackness closed in around me again. I was full-on crying, now, I wanted to howl and scream, but I couldn't draw air. I tilted my head back, fists clenched, closing my eyes in silent rage—

Just as they closed, I saw something that made them snap open again.

There was a faint glow coming from above, enough that I could see the rock ceiling. And it looked weird. Distant.

Distant as in *the ceiling was above the water.*

This wasn't a dead end at all.

I dived headfirst for the bottom, kicking as hard as I could. I followed the light from Rourke's lamp and wrestled his body into my arms. I felt him move in response, weakly pushing me away. There was still hope.

I kicked for the surface but we barely moved. Rourke weighed less underwater but he was still heavy and I was exhausted and out of air. I strained and pulled, kicking madly, my hands under his armpits, but we only rose a few feet. Then I remembered our weight belts and unbuckled both of them. Now we finally began to move...and as he felt us rise, he began to kick himself. I could see the surface coming closer but my lungs felt as if they were bursting, my vision going dark. *Kick, kick, kick kick—*

My face broke the surface and I drew in a huge lungful of air. Rourke gave a choking, rattling gasp and then did the same. For a few minutes, both of us were too weak to do anything but tread water, our faces lifted to the ceiling, huffing in breath after breath.

When I recovered enough to look around, I saw we were swimming in a pool at the center of a cave about thirty feet across. A shaft of light came from high in one corner and I could feel a breeze.

A way out! Relief sluiced through me. We wouldn't have to go back through the tunnels.

Rourke put his hands under my ass and helped me to lever my exhausted body out of the water. I slithered onto the rocks with as much grace as a heavily pregnant walrus and then started coughing and couldn't stop. But Rourke wasn't much better: he hauled himself just barely onto the edge and then rolled onto his back, groaning. We'd put our bodies through hell and both of us were utterly exhausted. All I wanted to do was sleep for a week.

We lay there for several minutes. It was me who finally got moving. There was too much at stake and I had to know. "Where's the treasure?" I rasped, my voice husky from coughing. I winced as I got up. My whole body felt like one big bruise.

The cave was full of stalactites and stalagmites. The floor was as smooth and slippery as ice, curving up to meet the walls at the edges. Water must have been dripping through the cave for centuries, slowly depositing minerals. It was beautiful...but I couldn't see a chest anywhere. Despite my tiredness, I started to move faster, searching the corners. Could someone have gotten here before us?

Rourke hauled himself up, stumbled a little on the slick floor, and limped over to join me. We searched the shadows, the walls, behind every stalactite. Nothing. "It's not here!" I said, my voice cracking. "Someone found it! Someone found it and took it and—"

Rourke put his hand up and I fell silent. He was frowning at something on my thigh. I looked down.

There was a patch of bright green on the dull gray of my wetsuit. At first, I thought I'd scraped against some algae during one of my impacts with the wall. But when I twisted and moved, the green patch stayed where it was. It was light, as if someone was shining a flashlight at me.

Rourke turned and walked across the cave, trying to figure out where it was coming from. The patch of green got bigger and bigger as I followed him. We eventually found the source: the shaft of sunlight from high above was striking something on the floor and throwing up a reflection.

No... Not something *on* the floor. Something *in* the floor. The surface was semi-opaque, like a frozen lake. But beneath the frosted layers, I could see something small and round and green. An emerald. And when Rourke shone his dive lamp down through the floor, I saw more colors next to it. The dark red of rubies. The deep blue of sapphires. And hard, bright points of white light that could only be diamonds.

We drew in our breath as we looked around the cave. "He spread them out for her," muttered Rourke in amazement. "Every jewel he'd taken over the years."

I closed my eyes, imagining the cave as it would have been centuries ago. A carpet of jewels. Esme would have been able to roll around in them....

Except Esme had never arrived. For whatever reason, she'd never followed the trail of clues we were following now. The cave had gone undisturbed for three hundred years and rain had dripped down, depositing minerals, slowly encasing the jewels beneath a new floor.

"There must be a message!" I said breathlessly. "We have to find it!"

We searched every inch of the floor and finally found the glass bottle, stoppered with wax like the others. We had to chisel it free with Rourke's dive knife before I could read the parchment inside. I immediately went to work figuring out the references. The first one was the number of times Captain Mace had brought Esme to—as he put it—*her peak,* one memorable night at an inn. I knew that because Esme had written a long, detailed description of it that still made me flush every time I thought of it. *Six.* And the other one was....

"The number of letters in the name they'd give to their first child, if she was a girl," I mumbled aloud. "*Harriet,* that's seven."

"She was going to have a bairn with him?" asked Rourke, sounding surprised.

That brought back what he'd said that morning and my chest tightened. He still didn't believe a man like Mace—or him—should try to make a life with anyone. I turned to him. "She loved him," I said tightly.

He stared back at me, half-guilty, half-defiant. "She was a bloody idiot," he muttered.

My chest contracted into a cold, hard knot. After everything we'd been through, he was still determined to push me away.

I turned away and marched over to the shaft of daylight. It was coming from a narrow, almost vertical tunnel that led towards a distant circle of blue sky. I began to climb.

Below me, I heard Rourke mutter a curse. Then those quick, uneven footsteps as he limped over to the tunnel. "Hannah!" he called. But I didn't look down. I didn't want him to see the way my breath was hitching, or the wetness in my eyes.

I reached the top and hauled myself out into open air and bright, warm sun. I'd come out near the center of the island, on a grassy rise overlooking the sea. I heard Rourke following, cursing as the climb forced him to use his injured leg. He hauled himself out onto the grass and I quickly turned away. I let the wind whip past my face and willed my eyes to cool because I didn't want him to find me all—

A big hand grabbed my shoulder and hauled me around to face him. I looked away and I tried...but I couldn't hide my pain from that fierce gaze. He cursed again and, when I met his eyes, I caught my breath. There was so much going on in those deep blue pools: anger at himself for having hurt me. Frustration at having to hold back. There was something he wanted to say *so badly.*

"I—" he began, then just glared at me.

My heart leapt. *Say it!*

For a second, we just stared into each other's eyes. He was so big, so strong...but in that moment, he looked absolutely helpless. He held my gaze for another second and then turned and scowled at the sea.

I *knew.* I knew what he wanted to say. But I knew he never would. He'd keep pushing me away instead. My only chance was for me to find out where all this anger came from. And this was the most open and exposed I'd ever seen him.

"You need to tell me what happened to Edwards," I said, my voice cracking.

He shook his head savagely.

"*Please!*" I put my hand on his arm.

He drew in a long breath, then turned and pinned me with his gaze. It was almost as if he was *trying* to be angry, using it as a defense. "Shouldn't have let you on board," he snapped. "Shouldn't have helped you. Shouldn't have bedded you. Shouldn't have—" He broke off and just stared at me helplessly.

What? My heart leapt again. *Shouldn't have what? Fallen for me?!* "Please," I begged. "Tell me."

His gaze softened. He opened his mouth to speak....

Then his eyes widened as he saw something behind me. He grabbed me and threw both of us full-length on the soft grass. I landed under him with the air knocked out of me.

Rourke pointed and I drew in my breath in shock. Ratcher's boat was a few miles offshore and heading straight for the island.

46

ROURKE

We ran for the far side of the island, where the *Fortune's Hope* was moored. It was downhill, the slopes steep but grassy. An easy descent...unless you have a gammy leg. I cursed up a storm as I stumbled and slipped. "Go on ahead!" I snapped at Hannah. It made no sense: she couldn't handle the boat on her own so she'd still have to wait for me. But I didn't care about sense: I just wanted her to be safe.

But she shook her head, grabbed my arm, and hooked it around her shoulder.

I snarled at her. "Let go of me! Dammit, I don't need your help!" Just as I said it, I staggered and almost fell.

"You help me plenty underwater," she panted. "You're in my world, now."

I cursed and we struggled on. I really didn't understand this woman. I was pushing her away as hard as I could and she was still trying to save me. *You bloody stupid woman—*

Except...she *wasn't* stupid. She was the smartest, bravest lass I'd ever met. And I didn't want rid of her. I wanted her by my side more than I'd ever wanted anything in my life. The sight of her next to me, the scent of her hair as it brushed my shoulder...I felt myself softening and that was dangerous. I'd come so close to telling her how I felt....

I had to find another source of anger. "How did he find us?" I snapped, jerking my head behind us. "No one knows we're here. Not even Hobbs!"

Hannah shook her head, as confused as me. We reached the shore and I sighed in relief as we began to wade. Now I was stable and she was shaky, the wet sand shifting under her feet. Without thinking, I grabbed her hand. Instantly, she looked up into my eyes. And as soon as she did *that,* it was almost impossible to keep looking angry and stern. *Dammit!*

I glanced towards our boat. "We have to swim out," I told her, forcing myself to snap. "Okay?"

She nodded, but suddenly hesitated.

I blinked, then looked at the *Fortune's Hope* again, this time seeing it with her eyes. I'd had to drop anchor a quarter-mile offshore: I knew she could swim that far but...for once, we were swimming out into the open ocean. The horizon was empty.

And huge.

God, it was everything the poor lass feared. And yet, as I watched, she nodded and took a step forward, her leg trembling a little. She was terrified and she was still doing it. My heart damn near melted.

I knitted my fingers with hers. "I'll be right beside you," I told her. "Just look at the boat."

And together, we dived into the water and started swimming.

47

HANNAH

We hauled ourselves up the ladder and onto the deck. After the run down the hill and the swim, I was ready to drop but there was no time to rest. I raised the anchor while Rourke scrambled madly with ropes and sails. Luckily, the wind was getting up.

"Will he see us?" I shouted over the noise of snapping, billowing fabric.

"Not if I can keep the island between us and him," yelled Rourke. We started to race forward, white foam forming at our prow. The island began to drop away behind us and, eventually, it disappeared from sight. Both of us let out a huge sigh of relief.

"But how did he find us?" I asked.

Rourke shook his head bitterly. "No idea." He led the way below deck. "Let's get a course laid in for the *Hawk*. The sooner we get the cure...."

He trailed off guiltily. I knew what he meant: not just *the sooner you'll be safe,* but *the sooner we can get back to our lives.*

We changed out of our wetsuits. I recited the numbers from the final clue while he bent over a table and plotted the course on a map. I suddenly saw his shoulders tense.

"What?" I asked, worried.

He shook his head. "Nothing." He rolled up the map and put it away, then stalked out onto the deck and began hauling on ropes, bringing us about. Soon we were flying along, the sails straining and the waves rushing past.

That's how I could tell something was very wrong. I knew that nothing made him happier than sailing but his jaw was set, his lips pressed together in a grimace. I sneaked a look at the map but it had so many lines and notes written on it, I couldn't work out where we were. *What did he see? What was on the map?*

Three hours later, I found out.

Rourke slowed the boat as we approached an island with towering cliff walls. He cursed, grabbed the map and compared it to the scene in front of us, then cursed again and angled the boat around it.

"What?" I asked. "What is it?"

He wouldn't answer, stubborn as a petulant child. We circled the island, which seemed to have sheer cliffs on all sides. I watched him consult the map again and then hurl it down in fury. "*What?!*" I pleaded. "Tell me!"

He sighed. Glared at the island with so much anger it seemed as if he wanted to move it through sheer force of will. "I was hoping the map was wrong," he muttered at last, still staring at the island. "But the heading leads here."

I blinked, confused. "Well...isn't that good? We've found it! Mace must have scuttled the *Hawk* just off the coast. Do we know which side?"

He closed his eyes and shook his head. "The heading is precise," he said. "And it doesn't lead to a point offshore, like the others. It finishes *on the island*. Right in the center."

"W—What?" I asked. The wind suddenly felt cold.

He finally opened his eyes and looked at me and my fear doubled as soon as I saw the worry on his face. He was scared. Scared for *me*. "The trail of clues doesn't lead to a wreck. Mace must have taken the treasure ashore and buried it, then scuttled the *Hawk* somewhere else."

I felt my face go pale. "Wait, but...if he just took the treasure—" I broke off, unable to finish the sentence. And saw from his expression that I was right, that he'd come to the same conclusion. He'd known as soon as he plotted the heading on the map. He'd just been praying he was wrong.

Our whole plan had hinged on finding the wreck of the *Hawk* because the cure was in the hold along with the treasure. But if Mace had taken the treasure and buried it instead, he'd have left the cure in the hold: as far as he'd known, it was just a worthless rock in a bottle. And the *Hawk* could be miles away: we had no way to find it. "But— But the map I found said it was the path to the *Hawk!*" I said, my voice cracking.

"Maybe that was to throw people off," said Rourke. "He let everyone think the treasure was on board: but he'd sneaked it ashore here. Then he scuttled the *Hawk* somewhere far away."

I let out a choked sob. It was the ultimate irony: Mace had gone to all this trouble to protect his fortune so it could go to the woman he loved...and we'd successfully negotiated every challenge, every clue he threw at us. We'd found the prize everyone had searched for...and it was useless to us. We needed the worthless junk he'd thrown away.

"*No!*" I croaked. I was trying not to panic but I could feel my whole world coming apart. *Katherine. Chrissie.* All those women, condemned to die. And me, too, probably within days.

I felt like I had when I'd first discovered the cure had been lost at sea. I'd come to the Bahamas for nothing. The whole thing had been a wild goose chase. Only this time, it was worse. Not only had I missed most of Katherine's remaining time with us but—my stomach lurched—I probably didn't have time to get home before the disease killed me. I wasn't even going to be able to see my family one last time.

I looked up at Rourke in hopeless despair. He'd been hauling on a rope, steering us around the island. But through a blur of tears, I saw him let go of it, leaving the boat to the mercy of the wind as he strode over to me. He wrapped me in his arms and crushed me to his chest, my head on his shoulder. "I'm sorry," he managed, his own voice choked. "I'm sorry, lass."

That did it: he was so strong, so unshakeable. I'd seen him stand against Ratcher, against the men in the bar, against sharks and darkness and the sea...to finally see him beaten was terrifying and it made the whole thing real. I pressed my face to him and sobbed, his shirt going damp and then wet. I felt him press his palms harder and harder into my back, hunching his shoulders so that he surrounded me completely, a barrier between me and everything that was trying to take me from him.

But there was one thing even he couldn't protect me from, because it was already inside me.

My sobs slowed as I felt it begin: a tendril of fire, rising to curl around the nerves in my right leg, hair-thin but flaring as hot as the sun. I let out a choked gasp that became a scream, long and loud, right into Rourke's shoulder. He grabbed me by the upper arms just in time to stop me falling to the deck as my leg gave way.

The tendril rose higher, looping itself around the nerves in my thigh. This time it cinched tighter and it felt like barbed wire was sawing into my flesh and bones. My whole body went stiff with agony and meanwhile my mind was still trying to accept what was happening. I'd known I was overdue for an attack but it had come on so fast and *now,* right when I was at my lowest, *oh please not now, please not now—*

A second tendril started spiraling up my other leg and now there was no hope of my standing. Rourke had to take my full weight as my legs kicked, every muscle straining in agony. A sweat broke out across my body and I could barely breathe, the pain stealing every bit of air in my lungs.

Rourke slipped a hand under my ass and scooped me up, cradling me like a child, then laid me carefully down on the deck. By now, the pain had risen to my stomach and back. It felt as if someone had punched right into my guts and was twisting and squeezing my organs. Meanwhile, sand had been poured between every vertebra of my back: the slightest movement was agony. And yet I couldn't lie still, not with the pain that was engulfing my muscles. I started to pant and choke: I wasn't in control of my lungs, anymore, my chest was spasming like everything else.

Rourke hunkered down over me, his muscled body blocking out the sun. "What can I do, lass?" he muttered between clenched teeth. "What can I do?"

But I couldn't answer him. Couldn't even reach for his hand, which was what I needed. This was worse, much worse, than the last attack. The pain wasn't just in my nerves and muscles, it seemed to be everywhere, in my bones and eyes and—

Oh God—

It was in my *skin!* Every inch of my skin was suddenly on fire. Wherever it touched anything, it was agony. The soft cotton of my blouse was like sandpaper dipped in acid. The elastic at the waistband of my panties was piano wire, cutting into my skin. Every point of pressure where I lay on the deck—my ass, my shoulder blades, and my heels—seemed to be crushing the skin into parchment-thin sheets and then slowly tearing it apart.

I was dimly aware that I'd started screaming and couldn't stop. I could feel my heart racing out of control and the sweat was pouring off me. I knew my body couldn't stand much more. Rourke was leaning over me, putting something to my mouth, and each time he did, I seemed to breathe a little easier, though it was still agony. There was a feeling of coldness on my forehead, too, the one part of my skin that didn't hurt.

It helped...but I knew it didn't matter. Whether I survived this attack or not, it was all over. Katherine, Cassie, me...we were all dead.

I felt myself doing the one thing I was most scared of. I felt myself giving up. The pain reached a peak. It hurt *so much.* It would be so much easier to just....

Stop.

My eyes closed. My aching lungs slowed their fight and then ceased moving altogether.

And then suddenly he grabbed my hand and squeezed it. It should have been unbearable: the grind of sand in my elbow joint as he lifted my arm, the scalding press of his palm against mine. And yet it wasn't. The pain was subsumed by something much stronger. I opened my eyes and looked up into his deep blue ones. And despite everything, I found myself squeezing back.

"*Don't,*" he snarled. "*Don't you give up on me!*"

I wanted to tell him that it was useless, that there was no hope.

"We'll find something!" he snapped. The emotion was making the Scottish in his voice even stronger, the words like flashing steel. "There'll be something, we'll find something!"

I wanted to hug him for his bloody-minded stubbornness. It was just enough to keep me going, to make me fight. I took an agonizing, rasping breath. I was sweating so much, it was running into my eyes. I twisted my face to the side for a second so that the wind could cool it and—

Without Rourke manning the sails, the boat was drifting. We were dangerously close to the cliffs: Rourke was putting his beloved boat in danger to tend to me. But as we spun and bobbed on the waves, I saw—

My eyes went wide. I hear Rourke give a guttural moan of horror: he thought this was it, that I was having a heart attack. But I'd seen something, something that changed everything.

For what felt like hours, I kicked and spasmed and screamed, my clothes wet with sweat. But Rourke stroked my hair and whispered to me to hang on and I squeezed his hand and focused on the strength in his voice. And finally, it came to an end and my body relaxed. I lay there panting, staring up into his eyes. I was utterly spent. I couldn't even lift my head, could barely speak. But I had to tell him.

"*In,*" I rasped.

He shook his head. "Shh," he said sternly. "Don't try to speak." His face was pale. I'd scared the hell out of him.

"*In,*" I insisted. With great difficulty, I lifted one hand to point towards the island.

"*Hush!*" he told me. He mopped my brow with the cold washcloth again. I could see a portable oxygen cylinder, too, with a mask. That must have been what he kept putting over my face. Probably the only thing that had allowed my spasming lungs to breathe.

"*In... side,*" I grated. And this time, I turned to look and he looked, too, finally seeing what I'd seen.

The cliffs towered fifty feet, all around the island. But one section was different to the others. It wasn't made up of solid, unbroken rock but a mess of boulders. They'd been lying there so long, they'd almost merged together, the gaps concealed by grass and plants. But if you looked hard enough, you could see the V-shaped gap they filled. A gap just big enough for a ship to pass through, when it had been open.

"Oh my God," muttered Rourke.

The *Hawk* was right where the map said it was. Captain Mace had sailed it inside the island.

48

HANNAH

"**D**ynamite?" I was sitting on the deck, my knees drawn up under my chin, and a blanket wrapped around my shoulders. It was mid-afternoon and the sun was still warm but I was sweat-soaked and shaky from the attack, and I wasn't steady enough on my feet for a hot shower, yet. "Actual...you know...*dynamite?*"

It sounded so ridiculous, to my ears. Dynamite was for cowboys, breaking out of jail cells, or for cartoon characters to swap for cigars. People didn't actually own it. Except Rourke did and he was talking about using it to clear the passage into the island. When he brought up a big, plastic case from below deck and carefully unwrapped several sticks, I was amazed to see it even looked like the stuff in cartoons, fuse and all. "And that's been just riding around with us in the boat?" I asked weakly. "Just rattling around, every time we hit a wave?"

Rourke just frowned curiously at me, as if it was all normal. More than anything else, more than the smuggling or the bribing officials or the sword or the rum or the living on a boat, it brought home how utterly different his life was. *I'm a librarian. He owns dynamite.*

He had to swim over to the island to place it. I watched through binoculars as he scaled the pile of rocks and shoved sticks into what I guessed were strategic locations. I was wincing the whole time, my body taut as a wire: one spark, one dropped stick of dynamite and he'd be gone.

When he finished and climbed down, I felt like I'd aged thirty years. Then, just as I was about to relax, he bent down, struck a match and a glowing, sparking ember began to rush along the fuse, terrifyingly fast. As Rourke dived into the water and swam around the side of the island, I pressed myself flat against the deck, hands over my ears—

There was a low rumble, like the loudest thunder I'd ever heard, and the whole boat shook. A hot wind rushed past the back of my neck. And then all I could hear were splashes.

When I raised my head to look, Rourke was halfway back to the boat, watching over his shoulder as the smoke cleared. The passage gradually came into view, now open...and beyond it was clear blue water, leading into the interior of the island. I gave a low moan of hope. It was just possible I was right.

Rourke could feel it, too. I could see the tension in his body as he climbed aboard: we had to get there, had to *know*. He didn't even stop to dress or get dry. As soon as he was back aboard, he just fired up the engine and took us in. He cursed under his breath as he eased the *Fortune's Hope* into the passage. The rock walls were worryingly close and yet our boat was much smaller than a pirate galleon. "Captain Mace was a romantic idiot," Rourke muttered, "but I'll give him this: he had balls."

The passage turned a corner ahead, blocking our view. My legs were still shaky but I grabbed the rail and heaved myself to my feet, then went to stand behind Rourke. As we began to turn the corner, I unconsciously put a hand on his back, letting the warm press of his muscles against my palm calm me. This was it: if I was wrong, it was all over....

We turned the corner. Rourke and I gasped together.

A sheltered bay lined with white sand beaches filled almost the entire interior of the island. The high walls meant there was little wind, the palm trees just barely rustling. Crystal-clear water was beneath us, the bottom too far down to see.

I looked behind us. The passage we'd re-opened was the only way in or out. No one had been here in three hundred years, not since Captain Mace blocked the passage behind him. *No wonder no one ever found the wreck.*

Rourke slowed us and then dropped the anchor. Before the boat had even stopped moving, he was up on the rail, powerful legs bending to leap. He stopped only when I scrambled up beside him. There was no time for swimsuits: I just pulled my t-shirt over my head and dropped my shorts, leaving me in bra and panties.

"*No,*" he said sternly. "You haven't recovered yet."

I shook my head. "You think I'm missing *this?*" I croaked. Strangely, it wasn't just the cure. It was the *Hawk* itself. It was everything we'd been through, this whole crazy adventure. I wanted to be there if we found it. My heart had started to pound in my chest and suddenly *I understood.* I got what drove him to be out here hunting for treasure. I understood the addiction: I was already a little addicted myself, against all my mouse tendencies. *What a life. Learning the history, discovering clues, racing to get to the treasure first....*

Except—my chest constricted—he didn't have that life anymore. It had all gone wrong, Edwards had died, and he'd given it all up, until I came along. What I'd seen was a glimpse into how he used to be. As soon as we were done here, he'd go back to that lonely, miserable existence...and I'd go back to Nebraska.

I took a deep breath...and we dived.

I got my bearings and kicked for the bottom. God, the water was so clear! And teaming with coral, small fish and other life, from anemones to starfish. When Mace sealed this place up, he'd created a wildlife preserve: humans hadn't fished or polluted these waters for three centuries. And the water was beautifully warm: the high rock walls made the island into a giant sun trap.

It hit me how much more confident I was, now. Open ocean still scared the hell out of me but in these sheltered waters I felt totally at ease. We dived deeper, descending towards the dark shadows at the bottom.

No. Wait: not just a shadow. There was something huge covering the bottom of the bay! I kicked faster, hands tearing at the water. I couldn't hold my breath much longer but I *had to know*. As my eyes adjusted, I started to make out detail in the darkness and then I saw something rising towards me—

Masts! Three huge wooden masts, one with a crow's nest still attached, now trailing long ropes of seaweed. And below them a wide wooden deck and a rising prow....

I twisted around to find Rourke. He was right behind me and I knew the expression on my face probably matched his: sheer, childlike joy. *We've found it!*

I flew into his arms and wrapped him into a hug, clinging to him. He held me there while he kicked us to the surface and seconds later we emerged panting into the sunlight.

He gripped my upper arms as we treaded water. "I know you want to get the cure," he said gently. "But let's just go slow. Okay? We need to be careful."

I nodded. He was right: I was giddy on adrenaline and so desperate to get into the hold and find the cure, I wasn't thinking straight. I let him lead me back to the boat and forced myself to be patient while we grabbed air tanks, flippers, and masks. By that time, my strength was mostly back and my shakiness had gone.

The warm, clear water made it an easy dive. There was enough sunlight filtering down from above that we could make out every detail of the ship. Protected from the ocean's currents by the rock walls, she'd stayed in amazing condition. We could see the huge hole in one side where Captain Mace had scuttled her, the figurehead at the front, even the name.

Rourke led me to the big, square opening in the deck that led down to the hold. We went cautiously, ready to back out fast. We didn't know what creatures had made their homes in the wreck.

At first, all I could see was barrels. Then wooden boxes and then—

I drew in a shuddering breath. Both of us came to a stop, floating above the floor.

A carpet of gold covered one whole side of the hold. It was like a beach made of doubloons, at least ankle deep. And that was just the money from chests that had broken open and spilled their contents. I counted thirty more that were still sitting undamaged. I couldn't even process how much money that was.

And it wasn't just coins. We passed over boxes too full for their lids to be nailed in place, stuffed with necklaces, bracelets, and rings. There were silver platters and goblets, ornate daggers and scimitars encrusted with rubies. I saw what looked like a full suit of armor, its entire surface intricately engraved, I opened a small chest at random and was immediately dazzled, my face lit up bright by the reflected sunlight. It took a few seconds of blinking before I could figure out what I was looking at: the velvet bags which had once filled the chest had long since rotted away and all that was left were their contents: a layer of diamonds as deep as my hand. I swished them between my fingers, amazed.

But none of this mattered. I closed the chest and swam on.

I couldn't find it at first. I was starting to panic: *maybe they just threw it overboard!* But then Rourke waved me over and showed me something. What I'd thought was the bottom of the hold wasn't even close. The chests and boxes were stacked at least three deep. My eyes widened. How much treasure *was there?!*

It took twenty minutes of searching before we found the trunk beneath two big boxes. Rourke used his brute strength to haul them out of the way. Both of them were full of gold but he didn't spare them even a glance, just swam straight back to watch me open the trunk. He wasn't acting like a man who only loved treasure and the sea.

I held my breath and lifted the lid. I saw the small wooden box immediately, nestled at the back. When I grabbed it, my hands were trembling so much I dropped it and it fell in slow-motion through the water. I got it open before it landed. Inside was a glass bottle, sealed with wax, and inside the bottle....

A black stone the size of a lime, rough on all sides except one, where it had been ground down.

The realization seemed to ripple up from my feet, growing stronger and stronger until it hit me full force in the chest, an explosion of emotion. *I've found it!* I was holding it in my hands, the same stone my ancestor had sent from Africa. Katherine would live. Cassie would live. *I* would live!

There was a knot in my stomach that had been there ever since the day Katherine had first collapsed. I finally felt it ease away. *Everything is going to be okay!*

My vision blurred and I realized I'd started crying. My whole body slumped, my arms and legs dangling from my body. Then a fear hit me: I was suddenly paranoid that I'd drop the bottle and lose it forever. I gripped it so tight the glass was in danger of breaking and hugged it to my chest, then nodded upwards to tell Rourke I wanted to surface. He nodded quickly: he understood.

Back aboard the *Fortune's Hope,* I carefully removed the stone from the bottle and turned it over in my hands. I had no idea what it was: some sort of mineral, maybe? But I followed the directions my ancestor had given, grinding a tablespoon's worth into a powder, and then mixing it with cooking oil. It made a thick, black liquid that smelled faintly metallic.

That was it. All I had to do was drink it. But—

But I had no idea what it would do to me, or even what the stuff was. If I had a bad reaction to it out here, hundreds of miles from a doctor, I was dead. My ancestor had been sketchy on things like side effects. All I knew was that it worked quickly.

After almost an hour of debating, I came to a decision. I dug in the boat's first aid kit and found a pill bottle just big enough to hold the liquid. I poured it in, then taped the bottle to what remained of the stone, and put the whole thing on a shelf next to the hammock. As soon as we got back to Nassau, I'd go to a hospital and then drink it: if anything went wrong, at least I'd have a chance. And if I had another attack before then, I'd grab it and drink it immediately.

There was still enough of the stone left to make a few more doses but what I really wanted to do was to get the stone analyzed by a scientist: if we could find out what it was, we could find more of it, enough for all the women in my family.

I found Rourke out on deck and filled him in on my plan. He thought about it, rubbing at his stubble, then nodded his agreement. But I noticed how he kept glancing at the sky. "What?" I asked.

He shook his head. "Weather's changing. Might be nothing, but we might need to get out of here."

I squinted at the sky. I couldn't see anything different, but if there was one thing he knew, it was the sea and the wind. "Then we should get the treasure up, as fast as we can."

He looked at me doubtfully. "I could come back for the treasure. Take you back to Nassau first...."

I shook my head, determined. "You got me to the cure. Now let me help you. This is the haul of a lifetime. Everything you ever wanted!"

The anger flared in his eyes for a second. He took a half step towards me and my heart leapt. I could see him fighting for control. His lips twitched as if they were going to form the words, as if treasure *wasn't* all he wanted—

But then he winced as his leg buckled under him and he closed his eyes for a second. When he opened them again, he looked bitter, resigned. All of the hope that had built in my heart twisted and died.

"Aye," he muttered. "You're right. Let's get it up."

Rourke spent a half hour setting up a winch and hooking it up to the boat's generator. It wasn't anywhere near as big as the crane on Ratcher's boat but it was enough to haul up boxes and crates from the wreck one by one. We got a system going: he'd stay underwater, loading the treasure, and I'd raise it up when I felt a tug on the cable. Then I'd push the chest into one of the cabins and send the cable down for the next one.

It took over four hours, with breaks for him to change air tanks and both of us to stretch our aching muscles, but we got it done. By the time I slid the last box into place, the sun had set. Every cabin was stacked with treasure right up to the ceiling: you could barely move, even in the main room. And all that gold and silver weighed a lot. Even I could tell we were riding lower in the water.

Rourke looked up at the sky again and cursed. "I was right about the weather," he said. "Going to be a big storm tomorrow."

"We could get out of here tonight," I said. One thing I'd escaped so far was rough seas. I really didn't like the idea of sailing back to Nassau through a storm.

But Rourke shook his head. "I don't want to try to get through that passage in the dark," he said. He looked up at the sky again. "We'll be alright, 'long as we leave first thing."

Leave. My stomach twisted as it sank in. We'd found the cure and now it was time to go our separate ways. Tomorrow, I'd be on my way back to Nebraska: no more sea, no more danger. It was exactly what I'd wanted, when I'd arrived.

I bit my lip and stared at him. He glared back: he knew what I was going to say. The silence swelled. I opened my mouth to argue with him, even though I knew it was useless—

He cut me off before I could begin. "We haven't talked about splitting the treasure," he muttered.

"I don't care about the treasure," I said, my voice tight. "It's yours. All of it. All I wanted was the cure." I took a step towards him. "And you got me to it."

He stared right into my eyes. That same anger was there that I'd seen on the beach the very first day. *Furious* with me for making him feel this way. "You can have half," he said at last.

I drew in a long, shaky breath. "I don't *want* half."

"You deserve it. Wouldn't have found it without you. All those clues."

"I don't *want*—"

"I'll sell it. I know people. I'll send you the money—"

"I don't—"

He pushed past me, limping towards the front of the boat. "Leave me a bank account number."

"I don't want the treasure, *I want you!*" I yelled.

Silence descended on the boat like a thick fog. When Rourke finally spoke, his voice was raw and bitter. "Believe me, you don't."

"I know what I want," I said in a small voice. And, maybe for the first time in my life, I really did.

He sucked in the air between his teeth. "You are the most stubborn.... Why won't you be told?" I opened my mouth to speak but he was suddenly in full flow. "I got you away from that bastard Ratcher, I ferried you halfway around the Bahamas, and I got you to the damn ship. All I want is to be left alone!"

I took a single step forward, my eyes hot with tears. "Is that really all you want?"

He stared into my eyes. I saw the facade crack open and the longing beneath it made my heart lift and swell. But then he squeezed his hands into fists and said, "I don't get to have you. That's not how it works."

I shook my head. "Why are you *so sure* that you deserve to be unhappy?" I could feel it *right there,* just beneath the surface: whatever had happened to him to make him like this. I just couldn't get to it.

He stared at me a moment longer and the *need* in his face made me give a strangled gasp. I swore I saw him lean forward for a second as if about to stalk over to me and gather me into his arms...and then he turned on his heel and stalked off. "Get some sleep," he threw over his shoulder. "We leave at dawn."

I stormed below deck and slammed the door. Threw myself into the hammock: I'd even mastered that skill, now. Yoyo hurled himself in to join me, scampered up my body, and stared in concern at my wet cheeks, riding my chest as it heaved in silent sobs.

I stared up at the ceiling, the wood blurring before my eyes. I knew he was doing it for me. He wanted to protect me from this crazy, dangerous life of his and he'd convinced himself that I could be happy with someone else, with some normal guy. *Maybe he's right.* I still shuddered every time I looked at the open ocean. I'd forced myself to face caves and sharks and men like Ratcher because I had to: I wasn't brave like him. Maybe I *did* belong with some guy back in Nebraska.

But I'd never met anyone else who made me feel like Rourke did and I knew I never would. It didn't matter how unsuitable I was, how shy and scared I was compared to the Esmes and Carlas of this world. We were *right* together.

And there was another side to it, a side I'd only glimpsed because he hid it so well behind that gruff exterior. Whatever had happened to Edwards, it had destroyed him. He couldn't take that happening again and his solution was to keep everyone at arm's length. He wouldn't let himself love again.

I had to make him see it was worth the risk or he'd be alone for the rest of his life. But I had no idea how to convince him. Trying to talk to him about it just made him close down more.

After hours of battling with it, I still didn't know what to do. And I was too worked up to sleep. So I did what I always did: I buried myself in a book. I'd read Esme's diary enough times that I already knew every detail but her writing was so descriptive that, every time I re-read it, I picked up something new.

I stopped on a page where she was raging about Captain Mace. He loved her but he was getting worried for her future. After almost dying in a sword fight, he'd started to push her away, much as Rourke had with me.

The crunch point had been when he had to journey to Boston: he'd be gone several months and refused to take Esme with him, saying it was too dangerous. He was even suggesting—my stomach twisted—that she didn't wait for him. *Find yourself a farmer or a carpenter,* he'd told her. *Some man who'll still be here in a year.* The more she'd argued with him, the more he'd raged at her, refusing to give an inch. *He was trying to protect her, just like Rourke....*

I leaned into the book, transfixed. The ink Esme had written in was blotched in circular patterns: she'd been crying when she wrote it. She only had one night to make him change his mind or she knew she'd lose him forever.

I turned the page. So that night, she'd crept from her bed, rode to where the *Hawk* was being prepared for departure and—

I stared, open-mouthed. It was exactly the sort of thing Esme would do...and it had worked.

I slammed the diary and turned on my side, staring angrily at the wall. *Why can't I be like that?* It had worked for Esme because she was confident. I was a mouse.

I closed my eyes and let out a bitter sigh. *Why can't I be like that,* I thought again.

Why can't *I be like that?*

My eyes snapped open in fear. *That's crazy.* I was as far from Esme as it was possible to be. I wasn't beautiful or strong or...*alluring.* I couldn't put myself out there like that.

Could I?

If I really wanted to convince Rourke to take a chance...didn't I have to take a chance, too?

49

ROURKE

I came awake and looked around in confusion. Everything was familiar: the deck under my back, the stars in the sky above. Everything but the sound. The sound didn't belong in my life. It wasn't part of my world of wind and waves and pain. It was softly feminine, hauntingly beautiful and it was calling. Calling to *me*.

I struggled to my feet, cursing my leg. The sound was coming from the back of the boat. I limped along the length of the deck, grateful for the light of the moon. I came to the bow and stumbled to a stop.

About twenty feet away across the water, a cluster of rocks the size of an SUV stuck up out of the water. Sitting on it was Hannah, but like I'd never seen her before.

She'd wrapped a white sheet around her, the fabric gathered in a band that crossed her breasts and wound around her hip. It just barely covered the essentials in a way that made me immediately want to rip the thing off her. Almost all of her gorgeous, naked body was on display and the moonlight made her pale skin glow. She looked like a statue celebrating the female form, her curves smooth and gleaming. Her long, golden hair fell around her shoulders, catching the light from the stars—

And she was singing.

I didn't know the song but it was about love, and needing someone, and being together. All that stuff I'd told myself was bloody nonsense...until I heard it like this. Her singing voice was everything I loved about that quick, sun-drenched Nebraska accent taken to the next level. It was light and sweet but with a deep, aching power that reached right down inside me. It bypassed my brain and all the anger and bitterness there. It went straight past the pain. It hit me where I lived and spoke to me on an age-old level.

When she sang about love, I understood.

I'm dreaming, I thought. I had to be. Hannah wouldn't do this. She'd flushed when I overheard her singing in the shower. But I didn't much care. If this was a dream, it was the best one I'd ever had.

The bay was utterly silent apart from her voice: it was as if all the wildlife had stopped to listen. Her voice was drawing me in across the water. I took an instinctive step forward and the movement must have caught her eye because she turned her head. She didn't stop singing, just locked eyes with me, willing me on.

I was a sailor, being lured by a siren. The wind had dropped away to nothing and there wasn't so much as a ripple on the water. The reflection of the moon on the surface looked so solid, I swore I could walk straight across it to her. *I am bewitched.*

I climbed up onto the rail. I knew that my leg must be hurting but I couldn't seem to feel it at all. I didn't question whether I should go. Just like when I'd kissed her, this had gone beyond choice, beyond any argument I could make to fight it.

I dropped into the water, dark ripples splitting the moon in front of me. I swam towards her with slow strokes, not wanting to break the spell. She watched me approach, her song never ceasing.

I clambered up onto the rock and moved towards her. The draw of her was incredible, a current I couldn't possibly fight. It had always been this strong, ever since the day I met her on the beach. She'd just found a way to cut through what was holding me back.

Still she sang and, as I drew within a few feet, the effect was even more intense. Hearing that voice, watching those blush-pink lips move and her almost-naked chest rise and fall as she sang of how her heart ached for me...something inside me opened, something that had been sealed shut for a long time.

She looked up at me, defiant. I'd tried so hard to protect her, to push her where she'd be safe. But she wouldn't *be* pushed. I'd finally met someone as stubborn as me. And there was fear in her eyes, too. This *wasn't* a dream. This was the shy, bookish woman I'd fallen for and doing this scared the hell out of her. But she was being as brave in this as she'd been in everything else. She was being brave for *me.*

I felt it inside, then: the deep, cold pain I always bury between the hot, simple pain of my leg. I didn't want to face that. *Couldn't* face that. But I was leaning down over her, now, her mouth so close to mine that I could feel the vibrations of her song on my lips. If I didn't stop hiding from the past, I couldn't have her.

And I had to have this woman.

I let out a long, low growl that contained every ounce of anger and pain that had built up over the last two years.

And then I just bloody kissed her.

50

HANNAH

He brought his mouth down on mine and the song died in my throat, the last vibrations playing against his lips. He was soft at first, reverent, tasting me as if for the first time. Then hard and savage, kissing me as if he couldn't get enough of me.

It was different to when he'd pounced on me next to the chest of coins. That had been an explosion, the pressure building up and up until we couldn't hold back any more. This was deeper, stronger, a wave that had been growing since we'd first met. It was now tall as a skyscraper and it *wasn't stopping*. Not ever.

He pressed me back against the cool rock, my breasts pillowing against the hard slabs of his pecs. I twisted my hips to one side, flattening myself against the rocks so that he could get closer, needing all of him in contact with me. He molded himself to me, groaning in need, until his whole upper body was tight to mine. He was only wearing a pair of shorts and I could feel the warmth of him throbbing into me, skin to skin. He buried his hands in my hair as he kissed me, open-mouthed but slow and deep.

His hands slid slowly down: my cheeks, my shoulders, and then right down my body. One slid beneath the sheet that covered my groin. The edge of it pushed between my thighs and I opened a little, gasping against his lips.

My head rocked back as two fingers began to rub slowly back and forth over my soft folds, his thick wrist keeping my legs open even when the pleasure made me try to close them. His other hand tugged at the top of the sheet. It fell away from my breast and then he was cupping me there, his thumb teasing my nipple to aching hardness, his fingers rolling and squeezing with just the right kind of roughness. He broke the kiss for a second and I heard him just *sigh*, as if I was the best thing he'd ever touched. "God, Hannah, you're perfect."

A flush went through me, rebounding and turning to liquid heat when it hit my groin. I was grinding my hips, now, his hand trapped between them as he rubbed at me. The pleasure was spiraling higher and higher, making me thrash and shudder. I had to respond, had to let it out.

I slid my palms along his shoulders, marveling at the width of them, the power. Then the hard globes of his biceps and the deep contours of his back. I stroked my fingers down his chest, then over the shark bite scar that arched across his abs: vicious tooth marks on smooth, sculpted valleys. I hated the fact it had hurt him. But there was some primitive, cavewoman part of me that went weak at the sight of them, and at the thought of the shark's jawbone on the boat: the idea that he'd slain the beast.

The hand between my thighs pushed under my ass and he stood, hooking his other arm under my shoulders. I clung to his shoulders as he lifted me into the air and deftly unwound the rest of the sheet, leaving me naked. He took a step back, to the edge of the rocks and then....

I cried out as he jumped. A second later, we hit the water together: still warm from the sun but blissfully cool against our heated bodies. We went under, already kissing, then surfaced, the water dripping down our faces. He opened the button on his shorts and kicked them free and then we were naked against each other.

We twisted together in the water, arms wrapped around each

other, kissing long and deep. He took control, using those powerful legs, and muscled ass to push us through the water. I was in his world, a woman from the land carried off by a man of the sea, and all I had to do was cling on.

One moment, he'd launch us up out of the water, kissing my breasts as we rose, making me arch my back and cry out before we splashed down again. The next, he'd let us gently sink beneath the surface and corkscrew down, our bodies entwined, kissing me to give me the air I needed. When I tired, he'd turn me so that we were floating on our backs with him half-underneath me. I'd gaze up at the night sky, my head on his chest, as his hands worked my body until I shouted my release up to the stars.

It was the most relaxed in the water I'd ever been: there was no fear at all, not now, not with his arms around me. I closed my eyes and lost track of which way was up and down, or whether we were on the surface or beneath. He brought me to panting, shuddering climax again and again and then, when my limbs were limp and shaky from pleasure, he swam us over to the beach. He laid me down in the surf, finding the exact point where the waves would lap over my breasts but come no higher.

He kissed me—God, I'd never, *ever* grow tired of the way he kissed, firm and decisive and in control and with that edge of raw heat, like I made him not quite able to control himself. Then he slid down the length of my body and used his shoulders to spread my thighs. I'd closed my eyes and I didn't realize what we were going to do until the first touch of his tongue. My eyes flew open and I arched my back, crying out in shock and delight. The waves struck the soles of my feet and washed over my legs as he kissed his way down each sensitive lip. The warm haze of pleasure suddenly deepened and focused, throbbing up through my body from my groin. My ass began to grind into the wet sand in slow circles.

His palms swept over my wet skin, rising until they captured my breasts. He began to squeeze at me, strumming my nipples with his thumbs in time with his expert tongue. The pleasure tightened and built and my fingers dug into the sand. Another wave swept over us, the warm water soaking him and splashing and foaming over my breasts, making me suck air in through my teeth as the bubbles burst against my skin.

He was using his upper lip to stroke at my clit, now, while he teased me open with his tongue and flicked and circled inside me. The rhythm was insistent, pushing me closer and closer to— I buried my hands in his hair, curling my fingers into his dark locks. My chest was heaving beneath his hands, breasts pressed hard into his palms as I arched my back. The pleasure rushing inwards, concentrating and heating, making me buck and tense beneath him....

I came just as another wave engulfed us, my cry rising into the treetops and echoing around the island's rock walls. He stayed there, his face pressed to me, as I rode it out, arching and trembling. Only when the wave retreated and I lay still did he move up my body and settle himself between my thighs. His body shone from the water and every hard muscle was outlined by the moonlight.

My hands slid from his hair to his stubbled cheeks and we gazed into each other's eyes as he slowly entered me. I could see that same raw lust I'd seen the first day I met him but the anger was gone, replaced by a deep, intense yearning. He'd stopped fighting it.

I felt my eyes widen as he filled me and I could see *his* eyes gleam in response, excited by my pleasure. The rest of the world seemed to disappear and it became a feedback loop: the deeper he moved, the more I bit my lip and narrowed my eyes in delight. The more I did *that,* the more turned on he became and the deeper he sank. My hands slid to his shoulders, then ran down his back to his ass as he finally buried himself to the hilt.

He rocked rather than thrust, grinding against me in just the right spot. Each contact made the pleasure spiral and tighten inside me, until I was panting and desperate. His lips went to my neck, nudging my wet hair out of the way so that he could drive me crazy with hot kisses all the way from my jaw to my collar bone.

For long minutes he stayed slow, as if relishing me. But when the pleasure made me helplessly circle my hips, he growled and began to thrust, his palms slamming into the sand either side of my head to support him. I gasped and grabbed onto his wrists, wrapping my sand-covered fingers around their thickness and squeezing tight.

He began to pound me, filling me in hard, silken strokes that made the pleasure coil like a clock spring, tighter and tighter, building to the point where it would have to release. My heels dug furrows in the sand as I drew my knees up. Wave after wave broke over our lower bodies, the spray misting on my face. I could feel myself rushing towards my peak....

The water receded for a second. I clung to his wrists, gasping and squirming under him as he thrust, drawing circles in the sand with my ass. My fingers climbed his forearms, digging into the sculpted muscle. *"W—Will!"* I hissed.

He slammed into me again, hilting himself. His lips sent a hot Scottish burr right into my ear. "Hannah...."

And the climax rocketed through me just as another wave hit us. I felt myself spasm around him, my back arching and my nipples grazing his chest. He growled, pressed tight against me...and I felt the explosion of heat as he came.

We stayed like that for a long time, the waves lapping at our bodies. He nuzzled gently at my neck, his dark hair gleaming in the moonlight. The sand was soft, the water was warm and neither of us wanted to move.

Eventually, though, he helped me up and we swam naked back to the *Fortune's Hope.* He threw some towels down on the deck and lay down on his back. I lay down beside him and half on him, and discovered that his chest made the best pillow in the world. With the deck slowly rocking under us and the stars above, it was incredibly restful.

Everything felt different, now. The barrier that had stood between us was gone.

For a while, he just gazed up at the stars. Then he lowered his head, staring intently at the prow of the boat. I didn't pick up on the significance of that, at first.

I shifted against him. The night was warm but the heat of his body was addictive and I wanted to put as much of me in contact with him as possible. I found a new, even more comfortable place for my cheek, nestled against the curve of his pec. I pressed my chest against him and wrapped an arm around him, a hot little thrill going through me as my damp breast kissed his body. I hooked one leg over his, entwining us. And realized that my toes were brushing his injured leg. I looked down at it and heard his head move: he was looking, too.

"Does it hurt all the time?" I asked. It was the first time I'd dared to ask.

He silently nodded. "In the water, it doesn't bother me," he said. "On land it does. Worse, the further I walk."

"What's....?" I tried to think of a tactful way of asking and couldn't. "What's wrong with it?"

He drew in a deep breath and then let it out. "Pirates," he said at last.

For a second, I thought he was joking. But no: he was staring up at the stars, his face stony. I pressed myself closer and waited.

"Seven years ago, off the coast of Somalia," he said. "It's mostly under control now but back then pirates were hitting a ship every few days, taking hostages, and demanding ransoms. I was captaining a Navy frigate at the time and they sent us in to bring some order back to the area. But the whole thing was a mess. The civil war had been sending things all to hell for years—people were desperate, just trying to scratch a living. The pirates had started off trying to protect their fishing grounds and a lot of the fishermen still supported them even when they were just doing it for the money." He shook his head. "You were never sure who was on your side."

"Anyway, we did what we could. Stopped a dozen or so attacks. A month went by and we felt...safe, I suppose. I mean, we were a state-of-the-art, armor-plated frigate and they were buzzing around in small boats. I was worried about my men getting shot when they boarded a pirate boat, or someone firing an RPG at us. But none of us ever thought—"

He closed his eyes. A second later, he sunk his hand into my damp hair and then sighed as if that brought him comfort. "We found out later that a lot of the pirates we'd been catching were financed by one particular warlord. He was pissed at us, and wanted to make a statement. Normally, he wouldn't have stood a chance but he was a wily bastard.

He waited until we were refueling. It was night and the sea was rough: I was having trouble just keeping the ship in position. Then we got a distress call from a fishing boat. Engine was out and it was drifting right towards us. I was worried a wave would carry it into us or the refueling boat. I sent people to try to tow it to safety but...." He took a deep breath, pain creasing his brow, and I knew he was there, in his mind. "But suddenly, it fires up its engines and shoots straight into the gap between us and the refueling boat. Right under the fuel lines. The crew bail out and a second later, it explodes."

I drew in a shaky breath. My hand gripped his shoulder.

"The explosion slams right into our frigate, above and below the waterline. I'm on the bridge and the metal wall next to me gets shredded like it's made of paper. Every light on both ships goes out. But outside, everything lights up orange." He paused, and when he restarted, the words were strained. "All that fuel, from the refueling ship. Thousands of gallons of diesel are burning, all around us. *The sea is on fire.*"

"Everything goes to hell very, very quickly. I know we're sinking and so is the refueling boat. Normally, we'd abandon ship but there's fire all around us. Communications are down, all my high-tech screens have gone dark. And the weather's getting worse: the sea's trying to smash the two ships into one another which'll finish us off for good. I have to keep us afloat until help arrives."

"So I stand there bawling orders and getting compartments closed. We have to do things the old-fashioned way, sending runners down to the engine room with messages, using torches to signal the refueling ship...Christ, at one point I'm using the stars to try to get us pointing in the right direction. We send up flares, we know there's a Chinese ship in the area that'll come, but it'll take a while. And we're already listing badly. So bad it sends me stumbling...and that's when I realize there's something wrong with my leg."

He looked down at it. "I hadn't felt it until then but when the wall was torn apart, some of the metal went straight into my calf. The deck's slick with blood and now I'm aware of it, it starts to hurt like *fuck*. But there are men who are hurt worse so I wrap a bandage round it and get on with it. We're taking on a lot of water plus there's a fire burning on one deck. The wind's gusting and the waves are trying to tip us over. If that happens, there's nowhere to run: it's drown or jump off into a sea of burning fuel. So I keep fighting the weather, keep her pointing the right way, until the Chinese arrive."

"Someone else could have done it," I said quietly.

"It was my ship," he said. "My men."

"How long did it take, before you were rescued?"

"A few hours, give or take. They cleared the refueling boat first, then us."

I looked up at him. "You waited until everyone else was off, didn't you?"

"I was the captain," he said simply. His eyes closed. "We lost eight men. Three more seriously injured."

"And your leg?"

As I watched, he lifted it slightly, then grunted in pain.

"The muscle was all torn up. Nerve damage, too. If they'd got to it sooner, they might have been able to fix it but..." He shrugged. "At least I can still walk. Some blokes aren't so lucky."

"But there's nothing they can do about the pain?"

He shook his head, then looked down at me and gave me that lopsided smile.

"What?" I asked, confused.

He kissed the top of my head and a warm flush went through me but I was still mystified.

"You," he said at last. The Scottish accent gave even that simple word warmth. "You, Hannah. When I'm around you...it doesn't matter."

My heart swelled and I bit my lip. It was the nicest thing anyone had ever said to me. I couldn't think of a response so I just cuddled in closer. When I next looked up, I saw that he was looking towards the prow again. "What's out there?" I asked.

He didn't respond.

I looked more closely at him. He wasn't looking out at the water at all: he was looking at the point where the rail curved round, right at the prow, the furthest forward you could stand on the boat. I saw the sadness in his eyes and remembered another time I'd seen that look: in McKinley's, staring at the empty seat.

My eyes widened. "Edwards?" I asked.

He blinked, his eyes liquid. "Edwards."

51

___

ROURKE

"He was my XO," I told her. "My executive officer. Served with him for years, but he saw sense and got out of the Navy well before I did."

I was watching Edwards as I said it. He lounged against the rail at the prow, watching right back.

"They gave me a medal," I said. "And a desk job. I told them they could have them both back: I just wanted to be out there on the sea again. But they wouldn't hear of it. Six months later, I'm going insane. Leg hurts, no matter what I do. Walls of my office feel like they're closing in. I inhale and all I can smell is copy paper and printer toner. And then I get a phone call from Edwards."

It felt strange, telling someone. I'd never told anyone this stuff, hadn't wanted to and hadn't thought I'd needed to. But now that the words were spilling out, I could feel a pressure inside me, like I'd lanced a boil and it was releasing its poison. It was her, the amazing woman lying next to me. She wasn't drawing it out of me: that wouldn't have worked. She made me *want* to get it out, when for so many years I'd been burying it deep and wrapping myself around it, using it as a source of anger.

"Edwards was...." I sighed in exasperation. "He was stupidly loyal. And kind. And... *good.*" I looked down at Hannah and shook my head. "I was the captain. My job was to lead, and the crew respected me but...they *liked* him. He was good at...people stuff. I'm not."

She looked up at me and our eyes met. "What? You thought I was only a grumpy sod since the leg?" I half-grinned, half-grimaced. "Worse, maybe. And a lot worse since Edwards. But I was never a people person like him. He made a great XO. He was good at talking and he always knew everything: he'd know if the crew were nervous or exhausted or if some guy was starting to lose it. He'd tell me I needed to go easy on some engineer because he'd just got a letter from home saying his dad had died, or that some gun loader was showing the strain and needed to be rotated out for some shore leave. He was...he was always *smiling.* Everybody liked him. And we were inseparable: we both got grouchy if we were apart. I loved him. Even when he drove me crazy."

I looked down at her, trying to see if she understood. I wasn't sure if I understood myself. It was like Edwards had filled in the bits of my personality I didn't have: he'd complimented me. *Lightened* me. I looked into Hannah's eyes...and she *did* understand.

A warmth filled my chest. She understood because she filled in those same parts.

"He was my friend," I said. My throat suddenly contracted and I had to stop for a second or I would have choked up. I wasn't ready for that: why was it happening now, before we even got to the painful part? I took a shuddering breath. "He was my only friend."

Hannah slid her hand across my chest and just the touch of her soft skin there eased things. After a moment, I was able to restart. "Anyway," I muttered. "He called me. Said he was out in the Bahamas, hunting treasure, making good money. Said he had his eye on a boat and he'd found good people we could work with...but they needed a captain."

I looked around us: at the night sky, at the softly lapping waves. I took a deep lungful of sea air. "So I came out here. The first day I arrived, I dived into the ocean...and my leg didn't hurt." I sighed. "It's hard to describe what that was like. It was the first time I hadn't felt pain in six months. I knew, straightaway, that I wasn't going home."

"Edwards and I bided our time. We worked for other people, did any little jobs that came up, but we had a plan. He'd already found Hobbs and we were scouring the Bahamas, tracking down wrecks no one else could find. A couple of months in, we got our big break. We managed to find the wreck of a merchant ship that had been transporting the personal possessions of a rich family who'd moved out here. Everything from mirrors with gold frames to hairbrushes inlaid with silver. Over two hundred items plus a fair amount of coins. It made us enough that we could buy the *Fortune's Hope* and hire a crew. We were in business."

"Who named her?" Hannah asked.

I grunted and rolled my eyes, but the memory made me smile. "Edwards came up with it after a few beers. He was very proud of it. He said we were doing this by the seat of our pants, so we better hope good fortune would see us through. And that we sailed in hope of the other sort of fortune." I shook my head. "I told him it was a bloody stupid name but his mind was made up."

"So we sailed. All over the Caribbean but down around Central and South America, too. Even made the passage to Africa and sailed there for a while. But Nassau was always our base, with stops in Havana to see Hobbs and Carla. The sort of people we sailed with...like I told you, we're not the most respectable. We're all a bunch of reprobates, in fact. But Edwards and I tried to keep everyone...honorable, if that makes any sense. It was good. Good times." My stomach lurched. "And then we found the sub."

Hannah heard the change in my voice and nestled in closer. Her soft warmth was what made it possible to go on. My muscles had tensed and I realized that, unconsciously, I'd been a half-second away from getting up and stalking away: my instinctual response, when this subject came up.

Not this time. She had to hear. The poison was coming out and it hurt like hell, but now that she'd helped me open the wound, I had to cleanse it completely.

"It had been a pet project for years," I said. "Something we'd talk about, late at night in McKinley's. Something we'd have long conversations with Hobbs about, when we went to Havana. We collected tiny little scraps of information: old letters, maps...sometimes, just rumors. But then we hit paydirt."

I closed my eyes. Instantly, I was there, my light reflecting off metal walls, the water cold around me. I knew that if I opened my eyes, Hannah would still be there and that made it bearable...just.

"The Nazis had spirited millions in gold out of Germany, during the war," I said. "Some of it on U-boats. And there was a story that one of those U-boats never made it to its destination. That it had sunk in the Pacific with all that bullion on board. No one knew where, of course. The crew tried to radio their last position but they couldn't reach their commanders so the sub was lost forever. *Except....* The sub's radio operator cracked under the pressure. Couldn't stand the thought of being trapped down there, running out of air. So he started radioing on civilian frequencies, begging for help from anyone. The sub's commander stopped him, but not before a fishing trawler heard him...and wrote down the coordinates. The fishermen wrote them down in a letter to his daughter...and Edwards and I got hold of it."

"It was a long way out to sea. So we decided to do a recon mission first, just Edwards and me. We'd dive down, take a look, and if it was real then we'd come back with a crew and any special equipment we needed."

I could feel the warm night air bathing my eyelids but, in my mind, it was brilliant sunshine. "The morning we arrived, it was a glorious day. Calm waters, perfect diving weather. We went down, thinking it might take a while to locate it. But—"—I shook my head in wonder—"it was just *there.* Just lying there on the bottom of the sea, waiting for us."

Hannah squeezed my hand. I could feel how much I'd tensed up and tried to relax, but I couldn't. I was seeing that huge, black cylinder appear before me, its conning tower rising above us. *Turn back!* I wanted to scream to myself. But it was already far too late.

"We got in through a hole in the hull," I told Hannah. "It was dark inside, and I mean pitch black: it was daylight, but there are no windows in a submarine. It was cold, too: the sun couldn't warm the water that was inside. But we'd brought lights and we'd been in worse places." I swallowed, remembering. "It wasn't like the wreck of some old pirate ship. It was only about seventy years old. There were still...bones."

Hannah drew in her breath and her hand squeezed mine a little tighter.

"It can be...tricky, underwater. Especially in the dark. Flashlights reflect off things and you think you see a light in an empty room. Your swimming pushes the water around and a skeleton six feet in front of you suddenly starts to move." I'd said *tricky*. What I really meant was *creepy as hell*. Especially with all the swastikas we kept seeing. "So by the time we get down to the lowest decks, we're both jumpy. But then we see a whole load of wooden crates. We get one open and...."

I could see it now. The wooden lid floating up in slow motion. The neatly-packed bars, the gold glinting and shining under our lights. Edward's face behind his mask as we both looked up in shock.

"The bars weighed five pounds each. That meant we were looking at something like half a million dollars *per bar*. Each crate held fifteen and there were eight crates. Sixty million dollars. And it was right there: all we had to do was bring it up."

I slowly shook my head, feeling my damp hair rub against the deck. "The plan had been just to check it out and come back with a team. But we hadn't thought it would be this simple. We'd thought there would be locked doors, or that we'd have to cut our way in through the hull. This was just so...*easy*. So we picked up a gold bar each: even underwater, they were heavy and we hadn't brought anything to carry them in. We swam up to the boat and dropped them on the deck and that was it: we were a million pounds richer, just like that. We'd been down less than fifteen minutes."

For the first time in a long while, I opened my eyes and looked down at Hannah. I needed her to understand. "We couldn't leave the rest of it just lying there," I said wretchedly. "It was...." I trailed off, trying to find the words.

"It was gold," she said quietly. And I saw in her eyes that she understood. She remembered the excitement, when we'd found the chest of coins. "It was a fortune."

I nodded. "It was a fortune. So we got fresh tanks of air and started figuring out how to get the rest of it up. We decided that we'd ferry it from the hold to the hole in the hull. Once we had all of it there, we could use the winch. We dived down and got to work. We'd brought bags this time and we found we could carry four bars each. Even so, it was going to take fifteen trips back and forth to get all of it."

"We planned to stay together for safety. But after all the creepiness of getting in there and then the high of finding the gold...God, we were drunk on it. Grinning like kids." My breathing was tight and getting tighter. It felt like a snake had coiled around me and was gradually crushing my chest. My words came slower and slower. "I got out of sync with Edwards: he'd still be offloading his gold near the hole and I'd already be halfway back for my next haul. We were almost through—"

And suddenly that was it. In my mind, I stopped swimming along the dark companionways of the submarine. I knew what would happen when I entered the next room and I couldn't face it. Not again. I closed my eyes. Opened them again and stared up at the stars. But it didn't help: it felt like I'd hit an invisible wall. I couldn't go on. Hannah felt it and pressed her body against mine but it felt as if I was feeling her through twenty feet of cold, cold water.

Then I looked towards the prow and locked eyes with Edwards. And he gave me that nod he always gave me, when something needed to be done.

"I'm filling my bag with my next load of gold," I said. "When I hear...I don't so much hear as feel it. A vibration. A big one. Like the whole submarine has shaken. I wonder if it's an earthquake—we *are* in the Pacific. I swim back towards the hole to check and when I get there...everything's changed."

My mouth was suddenly desert dry. "Next to the hole in the hull was a metal walkway. That's where we'd been stacking the gold. But now it's gone: the whole thing has torn away from the wall and fallen. And underneath it—" I pressed my lips together. "I could see an arm sticking out. Edwards."

Hannah was pressing her cheek against my chest as hard as she could, her arms locked fiercely around me. I smoothed her damp hair. "It was the gold," I told her. "We never even thought about the weight. When it was all stacked up in one place, on a walkway designed for people...."

I drew in a deep breath. "I swam down. Edwards was okay, just scared. I'm thinking, *Christ,* that was lucky. We'll get him out, both of us go topside and count our blessings, and then we'll carefully get the gold up. The bars were scattered around a bit, but we could collect them up. Then I try to pull him out...and I can't. The walkway's too heavy."

"Oh God," said Hannah. She'd lifted her head to look up into my eyes. She'd figured out how this story ended.

"I push all the gold off it: I don't care about the gold, anymore. But the walkway's thirty feet long and its solid metal. I can't move it even an inch. Then I think to check my air and I'm down to ten minutes. Edwards is the same."

"So I swim for the surface. Scramble on board, dump my tank, and get two fresh ones. Dive back down faster than I ever have. I manage to feed a tank under the walkway to Edwards and he gets the fresh mouthpiece in his mouth. Now I've got a half hour, maybe forty minutes if he can breathe slowly. But I still have no way to get him out. And that's when I start to panic."

"I think about calling for help: no good, we're way out at sea and it'd be four or five hours before the coastguard arrives. I know the winch won't lift something that heavy." I shook my head bitterly. "If we'd just stuck to the plan, scoped it out ourselves, and then come back with a full crew and equipment, we would have brought a heavy-duty winch with us. And we wouldn't have been stacking the gold there in the first place: it would never have happened."

It was difficult to talk, now, the tension working its way up my chest to my throat. "Over the next half hour, I try everything I can think of. I try and pull him out. I try to push it off him. I try to lever it off him. I even start undoing bolts, trying to take the damn thing apart. Nothing works. And I can see Edwards getting more and more scared: it's even worse for him, all he can do is lie there and watch."

"Our air runs out again. I go up and get fresh tanks...and I realize *these are our last two.* We didn't think we'd need more than six tanks. If we'd had our crew with us, we would have brought twenty or more. Enough that he could have held out until the coastguard arrived." I stopped for a second, my guts twisting in remembered terror. The years hadn't dulled things at all. "I'm standing there on the deck, looking down at the blue, and I realize *I don't know what to do.* As a captain, there's always a strategy, a tactic. But there was nothing. He had one tank of air left and then...."

"I go back down and give a fresh tank to Edwards. I'm trying to breathe shallow and calm but I can't: the sweat's pouring off me. My face is maybe a foot from his. A piece of steel maybe a quarter-inch thick is all that separates me from him but *I can't get to him.*"

"I get my hands under that thing, use my legs, and *heave.* I push like I've never pushed before because my best friend's going to die if I don't do this. My leg's screaming at me. I know that muscle isn't as strong as it should be. If I hadn't been injured...."

I could feel Hannah looking up at me in horror but I couldn't meet her eyes. If I did, I knew I wouldn't be able to continue. She knew now why I hated my injury so much, beyond just the pain.

"I push and I push and I push. Edwards is doing the same, we're giving it everything we've got. We don't quit until our muscles fail. But the fucking thing won't budge. I know we've both been gulping down air. I check our tanks: maybe a couple of minutes left. I stare into his eyes and we both know what's going to happen. He gives me this look, just *nods,* like he understands. And I can't...." My throat clenched up and I had to start again. "I can't speak to him. That's the worst part. I'm about to lose my best friend in the world and *I can't speak to him.* There's so much I want to tell him, so much I know he wants to say to me, and all we can do is look at each other." I stared determinedly up at the stars. They were blurring. "He grabs my hand and holds it tight. We just look at each other. And then his air runs out."

"I still have a minute or so left so I take out my mouthpiece and ram it in his mouth. I want him to have all of it, to give him as long as possible, but he keeps passing it back to me, won't take a breath unless I take a breath. Then my tank goes empty, too." I pressed my lips together tight. "He starts pointing to the surface, signaling for me to go. But there's no way I'm going. I'm not going to leave him there alone."

"He glares at me. He's furious, doesn't want me to drown too, and I think—I think he doesn't want me to see him go. But I'm not leaving him. I watch him hold his breath for as long as he can and then the fight begins. His body needs to breathe but there's nothing but water. He fights it, fights it...and then he takes his first big gulp of water and his body just goes wild, kicking and straining, trying to get to the surface. He's coughing and choking, water burning in his lungs, and every time he opens his mouth he's taking in more of it."

"Tears are running down my face under my mask. I grab hold of the walkway and give it one last heave but it's like trying to lift a truck. He's *scared.* I'd seen him walk through gunfire and fight sharks and jump off cliffs but *this,* this terrifies him. He grabs hold of my hand again and now he needs me to stay, and I grip it hard because I'm not going anywhere."

"He fights. He fights *so hard.* Thrashing. Clawing. His eyes begging me to help him, to find a way. I can see it happening, I can see the bubbles each time his mouth opens, air coming out, water going in. And all I can do is hold his hand and watch and not leave him, even though by now my lungs are bursting. I think that's the worst part, watching him thrash like that, but it's not. The worst part is when he starts to weaken. When his movements become all slow and dreamy.

When no more bubbles come out and there's just the occasional twitch. And then...nothing."

Hannah clung to me, squeezing me so hard it hurt, but it was exactly what I needed. Her face was wet with tears where it pressed against my chest and I could feel my eyes were wet, too.

"I just hang there in the water for a few seconds. My lungs are close to giving out: I know that if I don't go, I'm going to drown too. But part of me wants to. I deserve to drown, right there beside him. I don't want to go up to the surface because there's no Edwards, up there. But at last, I let go of his hand and kick for the surface. I almost don't make it: a few feet from the surface, I can feel my lips opening to take my first gulp of water...but then I break through into the air and cough it up. I drag myself aboard...and Edwards is right there, sitting on the deck, waiting for me."

Hannah lifted her head and stared up at me, her eyes shining with tears. She shook her head slowly and then just hugged me again. There were no words.

I went limp on the deck, exhausted from telling the story. Exhausted but...better, as if with the words had come a lot of the poison I'd been carrying around with me. We lay there in silence for a moment but then I had to speak, had to tell her that: "I know he's not...*real*. But I still see him." I shook my head and grunted. "I'm crazy."

Hannah smoothed her hand over my chest. "No. You're not." She looked up at me. "Will. It wasn't your fault."

Hearing that shouldn't have made any difference. I'd blamed myself every day for years. I'd ignored anyone who told me different: Carla. Hobbs. Edwards's family. Of course it was my fault.

Yet when Hannah said it...it wasn't like with the others. She was too close to me for me to discount it as bullshit or ignore it and push her away. I had to let myself believe that, just maybe, it was true. I felt the last of the poison ooze out of me and it was the thickest, darkest, and oiliest of the lot.

That left...emptiness. A void. It ached, but it didn't feel as if the pain was constantly being renewed.

I didn't say anything. I just put my arms around Hannah, hugged her to me, and nodded my thanks. When I finally spoke again, the words came more easily.

"I sailed back to Nassau. Went back with cutting gear and got the body so his family could bury him. I never took a single bar of gold from the sub. I even tossed back the two that we brought up. I told my crew I wouldn't be needing them anymore and took to just sailing. Going a little further out each time, hoping that the sea would take me. Didn't care about treasure, anymore. Didn't care about anything." I paused and looked down at her. "Until I saw you on the beach."

She looked up at me. I cradled her cheek in my hand. "Since you came along," I mumbled, "everything's different."

Hannah swallowed. Then, hesitantly, "Does Edwards...approve?"

I felt a hot swell of anger in my chest. Damn her. God*damn* her for being so understanding! I could actually feel my face getting hot: I was blushing like a child. "I know he's not real," I said again, looking away. I couldn't stand her thinking I was crazy.

She put a hand on my cheek and turned me back towards her. "I know."

I cursed under my breath and looked at her again. As soon as I saw those soft blue eyes looking up at me, all my anger melted away like clouds under a fierce sun. I couldn't get angry with her, not anymore. I'd lost that defense. Now I actually had to communicate with her. I couldn't put what I was feeling into words, though, so I just leaned down and kissed those blush-pink lips instead.

When I broke the kiss, she asked, "What happens when we get back?"

I found her hand with mine and knitted our fingers together. That was one thing I *was* sure of. I'd been sure from the second I jumped off the boat to swim to her. "We'll be together. If you can put up with a half-lame Scot with a foul temper."

She blinked up at me. "Can you put up with someone like me? I don't know if I'm...." She looked down at the deck as if ashamed. "...suitable."

I frowned. What the hell did she mean by that? I honestly had no idea. "Hannah," I said, and I could hear the Scottish thick in my voice, "I want you in my life. I need you in my life."

And I reached down, put my hands on her waist, and pulled her fully atop me so I could kiss her properly. It was a long time before we finally made it inside and fell into the hammock to sleep.

52

HANNAH

He was up before me. Whatever time we went to bed, he was always up with the dawn, usually doing things with ropes and sails while I was still warm and mumbling in the hammock. I'd have to get used to that. And that thought, of spending morning after morning together, made me thrill inside.

This morning, though, he didn't let me sleep. He knocked on the door and I slowly extricated myself from the hammock. I could feel the weight of Esme's necklace shifting against my chest as I stood. He'd put it on me again, just before we went to bed, and now I never wanted to take it off.

Rourke was sitting at a folding table and had breakfast waiting: fruit and bacon and eggs, with huge mugs of coffee. I pulled the blanket into a sort of toga and sat down, my eyes still half-closed. "What time is it?" I asked sleepily. The sky was still dark to the west and I am *not* a morning person.

"Early," muttered Rourke, sounding a little guilty. He passed me a mug of coffee.

I guessed it was about five a.m. I wrapped my hands around the mug, drank deeply, and tried not to yawn.

There were advantages to the early start, though. To the east, the sun was rising over the island's rock walls, lighting up the sky in glorious pinks and oranges. The water around us was millpond-calm and it acted as a giant mirror, so we were floating in the center of a second sunrise. It was one of the most beautiful things I'd ever seen and for a while we just sat there in wonder, watching it as we ate. Even Yoyo came to sit on the boat's roof, looking up at the sun as he nibbled on an orange. By the time I'd finished my coffee, I was feeling almost human. And when we hauled up the anchor and started to move, with both of us standing at the wheel, it really started to feel like *our* boat.

Rourke maneuvered us carefully through the narrow passage and we emerged into a calm sea. It was the first time in a while that I'd had nothing but ocean in front of me: normally, we'd been heading towards an island and I could focus on that. The sight of the endless water made me gulp and press closer to Rourke: my fear of the sea was slowly fading but I still felt so *tiny*....

Rourke noticed and slipped an arm around my waist. "We'll be alright, lass," he told me. "'Long as we get out of the way of *that*." He nodded to the horizon, where thick storm clouds were gathering.

"At least the waves are small," I said. The sea was almost as calm as the sheltered waters inside the island.

But Rourke shook his head. "That's because there's no wind." And I realized he was right: I couldn't feel even a breeze on my face. "We're stuck with the engine unless it changes. But we've got plenty of time."

I leaned my head against his shoulder. The engine might be slow but it had one advantage: it meant he didn't have to run around hauling on ropes. We could stand there together, at the wheel. "Why don't I make us another cup of coffee," I said. "And then you can show me how to steer and—"

A warm ball of fur landed on my shoulder. Yoyo grabbed hold of my ears. "*Eek!*" he squeaked urgently. "*Eek!*"

I scratched the special spot on his neck but for once that didn't placate him. "What?" I asked. "What is it?"

"EEK!"

He was looking at something behind us. Rourke and I slowly turned around.

Ratcher's boat was emerging from behind the island, belching black diesel fumes into the air as it bore down on us.

53

ROURKE

My first reaction was shock: it felt like the deck had dropped away from under my feet and I'd plunged straight into Arctic water. Then disbelief. Ratcher *couldn't* be here. There was just no possible way he could have found us.

And then, finally, the sick churning of fear. I hated the *Pitbull*. It was noisy and cumbersome and laden down with technology. It was no match for the *Fortune's Hope*, never would be. In any other weather, we would have outrun him no problem. But right now, with no wind, those big, stinking engines could easily out power us. And when he caught up with us....

I tried to push the throttle forward but it was already against its stops...and Ratcher was gaining fast. No matter what I did, they'd catch us.

If I was on my own, I'd have fought. It was suicide: Ratcher had upwards of twenty crew and all of them would be armed to the teeth. But I could at least make sure I took some of them with me.

But I wasn't on my own. I looked around at Hannah and saw her big, scared eyes. If I tried to fight, she'd wind up with a bullet in her. I couldn't surrender, either. This wasn't just about the treasure: Ratcher wanted *her*. And I wasn't going to let that happen.

I had to come up with something else. I ran below deck, Hannah close behind me.

"Can't we call for help?" she asked. "The Coast Guard?"

I'd just picked up my shotgun and was checking it was loaded. I picked up a fistful of cartridges and shook my head. "We're hours from anywhere. This is going to be over long before anyone can get to us. We need to get ready to be boarded."

"*What?!*" I saw her go pale. "But they can't—They can't just—"

My chest contracted. God, she was so beautifully, terrifyingly innocent. She really didn't understand how it worked, out here on the sea. *I should never have brought her out here!* I pulled her to me. "It'll be okay," I said with a confidence I didn't feel. "Just stay close to me."

I had to get her somewhere safe, somewhere a bullet wouldn't hit her when they swarmed aboard. I looked furiously around and my eyes lit upon the heavy door to the maintenance room. "In here!" I snapped. "Quick!"

The maintenance room is where all the wiring and pipes route to. It's barely more than a closet but it has one advantage: the door is steel lined, to stop fire spreading. I was hoping that would stop a bullet. And it has a glass window that looked out into the main room, so we could see what was going on. I pulled Hannah inside and called to Yoyo. As soon as he jumped onto Hannah's shoulder, I slammed the door.

Seconds later, I heard boots land on our deck. Then they killed our engines and we slowed to a stop. More boots came aboard, then a much heavier footfall I knew must be Ratcher's. The first man looked cautiously around the door. Not Ratcher himself, of course. He wasn't brave enough to lead the way. When the guy saw our faces through the window in the door, he leveled his gun at us. In answer, I raised my shotgun and pressed the barrels against the window's glass. The man cursed.

I'd created a stalemate. It was the best tactic I could come up with. If they came below deck, I'd shred them with the shotgun: in such a confined space, the blast would be devastating. They could probably win, if they sent down enough guys and put enough bullets in the reinforced door, but they'd lose a lot of men. And Ratcher's men weren't loyal enough to sacrifice themselves.

On the flip side, we were trapped until they left.

I heard muttered voices out on deck. Then Ratcher's bald head slowly appeared around the door frame. I had to resist the urge to pull the shotgun's trigger.

"All we want's the treasure," he yelled. "No one has to die."

"We didn't find it!" I yelled back. "The map was wrong!"

Ratcher threw back his head and laughed. "Right. That's why you're riding so low in the water, your balls are wet." I saw him eye some of the crates stacked around the room.

"You take a step into this room," I snarled, "and this shotgun'll cut you in two."

Ratcher's upper lip drew back in a sneer. "Fine by me. We'll pour gasoline all over your decks, then light a match."

Shit. He didn't want this to turn into a gun battle any more than we did. But if we denied him the treasure, he could just torch the whole boat from the safety of the deck. By the time he let us out, the fire would be out of control, and we'd either burn or drown when the boat sank.

Every fiber of my being was telling me to run out there with the shotgun and die in a blaze of glory. But when I was dead, he'd grab Hannah. Grab her and— *No. No way.*

There was only one other way out. It made me want to throw up, but it would keep her safe. I had to fight to speak, dragging the words up from an enormous depth. "Take it."

Hannah grabbed my arm. "*What?!*"

Ratcher grinned. "What was that, Rourke? Didn't quite catch it."

"Take it," I said bitterly. "Take the treasure. No one shoots. We all walk away."

Hannah grabbed my shirt. "*What are you doing? You can't let him take it!*"

I looked her right in the eye. "I don't care about the treasure," I said. "I care about you."

She stared at me, her eyes moist. Then she wrapped her arms around me and pressed her face to my chest.

"Sounds fair enough to me," said Ratcher, grinning. "You just stay there. Me and the boys will be out of your way in a jiffy."

There followed the toughest few minutes of my life as I watched Ratcher's men shamble inside and relieve us of the treasure. With so many of them, they could form a human chain and simply pass the crates out onto the deck and then onto their boat. What had taken days of effort and danger to find—not to mention the decades of research by Hannah's great-grandfather—became Ratcher's prize in just a few minutes.

I could feel the rage blossoming and heating inside me. It was the biggest find of my life, bigger even than the submarine I'd found with Edwards. And now the riches and the glory would be his. My finger was still on the shotgun's trigger. It would be so easy....

But if I started a fight, we were both dead. Ratcher wasn't kidding about burning the boat. He was willing to see it go to the bottom rather than let us keep it. He had nothing to lose but—I looked at Hannah—for the first time, I did.

I forced myself to lower the shotgun and watched, seething. They took everything, even the chest of coins and the ruby we found with the first clue. We'd be left with nothing. When I saw one guy walk off with my sword, staying put took every ounce of self-control I had.

Then, as they were preparing to leave, Ratcher grabbed something from the shelf beside the hammock. My heart sank. A pill bottle, taped to a stone. "What's this?" he asked.

I heard Hannah curse beside me.

"Nothing." I fought to keep my voice level but it suddenly felt as if someone was tightening an iron band around my chest.

Ratcher walked slowly to the door we were sheltering behind. He was frowning at the stone, rubbing his fat thumb back and forth over it. Then he held the pill bottle up to the light, sloshing the liquid inside it. He looked at me and raised a curious eyebrow.

All my anger about the treasure evaporated. None of it mattered: my entire attention was focused on what he had in his hand. And yet somehow, I had to pretend it wasn't important. "It's nothing," I said again. I was wracking my brain for an explanation he'd believe.

"It's a mineral," said Hannah suddenly. "I'm an amateur geologist. I found it on the island and ground some up to study it."

Ratcher leaned close to her, leering at her through the glass. She stared coldly back at him. I wanted to scream at him, tell him to get the hell away from her. I wanted to blast the shotgun through the window, right into his grinning face, or pull the door open and pummel him. But I forced myself to keep still.

"So it's not worth anything?" said Ratcher.

"No," said Hannah, her voice tight.

Ratcher turned away from us, his tank top stretched tight across his rounded back and sunburned neck. He marched across the room to the open door and drew back his arm as if to throw a ball. "So you won't mind if I toss it overboard, then—"

"*No!*" Hannah pushed forward and had the door half open before I could stop her. Ratcher turned, laughing, and I pushed her protectively behind me. But the damage was done.

"She needs it," Ratcher said victoriously. And then he read my expression. I couldn't help it: there was no hiding the look of fear on my face. I've faced death plenty of times and held it together but the thought of him throwing the cure overboard, dooming Hannah to an agonizing end...my eyes were wild, my knuckles white on the shotgun's stock. "And you've gone soft on her." He laughed. "You pathetic bastard."

"Just leave it here," I said. "It's not worth anything." And then, even though it made my soul burn to say it: "Please, Ratcher."

His face split into a huge, wet-lipped grin. He thought he understood: the half-lame, messed-up seadog, besotted with the beautiful blonde who was way out of his league. He shook his head and made to toss the stone into the hammock. My chest went tight: I'd take any amount of humiliation, as long as we got the cure back—

Then Ratcher frowned, his hand frozen in midair. I followed his gaze to Hannah, who in turn was looking at me. She quickly looked down at her feet, but it was too late. I'd seen the look of love and admiration in her eyes and so had Ratcher.

His grin disintegrated. "You're fucking him," he said. I saw his eyes go cold with jealousy. "You're fucking *him?*"

Hannah caught her breath and then set her jaw and glared defiantly back at Ratcher.

"I told you what would happen," he muttered. "I told you she was mine!"

He turned and stormed from the room. For a sickening second, I thought he was going to make good on his threat and throw the stone and bottle overboard, but he shoved it into his pants pocket instead.

I threw open the door and started after him, raising the shotgun in front of me. Hannah grabbed my arm. "*No!*" she screamed. "They'll kill you!"

I could hear Ratcher yelling orders above deck and boots moving around. "If they run off with the cure, you're dead," I growled. "And I'll not have that." I pulled myself free and ran for the door—

Halfway there, two of Ratcher's men leaned through the doorway and started shooting. Hannah screamed and ducked back inside the maintenance room, slamming the door. I fired the shotgun and the men ducked back, one of them clutching his arm. But as I reached the door, another man leaned in with a machine gun and let loose. I had to flatten myself against the wall and watch, ears ringing, as bullets tore apart the interior of the *Fortune's Hope*. Smoking black holes were punched through photographs of my Navy crew, my crew in Nassau, and the picture of Edwards and me. The polished woodwork shredded and splintered. In the maintenance room, I heard Hannah scream and her face disappeared from the window. I prayed she'd ducked down out of sight and hadn't been hit.

As soon as the guy had to reload, I stepped out from behind the wall and fired the other barrel of the shotgun out through the doorway. More gunfire drove me back and I scrambled to reload—

Then the machine gun roared again, outside, and I heard glass shatter and metal shake as bullets poured into it. What the hell was he firing at? Then more sounds: the hiss of rope followed by the heavy thump of cloth. I heard the engine of Ratcher's boat start up and men scrambling from one boat to the other....

And then all was quiet.

For a second, I waited, unsure if it was a trap. Had they left someone aboard to blow my head off as soon as I ventured outside? Hannah cautiously opened the door to the maintenance room but I waved for her to stay put.

At last, I crept out of the door and onto the deck. The *Pitbull* was already powering away into the distance, heavy now with treasure. The crew were on the deck, laughing and cheering, and Ratcher gave me a mock salute from the upper deck. I frowned. I didn't get it. Ratcher had been mad as hell: why hadn't he told his crew to finish us off, or torch our boat?

Then I saw Ratcher very deliberately shift his gaze and nod. *Look behind you.* I reluctantly turned....

The entire sky was black. The storm was almost on us and beneath the clouds, the wind was whipping the waves up into walls of water the size of houses. Even as I watched, the boat rocked like a toy as it began to enter the storm's influence. Ratcher was forgotten. I raced for the controls, to start the engine: I had to get us out of there. But when I got to the controls, they were a shattered, smoking mess. Now I knew what they'd been firing the machine gun at.

Hannah burst out onto deck. As soon as she felt the wind whip across her face she turned towards the storm...and gave a strangled moan of horror. My chest tightened: it was everything she feared: open ocean at its most merciless.

"Help me with the sails!" I yelled. Now that there was wind, we might still be able to outrun the storm, if we were quick. I grabbed for the rope—

And that's when I saw the main sail lying on a heap on the deck. They'd cut the line that would raise it and pulled it all the way out of the eyelet at the top of the mast. Until we got back to port, there was no way to rerig it.

We were dead in the water. We couldn't even turn the boat around. And the biggest storm I'd seen in my life was about to hit us broadside. We'd flip over and be torn to pieces like a child's toy. I ran for the radio but of course they'd shot that, too.

"You son of a bitch!" I screamed across the water. My heart was hammering with rage and fear. For years, I'd wanted the sea to take me. Now it was going to...but it was going to take Hannah, too.

By now, the *Pitbull* was tiny, easily pulling ahead of the storm. But I saw Ratcher wave mockingly in response to my cry.

Then he strolled below deck and left us to die.

54

—————

HANNAH

I stared at the approaching waves. They were straight out of my nightmares, cold and gray as iron and towering high above my head. I could feel the panic uncoil in my belly and start to spread through my body. In another few seconds, it would take over completely.

I tore my gaze away and faced Rourke. I could feel the chill wind lifting strands of my hair and working its way down the back of my neck and under my collar. "What do we do?" I asked.

And then my face fell because Rourke looked...*beaten.*

I'd never seen him back down or give up, no matter how useless the fight. That's why he won. But now he'd lost the treasure and was going to lose his boat. *All because of me.*

"There's nothing we can do," he said, his voice tight. His hands were bunching and unbunching in helpless fury. "We can't fix the sail out here. We'd have to get the line up through that hoop." He nodded at the mast and I looked. Right at the top, sickeningly high above the deck, there was a metal eyelet. "I used to be able to climb masts like that," he muttered. "Before—" He scowled down at his leg.

I grabbed the line and strode towards the mast. "I'll try." Just the thought of being all the way up there made me go light-headed with fear, so if I was going to do this I needed to do it *now,* before I chickened out.

Rourke grabbed me just as I got there, his hands warm on my waist. "*No!* If you fall—"

I glanced up at the height of the mast. At the hard deck beneath. "We don't have a choice," I said.

He stared at me, his blue eyes raging. But at last, he nodded.

I tied the line to a belt loop on my shorts so that I had both hands free. Then I wrapped my arms and legs around the mast, squeezed tight and dragged myself upward—

I got less than six feet before I slithered back down, my palms and inner thighs burning. I tried again and got a little further, then a third time and barely made it off the deck. *Shit!* It was just too smooth to grip and I didn't have the strength to hug it tight enough to stay on.

The wind lifted my hair and blew it out into streamers in front of me. For the first time, I heard it make that warning, shrill howl that everyone knows means *get to shelter.*

I *had* to look. Rourke and I slowly turned around.

I'd seen storms in Nebraska. I'd even seen tornados. But on land, there's always one safe haven, one thing you can cling to: the ground.

But we were on the water and it was as alive and as terrifyingly powerful as the sky. What was approaching didn't look like a flat ocean topped with waves. It looked as if the sea had torn itself apart into mountains and valleys: cliffs of towering gray slate and ravines so deep I couldn't see the bottom of them.

The noise was incredible: the slow, momentous crash of the waves topped with the rising wail of the wind. The sky was barely brighter than the water. Black clouds blotted out the sun and they were releasing torrential rain, so thick you could barely see through it. It was morning but it was as dark as night except when lightning lit up the scene.

And all of this was heading right for us. And there was no shelter, no cellar we could hide in. We were in a flimsy husk of wood and we were going to be in the middle of the chaos. The panic climbed up through my chest, stealing my breath. It was everything I feared about the ocean: I was tiny and powerless, about to feel its wrath. All of the confidence Rourke had been helping me gain evaporated. *I was right all along. This is no place for me.*

I felt for Rourke's hand and he grabbed it. But there was nothing either of us could do. We stood there on the deck staring up at the storm, the first drops of rain wetting our faces. I squeezed Rourke's hand tighter and tighter....

A warm, furry mass hit my leg and clung there. I looked down to see Yoyo glancing between me and the storm with huge, scared eyes. Then he jumped and in an instant had scampered up my leg, up my torso and onto my shoulder so he could nestle against my cheek. *How does he do that so easily?*

I turned and looked at the mast. "I bet Yoyo could get up there."

Rourke stared at me. "*How?*" he asked. "How are you going to...?" He looked between me and the monkey. *How are you going to tell him what to do?*

"He mimics us," I said, looking into YoYo's eyes. "Don't you?"

Rourke shook his head. But if he thought I was crazy, he didn't let it stop him. He grabbed some string and tied it to the end of the line, then tied a set of keys to the other end to give it weight. I found a fishing net and tore away the mesh to leave just the iron hoop. Then I picked up the keys and demonstrated. "Drop the keys through the hoop," I told Yoyo, my voice light and happy.

Yoyo stared back at me blankly.

"Drop the keys through the hoop," I said, doing it again. Then I pointed up at the hoop at the top of the mast. The monkey didn't even look.

"Drop the *keys*..."—I jangled them, forcing myself to keep my voice light—"through the *hoop*." I did it again. "*Up there.*" And I pointed. This time, Yoyo looked at the mast. But then he just looked at me uncomprehendingly, his little head tilted to the side.

"It's no good," said Rourke. His voice was gentle.

But I pressed on. "Drop the *keys*," I said, my voice strained, "through the *hoop. Please,* Yoyo." Spray hit the back of my neck and the boat suddenly lurched under my feet. The storm was right on us but I didn't dare turn to look.

Rourke grabbed my arm. "We need to get below." But there was an awful finality in his voice. He wasn't talking about surviving. He was talking about preparing for the end.

There was a rising roar behind me, a bass rumble that made my whole body vibrate. The wind whipped my hair across my face. Yoyo reached up and pawed it out of the way.

Rourke pulled on my arm. "We have to go. *Now!*"

"*Please,* Yoyo," I begged, tears in my eyes. "Drop the keys—"

Yoyo snatched them from my hand and darted away across the deck. When he reached the mast, his speed barely changed: he swarmed up it as if it was horizontal. I drew in my breath, barely daring to hope.

The boat began to tilt as the first big wave hit it. I stumbled but it was worse for Yoyo, halfway up the mast. The whole thing swayed, flinging him around, and he chirruped in fear. One paw came loose, then a leg: he was dangling. "Oh Jesus, no," I whispered and ran forward to catch him—

But as the mast steadied for a second he regained his grip and raced on up. Suddenly, he was at the top, holding the keys. I clasped my hands together in silent prayer—

He dropped them through. They hurtled down and clattered to the deck, trailing the string behind them. Rourke and I stared at them in disbelief. Yoyo raced down the mast even faster than he'd gone up, jumped the last six feet, and bounded onto my shoulder. I think I gave a kind of hysterical hiccup of joy. Then I cuddled Yoyo very, very hard into my chest and kissed the top of his furry head about twenty times. "*Good* monkey," I managed, panting with relief. "*Very good monkey.*" He snuggled into me as the rain began to soak us and the wind rose to a piercing scream.

Rourke hauled on the string and we watched as it pulled the line that carried the heavy sail. I ran over and took some of the sail's weight as it rose. If the string snapped....

But it held and Rourke pulled the line down to where he could grab it. He tied the two cut ends together and we had a sail again. I saw his lungs fill and his stance straighten: he was back. He nodded his thanks to me and Yoyo and then jerked his head below deck. "Get below," he said. "It's going to get rough."

Even as he said it, the wind caught the sail and almost tore the rope from his hand. He growled and hauled on it but he was being dragged along the rain-slick deck.

For the first time in a while, I looked at the storm. And immediately wished I hadn't. The black sky extended beyond us, now: we were *in it*. The only reason we hadn't capsized was that a huge wave was slowly building, right in front of us, and we were in the calm of its trough. But when it hit.... "You're going to sail through *that*, on your own?" I yelled over the wind.

He glared at me and gave me a push towards the door. "Get below, lass!" I could see it in his eyes, that fierce need to protect me. I glanced below deck. Even bullet-scarred and damaged, it looked warm and safe. It was so tempting....

But he'd die out here trying to save me, if I let him. "No." I pulled Yoyo from my chest, shooed him below deck and closed the doors tight. Then I stumbled across the lurching deck to Rourke. "I'm staying to help you."

His eyes burned into me. I could see him getting ready to yell, to tell me that *this was what he did*. That he'd had to be out here on his own ever since Edwards died.

But I pressed myself to his chest and stared right back at him. And at last, he got the message: he wasn't on his own anymore.

He drew in a long breath, his chest pushing against me. One hand cupped my cheek, his big palm gloriously warm on my rain-chilled skin. He shook his head slowly at me. "*Lass!*" he said in wonder. Then he leaned down and kissed me, his thumbs stroking over my cheeks, his hard lips working at my soft ones. A warm glow spread through me and my heart lifted and bobbed. The wind howled around us but, just for a second, it didn't scare me. Maybe we wouldn't make it through this, but if we went, we were going together.

Rourke stepped back from me, dropping his hand from my cheek only when he absolutely had to. "Tie yourself on," he ordered, throwing me a rope. "In case you go over."

Over?! I looked at the sea and my stomach plummeted to my feet. I'd been worried enough thinking about the boat being torn apart. Falling off into *that* hadn't even occurred to me. I passed the rope around my waist and tied it, then tied the other end around the rail as Rourke did the same. Then I struggled over to him. The wind was so strong, it was difficult to stand, difficult even to take a breath: it hit you in the face so hard it hurt.

"We've got to turn her around!" yelled Rourke. The wind was so loud now that it made my ears hurt. "We have to hit the wave head on!"

I nodded that I understood. I grabbed the rope he passed to me and we started hauling on the sail. But as the cloth caught the wind, I cried out in pain and disbelief. The rope just *stopped,* in my hands, as if I was trying to drag a building. I'd never known wind could be so strong.

"*Pull!*" yelled Rourke. I gritted my teeth and pulled. The rope rasped against my palms. My sneakers squeaked against the wet deck. Nothing happened. I heard Rourke curse.

I risked a glance at the wave and gave a strangled moan of dread. It was rising higher and higher, a skyscraper that was about to topple over onto us. And as we were forced up its side, we were leaning further and further over. I started to slide across the deck. The mast tipped lower and lower until the sail almost seemed to be touching the water. Any second, we would roll over and then the wave would crash down on top of us.

"When the wind eases for a second," growled Rourke. He wrapped the rope around his forearms to give him a better grip and I did the same. "Ready...."

The deck tilted even further and I slid again. There was nothing but water wherever I looked, now: the sea on one side as we were tipped towards it, the wave towering over us on the other. It felt like we were trapped in a tunnel of water that was about to crush us.

"*Ready....*" yelled Rourke over the wind.

I found my footing. I looked down and my stomach lurched. I was standing on the rail: we were so close to tipping over, it had almost become the floor.

The wind dropped a little, as if catching its breath. "*Now!*" yelled Rourke.

I pulled. I pulled like I've never pulled in my life, until my arms felt as if they were going to be torn out of their sockets. Next to me, Rourke had gritted his teeth and was almost snarling at the storm, the muscles of his back standing out through his shirt. We *heaved....*

And at last the sail came around. The boat righted itself, swung into the wind and began climbing the wave. But it was growing so fast: we were climbing a hill, then a steep hill, then what felt like a vertical cliff. The prow swayed alarmingly and it felt as if we were going to fall backwards to our doom. Rourke hauled on the rope, making tiny adjustments. All I could see in front of us was sky....

And then we were over it and the whole boat jolted as we slammed back into the water. My stomach shot up into my mouth: now we were hurtling down the far side of the wave into the trough. Water crashed over the prow, soaking us, and then we were working our way up the side of the next wave.

And, breathless and soaking, the wind screaming in my ears, I realized *that was just the first wave.* We had to ride each one to stay afloat. If we messed up even once, we'd tip over and be smashed to pieces. And the storm might last for hours.

"Next one!" yelled Rourke. "Ready?" And he grabbed my hand and squeezed it.

"Ready," I managed, terrified. And squeezed back.

For an hour, we swung the boat left and right, meeting each wave as it hit us. No other sailor would have stood a chance but Rourke had an instinctual feel for the wind: even as we crested one wave, he was already gazing off into the distance, figuring out where the next one would come from, getting us heading towards it even before it had rumbled out of the darkness.

But the storm was so strong. It blasted us with rain until my clothes felt like they were made of lead. It scoured my face with saltwater until my skin burned. It pulled at my hair so hard I thought it was going to rip out by the roots. It ate away at our endurance until our muscles were limp and useless, until our grip failed and our legs refused to carry us anymore.

But each time it got too much, Rourke was there. When I slipped, he'd throw an arm around my waist and brace me against him until I got my footing again. When my grip failed, he took up the slack while I rubbed the life back into my hands. When I was cold and shaking and about to pass out, he folded me into his arms and warmed me with his body.

"Just keep going," he said in my ear. His hot breath felt *so good* there after the merciless wind. "You're doing great. We just have to keep going until it blows itself out."

I nodded weakly. I wasn't sure how much longer I could go on but if he wasn't quitting, I wasn't quitting.

There was a creak from above. We both looked up to see the mast bending.

"*Shit!*" said Rourke. He quickly ran to loosen the rope but the sail kept straining against the wind, even when the rope was slack in his hands. *What the hell?*

Then a flash of lightning lit up the sky and we saw it: the knot he'd had to tie to fix the rope was jammed in an eyelet. We couldn't slacken the sail and the wind was building and building. The mast bent like a bow and a sickening vibration ran through the whole boat.

"Move!" bellowed Rourke. "It's going to—"

There was a tortured groan and then a *crack* and the mast snapped off. As it fell, the wind seized the sail and carried the whole thing across the deck.

Right towards me.

Rourke reached me a half second before the mast. He shoved me out of the way and then tried to scramble aside himself, but there was no time. The mast bounced, spun and—

It hit him square in the chest, sending him flying over the rail.

And then both he and it disappeared into the storm and I was alone on the boat.

55

HANNAH

For several seconds, I stood absolutely still, staring open-mouthed at the spot where Rourke had been standing. After everything we'd been through...he was just *gone,* quicker than I could blink.

Without a mast, the boat slewed off course and began to spin. A wave crashed over the rail and slammed into my back. Suddenly, I was on my face, choking and flailing, submerged beneath it. When it fell away, I managed to get to my hands and knees but then I just looked wildly around at the waves, the sky, the lightning—

I had no idea what to do. I was adrift on a crippled boat. Even Rourke couldn't sail this thing, with the mast gone, and Rourke was—

I drew in a low, shaky breath. *Rourke was—*

I felt something tighten around me as I inhaled. I looked down to see the rope that was tied around my waist.

The rope! Rourke had been tied on too!

I scrambled across the boat to where I'd seen him disappear. No sign of him in the water. And I couldn't see the rope, either, in the near-darkness. Had it snapped?

Then lightning split the sky and I glimpsed it, drawn tight against the hull. The far end disappeared beneath the black water. God, he was somewhere under the boat!

I threw myself full-length on the deck, grabbed the rope with both hands, and started pulling. Immediately, I could feel the weight of him on the other end. He was still attached...but it was like he was just a dead weight, being dragged behind us as the boat was tossed and spun. Was he unconscious? *Dead?*

I hauled him in inch by inch, the wet rope creaking and straining under my fingers. The boat was spinning like a carousel now, and lurching randomly as it did it. Waves crashed over me, and I had to hook an arm around the rail to keep from being washed sideways along the deck. "Come on, Rourke," I muttered aloud. "Come on!"

And then there was a sickening jolt, as if the weight I was pulling had hit something hard. His body had just caught on the keel.

Shuddering, I hauled him in faster. And then he broke the surface right beneath me, coughing and spluttering. There was a cut on his forehead and he was holding his side but he was alive, just too groggy to swim.

I *heaved.* But as he rose out of the water, he started to weigh his full weight: all that solid muscle plus his soaking wet clothes was way more than I could lift. "Rourke!" I yelled. "*Climb!*"

He slowly opened his eyes and focused on me. Then he started to haul himself up the rope while I gritted my teeth and held on. At last, he managed to get a hand on the rail and the rope slackened: another second and it would have slipped through my aching hands. I helped him pull himself over the rail and we collapsed together on the deck. I hugged him close.

"Thank you," he rasped, still coughing up seawater.

He managed to raise himself on his elbows and looked around. Then he untied the ropes from our waists and pulled me to my feet.

"What now?" I yelled over the wind.

"Nothing else we can do out there," he shouted. "We get below and pray we can ride it out."

He grabbed me and pushed me to the door, then into the main room. As soon as we got inside, Yoyo flew into my arms. Then Rourke slammed the doors shut behind us and the wind noise dropped away. My ears suddenly started ringing: I hadn't realized just how loud the wind was until I got some relief from it. I started shaking. I hadn't realized how cold I was, either.

In some ways, though, it was worse inside. The boat was still spinning and rocking and, now that we couldn't see the sky or the waves, it was like being in a box being shaken by a giant. I picked up several new bruises before Rourke muscled me down on the floor and then sandwiched me against the wall, using his legs to wedge us in place. I suddenly understood why everything on board was so neatly packed away in cupboards: loose objects would be deadly, in a storm like this.

The boat began to tip more and more wildly. My weight would change and shift as the wall behind me became a floor, then went back to a wall. I knew that, any second, we'd go all the way over and then we'd be finished.

Rourke wrapped himself around me, using his body to cushion me from the hard wood. His warm chest was pressed to my front, his strong forearms cradled my shoulders and the small of my back, and his thighs were tight against mine. We were so close that all I could see was him and, however much the deck rolled and lurched under me, I felt utterly protected.

He looked deep into my eyes. "I'm sorry, lass," he said.

"Don't say that," I told him, a lump rising into my throat. "You did everything you could. You did so much!" How could he feel guilty? He'd lost everything because he helped me.

The boat tipped again. This time, the wall became a floor for several seconds, leaving me white-faced and gasping in panic, before it tipped back again. He hugged me tight. We stared into each other's eyes—

"I love you," he said.

Just like that, clear and true and certain. I gaped at him for a second and then crushed myself to him, locking my arms around his back, tears running down my cheeks.

The boat lurched again. The wall behind me became a floor and this time I could feel I was pressed hard against it. Rourke had to support his weight on his arms so that he didn't crush me: *God, we must be literally on our side.* And then we tipped *further.*

"We're going over!" snapped Rourke. "Just hang onto me!"

I clung onto him for dear life. Felt myself slide sideways along the wall....

I heard water rushing in... and then all the lights went out.

56

ROURKE

I kept my body wrapped protectively around Hannah for a second, until I was sure we weren't going to tip back. Then I started feeling around, getting my bearings. There's nothing more disorienting than being in a boat that's upside down. Luckily, I knew the *Fortune's Hope* so well, I could literally walk around her with my eyes closed. I just had to reverse everything in my head: if the hammock hook is *here* then the cupboard must be *here* and the flashlight will be—

I found it and turned it on. The white light reflected off Hannah's terrified face...and a slick of water that was spreading across what was now the floor. Even Yoyo recognized that was bad, and chirruped in fear.

"It's okay," I said, gathering them both into my arms. "We'll float for a good while." I could hear the storm raging above our heads. The longer we could stay sheltered in here, the better. But the water was already rising and Hannah was shaking from cold and fear. I had to get her warm.

"Get your clothes off," I told her, stripping off my shorts and shirt. As soon as she was down to her bra and panties, I picked her up and pulled her into the hammock. One advantage of hammocks: they don't care which way up the room is. I pulled her against me and let my body heat warm her. Yoyo cuddled up to our feet. The hammock swayed as waves tossed us around. Hannah warmed...but she didn't stop shaking. I could feel how scared she was.

So I did the only thing I could think of, even though it went completely against the grain.

I talked to her.

I told her about growing up in Scotland, watching the submarines leave the shipyard, and seeing the Navy parades through my town. I told her about my mam—*mom,* Hannah insisted—and pubs with log fires in the winter. We argued over whether Nebraska or Scotland had "proper" winters. I taught her about supporting my soccer team, Celtic, and that it was *Seltic,* not *Keltic.* She tried to convince me that they called their college sports teams *Cornhuskers* and it took a good while before I realized she wasn't kidding.

I told her that she reminded me of a mermaid. I ran my fingers through those long blonde locks and explained how I never got tired of doing that. I talked about her breasts and the curve of her hips and the ripeness of her ass. Her blue eyes and the effect they had on me, the way just a bare shoulder or calf or the scent of her made me crave her. First I tried to be poetic, which she loved, even though I was clumsy as all hell at it. Then I switched to the language of sailors, hot and crude and honest. And that seemed to work for her, too.

We talked for hours, focusing only on each other, shutting out the howl of the wind outside. It was the most I'd talked to anyone since before Edwards died. It gave me a taste of what I could have had, if my life had gone differently. Just a taste. Because even if I got her through the storm, even if we somehow reached land, she was still going to die. That bastard disease would take her and we no longer had the cure.

I gathered her into my arms and crushed her against me. But even as I did it, I felt the water begin to soak the fabric of the hammock. The boat was half full and it was rising fast. "We have to go," I said. "We don't want to get trapped when she goes down."

I found a waterproof dive bag and convinced Yoyo to jump inside.

Hannah grabbed Esme's diary and slipped that into the bag, too.

I took a last look around. I'd spent years of my life aboard the *Fortune's Hope*. People can't understand how captains feel about boats: they're more than a place we work, more than a home. She had her own personality, her own spirit. She'd kept me safe in a dozen different countries around the world and now she was going to the bottom, all thanks to Ratcher. I never thought I'd have to say goodbye to her. I always thought I'd be going down with her. But I couldn't stay with her *and* be with Hannah.

I grabbed the logbook and added it to the dive bag, then sealed it shut. "Ready?" I had to grunt it around the lump in my throat.

Hannah jumped as a crack of lightning split the air right outside the boat. The wind screamed and I saw her face pale at the thought of going out there. She shook her head, mouth moving as she tried to put her fear into words, but nothing came out. "I'm not *like* you," she said at last. "I'm not used to storms and the sea and people with guns."

"You're doing grand," I told her firmly, taking her into my arms. "You've faced more, this last week, than most people do in a lifetime."

She pressed her face to my shoulder. "I'm not *brave*," she insisted. "I'm not like you and Edwards and... and Carla. I only did that stuff because I had to. I was scared the whole time."

I blinked and then slowly pushed her back so I could look into her eyes. *Carla?* It slowly sunk in that this is where all that bollocks about her not being suitable for me came from. Well, that ended right now.

I grabbed her upper arms hard. "Hannah," I said chidingly. "Being scared and doing it anyway...that's what being brave *is*." And I leaned down and kissed her hard. Hard enough that she knew she was the bravest, the most *suitable* woman I'd ever met.

When I finally broke the kiss, Hannah blinked back tears and nodded. We took deep breaths and then dived down into the black water, our way lit by the flashlight. We swam through the doors to the deck, kicked our way up to the surface—

And emerged into hell.

57

ROURKE

Water slammed into my face, leaving me gasping and choking. It was so dark I could barely see and the pounding rain and ear-splitting scream of the wind made it impossible to get my bearings. I grabbed hold of Hannah and pulled her to me so we didn't get separated, then looked around.

A flash of lightning revealed the scene and my heart sank. It was worse than I'd feared. The storm hadn't died down at all. The waves were the size of houses and without a boat we were just insignificant specks to be lifted and then smashed down into the water. The wind was so strong you couldn't take a breath: turn towards it and it rammed its way into your lungs; turn away from it and there was no air at all. It was driving rain and spray horizontally, stinging our skin and stealing every ounce of warmth from our bodies.

Hannah was panting in fear as she clung to me. This was about a thousand times worse than when we'd been above deck. Ask any sailor: there's nothing scarier than being overboard in rough seas with the waves towering over you.

We needed something, anything, to help us keep our heads above water. I pushed Hannah over to the upturned hull of the *Fortune's Hope* and helped her scramble aboard. The boat was sinking but it would be a while before she finally slipped below the waves and we needed every minute we could get. I climbed up next to her and—

My hand caught on something. A box the size of my fist that shouldn't have been there. I squinted at it, then cursed when I realized what it was. A GPS beacon. When I saw that diver swimming away, after we'd battled the shark, he hadn't been sabotaging us: he'd been placing this. That's how Ratcher had kept finding us. If I'd only remembered to swim down and check the hull, instead of getting all dreamy-eyed about Hannah.... I pulled the thing free and hurled it into the ocean.

The waves were carrying the upturned hull high into the air and then smashing it brutally down: it was like trying to cling on to a raging bull. Worse, I could hear cracking sounds over the wind and I knew it wouldn't be long before the boat broke up. Waves broke over it, threatening to wash us into the water, and the wind did its best to tear us free.

I helped Hannah drape herself over the hull and spread-eagled her so that she was clinging on like a starfish, making herself as hard to dislodge as possible. But she was still shivering from the cold and I was still worried she'd be swept off. So I covered her body with mine, giving her my warmth, and sealing her to the wood. I opened the neck of the dive bag just a little to make sure Yoyo had air and then there was nothing I could do except put my lips to Hannah's ear, tell her how much I loved her and that it was going to be okay.

I had no idea what time it was: the sky was so dark, it was impossible to tell. And I had no idea where we were: I knew the storm was carrying us with it, but there were no landmarks.

The sea wanted to claim me. It wet the wood under my fingers to make it slippery. It used the wind to claw at me, trying to lift me off Hannah and send me spinning into the waves. It soaked me with enough water that I felt I weighed a thousand tons, drove spray and rain down my throat until I coughed all the strength from my body. *It's time,* it whispered in my mind. *This is what you wanted.* To finally meet Edwards down in the darkness.

But I clung on. I clung on harder than I've ever held onto

anything in my life because if I went, she went. And I wasn't letting the sea get her. And for the first time in years, I didn't want it to end this way. I wanted a life on the water with her. Hell, I'd even take a life on the land, with her, and I never thought I'd say that about anybody.

The *Fortune's Hope* was as stubborn as me. For hours, it refused to sink. But the storm was merciless and my heart ached as I heard her beams begin to snap, a sound as intimate as bones breaking. She slowly slipped beneath the waves and I instinctively lunged beneath the surface down to grab hold of a rail or a rope. I had to save her, or go down with her—

But if I did that, I couldn't be with Hannah. I had to choose.

My fingers closed on empty water and I watched, chest constricting, as the *Fortune's Hope* disappeared down into the darkness. Then I swam for the surface. But as I grabbed hold of Hannah, the boat that had kept us safe for so long threw out one last gift: a ten foot section of her hull broke free and floated up to meet us.

I hauled Hannah aboard and we used it as a raft. As the wind howled and raged around us, we lay with our arms and legs wrapped around each other, clinging to each other for dear life.

And then, after God knows how many hours, the waves seemed to become a little less violent. The wind lost its howl and the rain eased and then stopped. The world lightened, beyond my closed eyelids, and my back started to feel warm.

We opened our eyes.

The sea was calming. The waves were settling and the clouds were beginning to break up. I could see an island in the distance.

We slumped on the raft in relief, taking deep lungfuls of air that was sweet and warm, not frozen and stinging. I opened the dive bag and Yoyo scrambled out and climbed up on Hannah's shoulder. It was evening, which meant we'd been in the storm an entire day. The sun was a glorious disc of molten copper, just sliding down into the sea. The best sunsets always come after a storm and this one was fantastic. For a moment, we just hugged and drank it in.

"What now?" asked Hannah.

I thought about it... and tried not to let my face betray how bad our situation was. We had no water, no food and no one was looking for us. Our only chance was to make our way to land: we were drifting closer to the island, but I had no idea what was there—

I squinted. The shape of the island looked familiar. It was surrounded by large rocks, sticking out of the water like teeth....

Oh, bloody hell.

As if to confirm my suspicion, a fin split the water only twenty feet away. The storm had carried us all the way back to the island where we'd found the second clue. The island that was nothing but a barren rock, surrounded by more rocks that would smash us to pieces if we tried to land.

And the injured shark we'd left behind was already sniffing around our raft, hungry for vengeance.

I was at breaking point. Of all the places we could have been carried to by the storm! To have survived *that,* only to be dumped here. And the *Fortune's Hope* was gone forever. That filled me with a despair I couldn't explain, even to Hannah.

Water lapping at my feet made me look down. Our raft was a section of the hull and the planks were starting to loosen and come apart. Already, one side was riding low, water sloshing onto our legs. I gave it a half hour at most and then we'd be in the water with the shark.

58

ROURKE

When I turned to Hannah, I could see the same realization on her face that millions of sailors have come to through the ages. That awful certainty. "We're not going to make it, are we?" she whispered.

I didn't answer. I pulled her into my arms and sat with her in my lap, her back to my chest and my arms wrapped around her. The shark circled and then shot forward and rammed the raft. A piece the size of my head broke off and floated away.

I've never been one to quit but I didn't see any way out of this. I'd used every last trick to get through the storm and now I had nothing left.

The shark charged us again. This time, a crack opened up along the length of the wood: another good hit and we'd split in two.

I kissed the top of Hannah's head, looked up, and saw Edwards sitting cross-legged on the corner of the raft.

It was the first time I'd seen him since I told Hannah about his death. I'd thought that maybe he was gone. Part of me was disappointed because it meant I was still crazy. But most of me was relieved to see him. "I'm all out of ideas," I thought. "You got any?" I squeezed Hannah hard. "Because I'm not ready to go. Not anymore."

And then I froze because I realized I hadn't thought it. I'd said it out loud.

Hannah twisted around in my arms, glanced at the spot occupied by Edwards and then threw her arms around my neck and kissed me. I kissed her back, hard, tasting the seawater on her lips, sliding my hands over her bare shoulders. When I broke the kiss, the shark was circling back towards us for a final run.

And Edwards was looking meaningfully at it.

I blinked and frowned. "*What?*" I asked aloud. There was no time to be embarrassed.

He looked at me, then looked at the shark again. It was flicking its tail, building up speed.

"*What?!*" I gave him a glare. The shark was close, now. I could see the spear I'd landed in its back when it attacked the launch—

It suddenly clicked. I knew what Edwards was saying. *Oh, you crazy, brilliant bloody idiot.* It was exactly the sort of hare-brained, chance-in-a-million scheme he'd come up with. It might get me killed. Or it might just save us. The important thing was, there was a hope, however slim, that I could save her. And that was better than quitting.

Hannah was watching the shark approach, backing away from it across the raft. When she saw me stand up, she grabbed my leg. "What are you doing?!"

I reached down and pulled my dive knife out of its scabbard. "Going fucking fishing," I told her.

And I dived into the water.

59

HANNAH

I scrambled to the edge of the raft and stared down into the water in horror. *What the hell is he doing?*

The shark darted forward and Rourke had to dodge to avoid it. This wasn't like when he'd fought it before: he'd had a mask and air tank, then, and flippers to help him move faster. Now he had to squint through the water and he could only fight as long as he could hold his breath.

I winced as the shark attacked again. It didn't manage to get its jaws around Rourke but it knocked him out of the way and its head thumped against the underside of the raft. The crack split wide open. We were breaking up!

The shark went for Rourke a third time and this time he dodged and then grabbed the spear that stuck out of its back. He clung on, at the same time stabbing at it with his knife. Blood clouded the water, blocking out my view. The raft chose that time to finally break up. I scrambled onto the biggest piece, which was barely bigger than a coffin lid, and hugged Yoyo to my chest.

And then everything went quiet.

The water slowly turned crimson. I started to panic-breathe as I counted the seconds in my head. Too much time went by. *He should have surfaced by now.* I stared at the surface, bracing myself for a severed arm or leg to float up.

The shark suddenly broke the surface, right next to the raft, and I screamed. Then Rourke emerged behind it, panting for air, and stabbing his knife down into it. The shark came to rest with its head on the raft, an inch from my knee. Its jaws snapped once, twice...and it went still.

Rourke was panting and exhausted. I couldn't decide if I wanted to hug him or kill him so I yelled instead. *"What the hell was all that for? Why did you—"*

He shook his head: he had no breath to explain. He grabbed the shark's tail and started to push. "Help me get it on the raft," he wheezed.

On the raft?! There wasn't enough room for both of us to lie on the raft. Why the hell....

But Rourke had never let me down yet. I slithered off the far side of the raft, grabbed hold of the shark's torso and pulled while Rourke pushed. It was so heavy we barely managed it. But eventually, we got it lying on the raft on its side. The raft was barely afloat under the thing and there wasn't an inch of space for us: Yoyo had to go back in the dive bag for his own safety.

"Okay," I said breathlessly. "Now *please explain* why we just did all that. You could have been killed!"

In answer, Rourke reached up and stabbed his dive knife into the shark's belly. Then he slashed right along its length. I screamed and turned away as everything in its stomach flooded out. But Rourke didn't back away. He shoved his hand in, groping for something.

When I dared to look again, Rourke was washing his hand off underwater. Then he held up what he was holding: the satellite phone the shark had swallowed, when we'd fought it on the launch.

I threw my arms around him and hugged him as he powered it on and lifted it to his ear.

~

The Coast Guard bundled us into a helicopter a little over an hour later. I sat next to Rourke, both of us wrapped up in a blanket. Yoyo nestled into my chest, his eyes just peeking over the top of the blanket. He'd been around boats his whole life but the sound and feel of a helicopter was new to him and he didn't let go of me until we landed at the Coast Guard station on Great Inagua.

Despite Rourke's protests, they insisted on dressing his wounds before they'd let him leave. He had a cut on his head, a suspected broken rib, and some fresh grazes from tussling with the shark. Like me, he'd picked up some bruises from being hurled around in the storm.

Then they turned to me. "Miss? Are you okay?"

I thought about it. It had been too long since I'd had an attack. I was due one anytime and this next one would likely kill me. But there was nothing they could do about it. The one thing that could save me, Katherine, and all the other women in my family was with Ratcher.

"Fine," I told the medic. "I'm fine."

By the time we got to Nassau, dawn was breaking. We headed down to McKinley's bar and borrowed a pair of binoculars from the bartender, who I learned was called Benny. The sun was turning the calm waters of the harbor to sparkling gold and it was clear enough that you could see for miles. Rourke pointed out the *Pitbull,* lying at anchor a mile or so offshore.

"She's riding low in the water," he said. "And he's posted guards. The treasure's still aboard."

I could just make out men with guns strutting around the deck. "So what do we do?" I asked.

He looked at me. "You stay here. I go and get the cure back." And he outlined his plan to me.

I felt my eyes bulge. "That's insane! Ratcher will kill you!" I shook my head. "It's too dangerous!"

Rourke pinned me in place with those deep blue eyes. His hand found my cheek, thumb brushing my lips. "That bastard's taken my boat," he said. "My treasure. But he's not taking you."

He leaned in and kissed me, slow and deep. His words had made a hot bomb detonate in my chest and the kiss turned the heat urgent: my hands grabbed at his shoulders and I clung to him. God, I loved this big, angry, Scottish seadog. But the way he kissed me scared the hell out of me. It was as if he was drinking me in, committing every press of my lips to memory.

He kissed me as if—

"R—Rourke?" My voice was shaking. I made him look at me. "*I need you to come back!*"

He nodded. But he wouldn't—couldn't—say the words I needed to hear. He couldn't promise. Before I could stop him, he was limping towards the rail that looked out over the sea.

"Rourke!" I called desperately.

But, stubborn as ever, he didn't turn around. And then he was diving over the rail and into the sea below. A few seconds later, I saw a faint shadow beneath the waves, swimming out towards Ratcher's boat. He was going on a damn suicide mission...*for me.* And I knew I might never see him again.

60

ROURKE

I swam a few feet below the waves, fast and silent. When I had to breathe, I twisted over and just barely broke the surface with my lips. Unless someone was looking in the exact right spot, I should be invisible.

My plan hinged on it being early. I figured Ratcher had probably dropped anchor the night before and the first thing he and his crew would have done would be to break out the beers and celebrate the find of the century. At this time in the morning, they'd still be sleeping it off. Even the men he'd posted as guards would be hungover...or they'd be bored and pissed off because they hadn't been allowed to join the fun, and that would make them sloppy.

But even if I was right, all that would only hold true for a little while. That's why I hadn't let myself get drawn into an argument with Hannah.

That, and the fact she was right to be worried. There was a very good chance I wasn't coming back from this one. Ratcher had upwards of twenty armed men. I had a knife. There are bad odds and then there's being plain stupid.

But I didn't have a choice. Hannah was dead if she didn't get that cure.

I saw the sea bed drop away beneath me. The *Pitbull* was anchored a good mile out: Ratcher was paranoid enough, with all that treasure on board, that he wanted some warning if he saw someone approaching from the shore. But it meant he was in deep water and that was a key part of my plan, too.

I surfaced beside his anchor chain and waited, looking up at the boat. A few seconds later, a cigarette butt came over the side and I heard a grumbled conversation: at least three men. As I'd hoped, the guards were resentful about having to be up and awake while the others slept. Instead of spreading out as they should, they'd gathered to moan and smoke.

I climbed the anchor chain, freezing each time I made the heavy links clank. But I made it over the rail and dropped silently to the deck without being seen. I risked a glance at McKinley's and saw a glint of sunlight on glass: Hannah was still up there, watching me. I waved in her direction but I had no way of knowing if she saw. Just the fact she was watching over me made me feel better, though.

I crept below deck...and stopped.

The room was a sea of snoring men. They'd drunk until they passed out and then just slept where they were: on the floor, slumped against lockers, lying across benches. Beer cans were everywhere. If my foot hit one, if I made the slightest noise....

The hardest thing for me is to walk slowly. I need to put my weight on my bad leg and then swing it quickly over to my good one. That's why I stalk around like I've got somewhere to be. But now I had to force myself to move at a snail's pace, gradually shifting my weight onto a foot, ready to freeze if the deck creaked. It was beyond agony. Before I'd gone six steps, I was sweating with the pain. But there was no other way to do it.

The room stank: unwashed bodies and stale beer, cigarette smoke and diesel fumes. Even this early in the morning, the air was warm and that didn't help.

I stopped. Ahead of me was the staircase I needed but four guys lay between me and it, so closely sardined that there wasn't an inch of floor visible...except where one guy had his hand behind his head, elbow out to the side. I'd have to step in that six-inch triangle formed by his arm, my toes right next to his ear. Worse, because they were right up against the wall, I'd have to use my injured leg.

This is without a doubt the stupidest thing you've ever done, I thought. If they woke and saw me, I was dead for sure. But Hannah had no other hope. And that meant I was doing it.

I gritted my teeth, stretched out my leg, and came down on my toes, right in the crook of the guy's arm. There was no room to put my heel down and spread the weight. It felt as if I'd put my toes down onto foot-long metal spikes and now I was forcing them—

Up

Into

My

Calf

I froze there for a second, teeth grinding so hard my jaw ached. I wanted to curse and scream but I couldn't. And now I knew it would get worse. I had to put all my weight on my bad leg and swing the other leg over the sleeping guys and onto the stairwell. I started to lift my back foot and—

I stopped. My brain's self-defense mechanism had kicked in. It wouldn't let me do it: not *all my weight.* Not on my toes, not slowly and silently. It would hurt too goddamn much.

I took a deep, silent breath and gathered myself. I thought of Hannah's soft golden hair and the way her pale skin gleamed when it was wet. I thought of those blush-pink lips and the way she opened under me, nervous and eager at the same time—

I stepped.

Every individual fiber in my muscles *screamed* as if they were being plunged into boiling water and then scrubbed with a wire brush. I wanted to be sick. I wanted to cry. That's how bad the pain was.

In my mind, I put my arms around Hannah, pulled her close, and buried my face in her shoulder. I focused on the feel of her, the smell of her....

My good leg came down on the first step of the stairwell. I took the weight off my bad leg and forced myself not to cry out in joy.

I took a second to take stock. My bad leg was agony, too painful to even put down, and I wondered if I'd permanently damaged something. I had to use my arms to support me as I struggled down the stairs. But it had worked: everyone was still asleep.

Downstairs, I mouthed a silent curse. The treasure was piled all around me in gleaming mountains, like Aladdin's goddamn cave. It sunk in just how rich Ratcher was going to be, even after he gave his crew their cut. There must be hundreds of millions of dollars' worth there. I reached into a crate brimming with gold coins. Just one fistful would fill my bank account....

I stopped with my fingers just brushing a doubloon. If I dropped one, or they jingled in my pocket, I was dead.

There was only one item that mattered. I searched the entire hold for the stone and the bottle taped to it: nothing. Ratcher must still have it in his pocket. Unless he'd thrown it away. *Don't even think that,* I told myself.

I sought out the locker where they kept the explosives. While I was old-school and stuck to dynamite, Ratcher had all the latest gear. It took me twenty minutes to figure out how it all worked, but eventually I got it done.

I crept up on deck and saw Ratcher near the other end of the boat, sprawled in a chair. His head was thrown back, his snores splitting the air.

I began to move towards him. My plan was simple: I'd confront him and tell him how I'd rigged the hold to blow. All I had to do was press the button on the remote detonator in my pocket and the whole bottom of the boat would be destroyed. The boat would take a while to go down but the treasure would drop straight out and sink to the sea bed. And the water was deep enough, here, that it would be out of anyone's reach. But all he had to do was give me the cure and I'd walk away and leave him with the treasure.

Ratcher wasn't dumb. He'd take the deal. And then I could get the cure back to Hannah and—

The muzzle of a gun pressed painfully against my scalp from behind.

Shit.

61

HANNAH

I watched through the binoculars as they searched him and took something small from his pocket: the remote detonator for the explosives, I guessed. Then they pushed him over to Ratcher and he staggered: his leg seemed even worse than usual, he didn't seem to be able to use it at all.

Then Ratcher had two of his men hold Rourke's arms, so he couldn't fight back, and he started to hit him with his ham-sized fists.

I lowered the binoculars, unable to watch anymore. I knew calling the police would be useless. By the time they responded and boarded the boat, Rourke's body would be at the bottom of the ocean. It was over.

Unless...

I looked at the sea and my stomach twisted. After everything I'd been through with Rourke, my fear had subsided a little. But diving with Rourke close to islands was one thing. Swimming out into the vast ocean...that was my worst nightmare. It would be exactly like when I lost my mom.

I looked at the rail Rourke had dived over: that was the fastest way to the water and I needed to be fast, now. They'd kill him, if I didn't stop them. *How the hell am I going to stop them?*

Time to think about that later. If I didn't go right now, he had no hope at all.

I kicked off my shoes, t-shirt, and jeans and then ran towards the rail. I ran because it meant less time to chicken out.

Ten steps away. The ocean below was endless, the *Pitbull* just a white blob in the distance. *I can't!*

I have to.

Seven steps and I started to falter. The drop was much, much further than I'd expected: twenty feet, at least. I gulped and slowed, glancing at the *Pitbull.*

Without the binoculars, Ratcher's men were dots, swarming like flies around the larger tan dot that was Rourke. It was twenty to one.

I had to save him.

I let out a wordless, desperate cry and picked up speed again. Three steps from the rail, it became real. *I'm actually going to do it. I'm actually—*

And then I jumped over the rail and flew out into space, arms pinwheeling. *Oh Christ, what have I done?!*

62

HANNAH

I plunged into the water and the sea forced its way up my nose and down my throat. I surfaced coughing and choking, just in time for the first wave to hit me in the face. The waves hadn't looked all that big from up on McKinley's terrace. Now, they rose far above my head: I couldn't even see the *Pitbull*. And I could feel the currents pulling at me, dragging me where *they* wanted to go.

I gave a strangled gasp. I'd been in the sea plenty, since this all started. But this was the first time I was out here, in the open ocean, all on my own.... And suddenly, the fear was rising up inside me, stealing my breath and numbing my muscles. It felt exactly like it had that night I lost my mom. The sea was so big and I was *so small*....

I twisted around. The shore was right there, a short swim away. *I don't have to be out there, this time. There's no current. I can choose to be safe.* I took one stroke towards it. A second.

Then I slowed. Stopped. Floated.

My man was out there, on that boat.

This is crazy. You can't do this! You're not brave like him!

Or maybe Rourke was right. Maybe bravery wasn't a lack of fear. Maybe it was being scared—

I sucked in a long, shaky breath and turned around to face the open sea.

Being scared and doing it anyway.

I threw myself forward, smacking into the next wave and then climbing it as it lifted me skyward. I'd barely crested that one when the next one started bearing down on me. It broke in my face and I coughed and choked, blinking salt water from my eyes and frantically trying to climb the next one. The panic started to rise. *Oh God, what am I doing?*

But then, as I reached the peak of that wave, I caught a glimpse of the *Pitbull* in the distance. And I saw the tiny smudge of tan I knew was Rourke.

I drew in a deep breath and wrestled the panic down. He was out there and I was going to get to him. One wave at a time.

That's how I did it. I didn't let myself think about how huge the ocean was, or how deep the water beneath me was, or how no one knew where I was, if I got into trouble. I just climbed the next wave, and the next wave, and the next wave. Until, shoulders aching and legs burning, I finally reached the *Pitbull*. When I glanced over my shoulder at the shore, I couldn't believe how far away it was, or how big the waves were. *I swam that?!*

I turned back to the *Pitbull*. I couldn't see anyone keeping watch on the *Pitbull*. Shouts and cheers from the far end of the boat told me they were all gathered in a crowd and my stomach twisted as I thought about what that might mean for Rourke. *I'm coming for you,* I thought.

I had no weapon. No plan. I thought for a second. *What would Rourke do?* Get aboard the boat. *How?* Climb up the anchor chain.

I swam around until I found it and then got my arms around it and tried to climb. God, how did Rourke *do* this? I hadn't climbed a rope since school gym class and the chain was wet and slippery, with steel links that dug into my palms. I let out a litany of curses as I clambered ungracefully up it. The only thing that stopped me falling was that I knew I'd make a noise if I fell and Ratcher's men would come running.

I rolled over the rail and landed, dripping and exhausted, on the deck. Everyone seemed to be on the upper deck. I decided to creep up there and see if I could grab a gun, and then try to force them to let Rourke go.

I crept up the stairs, slowly stuck my head around the corner and—

They were all clustered at one side of the upper deck. They'd found a piece of board and three of Ratcher's men were standing on one end, weighing it down, so that the rest of it could extend out over the water. And standing at the far end, hands tied behind his back, was—

My chest constricted in fear. His face was swollen and bloodied where they'd beaten him. His injured leg seemed to have failed him completely: he was barely able to stand. And now the bastards were making him walk the plank. I thought about drowning like that: your hands tied, unable to swim, seeing the surface rise away from you as you fell down and down...I couldn't imagine a worse way to go.

Ratcher was leaning out along the plank, prodding Rourke in the back with—God, he was using Rourke's own sword on him! The fear was joined by a dark, incandescent hatred. I wasn't going to let him do it. Not to my man.

Ratcher was only six paces away, his back turned to me. In the back pocket of his tan shorts, I could see a square bulge: I had to take a gamble that that was the detonator he'd taken off Rourke. I took a deep breath and sprinted out of the shadows. Heads turned towards me but Ratcher's men were too surprised at seeing a dripping wet woman in her underwear to react quickly. I reached Ratcher and shoved a hand into his pocket. He twisted away from me as he realized what was happening and for a second my hand was pressed tight against cool, unpleasant flesh. Then I pulled my hand out and snatched the thing to my chest.

I was in such a panic, I almost dropped it. Then I had to figure out how it worked and Ratcher was reaching for me, trying to grab it. His men were surrounding me, blocking my view of Rourke. There was a red button under a transparent cover. I flipped up the cover, put my thumb over the button—

"*Stop!*" I yelled.

And everyone did. They froze, their eyes locked on the button.

I stood there, heart pounding, staring into Ratcher's piggy eyes. His hand was an inch from the detonator. He slowly pulled it back. The men who'd been pushing in around me stepped back. I was almost as shocked as they were. *Oh God, what am I doing?*

"Rourke!" I called in a ragged voice.

The crowd parted and I saw him, still on the plank. He stared at me with a mixture of disbelief and that familiar anger, furious that I'd put myself at risk for him...but then he gave a rueful shake of his head and a big, relieved sigh. "I told you about the explosives down below," he told Ratcher. "If she presses that, the treasure's gone forever."

Ratcher sucked in air through his teeth, his face slowly turning scarlet.

"All we want is that stone you took," said Rourke. "You give us that, we walk away. You can keep the damn treasure."

Ratcher glared at him, then at me, as if he was running through all the grisly ways he wanted to kill us. Then he reached into another pocket and pulled out the stone. My lungs slowly filled: until that moment, I'd been worried that he'd tossed it overboard. He must have figured that it had some value, even if he didn't know what. He stared at the stone...then nodded.

Very slowly, Rourke started to move towards me. Everyone was on edge. The sight of my thumb on the button was holding them back, but I knew things could change in a heartbeat. We didn't trust them and they probably didn't trust us....

Rourke held out his bound wrists and one of the crew sliced through the rope with a knife, freeing him. Rourke motioned me to start walking back towards the stairs and I did so, keeping my eyes on him and trusting him to watch for threats behind me.

He drew level with Ratcher and held out his hand for the cure. Ratcher scowled at him and then slapped the stone into his palm. But he didn't let Rourke's hand go. He leaned in close, the rolls of fat on his neck bulging, and hissed something in Rourke's ear....

Just for that second, he blocked Rourke's view of me. I stepped back—

Two men grabbed my arms from behind. I automatically held the detonator above my head, trying to keep it away from them, but they started pulling my arms down.

Rourke pulled away from Ratcher but now more men grabbed *him. No!* It was all going wrong!

One of the guys holding me grabbed my wrist in two hands and twisted in opposite directions. I grunted in pain and the detonator danced through my fingers, almost falling. I grabbed it again but now my thumb wasn't over the button and that gave the men confidence.

"Fucking grab it!" yelled Ratcher.

More hands grabbed my elbows and dragged my hands down. I strained upward, trying to keep the little box out of their reach but more men were running over to me. Three, *four* pairs of hands were on my arms now. As they muscled my hands down to chest height, I pulled the detonator into my chest, bending and wrapping myself around it like a child protecting their favorite toy—

"*Press it!*" yelled Rourke.

I looked at him in horror. The explosives were a *threat.* A bluff. I hadn't thought we'd ever— I looked down at my feet. They were *right there,* one deck below me....

"*Press it!*" yelled Rourke again. "Or they'll kill us both!"

I took a deep breath, closed my eyes...and pressed the button.

63

ROURKE

I remember the deck heaving under my feet. I remember the sensation of flying through the air. Even before the explosion, I wasn't in a good way: my leg was still in even more pain than normal, Ratcher's beating had covered me in fresh bruises and my cracked rib felt like it had opened right up. So when I landed on my side on the hard wooden deck, it really, *really* hurt.

But I struggled to my knees, wincing in pain. Hannah. Where was Hannah?!

I spotted her lying a dozen paces away: alive, thank God. The upper deck seemed intact: everyone had been sent flying when the explosion rocked the boat and there was smoke pouring from below, but no one seemed hurt. The boat was going down, though. Already, the deck was starting to tilt. As Ratcher's men came to their senses, they started running for the rail and jumping overboard to escape.

The cure. Where's the cure? I'd had it in my hand when the explosion went off, but Ratcher had had his sweaty paw on it, too. I glanced around frantically. *There!* Lying on the deck. All I had to do was grab it, get Hannah, jump overboard and—

The stone started to slide away from me as the deck tilted. I threw myself forward and scrambled after it on my hands and knees, but it was picking up speed. If it went over the side, it was gone for good, just like the treasure. I got to my feet and stumbled forward but then the boat shook as more water rushed in below, and I went down hard. My eyes bulged as the stone slid away from me, straight towards the rail—

It hit one of the vertical supports and rebounded like a hockey puck, coming to rest only a few feet away. I let out a long sigh of relief and crawled towards it—

My world exploded into pain as Ratcher's boot hit me in the chest.

64

HANNAH

I'd been sprawled on my back since the explosion, my ears ringing. I seemed to be uninjured except for my left leg: there was a sharp pain there. Maybe I'd fractured a bone.

I lifted my head just in time to see Rourke scramble after the cure and Ratcher kick him in the chest. I tried to get to my feet but that made the pain in my leg worse. Weird: it didn't feel like a fracture.

I struggled to my feet, using the rail to brace myself. No one seemed to be looking at me. Ratcher's men were mostly abandoning ship. Ratcher was entirely focused on Rourke: he wasn't giving him a chance to get up, kicking him again and again. Rourke was trying to roll away, a hand on his side to protect his injured rib. Then Ratcher snatched the dive knife from the scabbard on Rourke's ankle. *He's going to kill him! I have to help him!*

Then I saw it: Rourke's sword, lying underneath a table. Ratcher must have dropped it when the explosion went off. I had to get it to Rourke!

Just as I started towards it, I saw the cure. It was still precariously close to the rail. If the boat tilted again, there was nothing to stop it falling overboard. But the cure and the sword were in two different directions....

I looked at Rourke. He was scrambling backwards, trying to buy time. Ratcher was advancing, brandishing the dive knife. Rourke kept trying to get to his feet but his bad leg just wouldn't hold him. And he had nothing to defend himself with.

He needs his sword! Now!

Mind made up, I staggered across the deck towards the sword. But after just a few steps, the pain in my leg blossomed and changed.

My leg wasn't fractured at all.

My leg buckled under me and I fell to my knees in agony. My calf turned to boiling, molten iron, shot through with lightning. I knew what this was. *No! God, not now! He needs me!*

I tried to shuffle forward on my knees. The sword was only ten feet away. But the pain was seething up through the muscles of my legs, every one swelling and straining with unimaginable heat, blistering my flesh from the inside out. I screamed and collapsed on my stomach.

This was it. I knew it. The pain was so much stronger: already, I was sweating and panting, eyes bulging with it. The idea of this spreading through my whole body was terrifying: my heart wouldn't be able to take it. And if I died, I couldn't help Rourke.

I looked across at the fight. Rourke was dodging and rolling, panting with the pain in his ribs each time he moved. He was using his arms to fend off vicious slashes from Ratcher and I winced as the knife sliced red lines across his forearms.

I turned back to the sword. Tried to bring a knee up under me so I could push myself forward. But moving just made the pain spread up through my legs and into my lower torso. I cried out again: I could actually feel the muscles locking tight, reacting to a nervous system gone haywire. My hamstrings were straining, the muscle fibers determined to rip themselves loose from the cartilage. I sobbed and choked, fighting the pain, trying to move my legs. But the slightest attempt to contract a muscle made the agony double.

I looked at Rourke. Ratcher had him pinned to the deck and was trying to stab down with the knife. Rourke was holding Ratcher's wrists, the point of the knife hovering an inch from his chest.

I looked at the sword and scowled. If I couldn't use my legs I'd use my arms, damn it.

I stretched out, clawed at the deck, and hauled myself along, letting out shuddering breaths as my legs were dragged, every jolt and scrape threatening to make me pass out. I moved six inches at a time: *left arm, right arm, pull....*

The pain rose up through my belly, up to my lungs. It felt like someone had thrust their hands inside my chest and was crushing the delicate balloons in their fists, squeezing the air from them. Then, to my horror, it reached my heart. It had been hammering but suddenly I felt my heartbeats stutter and.....

...pause. My eyes bulged. I was close enough to the sword now that I could see my own face in the shining scabbard. I'd gone deathly pale: not white but *gray.* The sweat was pouring off me but I kept clutching at the deck with my fingernails. *Left arm. Right arm. Pull.* My heart was beating but in short, rapid flurries, each pulse sending pain ringing through my body.

My vision blurred with tears. The pain flooded up through my shoulders and biceps, turning my arms to hooks and then my fingers to claws. It felt as if my flesh had been flayed away and I was scraping at the deck with raw bone. I'd never known anything could hurt this much. *Left arm! Right arm! Pull!* My vision was darkening. I couldn't go on any further. I was going to—

My fingers brushed metal. I grabbed the scabbard and pulled it to me. Then I twisted onto my side. The movement sent pain rocketing up my spine. The muscles of my back were locking so hard, I could hear vertebra click and pop.

Rourke was flat on his back, the dive knife pricking at his throat as Ratcher tried to push it home. He was staring at me, his face distended in horror at what he could see me going through.

I summoned up all my strength and hurled the sword. The throw used every bit of my body: my arms, my back, even my legs. And the pain fought back hard. It took control of my body completely: every muscle started to spasm, my mouth opening in a scream but my lungs no longer able to work. As the pain increased, my heart rate rose with it until the pounding of it filled my ears and the beats blurred into one continuous sound. But every few seconds, there'd be sickening nothingness as it locked up and missed a beat.

I couldn't move. I couldn't speak. And I could hear myself dying.

65

ROURKE

Thie point of the dive knife circled and dipped over my throat, the morning light glinting off the metal. Stopping it plunging into me was taking everything I had and, gradually, I was losing the battle. Ratcher was leaning forward, putting his weight into it, and the more I strained to push his hands away, the more my ribs burned and my chest ached. I had a feeling he'd really done some damage, with all that kicking.

The knife began to slowly sink, its point pricking the skin of my throat.

Something thumped into my side with a clatter of metal. I glanced down to see my sword.

I pushed the knife with all my might and then snatched one hand away to draw my sword. The knife started to come back down but then I stabbed and Ratcher had to jump back or my blade would have sunk right into his stomach.

I had to use the rail to pull myself to my feet. I could barely stand, between my leg and my ribs. But I was up. "Alright," I muttered. "Alright, you fucker."

I advanced on him, panting and staggering, one hand on my ribs. I was a mess but I know how to use a sword. Every time he stabbed with the knife, I was there to block it. I drove him back, back...and then I managed to hook the knife out of his hand and it clattered to the deck. He reached down and grabbed at something: the knife, I presumed. I brought the point of the sword to his neck, pinning him between it and the rail.

"*Wait!*" he snapped. Then, "Look."

Not moving the sword a millimeter, I looked at what he had in his hand. It wasn't the knife. He'd grabbed the stone. *Shit!*

"Thought it was to do with rocks, at first," said Ratcher. "Maybe evidence of oil, or diamonds, and you were going to make a deal with some big mining company. But it's *her*." He looked across the deck and when I followed his gaze, my heart clenched tight: Hannah was lying on the deck, her spine arched and straining, her mouth open in a silent scream. "She's dying, isn't she? This'll save her."

"*Yes,*" I growled. And held my hand out for it.

But his lip twisted in a scowl. And I saw too late that this was about more than just revenge for the fortune I'd cost him, more than just our rivalry, even. This was about Hannah liking me, not him. Maybe about *all* women not liking him.

"Fuck you," said Ratcher. And threw the stone.

I raised the sword and brought the pommel down hard on his forehead. He went limp and slid to the deck but my attention was on the stone as it fell through the air. I lunged forward, arm outstretched, but I wasn't close enough—

The stone hit the water and sank towards the bottom of the sea.

66

ROURKE

I wasted time. Three beats of my heart, the enormity of it flooding through me.

Then, gasping and wincing in pain, I climbed up onto the rail.

Behind me, I heard Hannah rasp *"No!"* And I knew she was right. Even if I was at full strength, this would be a bad idea. *If* I could catch the stone, by the time I got it, it would be deep. Far deeper than would be safe to free dive. With my leg barely working and my ribs broken, it was suicide.

I didn't care. My only regret was that I didn't have time to kiss her goodbye.

I dived off the rail and plunged into the water, my eyes searching for the stone. I couldn't see it, at first: I had to just swim like crazy and pray that I had the spot right. The fear was rising in my chest: it was already out of sight and dropping fast towards the same bottomless pit the treasure had sunk to.

But it could only fall. I could power my way down. I aimed myself straight down and *kicked*, clamping my arms to my sides to make myself as streamlined as possible. My injured leg was a solid mass of pain, muscles swollen and throbbing, and every time I kicked the movement hammered metal spikes into the tissue. But I wasn't giving up.

There! I could see it in the distance. I was catching up to it...but too slowly. Already, the water was getting darker and colder, the black stone becoming difficult to make out. I could feel my shattered ribs moving as if kneaded by invisible hands and it was agony. I knew it was the water pressure crushing my chest. I couldn't go much deeper.

There was one thing I could do. My buoyancy was trying to draw me up to the surface and that was slowing me down. To catch the stone, I had to get rid of the air.

I blew it out in a stream of bubbles, feeling my lungs contract. Immediately, I felt gravity take me. I picked up speed, the stone drawing tantalizingly close. I stretched one arm out in front of me. I was so close that I could feel its wake...but not close enough for my hand to close on it. I was gaining, but only an inch for every ten feet we descended. And we were dangerously deep now: well over a hundred feet and going down fast...and I had no air.

Below me was blackness. The sunlight from above couldn't penetrate that far. I could barely make out the tumbling stone, had to just keep kicking and trust that it was there. My mind started to go hazy and sleepy and I knew, on some level, that my brain was being starved of oxygen. Worse, my chest and lungs felt...weird. I had no idea what damage Ratcher had done with his kicking, but something wasn't right.

I kicked faster, faster, my body straining for speed. But the deeper I went, the more my mind relaxed. There was blackness all around me, now, and the water hugged me, cold and tight. It hurt my ribs but it was an embrace like no other. One I'd been waiting years for....

The sea had me. Just as it was always meant to be.

I kicked on and on, knowing what I'd find. And finally, my fingers brushed something. Not the stone. A hand. It clasped mine.

I stared into Edwards' eyes.

I was dimly aware that I was still swimming, that I was descending and he was keeping pace with me. But it didn't feel like that. It felt as if we were standing still in the blackness.

I'd heard his voice plenty of times since he died. I'd even answered: hell, I'd had whole conversations. But that was up on the surface. I'd never visited him down here, where he now lived. Here, my lips didn't have to move and I could hear him just fine despite the water between us. And here, I could stop talking to him about gold and McKinley's and working on the boat. I could say what I'd been wanting to say all along.

I'm sorry.

Edwards hugged me tight, wrapping me in an embrace even tighter than the ocean's. And I felt my eyes go hot and then I was sobbing like a bairn. I don't know how long he held me like that. I just know that it was enough.

He moved back and I reached for him: I didn't want him to go. But he just looked at me and then looked up to the surface, towards sunlight and golden hair and an accent like sweet, fresh, country air. A place he no longer belonged.

Then he took my hand, stretched my arm out into the darkness, and closed my fingers. I felt something hard and stared down at my hand. When I looked at Edwards again, he was gone.

And suddenly I was swimming straight down into the black, the stone in my clenched fist. The hazy, slow feeling lifted and I stopped and looked around.

I was *deep*. Deeper than I'd ever been, without breathing equipment. And I had no air.

I turned tail and kicked for the surface as fast as I could. My chest felt as if an elephant was sitting on it and my ribs were being crushed by a tightening ring of iron. Things were moving in there, things that shouldn't move. I could taste blood. Something was very, very wrong.

I kicked hard but I'd gotten rid of my buoyancy so every foot had to be earned. I started using my arms as well, clawing at the water. Already, my lungs were screaming at me to take a breath. My mouth wanted to open, to suck down a cool refreshing lungful of seawater, and it took all my willpower to resist.

Above me, I could see it getting lighter. But I still had a good way to go and now I was starting to see spots in front of my eyes. As I rose,

I felt the fear begin to swell and leap inside me. Needing to breathe but not being able to: it's a primal fear you can't fight. But panic would drain what scraps of oxygen I had left even faster.

The water was definitely lighter, now, but my pace was slowing. My arms and legs felt like lead and my lungs were on fire. But if I was going to reach the surface, I couldn't let the fear win. I had to think about—

The scent of her hair when she passed me in the narrow gangway—

The way her breasts moved under the sweater I gave her—

The water-slick curves of her body as she sat on that rock, singing. I remembered the song, every word burned into my memory. My heartbeat slowed. I kicked and clawed and rose towards the light and—

I gulped in air as I broke the surface, eyes screwed shut against a dazzling sun. I filled and emptied my lungs three times before I even opened them and it took another few breaths before my brain had enough oxygen to think. Something was wrong with my breathing. Inhaling should feel good but it *hurt,* a dull pain followed by a sharp one that doubled me over in the water. And instead of my strength coming back, it seemed to be fading.

I was dying.

I gritted my teeth. *No time for that now.* I'd surfaced not far from the *Pitbull,* which was listing badly and going down fast. The water was already halfway to the upper deck. I swam aboard and then climbed the stairs—God, even that was an effort. I was weak and shaky and my vision was blurring.

I found Hannah, staggering towards her as if I was drunk. She was horribly pale and her face was wet with tears. When I pressed my fingers to her throat, her pulse was faster than I could count and kept giving out entirely for long seconds.

I tore the pill bottle away from the stone and uncapped it. A thick, oily black liquid. It seemed insane that this could do anything. We didn't even know what it *was.* But we were long past the point of playing it safe.

I lifted her head, opened her jaw and poured in the whole bottle, then made sure she swallowed. She coughed and choked, her lips coated in the stuff, but she kept it down. I laid her head gently down and took her hand.

And wavered, and nearly collapsed on top of her. I coughed and blood splattered onto the deck.

I slumped down next to her on my back, my hands going to my throat. I was on the surface, in clean, sweet air.

But I couldn't breathe.

67

HANNAH

I was in hell. I couldn't see beyond a blue sky blurred by tears. I couldn't move, couldn't think. Every muscle was strained beyond its limits, every nerve ending close to burning out. Everything was pain. The world was jagged slivers of glass and I was being pushed through it faster and faster, powered by my racing heart.

I was aware of Rourke's hand sliding into the mass of blonde hair behind my head, because it felt good. Then I was aware of him lifting my head because every tiny movement of my spine felt like the bones were being ground away with power tools.

A bottle pressed against my lips. *The* bottle. The contents glugged down my throat. It tasted of the olive oil I'd used to mix it but there was a sharp, metallic tang, too, like licking a coin.

My heart thumped harder and faster, deafening inside my head, and the skipped beats were coming more and more often. My veins throbbed and ached as if about to burst. I knew it wouldn't work. Even if my ancestor's story was true, we'd left it far too late. Nothing could work in time to—

It stopped. Not instantly but with such breathtaking suddenness that it felt that way. It felt like an army surrendering, one soldier throwing down his gun and then the action spreading through the ranks, moving in a wave. My muscles went limp one by one, my body loose and floppy on the deck. Almost immediately, there was a new wave of pain and I tensed...but it was just the muscles twitching and cramping after having been under strain for so long. I felt my heart begin to slow. I could breathe again. *Oh my God....*

I wasn't *okay*. Every single part of me ached and throbbed. It felt as if I'd done something to my back: I could move, but it made me grunt in pain. A couple of fingers were bent at an unnatural angle and I figured I'd dislocated them while I'd been clawing at the deck. But I was alive. *What the hell is that stuff? How did it work so fast?*

Soaked in sweat and panting, I managed to roll onto my side to look at Rourke.

He wasn't moving. He just lay there staring up at the sky.

"Rourke?" No response. "*Rourke?!*"

I put my ear to his chest. There were sounds, but not like any breathing I'd ever heard. Then I saw the blood on his lips. *Oh Jesus.* He'd injured himself, somehow, diving down to get the stone. His face was going rapidly pale. Then I looked down. *Oh Jesus!* His chest was swelling. A lung must have been damaged and air was escaping inside him, squeezing his heart.

He was going to die, right in front of me.

"Rourke!" I yelled. "What do I do?!"

But there was no reply. He was only semi-conscious and he couldn't speak. I looked around frantically but we were alone. Every member of Ratcher's crew had deserted him and Ratcher himself still lay unconscious against the rail. The Coast Guard would be coming, but they weren't here yet: it felt like hours but it had only been minutes since the explosion.

"Rourke!" I yelled, close to tears. "Tell me what to do!"

His breathing was getting weaker, his skin paler. His eyes were closing. "*Rourke!*"

I started sobbing. *I don't know any of this! I'm not a doctor! All I do is read books!* And he needed help *now.* I had to—I had to—

Not delay.

I heard a somber Scottish accent intone the words. *In the case of *air in the chest cavity compressing the heart, do not delay. Thrust a hollow needle into—*

I drew in my breath. God bless *The Shipboard Doctor.*

I surged to my feet...and almost fell. The ship was going down and listing to one side. I half-staggered, half-crawled downstairs to the semi-submerged lower deck. Thigh-deep in water, I found a locker marked *Medical* and grabbed the bag inside, then hurried back to Rourke.

The bag held a bewildering array of equipment but I knew what I was looking for because the picture had given me nightmares for days afterwards. I grabbed a hollow needle, tore off the packaging, and used my fingers to find the right spot on his chest. *Jesus, if I'm wrong, I'll kill him—*

There was no time for doubt. I prayed and *thrust.*

Air hissed out. And Rourke drew in a breath. It was shaky and labored, but he was moving air again. After a few seconds, his eyes fluttered open.

"It worked," he said.

I nodded and smiled and then realized he was talking about me, about the cure. "That too," I told him weakly.

I was too exhausted and ached too much to stay sitting so I lay down on the deck next to him, nestling my head on his shoulder because I didn't want to press on his chest or ribs. Every part of me hurt...and I didn't care at all. Clutched tight in my fist was the stone that would save Katherine and all the other women. There was a rattling, buzzing noise in the distance and I realized it was a helicopter. The Coast Guard was coming.

Rourke slid his arm around me and pulled me tight against him. From the way he hissed through his teeth, it hurt a lot to do it. But he did it anyway.

"Sorry about the treasure," I said into his neck.

He gave a low grunt and hugged me even tighter. "Got everything I need right here."

EPILOGUE

Hannah

At the hospital, we discovered that Rourke had indeed suffered a major trauma to a lung, together with broken ribs. I had two dislocated fingers, muscle tears in several places and too many bruises to count.

There was no way Rourke could leave the hospital for a few days but I had to get going: I wasn't prepared to let Katherine suffer a day longer. So, that night, dosed up on heavy painkillers and with one hand in bandages, I left against medical advice and got a flight back to Nebraska.

On the plane, I thought about the approach I'd take with Katherine's doctors...and quickly decided the best strategy was not to tell them at all. If I started telling them about shipwrecks and gypsy lovers and a curious stone lost for three hundred years, they'd have me locked up.

I'd prepared a bottle of the cure before I flew so, as soon as I got to the hospital, I ran to Katherine's room. I hadn't been able to get through on the phone before I left and I'd been out of touch for days. *What if she—What if she's—*

To my relief, Katherine was sitting up in bed, paler and weaker than when I'd left her but alive. Her eyes widened when she saw me. "Where have you *been?*" she asked.

I thrust the bottle of oily black liquid at her. "Tell you later," I said. "Drink this."

She stared at it. "What—"

"Just *drink it.* Now. Before you have another attack." I'd never heard myself be so forceful. *I'm not a mouse anymore.*

She looked at me doubtfully and then uncapped the bottle and downed the whole thing. I slumped in relief. It was over.

Katherine frowned as she licked the liquid from her lips. "You've changed," she said suspiciously.

I sighed and lay down next to her on her bed. The relief of knowing she was safe was incredible, like a huge weight had been lifted from me. "More than you know," I told her.

Several days and many tests later, the doctors confirmed that we were cured. The stone turned out to be a rare mineral containing huge quantities of a chemical the body needs to produce neurotransmitters: specifically, the ones related to shutting off pain once it's been triggered. More tests and they figured out that our genetic condition means we can't store that chemical like other people do. Our bodies use up their supply too early: typically, in our mid-twenties. When it runs low, pain starts spiraling out of control.

The ground-up stone gave us several lifetime's worth of the chemical all in one go, which explained why it worked so fast and why it was a permanent cure. The chemical was easily available and the other women in our family could easily be treated: a simple injection would top them up for life. My family was safe and I stayed long enough to celebrate with them...but there was someone I needed to get back to.

Back in Nassau, Rourke was recovering. His leg was healing from the hell he'd put it through aboard the *Pitbull* but the original pain was still there and always would be. "Doesn't matter, though," he told me as I sat on the edge of his bed. "As long as I've got you."

I kissed him long and deep...but I still felt guilty. He'd lost a fortune in treasure, plus his boat—and that meant he'd also lost his home. For a while, our future looked bleak.

Then Benny brought Yoyo to visit, breaking about a million hospital rules in the process. As the warm little bundle of fur sat on my shoulder, he started playing with my necklace. I'd gotten so used to wearing it, I'd sort of forgotten it was there. It was only when he drew the ruby pendant out of my blouse and I looked down at it that it sunk in. *Esme's necklace.* It was worth at least a hundred thousand dollars.

"Sell it," I said immediately. I didn't want to part with it but I owed him. "You can use it to buy a new boat."

But Rourke shook his head. "Got a better idea," he told me.

There was something else I'd forgotten about. All the treasure from the *Hawk* had gone to the bottom of the sea, together with the chest of coins we'd found and even the ruby we'd found with the first clue. But there was still the fortune in jewels hidden in the cave. Using the necklace as collateral, we were able to mount a small expedition with a couple of trustworthy workers and a set of power tools. Within a day, we were cutting rubies and diamonds out of the rock. In three days we'd cleared the cave and set ourselves up for life.

Ratcher was facing a very different future. He'd been evacuated from the *Pitbull* still unconscious. And when his crew saw that their captain was penniless and without a boat, their meager loyalty disappeared entirely. They turned on him and between their testimony and ours Ratcher was charged with multiple counts of attempted murder and sent to jail for a long, long time.

Six Months Later
Hannah

"Right five degrees," Rourke called. "Bring her into the wind and let's pick up some speed."

"*Aye-aye, Cap'n!*" I yelled, a little too enthusiastically.

Rourke muttered something under his breath but he grinned, too. I hadn't got tired of calling him *Captain* yet and I wasn't sure I ever would.

The *Fortune's Reward* leaned as I brought her out of the harbor, her white sail bright against the glittering water. She was a similar size to the *Fortune's Hope:* we could take a crew but today it was just Rourke, YoYo and me.

We'd moved into my great-grandfather's house in Nassau. The first night we'd slept there, lying in bed with my head on Rourke's chest and the waves crashing outside, I'd finally told him what had happened to my mom. He'd held me tight while I relived it one more time...and when it was over, the sound of the waves didn't make my chest clench up, anymore. I'd let something go.

Rourke was still getting used to sleeping in a bed, not a hammock, but he said I eased the transition. There was no way I could make him live on land full time, though: that wouldn't be right. So we'd found a balance. He'd re-hired most of his old crew plus a few new faces and we were starting to mount treasure-hunting expeditions. Once a month or so, we'd all pile onto the new boat and we'd head out to a wreck, usually on a tip Hobbs supplied.

The expeditions were crazy: sort of like a road trip with a colorful, eccentric bunch of friends. Every cabin was full and meals were eaten out on the deck with a plate on your lap. I gradually became a competent diver but my real strength was in being our on-board researcher, deciphering old log books, letters and maps. And however crowded the boat was, I always made sure Rourke and I had the master stateroom to ourselves. There have to be some advantages to being the captain's woman.

For the first time, I got to see how he treated a crew: tough but fair, always willing to listen, and the loyalty they showed him was powerful and moving. He made sure they were well paid, even if we didn't find treasure, though we got lucky more often than not. And I found I could help. When someone was down because he'd broken up with his girlfriend, or was feeling overworked, or just stressed, I picked up on it, and nudged Rourke to go easy on them.

Between expeditions, we explored Jamaica and Haiti and visited Hobbs and Carla in Cuba. I'd become good friends with both of them and now had plans to matchmake both of them as soon as I found good matches. We'd also made a few trips back to Nebraska so that Rourke could meet my family. Being so far from the sea was hell, for him, and when I saw the discomfort on his face when he first looked out across the wheat fields, I almost abandoned the whole thing and bundled him back onto the plane.

But he squeezed my hand, called us a cab and made it through the whole weekend without a single complaint. And to my surprise, he and my dad hit it off immediately. They were worlds apart but they were both tied so tightly to the physical—the sea, the earth— that they were on the same wavelength.

We'd also been revisiting all of the places on the trail of clues and had tracked down some of the other locations Esme referenced in her diary. The inn, where Mace made her come six times? That turned out to be McKinley's. There were a couple of rooms upstairs that used to house guests: Benny hadn't used them in years but he let us stay over one night. And...well. We set a new record. And the island where the wreck of the *Hawk* lay was one of our favorite places, now. With its hidden, sheltered waters, it was romantic and private: perfect for moonlit skinny dipping.

We'd also cleared up something that had been bothering me all along. I'd been sad that, after all the trouble Captain Mace went to to make sure Esme got his treasure, he'd died and she'd never found it, never even found the first clue. I must have told Rourke how unfair it was about fifty times before, one night in Havana, he'd finally said, "He *was* a pirate, you know."

I'd blinked. "What?"

Rourke shrugged. "Pirates were wily. Full of tricks. This plan to go down with his ship and leave Esme his treasure: very noble but...what if that was his plan *B*?"

I'd frowned, knocked back my mojito and shut myself in a room at the library for almost a week, refusing to come out except for food until I'd solved the puzzle. What I found was the arrival of a new couple in London society, just a few months after the *Hawk* sank: supposedly a long lost Count and his Countess, but they bore a striking resemblance to Captain Mace and Esme and the dates matched. Rourke had been right: Mace's plan B had been to go down with his ship and leave Esme his treasure...but he'd never needed that because his plan A had been successful. He'd taken as much of the treasure as he could carry, scuttled the *Hawk* and then escaped, probably in one of the ship's lifeboats. It must have been a perilous journey to an inhabited island in such a small boat, but then he was a legendarily good sailor.

Once there he'd met up with Esme and they'd escaped together and started a new life in London, leaving the rest of the treasure where it was. I liked the way it had worked out. If they hadn't found their happiness, we wouldn't have been able to find ours. And although the treasure was out of reach, nothing's ever really lost forever. Technology was improving all the time. Someday, a hundred years from now, someone would find it.

As the harbor fell away behind us and we picked up speed, I turned and looked at Rourke. He looked as gorgeous as ever, wearing nothing but a pair of shorts, his tanned body hard and perfect. He was happier, these days. He still had the limp, but he said I helped with the pain. And like the shark scars, it was part of who he was. Edwards wasn't forgotten but Rourke had finally allowed him to become a memory.

YoYo climbed my leg, swarmed up my body and settled himself on my shoulder. I let out a long, contented breath and gazed at the endless blue ahead of me. My fear of the ocean was gone: all I felt was giddy excitement. Two-thirds of the world is water and there were a million adventures waiting for us out there. My life stretched out ahead of me: crisp, blank pages ready to be filled. "Where shall we go?" I asked.

Rourke put his arms around me from behind. His cheek pressed against mine as he wrapped me into his chest and then his lips were brushing my ear. "Let's see where the wind takes us," said Captain Rourke.

THE END

Thank you for reading.

You may also like *Alaska Wild.*

Mason Boone. A former Navy SEAL who lives in isolation in the Alaskan mountains. He's rugged, untamed...and gorgeous. I'm an FBI agent; he's a fugitive on his way to prison. But when our plane crashes deep in the Alaskan wilderness, Mason becomes my only hope.

To survive the cold, the wild animals and the terrain, we'll need to stay close. But every time he touches me, I melt inside. He makes me feel protected like no man ever has and the way he looks at me, as if he just wants to push me up against a tree and rip my clothes off.... Could he be innocent of his crimes and can I help him escape the demons of his past? I'm a city girl but I'll need to learn to live as wild as him...because the other prisoner from our flight and his gang are out there...and they're hunting us.

Alaska Wild is out now.

Find all my books at helenanewbury.com.